HUNGER

DEREK MUSE

This book is dedicated to my wife and best friend Emily, who's countless hours of listening, encouraging, and helping with editing have made this book so much more than it ever would have been.

CHAPTER 1

DARKNESS WRAPPED AROUND every object in the narrow alley. Graffiti-covered, misshapen, and overfilled dumpsters with ill-fitting lids were strewn haphazardly along the crumbling brick walls. Trash overflowed from the dumpsters onto the grime-encrusted pavement. Like a blanket that could not be thrown off, the lingering heat of the day wrapped itself inextricably around the objects in the alley. The pungent odors emitted by layers of rotting food in and around the dumpsters would have sent most humans running with their nostrils pinched closed tightly between thumb and forefinger. But there was one subset of the human race that could tolerate this hostile environment without complaint.

Fred Barnes tilted his head back and tipped the whiskey bottle as high as it would go, waiting patiently for the last drops to drain out of the amber bottle and onto his tongue. It amazed him how quickly a fifth disappeared. He'd just gotten this one this afternoon. Or had it been this morning? After a fifth of whiskey, it was hard to remember. At Fred's current alcohol level, notwithstanding the tolerance that had built up in his brain for high levels of ethanol, he only vaguely remembered the pain caused by the loss of his business, his crooked ex-partner, and his backstabbing ex-wife.

Sweat matted his overly long and thinning gray hair to his deeply wrinkled forehead. The food-spattered long-sleeve shirt he was wearing was fastened with its few remaining buttons in the wrong buttonholes. With his pants sporting gapping and tattered holes in both knees and his right big toe visible through a hole in his grimy old tennis shoes, he looked little different from the hundreds of drunks that lay sprawled on sidewalks and in alleys throughout the city.

The corner where he sat was in the farthest reaches of the alley, next to some dumpsters that belonged to a small market. The name of the market escaped Fred for the moment. He had enough trouble remembering what city he was in.

A sharp pain flared in his left buttocks. Fred rolled his eyes in frustration. The fact that he could feel pain at all meant that he still wasn't drunk enough. He grunted and shifted a little to take the weight off the bruise on his left buttocks where some punk kid had kicked him hard a few days before.

Suddenly, he heard male voices. They were talking faster than he could think. That scared him. People that talked fast weren't drunk, and the only reason they would be here this time of night was to rob him, beat him senseless, or both. He saw movement and blinked in the misty darkness. The hazy outlines of two approaching men slowly became more distinct. The men stopped a few feet from his corner. He couldn't see their faces or tell what they were wearing because their backs were to the only streetlight in the ill-lit alley, leaving their faces hidden in shadows. One of the men was holding what looked like a whiskey bottle in his hand. The man started to raise the bottle and Fred threw his arms clumsily over his head for protection, waiting for the blows and the broken glass.

However, instead of a blow or slash from the bottle, he heard a male voice say, "Put your arms down, old man. We're not going to hit you with this bottle. We want to give it to you."

Fred lowered his arms only a little while he kept a wary eye on the men. The same voice continued, "Come on. Put your arms down." With his arms getting pretty tired, Fred finally lowered his arms to his knees.

"Good," the man said. "Now this is the deal. You'd like this whiskey, right?"

Fred hesitated, wondering if it were a trick question. However, his craving for more whiskey was intense. Unable to hold back, he answered weakly, "Yeah."

"Then all you have to do is try a little of this nose candy, and we'll give you the whiskey."

Fred squinted at the bottle. He couldn't make out the label in the dim light. Whatever it was, it would be nice to get a brand-new fifth without having to beg for money to buy one. He could almost taste the warm liquid going down his throat. His mouth went dry in anticipation. *But nose candy has to be cocaine, and drugs are bad.* He didn't do drugs. Drugs would fry his brain. A man had to draw the line somewhere. Gathering strength that he barely knew he had, Fred replied as loudly as he could, "I don't do drugs."

The second man snorted and said, "Sure, you don't."

Struggling to get up to his feet, Fred said, "Now, if you'll excuse me, I'll just get out to the street and get my own—"

Like lightening, the second man stepped behind Fred just as he finished standing. The man encircled Fred's neck with his right arm and thrust his right hip forcefully into Fred's back. Simultaneously, the man yanked Fred's head back hard by his hair. Snarling in Fred's ear, the man tightened his lock around Fred's neck with his arm until it hurt as he said, "Wrong answer." The man then barked out to his companion, "Do him!"

The first man reached out and shoved something sharp into Fred's right nostril. Fred felt something spray into his nose. Just as fast, the same thing was done to Fred's left nostril. The pain caused by the spray made Fred's eyes water. A moment later, the arm around his neck loosened and the man that had been behind him was suddenly gone. Off-balance and with his normal reflexes blunted by too much whiskey, Fred fell back in a crumpled heap in same the corner, striking his head hard on the brick wall of the alley as he went down.

"What the..." Fred exclaimed. He awkwardly pushed himself up to a seated position with one arm while he rubbed the back of his head with the other hand. "What was that stuff you sprayed into my nose?" He wrinkled his nose and sniffed twice. "I don't smell anything," he said as he looked quizzically at the two men. They were both once again standing in front of him.

"Here's your booze, ya old drunk. Just like we promised you," the first man said as he held out the bottle. Fred snatched the bottle from the man's outstretched hand.

"It really stinks in here," the second man said.

"Yeah, let's go," the first one agreed. They turned and disappeared quickly into the dark mists of the alley.

Fred's attention span was only as long as the time it took to open his next bottle. He clumsily screwed off the lid and then drank deeply until he had to come up for air. "Ah, that's good," he mumbled to himself as he wiped his mouth with the back of his hand.

Nestling back into his dark corner, he savored the warm glow of the whiskey. Since nothing had happened after the men gave him the painful sprays up his nose, his worries about the two men and their nose spray began to fade. His mind wandered back to happier times. He remembered his ex-wife, Sandy. She had been five years younger than him. He had first seen her in an ice cream parlor on a hot summer day. She had been eighteen years old and had looked so hot in that short halter dress with—

Without warning, he felt that he couldn't breathe. His chest wouldn't move, and he couldn't get enough air. The skin of his forehead rapidly beaded with sweat. Even with all his senses blunted by the alcohol, he felt extreme panic billowing up in his chest. Before he even had a chance to cry out, the world rushed away from his eyes and ears. Fully unconscious in less than a second, he fell back against the wall of the alley, striking his head hard against the brick for a second and last time.

Thirty minutes later, the two men returned to the dark entrance of the alley. They glanced around briefly to be sure no one was watching and then disappeared into the alley's shadows. They walked slowly down its length, checking to see if any other drunks were half buried in the darkness amongst the heaps of trash. At the end of the alley, the old drunk lay slumped in the same corner. The drunk's head rested at an odd angle on one shoulder.

The taller of the two men pulled a pair of latex gloves out of his trench coat pocket, donned them, and then briefly checked for a pulse at the drunk's neck. He straightened, saying, "He's gone."

The other snickered and said, "Way cool! That was so easy."

The tall one popped off the gloves and shoved them back into the same pocket. As he turned away from the body of the old drunk and started for the entrance of the alley, he added, "Yeah, but anyone can waste a drunk. What really matters to the boss is how the police are going to rule this one, natural causes or homicide."

CHAPTER 2

NICOLE WRIGHT—A THIRTY-FOUR-YEAR-OLD, overweight patient—cried as she told Dr. Trevor Davis how depressed she was about her weight. As she poured out her frustrations, Trevor summarized her concerns in her electronic medical chart. He avoided the words "obese patient" as he typed, since that would be offensive to her if she ever accessed her chart online and read his note. Studies had indicated that the word "obese" was second only to "fatty" on the list of the most offensive terms that could be used to describe an overweight patient.

"I reached my full height of five-foot-five at age fourteen. I weighed one hundred and twenty-five pounds then and had no trouble maintaining my weight through high school. When I got married at age nineteen, I still only weighed one hundred and thirty pounds. I felt and looked great. But then I gained twenty pounds with each of my three children and never lost any of the weight between the births. After my last child, I went back to eating like I always had, but instead of maintaining, I continued to gain weight. I'm so embarrassed that I'm two hundred and twenty pounds today. That's the most I've ever weighed. I'm exercising five times a week at the gym, but it is only taking off inches, not pounds. Something has to be wrong with my metabolism. I just keep gaining weight, but I'm not eating any more than anybody else. My husband eats more than I do, and he doesn't gain weight.

"Recently, my husband has started making little irritating comments about my weight. And last week, he made it pretty clear that sex wasn't as much fun now that I was so heavy. His criticism about my weight has been bad enough, but his comments about sex have about killed me. I have been crying ever since. I don't even let him see me undress anymore. I'm jealous all the time about the thin girls he works with at his office. I can't help but think that he'll have an affair with one of them." The tears started again. "I've come to you for help with my weight because my friend told me that you helped her lose weight. I'm desperate, Dr. Davis. Please help me."

"First of all, you're a beautiful woman no matter what you weigh," Trevor stated. "I'm sorry if your husband doesn't recognize that. And as long as your labs and electrocardiogram come back normal, I should be able to start you on weight-loss medication within the next few days to help you lose weight."

There was no question in Trevor's mind that the woman needed to lose weight. With her medium frame, her ideal weight range was 125 to 140 pounds. With eighty pounds to lose to make it to 140 pounds, she far exceeded the guidelines that governed the appropriate use of weight-loss medications. Trevor had already ascertained that she was healthy and not pregnant. There was no history of past anorexia or bulimia.

One of Trevor's favorite parts of practicing medicine was helping patients lose weight. He had a lot of empathy for overweight people since he had fought his own obesity all of his life. His own self-image still suffered over an extra twenty pounds that he just couldn't lose. Even though he played racquetball or jogged three to four times a week and watched his carbohydrate intake, he just couldn't get the extra weight off. He was six feet tall and with his medium frame, the weight charts said he was supposed to weigh 175 pounds. Even

185 pounds would be an okay weight for him, if he could ever get there. At 205 pounds, it was still hard for him to look in the mirror in the mornings after a shower because he was too ashamed about his protuberant belly.

Trevor had turned to weight-loss medications for help eighteen months previously when he had been twenty pounds heavier at 225. A pharmaceutical representative had left samples of a new weight-loss drug called Reductol for Trevor to try on his patients. Instead, Trevor had decided that he needed the Reductol just as much as his patients. After first visiting with one of his partners in his clinic to document that his using the Reductol would be appropriate, his partner had started him on the Reductol samples. With the help of the Reductol, he had lost twenty pounds in six months, but then he had plateaued. The Reductol was helping him to maintain but hadn't helped with the final twenty pounds that was still there.

Just as the Reductol had helped him, he knew that it would also help Nicole. He said, "I'd like to do a brief exam first just to make sure that you are healthy." He patted the exam table.

Nicole smiled through her tears and sat on the exam table.

As Trevor began by checking her thyroid, he added, "After I finish examining you, we'll go over the diet plan that I want you to follow while you're on the weight-loss medication."

Trevor had treated about 500 patients with Reductol, as well as a handful of patients with a newer weight-loss drug, called Waitno-mor, that was similar to Reductol. The results from both had been impressive. Some patients had lost up to 100 pounds in six months, although the average weight loss was closer to thirty pounds in six months. Prior to losing weight, many of those same patients had suffered from poorly-controlled high blood pressure, type 2 diabetes, and sleep apnea. After their weight loss, the same patients were doing so much better that many had been able to go off of most, if not all, of their medications. Sure, there were rare risks, but the physical and social benefits far outweighed them. He himself had been so unhappy two years ago when he had been heavier. Getting dates had even been more difficult. Even though he had lost weight, he still hadn't been out on a date for months. His workload at his practice was just too large to leave time to meet anyone new.

CHAPTER 3

BRITTANY ADAMS GUIDED her late-model cherry red Chevy Corvette to the front entrance of the Saint James Hotel in Portland, Oregon. The six-story hotel wasn't much to look at from the outside. It was box-like in appearance and its feature-less gray marble walls were interrupted only by columns of small windows and diminutive stone balconies that were accessed from each hotel room by sliding glass doors. In spite of the drab exterior, more than a few of her wealthier clients stayed here, in part because of its proximity to the downtown area, but also because its interior trappings were exquisite, and its service was unequaled. Glancing at the red, two-foot-high block letters that spelled the hotel's name on the top of the front of the hotel, Brittany smiled wryly at the irony of seeing the name of a saint on a building where less than saintly activities were often the norm. As she approached the front entrance, her smile was stolen by the sudden memory of a recent and distinctly unpleasant event that had occurred at the hotel a few months ago. She shook her head to clear the horrid thought from her mind. The need to work and to get paid well demanded that she be mentally focused and unencumbered by the past.

Slowing to a stop at valet parking at the front entrance, she ignored the stares of the young men in maroon jackets, white shirts, bowties, and black tennis shoes that were waiting to park or retrieve cars. Three of them almost fell over each other as they jockeyed to be the first one to her door. The lucky valet that got there first opened Brittany's door while Brittany reached to grab her purse out of the passenger seat. Brittany turned back toward him and stepped out of the car. Her twenty-one-year-old ankles were thin and graceful; her calves were slender, and her knees were perfectly shaped. As Brittany straightened, the hem of her dress, aided by gravity, quickly assumed its normal position over her mid-thigh. Brittany couldn't help but notice the valet's eyes as they swept up her torso.

Brittany was neither irritated nor flattered by the obvious visual undressing she had just received. As she turned and walked toward the hotel's front revolving door, she didn't even look to see if the valet's eyes were following her. She already knew that they were. Male ogling had been part of her life ever since she had started junior high.

Brittany pushed through the revolving door of the hotel. Flashing a smile at the same aging concierge that had been on duty ever since she could remember, she walked directly to one of the four elevators that serviced the hotel's upper floors. She got out of the elevator on the sixth floor and walked to room 603, where she had been told to show up for a job interview. She knocked twice on the door. She was applying for this job because she had gotten a tip that the company that she was going to interview with would pay her twice as much as she was now making as an escort. Trying to pay for college and for her expenses was hard, even though she was the most requested escort at Bambi's, the escort company where she worked. If what she had heard were true and if she could get this job, she wouldn't have to worry about money, and she wouldn't need to work as escort anymore. Ever since one of her clients had sexually assaulted her, she had known that her days as an escort were numbered.

The door opened suddenly, and a tall, tan, attractive man in his later thirties answered the door. He was talking on his cell and motioned to her with his unoccupied hand to step into the room. Seeing no one else in the room, Brittany hesitated. She had expected to be meeting with more than one person.

After a moment, the man tore the cellphone from his ear and quickly said, "Hi. Come in." He then resumed talking on his cell, cutting off Brittany's half-formed "hello." The man backed away from the door into the middle of the room to let her in.

Brittany followed tentatively and stopped just inside the still-open door.

The man put his hand over the microphone of his cell phone and said softly, "I'll be just a minute." He then turned away and resumed talking on the cellphone as he stepped into an adjoining bedroom and closed the door.

Brittany took another step into the room, allowing the door to close behind her. She quickly looked around the living room of the spacious penthouse suite. This particular room was quite familiar to her because she had been here with clients a number of times before. However, the expanse of carpet just in front of her seemed to be an invisible barrier to her, blocking further entry into the room. She shivered involuntarily. Try as she might, she couldn't put the memory out of her mind of what had happened to her there. When she had been told that today's job interview was going to be in the very room where the assault had happened, she had hoped that it wouldn't bother her too much. But now that she was here in the entryway of the penthouse, she couldn't fight back the revulsion.

That evening six weeks ago had started out pleasantly enough. However, after an enjoyable night at the opera, Clint, a gentlemanly first-time client from Texas, had suddenly transformed into a self-centered sweating beast as soon as the door had closed behind him. Without a word, he had thrown her on the carpet right in front of where she now stood, torn her clothes off her body, and had forced himself on her. When she had tried to push him off and tell him no, he had pinned her to the floor even tighter and had grunted out, "It ain't rape if you do it with a prostitute."

The ordeal had ended quickly, and he had staggered to a nearby couch and had fallen asleep within moments. She had collected her clothing and purse and had retreated to the bathroom. As she had slowly gotten dressed, she had decided that as much as she needed the money, she felt too violated to want to wake the jerk to request payment. Slipping out of the penthouse quietly, she had gone directly home. Showering for almost an hour had left her still feeling dirty.

With her heart pounding in her throat, Brittany forced herself to walk quickly around the place where it had happened. She took a seat on the edge of an armchair that was opposite the couch where Clint had fallen asleep weeks before. Being back in this room with another man that she had never met before was unnerving, to say the least. It took all of her energy just to stay seated on the chair. She constantly had to suppress the thought that she should just run out the door and never come back. She reminded herself sternly that this job just might be the ticket she needed to get out of the unhappy life that she was trapped in. With great effort, she placed her hands in her lap and forced them not to tremble. She hoped the man wouldn't take too long on the phone. She wasn't sure how long she was going to be able to sit here.

She didn't have to wait long. The door to the bedroom opened. Brittany rose to greet the handsome gentleman.

They shook hands briefly as he introduced himself, "Hi, I'm Austin Vernon."

Brittany said, "Hello. I'm Brittany Adams."

"Please have a seat."

She returned to her perch on the edge of the same chair. She held her knees tightly together and clenched her hands on her lap.

"I recognize you from your picture." He lowered himself onto the couch opposite Brittany. "You are even lovelier in person."

"Thank you."

"So let's get right down to business. I'm sure you're curious about our company and about the position that you're here to interview for, but I would like to ask you to bear with me for a few minutes. I need to ask you a few questions first."

"Okay."

"How much notice would you need to leave town for training if I hired you today?"

Brittany hesitated and then replied, "Oh, I don't know. How soon do you need someone?"

"If I hired you today, I would need you to leave this evening for the training that starts tomorrow morning. I would take care of all your travel arrangements and expenses."

"I would have to leave tonight?" That was a shock. She had a client scheduled for that evening.

"If hired, I would need you to leave tonight. Otherwise, I'm afraid I won't be able to offer you the job."

Brittany looked away for a moment. *How can I trust this guy?* He seemed like a legitimate businessman, but so had Clint. Brittany looked Austin directly in the eyes again. She wasn't sure why, but she at least felt a little comfortable with him. His looks weren't bad either. He was trim and clean-shaven, and his light brown hair was well groomed. His green eyes matched the green in his dress shirt in a way that made his eyes quite attractive. She made her decision and answered, "Okay. I can leave this afternoon, if I am hired and if I decide to work for you."

"Would you need to notify anyone, such as a landlord, family member, boyfriend, or a close friend?"

"No, I can just leave if the job is right for me."

"Do you have any sales experience?" Austin paused as he looked through Brittany's resume. "Oh, it's right here. You don't."

That made Brittany nervous. Did the job require sale experience? No one had warned her.

He looked her directly in the face and asked, "How do you feel about a job in sales?"

Searching for a quick and satisfactory answer, Brittany winged it. "Since you know that I work for an escort service, you probably know I have to sell myself to each new client in order to get their repeat business. I'm good at selling myself and have a busier schedule than all of the other girls at our service. I have no doubt that I would be good at sales."

"Great. This next question will be a tough one. Let's assume that you have a sales job where you are paid a salary plus commission. If you came to realize that the chances of selling your product would be enhanced by sexual involvement with the potential purchaser, would you then be willing to use it to improve your chances to make a sale?"

"That's a pretty bold question. But, then again, that's what I do on a daily basis with my clients at the escort service. I really shouldn't answer your question without knowing more about what I'll be selling."

"Sounds good," Austin said, avoiding answering her question about what she would be selling. "Now, for one last question. We realize you are not a college graduate. After being thoroughly trained in all aspects of our product, would you be willing to present yourself as an expert, even one with a college degree, if necessary, to your potential customers? We would provide you with an authentic looking diploma to back up your claim."

Brittany took a moment to think this one through. *This is so strange! I don't even know what I'm going to be selling. What should I say?* She really wanted the job, but how could she be sure it was right for her without knowing what she would be selling? Brittany replied, "As long as I know that the product I am selling is legal and that it's in my customer's best interest to buy it, I guess I would be willing to do that."

"Good. This sales job is a great opportunity for you. We can pass you off without difficulty as a college graduate, enabling you to make upwards of one hundred thousand dollars per year. You can almost double that with commissions and bonuses that will be based on how well you sell our product.

"Okay. Now I want to get to a more difficult part of the interview. My boss insists that this part be done before any candidate can be offered the job. I need to see you completely undressed for just a moment. It's so my boss can be sure that you don't have any unacceptable physical blemish that might turn off our clients. If that's okay with you, then you can use the bedroom to get undressed. There's a robe on the back of the door. Please step back in here when you are ready."

His unusual request made her just a little nervous. "No, I won't need the bedroom. But I really have to protest. I know nothing about the company you represent. I don't really even know if it's safe being in this room alone with you." Brittany was careful to finish with a faint smile on her face. She hoped he couldn't see her heart beating out of her chest.

"You appear to be an excellent candidate for this job, but I must be firm on this one. I can't give you the job until we do this. I've been doing this exact interview all across the United States for months now, and I promise you that I have been very careful to be as inoffensive as possible during the whole process."

Brittany hesitated. *Can I trust him?* She finally decided that getting this job was worth the small risk of complying with his request. "Okay then. Let's get it over with." She stood up and reached behind her back to undo the zipper of her dress.

CHAPTER 4

BRUSHING HER SHOULDER-LENGTH auburn hair behind her ears with her fingers, Melanie Baker opened the door to East Camelback Family Practice. She was dressed in a beige business suit with a cream blouse. Once inside the clinic, she walked directly to the front desk.

"Hi, Melanie. How are you today?" the receptionist asked with a warm smile.

"I'm doing well today, Sally," Melanie replied with a happy smile of her own. "Thank you for asking. How's the new baby doing?"

"She's doing just fine, but she's not so new anymore. She's already five months old and is cutting her first tooth." Sally paused, then continued. "I like your hair that way. When did you get it cut?"

"A couple of weeks ago. I was ready for a change, especially in this heat." For years, Melanie had been curling her long hair. Two weeks ago, her mother had finally convinced her that she needed a newer, more stylish look. The shorter style was really helping to keep the sweat from dripping down the back of her neck. However, she wasn't sure if she liked the cut. It was nice to hear a compliment.

"Is Dr. Davis in the office this afternoon?" Melanie asked. As soon as she finished asking the question, Melanie realized that she had never before asked specifically for Dr. Davis's status. Instead, she had always asked what medical providers were in and were they free to meet with her. She hoped that the directness of her question hadn't revealed her interest in Dr. Davis.

Melanie was a pharmaceutical representative for Medicon Pharmaceuticals. She had been calling on East Camelback Family Practice for the past year. Today was her usual semi-monthly visit. She enjoyed interacting with the medical providers as she detailed them on the medications produced by her company. And although she found it difficult to admit, she was becoming more and more interested in conversing with Dr. Trevor Davis. She found herself attracted to his easygoing and gentle personality and to his keen intellect. He was sensitive and caring. His dark brown eyes were warm and attractive. In truth, she liked everything about him. When she talked with him, even though she tried to conduct herself in a professional manner, she couldn't quite ignore the subtle thrill of excitement that she felt. Her growing attraction for Dr. Davis was problematic since it was against Medicon company policy to date one of her medical providers. On top of that, she didn't even know if Dr. Davis returned the attraction. She reminded herself to try even harder not to let her feelings for Dr. Davis show to him or to his staff.

"Dr. Davis wasn't here two weeks ago when I dropped by," Melanie continued quickly in an effort to disguise her initial blunder. "I want to give him some information about Posivasc, and I wanted to be sure that he was here."

"Dr. Davis is here this afternoon," Sally replied with a smile.

Did Sally already suspect her attraction to Dr. Davis? Melanie was sure she'd die of embarrassment if Sally ever said anything to Dr. Davis.

Sally just kept on smiling as she continued, "Dr. Fife is here also. But Dr. Quintero, our new physician, is off today. We also have two of our mid-level practitioners here as well. I'm sure Dr. Davis, Dr.

Fife, and the mid-levels will have time to see you. You can wait for them by the nurse's desk."

"Thank you, Sally. And give that baby a hug for me." Melanie headed for the door to the back office, still feeling embarrassed for being too obvious about wanting to be sure that Dr. Davis was in the office.

Melanie walked down the hallway toward the nurse's desk. Even though East Camelback Family Practice had been in this building for ten years, the interior was so well maintained that it seemed brand new. The walls were painted in a light mauve and the thick, trackless carpet was two shades darker than the walls. The doors, door frames, baseboard, and crown molding were made of richly finished cherry wood. Compared to other offices, East Camelback Family Practice was one of the nicest. The rooms and halls were spacious. The counters were uncluttered.

As Melanie arrived at the nurse's desk, a redheaded nurse looked up and smiled in recognition. "Hi, Melanie. It's good to see you."

"It's good to see you, too, Laurie. It looks like you're keeping busy."

"We're always busy," Laurie replied with a smile. "But we're never too busy for a visit from you. How are you doing?"

"I'm having a great day. To top it off, I get to visit my favorite office this afternoon."

"Oh, and which office might that be?"

"Well, since this is the only office that I'm visiting this afternoon, I guess it must be you guys."

"You're too kind."

Melanie asked, "Is it all right if I wait here for the medical providers to see if I can catch them in-between patients?"

"Sure, one of them should be out in just a moment."

They were interrupted by Sally's voice emanating from the phone system. "Is there a nurse available?"

"Yes," Laurie answered.

"There's a patient call on line five," Sally said.

Laurie turned back to Melanie and said, "I'd better take this call. Go ahead and wait right there."

Laurie picked up the phone and began conversing as Melanie turned toward the rooms where Dr. Davis usually saw his patients. She hoped she wouldn't have to wait too long. She could feel her heart beating a little faster than usual. Her palms were slightly moist from anticipation. *What is going on with me? I can't believe it. I'm acting like I'm in junior high!*

Just then, Dr. Erwin Fife, the founder and senior partner of East Camelback Family Practice, stepped out of a room down the hallway and rushed toward the nurse's station. He was diminutive in height, but he made up for it with his intense personality and keen intellect. Although he was fifty-nine years old, he appeared younger because of his youthful vigor, smooth skin, and well-toned body. His light brown hair had receded only a little, although Melanie suspected that he dyed his hair to hide the gray. He smiled thinly as he noticed Melanie standing in front of the nurse's desk and asked briskly, "Do you need me to sign for some samples?"

"I do, Dr. Fife. Could you sign here for some Posivasc and Reductol?" Melanie put her drug company's tablet on the reception counter of the nurse's desk in front of Dr. Fife. She pointed to the line where he needed to sign with his finger.

"Melanie, you know how I feel about Reductol," Dr. Fife stated firmly. "I'm absolutely not going to prescribe potentially dangerous medications for patients that really just need to learn how to eat properly and exercise. Just leave me a few boxes of Posivasc, but no Reductol," he said as he quickly signed the tablet.

Melanie retrieved the tablet and removed the number two in the blank for Reductol sample boxes on the next screen on the tablet. With a friendly, yet determined, smile, Melanie said, "I know how you feel about weight-loss medications. It's just that we're having so much success with Reductol in patients that have obesity-related type 2 diabetes and high blood pressure that I thought you might have reconsidered."

"No, I haven't reconsidered, and I never will. I'm coming to your speaker presentation tonight at the Philadelphia House Restaurant to be sure that your speaker doesn't mislead the other medical providers at Good Hope Hospital into using dangerous and unnecessary weight-loss medications. I'm sorry that I'm so against weight-loss medications. It has nothing to do with you and how you detail me on your medications. It's just that I sincerely believe that weight-loss medications are the wrong thing for our patients."

"I understand, Dr. Fife. I don't want you to use any medication that you don't feel comfortable with." Melanie knew that pushing Dr. Fife any further concerning Reductol would be fruitless. "Thank you for your support in using Posivasc."

"I use Posivasc because it is good for my patients, not out of loyalty to you or your company," Dr. Fife replied with just a hint of indignation. Dr. Fife turned away from Melanie and gave a series of hand signals to Laurie that indicated that she needed to get off the phone and help him in one of his patient rooms. He then walked back down the hallway to the room he had last come out of, opened the door, and disappeared back into the room.

Although Melanie liked Dr. Fife, she found him highly intimidating and difficult to talk to. He made her feel like a teenage daughter that had stayed out too late on a date. It didn't help that he was the president of the medical staff at Good Hope Hospital. He was well respected by all of the medical providers at the hospital. If he came out against a new medication, which he was apt to do, then the hospital staff usually followed his advice and didn't use the medication. She was more than grateful that he was willing to prescribe Posivasc but was disappointed about his refusal to even consider trying Reductol for his patients. And now, after today's exchange, she was quite concerned that he was going to undermine her speaker at the lecture that evening to be sure that the other medical providers in attendance didn't start prescribing Reductol.

As Melanie continued waiting for the other providers to come out of one of the exam rooms, her mind wandered, and she began daydreaming about what her father would have looked like had he lived to be Dr. Fife's age. Her father had died of colon cancer at the age of thirty-eight. Melanie had been only nine years old, the fifth of six children. The first year after her father's death had been difficult for Melanie. But the overall impact of the loss of her father had been minimized by the loving relationships that Melanie had with her mother, her siblings, and her grandparents. Each of her grandfathers had visited her family's home two or three times a week in the first year after her father's death and had made a special effort to spend time individually and collectively with Melanie and her siblings.

Melanie's reverie was interrupted when the door to exam room three opened and a woman walked into the hallway, heading toward the front desk. Dr. Davis followed the woman out of the exam room moments later. He smiled broadly the second that he saw Melanie. Melanie smiled back and immediately felt just a tiny bit lightheaded.

Dr. Davis walked directly up to Melanie. "Hi, Melanie. What brings you to this neck of the woods?"

"I'm on my usual visit to your office." Melanie's voice cracked as she finished the sentence. She inwardly cringed and hoped that it wasn't too obvious that she was nervous and excited at the same time. Clearing her throat, she continued, "I'd like to check your samples to see if you have enough and to see if you have any questions about Posivasc and Reductol."

"And I thought that you were here to extend a special invitation to the dinner and lecture tonight at the Philadelphia House Restaurant. I'm hurt that you haven't personally invited me."

"Dr. Davis, I received your RSVP last week," Melanie replied, playfully chiding Dr. Davis for his mock offense. She pulled up his email of acceptance on her tablet. "I have your confirmation email right here. You had also requested a seat for a guest. Is one of your staff going to be attending?"

Melanie hadn't thought too much about Dr. Davis' request to bring a guest. She had assumed that he would be bringing one of his partners or his nurses since medical providers knew that the only guest that they could bring to drug company sponsored dinners was another medical professional. The whole pharmaceutical industry was currently under very tight control on what they could and couldn't spend on medical providers.

"Well, I was hoping to bring a guest…" Dr. Davis paused.

Was he asking if he could bring a date? She was supposed to tell him no if that was the case. But she couldn't bring herself to open her mouth to say it. With butterflies in her stomach, Melanie explained, "I need to know so I can confirm the number of attendees with the restaurant."

Trevor smiled. "Well, to tell the truth, there's no one coming with me tonight, at least not yet." He paused. "Will you be at the lecture?"

"Yes, of course I'll be there," Melanie replied, feeling light as air now that her fears appeared to have been proven groundless. Why was she letting this whole thing get to her? She was a grown woman and a professional. "I'm the one that is organizing the whole thing. I have to be there."

"Then it's only fair that I ask if you're going to bring a guest."

"No. No guest for me tonight either." She didn't add that she couldn't bring a guest. It was company policy. Besides, she wasn't dating anyone at the moment.

Trevor replied teasingly, "I can't believe a beautiful woman like you doesn't have someone to accompany her to one of the finest restaurants in town, especially since your drug company is footing the bill."

"Who needs a date when I will be hanging out with so many

handsome medical providers? Anyway, the company doesn't let me bring guests to these dinners."

"I'm sure that we'll have a chance to talk more this evening. I'm running pretty far behind right now, so I'd better get going. By the way, things are going great with Posivasc and Reductol. I've also been using Reductol's competitor, Waitnomor, a little, and it's been working well, too."

Melanie smiled as she took on his challenge to her drug. "Remember that Reductol has been on the market for three years and has proven itself to be safe and effective. Waitnomor has been out for a year and still has only garnished a ten percent share of the market for branded weight-loss medications. It just hasn't been around the long enough for medical providers to be sure of its safety profile."

"True, but it is in the same drug class as Reductol; it does seem to work just as well, and it appears to be safe. In a few of my patients, it has even worked better than Reductol." Trevor signed the drug sample tablet that Melanie had placed in front of him.

"I'm sure we could talk further about weight-loss medications, but I'd better let you get back to your patients." There was nothing that she wanted to do more than stand there and talk to Dr. Davis for the rest of the day, but she knew she had to let him get back to work.

"Thanks. I'll see you tonight at the lecture." Smiling, he turned back toward his patient exam rooms.

CHAPTER 5

BRITTANY STEPPED OUT of the Saint James Hotel into bright sunlight, a rarity for Portland. The splendor of the clear blue sky only added to her elation. She had gotten the job!

Austin had spent no more than ten seconds checking her body for "blemishes." The thought made her smile. Blemishes? Her body was flawless. In fact, men praised her body so much and so often that Brittany had grown a bit tired of hearing it.

After she had dressed, Austin had offered her the job. She had only thought for a second, and then she had gone for broke and accepted the offer. Austin had finally explained that she was going to be working for a company named Hughes Pharmaceuticals and that she would be training as a sales representative for a new pharmaceutical product. If she completed her training successfully over the next month, she would be relocated to somewhere in the Southwestern United States where she would begin work immediately. He had reiterated that she would need to be ready to leave that afternoon at 3:00 p.m. sharp for the training seminar.

Austin had told her to pack for warm weather for seven days. He had also instructed that everything she was taking should fit in one suitcase and one small carry-on bag. If she brought anything else, it would have to be left behind. Because of concerns caused by past attempts at corporate espionage at Hughes Pharmaceuticals, Austin had told her to tell no one where she was going and why she was leaving. He had smiled when she had objected at not knowing where she was going for training. He had just replied, "South. You'll find out when you get there."

In spite of her excitement over her new employment, Brittany couldn't help but feel puzzled by the degree of secrecy that Hughes Pharmaceuticals insisted on maintaining. *What was so secret about a new prescription drug? Was Hughes Pharmaceuticals up to something illegal?* Austin had seemed like an okay guy. She felt that she could probably trust him, although he had said that they were going to give her proof of a college degree when she clearly hadn't graduated from college. She was only a sophomore and hadn't yet declared a major. He had said that if the training seminar, or if working for the company, weren't right for her, she could quit at any time and the company would fly her back to Portland. That part had been reassuring to some degree.

Besides, just the thought of all the money she was going to make working for Hughes Pharmaceuticals helped her forget her concerns and brought a smile of anticipation to her lips. After so many years of being in debt, she would be able to buy the things that she had always wanted. She wished that her mother were still alive so that she could tell her about her new job. Brittany was quite sure her mom would have told her that this was the right thing to do. Her mother had always wanted Brittany to succeed in life. And Brittany would do almost anything to achieve that success.

CHAPTER 6

LEANING BACK INTO the overstuffed, high-backed burgundy chair, Rick Newberry allowed a quiet sigh of boredom to escape his lips. Although he enjoyed his job as the Southwest area manager for the pharmaceutical company Pharmplus, sitting through the endless array of meetings sometimes became tedious. The meeting he was in right now had to be the worst. It was held weekly and was a reporting session on the status of the company's medications that were in the research and development pipeline.

Gazing beyond the cherry-wood table and over the heads of the twelve people that were seated at the boardroom table, his eyes searched beyond the glass windows that were opposite him for anything that was more interesting than this meeting. However, all he encountered was the unbroken pattern of the tinted-glass panels of the skyscraper on the other side of the street. It was a toss-up which was more monotonous: the featureless glass of the skyscraper across the street or the voice that belonged to Jim Ford, the short and balding researcher that currently stood behind a podium at the head of the table. Still doing his best to ignore Jim, Rick noticed his own faint reflection in the window of his building and couldn't help but admire his wavy black hair and his athletic shoulders.

Rick sat up straight and forced his tailbone against the back of his chair in an effort to force himself to stop daydreaming and pay attention. Jim was in mid-sentence when Rick tuned back in for the umpteenth time, "… might be promising in our efforts to discover an agent that has a greater affinity for the F-2 receptor."

"I'm sure you'll have more to tell us at our next meeting," Don Jamison, the director of research at Pharmplus, remarked. "Hopefully, this compound won't have the same unusual properties as the compound R-648 that bound irreversibly to the rat leptin receptor."

The group of bored people seated around the table suddenly came alive, responding with sly smiles and stifled laughter.

The director continued with a smile of his own. "Now, let's move on to the status of research on R-753. Jane, could you tell us about the in-vitro studies…"

Instead of focusing on the director's voice, Rick's mind wandered back to the research meeting six months ago when he had first learned that R-648 caused weight gain instead of weight loss. While the rest of the group had passed off the weight gain on R-648 as a humorous joke that nature occasionally played on researchers, Rick's interest had been piqued. The next afternoon, Rick had visited the laboratory where R-648 had been developed and tested. Cornering Jim Ford, who had been the lead researcher for R-648, he had listened with interest as Jim had described his initial elation and then disappointment with R-648. Jim had attached a mildly radioactive chemical to the R-648 and had injected it into rats. He had been pleased to see that that the radio-labeled R-648 concentrated in the rodents appetite control centers as he had hoped. However, almost immediately the rats began gaining weight rapidly. He had reported his unexpected results to his superiors. Two days later, funding for his research into R-648 had been withdrawn. The board of directors for Pharmplus, pushed by Rick himself, had decided instead to put the money saved into aggressively marketing their new weight-loss drug, Waitnomor.

Jim had been deeply offended by the loss of funding for his research. It had felt like years of his life had been wasted. Rick had been more than willing to exploit Jim's anger and frustration to accomplish his own designs. When Rick had asked for a copy of Jim's notes on the synthesis and testing of R-648, Jim hadn't cared enough to even ask him why. Rick had received a summary copy of Jim's research by interoffice email the next day. The accompanying text had read, "I hope that this is the last time that I ever have to hear about this compound. Maybe this material will be of some use to you, although I can't imagine for what."

Still seated at the chair in the boardroom, Rick smiled to himself as the speaker droned on about her research. He obviously had a much more active imagination than Jim.

CHAPTER 7

BRITTANY GOT OUT of the ride service car in front of the executive terminal at the Portland airport and waited as the driver retrieved her two pieces of luggage from the trunk. She thanked the driver and headed toward the entrance to the terminal.

While she had been getting packed, she hadn't been able to keep from worrying about the risks that she was taking by leaving suddenly for an unknown destination with a man that she had only just met to take a job that she knew little about. She had finally sat herself down and had listed on a piece of paper the worst things that could possibly happen to her if she went with Austin that afternoon. She had listed kidnapping, murder, being forced to be a drug mule, forced prostitution, and slavery. Kidnapping was out of the question, because her alcoholic father didn't have a dime to pay in ransom. Murder had seemed just as unlikely. Forced prostitution had concerned her, but again, Austin just didn't fit the profile of a violent, small-time pimp. There was the possibility of being forced to be a drug mule. But, if that ended up being what this was all about, she would play along until she was sent out on a shipment. Then she'd just disappear.

Slavery in a foreign country had been the only item on the

page that had seemed to be a scary and real possibility. But she had pretty much ruled that one out by calling the airport one hour ago and asking the clerk at the executive terminal if there were a private jet registered to Hughes Pharmaceuticals that was flying out in just over an hour. The clerk had confirmed that the jet was there and was being fueled as they were speaking.

Just to be sure, she had searched for Hughes Pharmaceuticals on the web. The home page for Hughes Pharmaceuticals had popped up first on her search list. The website had looked legit enough. She had called the number listed on the "Contact Us" button on the webpage. The woman that had answered the phone had been very friendly and had confirmed that Austin Vernon did in fact work for Hughes Pharmaceuticals as the assistant manager of the Southwest region. Seeing the website and confirming that Austin was who he had said he was had helped a lot.

With less than an hour left before she had to be at the airport, Brittany had decided that she would stick with her decision to take the job. For her, the potential benefits clearly outweighed the risks. She desperately wanted financial independence. Since the rape, it had become painfully obvious that she couldn't bear to work as an escort any longer. But without the income from her escort job, she couldn't afford to pay her living expenses and still buy the things she wanted.

Upon entering the terminal, it took only a few moments for her to find Austin standing by the pilot's flight-registration counter. He was conversing with an attractive male in his mid-thirties with wavy dark hair and a jet-black mustache. She walked directly over to Austin and said, "I made it."

"Good," Austin said as he turned to greet her with a smile. "I'm glad you're here. I'm sorry again about the short notice. Now let me introduce you to John Costa, the pilot of our corporate jet."

Brittany reached out and shook the pilot's hand.

Austin continued, "John, let me introduce Brittany Adams, our newest employee."

"It's good to meet you." Brittany looked carefully into John's eyes for any hint of ill intent, but instead she found only warmth.

"John has already filed the flight plan and fueled the plane," Austin said. "Brittany, if you're ready to leave, then let's get on our way. Do you have any questions before we go?"

"I do have one question. Would you please tell me where we're going?"

"Since you've been willing to come this far, I can tell you that John is going to fly you to our corporate training center in Mexico, which is just outside of Mexico City. You are the last of forty women that we have hired for this job. Training begins tomorrow at 8:00 a.m. so we need to get you there as quickly as possible so that you can get settled and get a good night's sleep before beginning your training."

"I had already worked through any misgivings that I might have had before I got here, or I wouldn't have come. After we are in the air, maybe you could answer a few more of my remaining nine hundred and ninety-nine questions."

Austin chuckled. "We'll do just that as soon as we're in the air."

He and John led the way through the doors and out onto the tarmac where a sleek, ten-passenger corporate jet was waiting. The words "HUGHES PHARMACEUTICALS" were painted on the tail of the airplane.

As Brittany boarded the plane, she took a last look over her shoulder at Portland. As she turned and entered the plane, she thought to herself, *I'm not going to miss Portland one bit. I'm going to make this new job work for me, no matter what it takes.* She took a seat across the aisle from Austin as John shut the door of the plane with a loud click.

CHAPTER 8

TREVOR HURRIED TO the front desk at the Philadelphia House Restaurant. In spite of his best efforts, he had ended up being over an hour behind schedule at the office for the rest of the day and had finished with his last patient at 7:15 p.m.

"Will you be having dinner with us tonight, sir?" the receptionist at the desk asked.

"I'm here for the pharmaceutical company dinner and lecture," Trevor replied quickly. After he saw the puzzled look on the greeter's face, he added, "It's sponsored by Medicon."

"Ah, yes. They're in the conference room." He gave Trevor directions to the conference room, and Trevor lost no time in heading that direction.

Upon entering the room, he noted to his relief that he wasn't too terribly late because the salads were just being served and the speaker hadn't started yet. He spotted the only empty chair at a table near the front. As he walked to the table, he was pleasantly surprised to see that Melanie was seated next to the empty seat. She looked up and smiled as he approached. She then got out of her chair and greeted him with a firm handshake.

"I'm glad that you were able to make it, Dr. Davis," Melanie said. "I hope you don't mind sitting by me since it's the only seat left."

From the moment that Trevor had seen Melanie rise from her chair to greet him, he had noticed that something was different about her tonight. In the year that Melanie had been visiting him as a drug rep, she had always dressed conservatively with her hair pulled back and with a minimum of makeup. But here she was looking absolutely gorgeous. He couldn't tell if it were just the silk dress that she was wearing that showed off her trim figure or if it were the different hairstyle. Her eyes were striking. Whatever she had done differently, it was enough to immediately command his complete attention.

"Not at all," Trevor said. "I can't think of anyone else here that I'd rather have dinner with tonight."

Trevor waited until Melanie had taken her seat and then sat and greeted the other three medical providers and one of their wives that were seated at the table.

"Sorry that I'm late," Trevor stated as he turned back to Melanie.

"Oh, no problem," Melanie said. "They've barely begun serving the salad. You must have had a busy day at your office. I hope I didn't take too much of your time today."

"You were only there for a few minutes. I was already an hour behind when I talked to you, and it didn't get any better for the rest of the day. On top of that, my last patient was very dehydrated from food poisoning, and it took a long time to give him enough IV fluid."

"Is he going to be all right?" Melanie asked.

"He'll be fine as long as he keeps up his oral fluids."

Melanie picked up her fork and began sampling her salad. "Did you see that Dr. Fife was here when you came in?"

"He's here, all right. He's at the table kitty-corner from us. I don't think he'd miss a lecture on medication-assisted weight loss for anything. I talked to him before he left the clinic this evening and he was pretty worked up about this lecture. He is so against weight-loss medications. I hope he doesn't embarrass us all by arguing with the lecturer like he did at that lecture on Waitnomor two months ago."

"You told me a little about it. And I got the whole story again from Becky Morales, the Phoenix area representative for Pharmplus. You know who she is, don't you?"

Trevor nodded.

"Becky was so embarrassed by the way that Dr. Fife treated the lecturer. Apparently, Dr. Fife interrupted the speaker five or six times with difficult questions about the long-term safety of Waitnomor and the lack of long-term data for weight maintenance. I felt really bad for Becky. She and I have been friends since college. We were so excited last year at graduation when both of us got jobs in the Phoenix area. But now, after one year with Pharmplus, Becky is frustrated and is thinking about giving notice. Sales of Waitnomor in the Phoenix area have been flat for the last six months."

"I'm surprised to hear that Waitnomor is not doing well," Trevor said. "I have been using it more and more, and I am pleased with how it is working. It's at least as good as Reductol."

"Trevor, it isn't polite to praise my competitor's drug when I am paying for your dinner," Melanie said teasingly. "Besides," she continued in a slightly hushed tone, "There have been some uncon-firmed reports that Waitnomor is causing sudden deaths. I haven't said anything since the deaths are just scattered case reports, and I'm not FDA-approved to say anything about it to my medical providers. Becky, however, is worried sick about it. One of the doctors that she calls on in Flagstaff had a previously healthy, twenty-five-year-old patient that died suddenly last month. I have been concerned about Reductol, too, because it's in the same drug class as Waitnomor. Yet, as far as I know, there haven't been any sudden deaths that have occurred with the use of Reductol."

"We already know that this drug class," Trevor said, "the sympa-thomimetics, can cause sudden death in an extremely rare person.

Most likely, they'll find out that Waitnomor and Reductol don't cause any more sudden deaths than the extremely rare deaths that have happened with use of over-the-counter decongestants. They're all in the same drug class."

"All I know is that Becky is worried that Waitnomor might be causing more sudden deaths than the company is letting on," Melanie said. "I don't know if she's right or not, but it would be hard to detail a drug to medical providers when you are worried that it could be harmful to people."

"Melanie, I think your friend Becky is overly concerned. I'm sure that these drugs will be proven to be safe. I haven't had any trouble with my patients, and the drugs have definitely been useful in helping my obese patients to lose weight and achieve better health."

Melanie and Trevor's conversation was interrupted by the arrival of their waiter to pick up their partially-consumed salads. As the waiter was clearing their salad plates, one of Melanie's fellow drug reps stepped to the podium and began introducing the guest speaker for the evening. He explained that it would be best for the speaker to begin while they were eating their main course so that adequate time would be available at the end of the lecture for questions.

"We'll have more time to talk after the lecture," Trevor whispered to Melanie. He could hardly tear his eyes away from her.

CHAPTER 9

RICK ARRIVED AT the door of his office at Pharmplus thirty minutes later and unlocked it. He opened the door, flipped on the lights, and walked across the plush carpet to his desk. The desk was made from imported mahogany. He sat in his burgundy; high-backed; executive chair, reached across his desk to his laptop computer, and flipped up the lid. Rick double-clicked on the icon on the screen for internet access. He typed "tvtrucking.com," requested a video call with Austin and then sat back to wait. He was sure that Austin would log on in the next few minutes.

A soft bell-like tone sounded from the laptop. He sat up in his chair and focused his attention on the computer screen. "Hello, Austin," Rick said.

"Hey, Rick. How are you doing?"

"I'm doing just fine." It was good to hear from Austin. They hadn't seen much of each other for the last month while Austin had been traveling around the nation interviewing and hiring escort girls to be their new pharmaceutical representatives.

Rick continued, "Are your people sure that this is a secure connection?"

"This video link is protected by the best encryption software that is available anywhere in the world, thanks to my connections with dealers in stolen military equipment. In fact, this software comes to us via the United States Army."

"Well, at least we're being patriotic by using something that is made in the US. I just hope that it works as well as you say it does."

"Rick, you're being paranoid."

"You're right. It's just that things have been going so well. The last thing that we need is for some computer hacker with the police or FBI to listen in."

"Everything is going to be just fine."

"Were you able to hire the last girl?"

"She flew down with me from Portland. I think you're going to like this one."

"You haven't picked a bad one yet, at least as far as I can tell. I'm sure she'll be fine."

"I thought you might want to know that the test on the nasal delivery of the octopus venom went smoothly. We found a drunk in the end of a deserted alley last night and gave him two sprays. He was dead when we checked him a half an hour later. No one saw us, and no one suspects anything. I called the coroner's office anonymously. The preliminary result of the autopsy was death by natural causes."

"Perfect. Our men in Mexico have also tried out the octopus venom on a small-time dealer that had crossed us one too many times," Rick said. "It was delivered through the earpiece of a stethoscope and was highly effective. All we had to do was to leave the stethoscope on the desk in his cell in the dungeon. The punk kid couldn't resist playing with the darn thing. Of course, an autopsy wasn't done. However, it's unlikely that any coroner in North America would ever be looking for the venom of the Australian blue octopus in someone's ear."

"That's good news," Austin said.

"Our priority is to get the women you've hired trained as soon as possible. Sales of Waitnomor are still not good enough. We really need these girls out there increasing sales."

"I'll be sure that they're ready within the month."

"I'm working on another idea that might help boost sales of Waitnomor even higher."

"Oh, and what's that?" Austin asked.

"I'm going to hold off on telling you about it until I know for sure that the person that I am dealing with can make good on their promise."

CHAPTER 10

"UH-OH. HERE IT comes," Melanie said under her breath to Trevor. "At least he waited until after the lecture." Dr. Fife's hand had shot up as soon as the speaker had finished his lecture and the moderator had announced that there was time for a few questions. Melanie thought that the lecturer had presented the topic of medication-assisted weight loss in a down-to-earth and unbiased manner. That was exactly why she had requested this particular speaker. She knew that Dr. Fife would have come unglued if she had brought in a speaker that was flamboyant, arrogant, or didn't stick exactly to the FDA-approved slide deck, like some speakers couldn't help doing. Her plan seemed to have worked thus far because Dr. Fife had not interrupted the lecturer. But now, with his hand waving ominously in the air, she braced herself for the worst.

The speaker pointed to Dr. Fife and asked, "Your question, please?"

Dr. Fife stood and cleared his throat. "Weight-loss pills are dangerous. You said so yourself just a few minutes ago during your lecture. Why in the world would you suggest that I put my patients in danger with a treatment that helps them lose weight, but then they just put it back on again when they stop the drug? Learning to eat right and exercise are much cheaper, safer options. And they are just as effective in the long run." Dr. Fife's voice had increased in volume with each sentence. When he stopped speaking, there was silence in the room.

The lecturer responded, "Weight-loss medications are only recommended for significantly obese patients that are at risk for serious medical problems and death from their obesity. In those patients, the risks related to obesity are significantly greater than the risks associated with weight-loss medications."

"Obese patients just need to learn to eat right!" Dr. Fife said. "They are just food addicts. Millions of people in America eat correctly and remain thin throughout their lives. There is no difference between obese people and thin people except that obese people just don't push away from the table. Obese people don't need drugs. They just need self-control."

Scattered applause was heard from the audience. Looking around, Melanie recognized that the applause was coming exclusively from the thin medical providers that made up the majority of the attendees. The few significantly overweight physicians in the room were studying their fingernails or staring off into space.

The lecturer was determined in his support of Waitnomor. "We have been trying for fifty years to get our obese patients to eat correctly. We have sent them to commercial weight-loss programs, had them buy book diets, and have preached control of food intake as well as exercise. Our long-term success rate with the significantly obese after fifty years is close to zero. How many medical providers in this room can name more than five significantly obese people in their personal lives or in their practices that have lost at least fifty pounds without surgery and have kept it off for more than five years?"

The lecturer paused, waiting for response. None came, even from Dr. Fife.

After a moment, a hand shot up near the back of the lecture

room. Dr. Adams stood and began speaking. "You and the company that you represent, as well as the whole weight-loss industry, are making life miserable for my patients," she said with bitterness in her voice. "I have a practice full of mostly happy and well-adjusted women. Some of them are more on the thin side, and some are little heavier, but they are all successful in their fields of endeavor. Then along comes your pharmaceutical industry, along with Hollywood and women's magazines, that tell my patients that unless they look like the ultrathin actresses and models that are in advertisements and movies, they are fat. Your industry tells my patients that they are unattractive and that they are failures as women. These women then come to me in tears for help because their self-esteem has been destroyed, and they are suffering from depression. But instead of wanting psychotherapy and antidepressants, they want me to give them dangerous and frequently ineffective weight-loss medications to help them look like your industry's bulimic and anorexic role models. Obese patients that are reasonably healthy don't die young of their obesity. But they are definitely being injured physically and psychologically by pursuing the false stereotypes propagated by your industry."

Again, a smattering of applause was heard, although, this time, it was a little louder. One physician yelled out, "Hear! Hear!"

Melanie looked at Trevor and whispered, "This is awful. Why isn't anyone brave enough to say something positive about these medications?"

"With the mood in this room right now, any effort to say something positive would be like throwing one's self into a den of starving lions."

The lecturer attempted to regain control of the audience, "I never said that these drugs should be used for cosmetic weight loss. They should only be used for significantly obese people that are at risk for developing serious medical problems from their obesity."

A voice came from the other side of the room, "But that isn't keeping medical providers from prescribing these drugs to anyone that asks for them."

"I can't comment on the prescribing habits of physicians that don't follow the FDA-approved prescribing guidelines," the lecturer replied as calmly as he could. He glanced over at the drug rep that had introduced him with a hint of concern in his expression.

Dr. Fife stood again. "No self-respecting physician should be prescribing weight-loss—"

Mercifully, the drug representative that had been functioning as the moderator quickly stood, took the lapel microphone from the lecturer, and spoke louder than Dr. Fife into the microphone, "Thanks for coming, everyone. That's all the time we have. I'm sorry that we couldn't get to everyone's questions."

Dr. Fife slowly sat back down.

The drug representative continued, "Our speaker would be glad to stay for a few minutes to answer any additional questions individually in the front of the room."

Out of politeness, some members of the audience briefly applauded. With the dinner and lecture over and with the tension in the room still crackling like a live electrical wire in a pool of water, the attendees stood to leave, almost in unison. Melanie noticed that only one physician approached the lecturer to ask a question. After most successful lectures, the speaker had a field of six to eight attendees hovering around, waiting for their additional questions to be answered.

"Well," Melanie said to Trevor, "that went over like a lead balloon."

"Most of the medical providers that were here tonight are very much against weight-loss medications. I doubt that any medical provider that wasn't prescribing weight-loss medications before this lecture will start, but I also doubt that anyone that is already prescribing these medications will stop. I'm not going to stop prescribing them or taking them myself."

"Dr. Davis, I didn't know that you were taking a weight-loss medication," Melanie said. "You don't look like you need it at all."

"I am taking half a tablet of Reductol a day to keep from regaining the thirty pounds that I lost last year. You haven't seen me when I'm heavier. Every time I try stopping the Reductol and try to prevent weight regain by diet and exercise alone, my weight starts to go up one or two pounds a month. When I take the Reductol every day, my weight stays the same." Trevor scooted his chair away from the table and said, "Why don't I walk you to your car?"

"Sure," Melanie answered as Trevor stood. "I just need to talk to the lecturer for a moment before he leaves. Can you wait?"

"Yes, I can. Rather than wait here, do you mind if I accompany you while you finish up?"

Melanie smiled warmly as Trevor pulled her chair back. She stood and said, "I'd be honored." They headed for the podium where the lecturer was just finishing up with the lone physician's question.

Trevor held the door open as Melanie exited the Philadelphia House Restaurant. It felt good to be with Dr. Davis. At the same time, Melanie had to school herself. He was probably just being a gentleman by escorting her to her car. She couldn't hope that it meant he liked her.

They walked toward the parking lot. The night was pleasant, and there was a gentle breeze. The rich scents of summer wafted past their noses, carrying hints of nearby oleander bushes and freshly-mowed grass.

"My car is over there," Melanie said as she gestured to her right. "It's such a beautiful night, isn't it?"

"It's beautiful enough that we should enjoy it a little longer. How about taking a walk with me around the block? We can finish discussing how the lecture went tonight."

"That sounds wonderful, although can we please talk about anything besides the lecture?" Melanie was thrilled that Trevor wasn't going to rush off. Even though it wasn't a date, and even though they were just colleagues, she wasn't ready for the evening to end either.

"It really didn't go that well, did it?" Trevor said with a chuckle. "How are sales of Reductol going?"

"Sales of Reductol are up five percent in Arizona, which is good news. Sales have decreased in Phoenix over the last year, however. Even though some medical providers, like you, are using it more and more, others have never used it and don't want to start. Or they have stopped using it due to concerns over side effects and long-term effectiveness."

"I'm sure that Dr. Fife is one of the main reasons for slow sales of Reductol in the Phoenix area," Trevor said. "Most of the medical providers in this area know and respect him. His opinions are given more weight by the fact that he is the president of the medical staff of Good Hope Hospital. When he decides he doesn't like a medication or a treatment, he's as tenacious as a pit bull in thwarting its use. I should know. I have to talk until I'm blue in the face just to get him to try anything new at our office."

"He is quite strong-willed," Melanie said with a smile. "How did the two of you end up as partners?"

"You remember that I did my residency at Good Hope Hospital, don't you?"

Melanie nodded.

"He was one of my favorite attending doctors. I looked up to him a lot and jumped at the chance to practice with him when he invited me."

"Have you liked being a family doctor?"

"Being a family physician is wonderful. The patients are fascinating, and there's a lot of variety. When I started medical school, I wanted to be a doctor to make a lot of money, to help people, and to be intellectually stimulated. Since then, I have realized that I will never get rich practicing medicine. I do like the variety of the cases that I see in family practice, but most of what I see is the same thing over and over again. I guess that the most satisfying part of being a family doctor is interacting with my patients. Each one is so different, and each is fascinating in their own way."

"Dr. Davis, that's why everyone loves you as their doctor because they know that you really care about them as people and not just as a disease on two legs. I know a lot of people that come to you. They all think you're wonderful."

"That's kind of them to say such nice things. And, please, call me Trevor."

"Okay. As long as I not seeing you professionally in your office. I do like your name."

"I like it, since it's the only one I've ever had." Trevor chuckled.

They walked in silence for a few moments, enjoying the pleasant evening and the pleasure of each other's company. Still unsure about whether Trevor was just treating her kindly because he was kind to everyone or because he actually liked her, Melanie waited and hoped that Trevor would ask her out. He definitely seemed to be happy to be with her. As they finished their walk around the block, Melanie felt a little crestfallen. What was he waiting for? She decided to not let him off so easily. She would invite him to the speaker program that she was putting on in two weeks at the Sunrise Point restaurant in North West Phoenix. She hadn't even thought to invite Trevor before since the restaurant was on the other side of the Phoenix area.

Arriving at Melanie's car, Trevor said, "Thanks for making just another drug lecture a pleasant evening."

"And thanks for sitting by me at the lecture. You really helped me to not get too stressed about what happened tonight. Also, thanks for taking me on a walk. It's so beautiful outside tonight. By the way…" Melanie sensed that it was now or never. "I'm putting on another lecture in two weeks. Luckily, the topic will be hypertension and will have nothing to do with weight-loss medications. It's going to be held at the Sunrise Point restaurant. Have you heard of it?"

"Isn't that the restaurant in North Mountain Park?"

"It is. I guess you actually do get out of Scottsdale once in a while."

"Ah, come on. I'm not all work and no play. I'd like to come, at least as long as you save the seat next to you for me again. Plus, who knows? You might need protection from a medical provider with an axe to grind."

It worked, she thought to herself. At least she knew that Trevor didn't mind hanging out with her at medical lectures at restaurants. Melanie waved goodbye to Trevor as she drove off. She couldn't help but hope that he would ask her out on a real date after the lecture in two weeks.

CHAPTER 11

BRITTANY'S FLIGHT FROM Portland to the training center in Mexico had been uneventful. Austin had slept for the whole trip. The sun had been going down as the plane began descending. The plane touched down and came to a stop at the end of a private airstrip. A company car was waiting on the runway and took Austin and her directly to the training center. When she asked about going through customs, Austin assured her that the company would take care of all of the necessary arrangements with the Mexican government for a temporary visa. That seemed odd to her, but she was getting tired of asking questions that weren't being adequately answered.

Once at the training center, the driver parked in front of a row of fourteen identical, white mobile homes that were spaced exactly six feet apart. Each sported an orange tree planted to one side of a dark red gravel front yard. A matching concrete sidewalk led from the parking lot to identical raised landings covered with green artificial turf.

Austin escorted her to a trailer that was identified as "Number Seven" by a wooden plaque that was attached to the front end of the trailer. The driver carried her luggage.

A tall, beautiful and brunette young woman dressed in pale lavender pajamas with a matching robe tied at the waist answered Austin's knock. "Hello, Austin. And hello to my new roommate," she said to Brittany.

Brittany said, "I'm Brittany Adams. Nice to meet you."

The woman said, "I'm Sarah James. Please come in."

Once inside, another young woman with long, blond hair that was also quite beautiful joined them from the mobile home's hallway. She was wearing a lime-green bathrobe tied at the waist and was combing her wet hair.

Austin said to Brittany, "This is you other new roommate, Amanda Thomas."

"It's good to meet you," Amanda said.

Tom said, "The three of you will be roommates for the duration of the training. There are thirty-seven additional women that will be attending the training meetings with you that were housed in the thirteen other mobile homes. Breakfast will be at 7:30 a.m. sharp." He bid them good night and he and the driver left.

Brittany's roommates took her on a short tour of their mobile home.

"It's good to have you here," Amanda said as they had finished the tour in what they informed Brittany was her new bedroom.

"Thanks. It is good to be here, at least I think so," Brittany said. "Everything has happened so quickly that I'm just a little out of sorts. This morning, before my job interview, I had no plans on leaving Portland. Now here I am."

"They did the same thing to Sarah and me," Amanda said. "Austin hired us and told us that we had to leave the same day."

"Believe me, we were both nervous at first," Sarah said. "But now that I have been here for five days, I'm not so worried. Even though the staff appears to be all men, they have been nice and have treated us with respect. I think that Amanda feels the same way."

"I do," Amanda said. "Everything will be fine. Would you excuse me while I finish getting ready for bed?"

After Amanda left the room, Sarah said in a low voice, "I'm glad to know that I'm not the only one that is a little uneasy about this whole thing. Sure, the men here have been perfect gentlemen. It's just that some of them, in fact a lot of them, have a coldness about them that makes me wonder what they would do if we stepped out of line even a little bit. On top of that, I have seen some of them staring at us like we are meat at a market."

"It never ends, does it," Brittany said.

"In truth, every one of the forty women are gorgeous. But, get this. Every one of us was working for an escort service at the time we were hired. Were you working as an escort?"

"Yes, I was."

"It makes me wonder if we're really here to be trained as pharmaceutical representatives or if the men have other plans for us."

Brittany said, "I really doubt that they would have gone to all the expense of flying everyone here and putting us up in brand new trailers just to sell us as sex slaves."

"That helps to hear it from someone else that everything is going to be okay."

"Hey, I'm getting pretty sleepy," Brittany said. "Let's call it a night and we can talk more tomorrow."

Brittany got ready for bed but wasn't able to sleep for hours because her mind kept wandering, imagining dozens of scenarios of what might occur over the next few days, some of which had less-than-pleasant outcomes. Exhausted, she had finally fallen into a troubled sleep.

The next morning, all forty girls, each one just as pretty as Sarah had said, had shown up for breakfast in the training center cafeteria. Looking around room, Brittany felt like she was in a beauty pageant, except that here every girl was pretty enough to be the queen.

Brittany was chagrined that, for one of the first times since junior high, she actually felt a little insecure about her looks.

At 8:00 a.m. sharp, the food was cleared, and the lectures began. Austin was the first speaker and welcomed the girls to the Hughes Pharmaceuticals training center.

"Even though each of you lacks the proper college degrees and job training, the purpose of this training seminar is to prepare you to function as full-fledged pharmaceutical representatives. Although a lofty goal, the potential earnings will make it all worthwhile. To drive home this point, starting at 8:00 a.m. this very morning, you have all started earning six thousand dollars a month. The first payday will be two weeks from today."

Using the chalkboard, Austin then outlined how each one of them could double, triple, and even quadruple their starting salary as sales of the medication that they were going to promote increased. Many of the girls buzzed to each other like bees in their excitement over the prospect of making more money than they had ever made.

Austin continued, "Let me next explain the course outline for the next month. You will be taught in four areas: pharmaceutical-product marketing, human anatomy and biology, pharmacology, and accounting. Each area will be covered for a half a day at a time, on a rotating basis, six days a week. All books and supplies will be provided. There will be homework assignments in every class each day." That announcement had produced a few groans from the audience.

"Testing will be done during the first hour of class each Friday and Saturday. In addition, lectures specific to the product that each of you are going to be selling and the methods to be used in its marketing will be held from 8:00 to 9:00 a.m. on Monday, Tuesday and Wednesday.

"I want to reassure you that I am certain that each of you will do well in the training since each of you has completed at least your first year of college with at least a C average. Finally, I will be available throughout the month in my office, if there are any questions or concerns."

One of the women asked about the name of the product that they would be selling. Austin stated that they had plenty to learn for the time being and that specific information about the product that they would each be selling would be presented in a few days at one of the 8:00 a.m. lectures.

A balding, retired professor of anatomy from Cornell University gave the rest of the lectures for the morning. By noon, Brittany had developed a headache from the strain of being back in the classroom and her wrist hurt from taking copious notes. Lunch time was a welcome relief. Not feeling hungry because of her headache, Brittany went outside to seek refuge from the incessant chatter and laughter in the lunchroom. The rest of the women stayed inside, whining that the heat outside was just too much. The midday heat on the patio didn't bother Brittany. She sat at a table and leaned back in her chair. *This month is going to be a long month. But no matter what they throw at me, I'm going to succeed, and I'm going to make a lot of money doing it.*

CHAPTER 12

MELANIE STOOD UP from the sandbox where she had been helping Becky's three-year-old son, Christopher, build a small mountain of sand. As she brushed the sand off of her knees and hands, she smiled as she saw Christopher run toward the small pile of sand, jump, and land in the middle of it, scattering the sand in all directions. Sitting down in the middle of the ruined mountain of sand, he grabbed two fistfuls of sand and threw them in the air over his head as he yelled, "Volcano!"

"No, Christopher. No throwing sand." Melanie tried to be stern, but she couldn't wipe the smile off her face. He was so darn cute even when he was misbehaving. In response, Christopher giggled, grabbed two more handfuls of sand, and sent them airborne.

"Okay. That does it." She walked toward Christopher as she continued," I'm going to have to take you back to your mommy." Before she could reach him, he hopped up and started running as fast as he could in a beeline away from Melanie.

"Christopher, come back here," Becky called out sternly as she came to the rescue. Christopher stopped, hesitated for moment, then turned and ran straight back to his mother. Becky picked him up, and Christopher gave her a big hug.

"How do you do that?" Melanie asked. "He never does anything that I say."

"It takes practice. Besides, he knows that you won't put him in a time-out for not listening like I will." Becky was the same height as Melanie and had short, dark brown hair and brown eyes. She looked fit and trim from daily exercise. "Why don't we head back to our table and see if George has gotten back with the fried chicken? We don't want to leave it in the hot sun for too long."

The two women, with Becky carrying Christopher, walked toward their picnic table that was hidden from view by a man-made rise in the terrain of the park. Becky and her husband had been inviting Melanie to join them for Labor Day for the past five years. For the first four years, they had gone to a park in Las Vegas where Becky and Melanie had been attending UNLV. They had both graduated in marketing and decided to seek employment as pharmaceutical representatives. It had been a thrill when they had both found jobs in Phoenix.

"How are things going with Pharmplus?" Melanie asked as they walked. Melanie knew that in spite of the fact that they were detailing competing products, Becky wouldn't be offended by her question. Their friendship was more important than success or failure at work.

"You don't want to know."

"Is it that bad? Are you still having problems with your manager?"

"Yes, it's bad. My regional manager at Pharmplus, Rick Newberry, is the problem. All of the Arizona reps met with him here in Phoenix last week. He's pretty mad about how poorly Waitnomor is selling in Arizona, especially in Phoenix. He met with each one of the Phoenix area reps individually. Unfortunately, I was the last one to meet with him. I already knew that it was going to be bad from the looks in the other rep's eyes as they had walked out of his office. Even then, I wasn't at all prepared for what he said." Becky swallowed hard, and she had to stop talking for a moment.

Melanie could tell that Becky was deeply troubled. Her friend was rarely ever at loss for words.

Becky was finally able to continue, "At first, he demanded to know why I wasn't selling enough Waitnomor. When I tried to explain the difficulties that I have been having, he interrupted me and insisted that my inadequacies were the problem. He told me that if I wanted to keep my job, I would have to begin using new techniques to sell Waitnomor. He told me that I would need to wear more makeup, shorter skirts, and lower tops and that my hairstyle had to go. He told me that he had already made appointments for me for that afternoon with a wardrobe consultant, a hairstylist, and a makeup artist."

"You've got to be kidding!"

"You haven't heard all of it. He said that I would have to be friendlier with the medical providers that I detailed and that I would have to take them out to dinner, concerts, symphonies, or whatever else it would take to earn the provider's prescriptions for Waitnomor. I tried to interrupt to tell him that what he was asking violated PhRMA guidelines, but he ignored me and kept going. He told me I needed to stand closer to the male medical providers, invade their personal space a little, and make an effort to get them to be attracted to me physically. Finally, he even suggested that I use whatever feminine ways I could to entice my male medical providers to use Waitnomor. Without really coming out and saying it, he suggested that going all the way with a male medical provider, if necessary, was not out of the question, if it was what it took to sell Waitnomor."

Becky had spoken hesitantly at first but had talked faster and faster as she had recounted her meeting with her manager. Tears were flowing as she finished, "Last of all, he told me that I had one week to decide whether I would be willing to implement these 'techniques' in selling Waitnomor, or I would lose my job."

"That's horrible," Melanie said. Becky was attractive and very feminine, but she would never stoop to the measures that her boss was asking her to use. Melanie put her arm around Becky's shoulders, and Becky began to sob.

Christopher reached over to Melanie and then hugged them both, one little arm around each of their necks, as he said "I love you, Mommy, and I love you, Melanie. Be happy, okay?"

"We shouldn't talk about these things around Christopher," Becky managed to say as she wiped her eyes and tried to compose herself.

"Here, let me hold him," Melanie said. Becky relinquished Christopher into Melanie's arms.

"I'm just going to have to tell Mr. Newberry no," Becky said firmly, although her voice was still quivering from her tears. "I can't even consider continuing to work for Pharmplus if that is what I'm going to be required to do. George and I are tight for cash so I'm hoping that I can finish out the month. Hopefully, by that time, I will have found a new job. The sad thing is that it probably won't be here in Phoenix, which will mean that we'll have to move. George will have to quit his job, and I won't live close to you anymore. That last part will probably kill me." Tears welled up in her eyes again.

"Becky, everything is going to be okay. I wish that I weren't going out of town for the next few days to detail my docs in my northern territory. I really want to be around to help you get through this. You haven't told George yet, have you?"

"No, I haven't dared."

"Talk to him about it. George will understand. He loves you a lot and would never want you to put up with what your boss is asking you to do. And I will understand if you have to move, even though it will probably kill me, too."

"A lot of good that would do us, dying because we miss each other," Becky said, laughing a little in spite of the tears in her eyes.

"Oh, come on. Neither one of us is going to die. I'll always be there for you, no matter what happens."

"And I'll always be there for you, too, through thin or thick, or is it thick or thin?" Becky asked, and they both laughed.

Melanie pushed open the door to her apartment with her shoulder since her hands were occupied with a suitcase and a heavy computer bag. Setting everything down by the door with a sigh, she closed and locked the door. The trip back from northern Arizona had been tiring, and her phone had died right after she had gotten in the car. The phone charging cable must have been knocked off the phone before she had fallen asleep the previous night at the hotel. Wanting to get home, she had decided not to stop and plug her phone into the car's powered USB port. Now that she was home, she tried to resist the urge to immediately pull out her charger, power up her phone, and check her voicemail in hopes that one would be there from Trevor. She tried telling herself that it didn't really matter whether he had called or not. Curiosity won out over restraint in about three seconds, and she plugged in her phone charger, attached her phone, and waited impatiently for it to restart. Finally, she was able to open her voicemail to see that there were three missed calls. The first missed call was from her mother, asking how she was doing and if she had met any nice men. Her mom's interest in her well-being had been a mild annoyance in Melanie's early twenties, but by her thirties, she was glad that her mom hadn't completely cut the apron strings. It meant a lot to Melanie that she cared enough to call and check up on her. Melanie mentally planned to call her mom later that evening.

The second missed call was from an unidentified number. Since one her the medical providers that she called on might be calling to confirm for the dinner at the Sunrise Point restaurant, she pressed play and discovered it was a robocall for a fundraiser for the local fire department. Melanie punched the pause button as fast as she could, and then she blocked and deleted the number.

The third missed call was also from an unidentified number.

It was from George, Becky's husband. That got her attention right away since George had never called her before.

"Melanie," he began with tightness in his voice. He paused for a moment, and Melanie could hear him sniff his nose. "Becky left us yesterday." He paused again and she could hear quiet sobbing. Melanie's heart began pounding with sudden anxiety. After a moment, George continued, "I need to talk to you. I'll be waiting for your call." George announced his number, and the message ended.

Melanie punched George's call back number. As the line began ringing, Melanie's mind raced. What had George meant when he had said, "She left us last night?" Maybe he had meant that she had left for a long business trip and that he was lonely. However, that didn't make any sense. Maybe she had been killed in a car accident. The pain of that thought hit Melanie in the pit of her stomach like a boxer's gut punch. Her eyes began to tear, and her throat tightened more and more as her mind continued to race through the possibilities. Had Becky been kidnapped or even murdered?

Mercifully, George answered the phone on the fourth ring. "Hello." It was George's voice, but he didn't sound like his usual jovial self.

"George, it's me, Melanie."

"I'm so glad that you called. I'm sorry I got so choked up when I called earlier. I've got things a little more under control now."

"What happened?" Melanie asked quietly. "What did you mean when you said that Becky left?"

"I got a text from Becky about three hours ago while I was at work. Becky was out of town for an overnight trip to southern Arizona to visit her medical providers. I was expecting the usual flirting with hearts and smiley faces like she always sends me when she's traveling, but instead, her text blew me away. She told me that she was leaving me and that she wasn't coming back. She told me to not forget to pick up Christopher from daycare and to take good care of him. She said she didn't want me to come looking for her because it would be a waste of my time. She finished by saying that her attorney would be in touch with me to discuss getting the divorce papers signed and negotiate the custody of Christopher."

He paused, and Melanie couldn't help but exclaim, "Oh, George!"

"That was it. That was all she said. I can't believe it. I thought she was happy with me and Christopher. I had no clue this was coming. It really hit me when an attorney called an hour later and stated that he was representing Becky in our pending divorce proceedings. He asked me if I would be contesting the divorce, and I lost it. I yelled at him that I didn't want to divorce Becky and then I hung up on him."

As George had been relating the particulars of Becky's text and the attorney's call, Melanie's mind raced. *Why in the world would Becky suddenly do this, especially without letting me know that something was wrong? It didn't make any sense. This couldn't be a cruel practical joke because Becky has always disliked practical jokes.* The cramping pain in Melanie's gut intensified. *Why didn't Becky call me to let me know what was going on? We are best friends, or so I thought.*

Realizing that George was sobbing quietly on the other end of the phone brought Melanie out of her sorrow. His heart was breaking, and he needed her help.

"George, have you and Christopher had dinner yet?"

"No," he said. "It hurts so bad that I don't feel like eating."

"Well, you do need to eat, and I'm sure that Christopher is hungry, too. I haven't had dinner yet, either. I'll pick you up in ten minutes, and we'll go out to dinner. We can talk more then."

George hesitated for moment and then replied with a little more composure, "I guess you're right. I really need to talk to someone about this, and you have been such a good friend to Becky and me. Also, it will be good to get out of the house. Everything here reminds me of Becky and makes me cry. When Christopher sees me crying, he gives me hugs and tells me that everything will be all right. He has no clue about what has happened, and I haven't had the heart to even try to tell him anything."

"I think it is best to let him think his mother is just on a business trip. I don't think he would understand if you tried to explain it to him anyway. I'll see you in ten minutes, okay?"

George replied that they would be ready. Melanie ended the call. She quickly found Becky's number in her contact list and called her. It rang but went to voicemail. Melanie sent Becky a text asking where she was and why she had left George, followed by a frowny emoticon. After waiting thirty seconds and getting no answer, Melanie grabbed her purse and keys and headed for the front door.

CHAPTER 13

DECIDING NOT TO visit the first medical office on her usual route, Melanie had gone straight to East Camelback Family Practice. In spite of still feeling horrible about Becky's disappearance, she had put on a cheery face as she had passed the receptionists and then had happily greeted the nurses at Dr. Davis's nurse's station. She had been informed that Dr. Davis was with a patient but would be out soon.

Now as she waited, she tried to force herself not to think about Becky. She concentrated on remembering the pleasant moments that she had spent with Dr. Davis over the past year. As pleasant as the memories with Dr. Davis were, it didn't work, and her mind jumped back to her concerns about Becky. Could Becky really have run off with another man? For the life of her, Melanie couldn't imagine when Becky would have found the time to even get to know someone else. Melanie knew that Becky had been on the internet a lot lately, ever since she had learned that a patient in southern Arizona had developed a serious heart arrhythmia after taking Waitnomore for a year. Becky had been trying to find other reports of serious problems in Waitnomor users. Maybe she had fallen in love with some guy over the internet and had gone to meet up with him.

"Hello, Melanie," Dr. Davis said right in front her, startling her. "I caught you daydreaming. It must have been interesting because you didn't notice me until I was right in front of you."

"You caught me. I was thinking about something very sad that happened to good friend of mine yesterday."

"What happened?"

"You know Becky Morales, don't you? She's one of the drug reps for Pharmplus. She details you on Waitnomor."

"Yes, I know her very well."

Melanie told Dr. Davis what had happened with Becky. As she finished, Melanie's eyes were filled with tears.

"This is really sad news."

"I can't believe that she didn't even call me and tell me that she was leaving." Melanie's tears were now flowing freely.

Trevor offered her a tissue from the box that was on the nurse's desk and then asked, "Why don't we talk about this in my office?"

Melanie nodded in agreement and Trevor led the way to his office. Melanie sat in the chair that Trevor offered, and he sat next to her.

"I'm sorry that I'm such a crybaby," Melanie said as she dabbed her eyes with the tissue. "I know that I'm interrupting you right in the middle of a busy day. All I really came for was to remind you of the lecture at the Sunset Point restaurant tomorrow. Are you still planning on attending?"

"Yes, I'm coming."

"The dinner and the lecture start at 6:00 p.m." Melanie reached into her computer and pulled out a sheet of paper. "All of the details are on this invitation."

Trevor took the invitation and slid it onto his desk. "Thanks, but I probably won't need the invitation to remember where it's at."

Suddenly feeling embarrassed for crying in front of Trevor and his staff, she decided that it would be best to leave before Trevor asked any more questions about Becky and made her cry again. "I feel so bad for interrupting you. I really need to let you get back to your patients." She stood and walked out of Trevor's office into the hallway.

Trevor followed. "I wish that we could talk longer, but it is true that I am fifty minutes behind. I'm sure we'll have more time to talk tomorrow." Melanie smiled, thanked Trevor for his kindness, and then walked down the hallway toward the front office.

CHAPTER 14

"I CAN'T BELIEVE THAT none of the medical providers have arrived yet," Trevor said to Melanie. They were seated at a large dining table in a private room at the Sunset Pointe restaurant.

"Oh, they'll be here in twenty minutes or so, right before the lecture is supposed to start. You came really early."

"I came early to see if you needed help setting up."

"Is that the only reason that you came so early?"

"Okay, I confess: I really just wanted a few minutes with you when we aren't so rushed, like we always are at my office."

"So what's on your mind? We've got at least twenty minutes."

"I don't really have anything specific to say except that I enjoy being with you."

Melanie's heart jumped for joy. Trevor did like being with her. Keeping her excitement to herself, she said, "I enjoy talking with you as well. But I bet that you say that to every woman that you meet."

"Contrary to popular belief, I don't say that to every woman that I meet. And, I haven't met any women recently that were as interesting to talk as you are."

"You're such a flatterer. How is it that such a nice guy like you isn't at least being pursued by a dozen women?"

"I guess I'll take that as a compliment."

"I am curious. How have you resisted settling down with the girl of your dreams for all of these years?"

"Well, since you're so persistent, I'll tell you. The truth is that I have been married once before. My wife died of breast cancer four years ago."

"Oh, Trevor, I'm so sorry to hear that."

"We had been married for two years and had started talking about having a baby. She had gone in to get checked out before trying to get pregnant, and the doctor found a breast lump. The biopsy indicated that it was an aggressive breast cancer. She was only thirty years old…" Trevor was unable to continue.

Melanie asked softly, "What was her name?" The fact that he was willing to share such a private matter with her touched her deeply.

"Vanessa," Trevor said weakly through the lump in his throat. He did his best to try to clear his throat by swallowing hard and then struggled to continue. "Her name was Vanessa. Within a week of her diagnosis, she had a lumpectomy with an axillary node biopsy. The tumor was found to have already spread to the lymph nodes. She started radiation and chemotherapy almost immediately. Our plans for a child were put on indefinite hold. Her hair fell out and she lost so much weight.

"After the chemotherapy and radiation, she recovered well. Everything seemed to be okay for the next year." Trevor swallowed hard again.

Melanie could see from the pain in his eyes and face that his loss was still causing intense grief.

He continued, "A year later the cancer came back. She died six months later."

"That's terrible." Melanie desperately wanted to console Trevor and was trying to think of the right words. "I can tell how much you're still grieving for her. You must have loved her so much."

"We were very much in love." Trevor stared straight ahead,

clearly lost in the memory of a love now far out of reach. He sighed heavily once and then turned and smiled at Melanie. "It has been four years. The first few years were hard, but I've gotten over losing Vanessa as much as a person can get over the loss of a loved one. I don't bring up the subject very often."

"I am glad you thought enough of me to share it with me. She must have been quite the woman."

"It still amazes me that she chose to be my wife. She could have had any number of guys. I guess that I was just lucky."

"I have a hard time believing that."

"It's true. I was really overweight when I first met her."

Melanie's disbelief showed on her face.

"I know that it's hard for you to believe, but I'm a fat person in recovery. I have had a weight problem on and off for years. I eat when I'm stressed. I gained fifty pounds in medical school and then thirty more after Vanessa died. A year after she died, I looked at myself in the mirror and decided that enough was enough. I started exercising and dieting and lost the thirty pounds that I had gained in the previous year, but I just couldn't lose the other fifty pounds that I had gained in medical school. I first learned about the diet drug phentermine from a doctor that I met at a conference two years ago. It was the answer I was looking for. I started taking phentermine almost immediately. It gave me the edge that I needed, and I was able to drop thirty pounds over the next six months. However, like most people that take phentermine, my weight plateaued for the next six months, even though I was still taking the phentermine. About a year ago, I tried your drug Reductol. I was hoping that it would help me to lose the last twenty pounds. Forgive me for saying so, Melanie, but I didn't lose any more weight on the Reductol."

"I don't mind."

"Anyway, that's why I just haven't dated much since Vanessa died. I have tried, but my heart just hasn't been in it. It's still hard for me to accept the fact that Vanessa's gone. Sometimes I think it's all just a bad dream, that I'll wake up and she'll be back, like she's been away on a long vacation and now has returned home. Intellectually, I know it isn't true. It's just been hard to convince my heart otherwise."

Melanie reached out and put her hand on Trevor's arm and smiled warmly. Letting her hand drop, they stood quietly for a few moments. They were interrupted by the arrival of the first medical provider.

"What did you think about the lecture?" Melanie asked. She was walking with Trevor to her car after the lecture.

"It was interesting," Trevor said.

"Oh, come on, Trevor. Is that all you're going to say?"

"Well, his presentation was a little one-sided."

"I was afraid that you would think that," Melanie said as they arrived at her car. "I was thinking the same thing that you were thinking. This guy is definitely not my favorite lecturer. I know that medical providers ignore lecturers that show the slightest bias toward the company that is paying for the lecture. In truth, I was really hoping to get Dr. Alan Peterson, the editor of *Cardiology Today*. He's interesting to listen to and presents the pros and cons of all the medications that are used for the disease on which he's lecturing. Unfortunately, my company informed me last week that he suddenly wasn't available. They sent this guy in his place at the last minute."

"I'm glad to hear you say that. I was worried that I would offend you by telling you how I really felt."

"Thanks, but you don't have to worry about me. I need to be sure that these lectures are top-quality or else medical providers are going to stop coming."

Trevor asked, "I know that this is out of the blue, but how about going with me to a Camelback State football game two weeks from today? I know that the game is a few weeks away, but I wanted to ask you now because I am going out of town tomorrow to visit my family. I'll be getting back the Thursday before the game."

"That sounds like a lot of fun. I can't think of anything that I have scheduled for that day."

"The game starts at noon. Can I pick you up at ten?"

"That will be great! I'm excited to go. And thanks for coming early to help me today."

"Melanie, I don't know why I let myself tell you about my struggles with my weight. Sorry that I revealed so much about myself."

"I'm glad to know that you consider me someone that you can share those things with."

Suddenly, Trevor leaned forward and kissed her on the cheek. "Thanks for a wonderful evening. Drive safely and I'll see you in two weeks."

Barely able to think straight, Melanie got into her car and turned on the motor. Trevor waved goodbye and turned to walk toward his car. Melanie felt like getting back out of her car, running after him, and asking him to spend the whole rest of the evening with her. Instead, she put her car in gear and drove out of the parking lot. Still, she couldn't keep the happy grin off her face, nor did she want to.

CHAPTER 15

AS A WELCOME change from the usual boring first-hour lecture, Brittany was pleased to see that Austin would be the speaker. Austin began, "Hughes Pharmaceuticals is not the real name of the pharmaceutical company that hired you. We used the name Hughes Pharmaceuticals to lend credibility to our recruitment efforts while at the same time keeping you from connecting any of the activities here with our real company. That way, any woman that decided to quit would have no clue as to the real name of the company that had sponsored the seminar. The real name of the company that hired you is Pharmplus, a worldwide leader in pharmaceutical research, manufacturing, and sales. The company recognizes that each one of you that is still at the seminar is doing well in your training and is committed to long-term employment with the company. Pharmplus is committed to you, and at this stage of your training, there is no reason for you not to know for whom you are really working. I do want to apologize for this deception, the fake Hughes Pharmaceuticals website, and the operator that you might have called at Hughes Pharmaceuticals that was really just my colleague. However, due to the nature of the training and preparation that we were planning to give you for your new jobs as pharmaceutical representatives, we felt that we had no choice.

"The drug that you are going to be detailing is called Waitnomor. It is a weight-loss medication. Since it's important that each of you understand how Waitnomor works, the rest of the 8:00 a.m. lectures for the next and last week of your training will be about Waitnomor itself and how to market it successfully.

"Each one of you will need to assume a new name and identity. This is important because none of you have college degrees and a college degree is pretty much a standard requirement for being employed as a pharmaceutical representative. I want to remind you that each one of you said at your initial interview that such a possibility was acceptable to you. I want to assure you that each of your new names and identities have been thoroughly researched. These names and identities will stand up under close scrutiny. The new identities that you are going to receive are for women, obviously, between twenty-four to twenty-eight years of age, putting you a little closer in age to the medical providers that you will be visiting and consistent with a college graduate with at least two-years' experience as a pharmaceutical representative."

Pausing for a breath, he then asked if there were any questions. There weren't any. Brittany was sure it was because they were all still trying to wrap their minds around what he had just told them. "Your fact sheets of personal information about your new identities will be handed out at the end of my lecture. You are required to memorize all of the items on your fact sheet by next Friday. You are also required to use your new names and identities twenty-four hours a day from the moment you leave this lecture, even in the trailers. The penalty for not doing so will be one hundred dollars for each infraction, which will be taken out of your next paycheck. Each of you will be provided with a new driver's license, passport, and social security card under your new identity at the completion of your training. You will also be given a major credit card in your new name that will be used to cover all of your expenses in your new area."

A few hands finally shot up, but Austin ignored them as he continued, "Along with the information about your new identities, you will be given assigned locations after the completion of your training. Each one of you will have twenty-four hours to get back with me on whether your new identity and your future area of employment is satisfactory. Changes will be accommodated, if possible."

Austin then spent the rest of the hour lecturing on techniques that they were to employ to increase sales of Waitnomor. They were to dress and act provocatively, befriend their medical providers on more than a professional level, and use their bodies as a marketing tool. None of Austin's revelations were surprising to Brittany. She had known all along that there had to be a reason why they had hired forty beautiful escorts to help sell their product. The marketing techniques that he was suggesting that they use were no different from what any of them had already done to service their customers in the past.

At the end of the lecture, their new names, identities, and assigned territories had finally been handed out. Brittany was a little frustrated to learn that she was going to be working in the Phoenix, Arizona, area. She had never been there and all she knew about Phoenix was that it was in a desert and that it was hot, which was about as opposite of Portland as she could imagine. Her new name was going to be Shannon Lowry. *That name doesn't fit me at all.* She'd just have to get used to the name and the desert. She didn't want to be labeled as a complainer.

"You've scored higher on the tests than all of the other girls," Austin said to Brittany. Austin had pulled Brittany aside after his lecture that morning and had asked her if she would meet with him in his office during lunch. Austin was seated behind his desk in his office.

"Thank you," Brittany said.

Austin continued, "Your performance in the practice sessions indicates that you have an excellent aptitude for sales. You think and react quickly. Because you're our top graduate, we have decided to send you to one of our most difficult territories. Phoenix at the bottom of the list with respect to sales of Waitnomor. I wanted to sit down with you to help prepare you for the challenge that you are going to be facing. Waitnomor sales in Phoenix are down largely due to the efforts of one man, Dr. Erwin Fife. He practices in Scottsdale. As the president of the medical staff of one of the largest hospitals in the city, he is a powerful man. His influence has spread to the medical providers of the other hospitals in Phoenix through meetings that he has attended where he has been very vocal and quite effective in his efforts to squelch the local use of weight-loss medications. I put a list of the medical providers in Phoenix and the clinics that they are associated with in the packet that you were given this morning. I'd like to go over it with you."

Shannon retrieved the list from her packet and then moved her chair next to Austin's chair so that they could both see the list.

Austin continued, "Using the information from the previous Waitnomor representative, I have highlighted the medial providers that are already prescribing weight-loss medications in green. As you can see, there aren't very many. I have also highlighted the medical providers that are least likely to prescribe weight-loss medications in yellow. In Doctor Fife's clinic there is another physician, Dr. Trevor Davis, who is one of the biggest prescribers of weight-loss medications in the Phoenix area.

"We believe that in order to increase sales of Waitnomor in Phoenix, you're going to have to concentrate your efforts on Dr. Fife. You need to use whatever means you can to convince him to stop speaking out so strongly against weight-loss medications and to convince him to begin using them in his practice. Possibly, the key to accomplishing this is through his partner, Dr. Davis." He paused and asked, "Any questions so far?"

Brittany said, "No. No questions."

"Use this list," Austin said, "And visit the medical providers that are already prescribing weight-loss medications first. The information and techniques that you have learned here will help you to get them to abandon the other weight-loss medications that they are using and switch to Waitnomor. Then use your successes with those medical providers to try to influence the other medical providers on this list to begin using Waitnomor. Leave the medical providers that are highlighted in yellow for last. Their track record of being strongly resistant to using weight-loss medications will most likely result in your time being wasted.

"My manager and I will be in Phoenix for a district meeting in one month to meet with you and the other three representatives from Arizona. We're going to want to see how things are going. I'm sure that you'll have good things to report."

"It all seems pretty straightforward to me," Brittany said. "I do have a question, however. Is it alright with you if Jennifer and I room together in Phoenix?"

"Brittany, who is Jennifer?"

"This new identity thing is hard even for you, isn't it?" Brittany said with a smile. "I'm Shannon Lowry now, and not Brittany anymore. And, before her new identity, Jennifer was my roommate, Sarah James."

"That's right. Sorry. It is hard to keep all of these new names straight. Sure, it's okay if you room together in Phoenix."

"She's more adamant about rooming together than I. I think she's feeling nervous about being dropped off alone in an unfamiliar, big city."

"Are you feeling nervous about this whole thing?"

"Not at all," she declared confidently with a dazzling smile. "This is going to work out wonderfully. I'll make sure that it does."

CHAPTER 16

TREVOR CHECKED THE address in his phone to make sure that he was at the right apartment and then knocked on the door. Sticking his phone back into his pocket, he stepped back to wait for Melanie to answer the door. He had been looking forward to taking Melanie to this football game for two weeks and was excited and nervous now that the time had finally arrived. In keeping with the spirit of the game, he had donned his Camelback State T-shirt, along with a pair of tan shorts.

Melanie still hadn't answered the door, so he took a second to check out his mud-stained tennis shoes. He hadn't been thinking when he had worn his new tennis shoes fishing with his father last week when he had gone home to visit. The shoes had gotten muddy when he had slipped off a rock while crossing a stream. At least they looked better than when he had gotten back, thanks to a trip through his washing machine.

His moment of self-inspection was interrupted by a cheery, "Hi! Come in," from Melanie as she opened the door. She was wearing light blue jean shorts with a white top that was embroidered with patterns of tiny, white beads. Her hair was pulled back with a white hair clip. She looked amazing.

"I'm almost ready," Melanie said with a smile. She gestured to a couch in her living room and added, "Have a seat and I'll be just a minute."

"I'm sure I can manage to keep myself occupied," Trevor said as Melanie turned and headed down the hallway of the apartment. It was impossible for him to resist stealing a quick, but appreciative, glance at her cute figure and well-shaped legs before she disappeared.

Looking around the living room, Trevor noticed a wicker bookcase against one wall. Its shelves contained several framed photographs. Stepping closer to take a look, he recognized Melanie in most of the pictures. One was a family picture and showed Melanie standing behind an older woman that looked to be her mother. On each side of Melanie stood what appeared to be Melanie's brothers, sisters, and their spouses. A half-dozen children of various ages were arranged in front of the adults. The picture had to be recent because Melanie didn't look any different now than she looked in the picture. Trevor felt a little sad as he remembered that Melanie's mother had been a widow for years. It had to have been hard to raise the kids alone after her husband's death. At the same time, Trevor could tell from the happy smile on her face in the pictures that Melanie's mother loved her family deeply and that they loved her just as much.

"Okay. I'm ready," Melanie said as she returned from the hallway.

"You've got a great looking family," Trevor said as he turned toward Melanie. "They all seem to be so happy. Your mother is quite the lady to have raised all those kids by herself."

"You're right, she is a neat lady." Melanie opened the outside door of her apartment and stepped through the door.

"Just like her daughter," Trevor said as he followed her.

"Thank you, Trevor," Melanie said as she locked the door. "That was a sweet thing to say. I guess that flattering the women that you date is one of your specialties, also."

"You caught me. And I thought that women liked compliments."

"They do like compliments, even if they tease you about giving them. A compliment a day keeps your date from running away. So, I'll race you to the car," Melanie said suddenly, and she was gone.

"Thanks for the head start!" This was another side of Melanie that he had never seen. He sprinted after her down the outside walkway. He figured that with a little luck he'd get there first, mainly because he knew where the car was parked, and Melanie didn't. Grinning as he ran, he couldn't help but be excited about spending the rest of the day with a woman that was so much fun.

CHAPTER 17

THE THIRTY-SEVEN REMAINING women at the Pharm-plus training seminar finished their month-long training with one last lecture from Austin. Near the end of his lecture, he said, "You will be given a company credit card as you leave today that you will use for all personal and business-related purchases. Each of your credit cards currently has a $12,000 credit balance, which is equal to the amount of the two paychecks that you earned while at this training seminar. I wish each of you well in your new territories and thanks for all your hard work this past month. This ends our seminar. Please head to your rooms to pack and get ready to leave."

Shannon was excited about the prospect of having so much money to spend. She hoped the shopping was good in Phoenix. She stayed in the lecture hall for a few minutes and said good bye to a few of the other women she had gotten to know. She avoided the thronging mass of crying and hugging women in the center of the room and headed to her trailer. Grabbing her already packed bag, she headed for the buses that were ready to take them to the airport. She didn't give much thought to the fact that she felt little attachment to most of the other women at the seminar. It hadn't been any different at the training seminar than it had at been at any other school she had ever attended. To her, it made no sense to stay around to witness sentiments that she didn't feel. True, she had become acquainted with Jennifer because they were roommates, but that was as far as it went. When Jennifer had asked Shannon to be her roommate in Phoenix, Shannon had agreed, but only because she was concerned that Jennifer's poor performance at the seminar might result in her being a poor pharmaceutical representative. With Jennifer as her roommate, she could keep an eye on her and do damage control, if needed.

Shannon and Jennifer flew from the training center in the same private jet that Shannon had arrived in to Tucson where they cleared customs easily with their new passports. They then flew commercially in first class from Tucson to Phoenix.

Phoenix International Airport was no different from any other airport she had ever been in, Shannon decided. There were endless concourses lined with innumerable gates for faraway destinations interspersed with small, high-priced stores that would have never survived outside of the airport's captive environment. Shannon and Jennifer headed straight for one of the high-priced clothing outlets that looked like it sold more than T-shirts and mugs. Their bags in baggage claim could wait while they flexed their newfound financial muscles by trying out their brand-spanking-new company credit cards.

Although Shannon was calm and cool in most circumstances, she did let her hair down a little when she went shopping. The exhilaration showed on her face as she selectively moved through the racks of costly clothing in the small shop. It only took moments to pick out a casual dress, a couple of pairs of shorts with matching tops, and a new bikini. She presented the merchandise to the clerk and then waited as calmly as she could while the clerk ran the company credit card through the machine. She had $12,000 to spend! It was a dream come true.

The credit-card machine paused and then seemed to wait forever to start printing the approval for the purchases. The clerk just stood there, staring at nothing. With her heart in her throat, Shannon almost rushed out of the store. Maybe there was something wrong with the credit card. The store clerk was going to find that the card was illegal somehow and call the authorities. Before Shannon could bolt, the receipt printer suddenly sprang to life and spat out the approval slip. Relieved, Shannon quickly signed her name effortlessly as Shannon Lowry, just as she had practiced hundreds of times during past week. The request for a picture ID also brought a small pang of anxiety. Shannon forced herself to calm down. Austin and his boss, Rick, knew what they were doing. Her new identity was solid. Everything was going to be just fine. Providing her brand-new driver's license, she had only to wait a moment, and the satisfied clerk handed both cards back to her with a smile.

Shannon stepped out into the concourse and waited for Jennifer. Moments later, Jennifer joined her from the same store, and the two women laughed as they compared receipts to see who had spent the most. Shannon had spent the most, of course. The women's elevated moods carried them through the tedious process of getting their baggage and then renting a car. Minutes later, with Jennifer driving and Shannon as navigator, they were on Interstate 10 heading east toward Tempe, a suburb in the southeast part of the Phoenix area. They had already agreed that an apartment near Camelback State University in Tempe would offer a greater variety of social opportunities with people their own age, like parties and dates, and would still be centrally located.

CHAPTER 18

THE SETTING SUN lit up the sky over West Phoenix with brighter yellows near the horizon that transitioned to deeper colors of amber higher in the heavens. A few stray clouds that were near the horizon where the sun was setting were ignited into flaming red nebulae. What Phoenix didn't have in beautiful fall colors, it had in abundance in gorgeous sunsets. The intense heat of midday was slowly abating, and the evening air was pleasant.

Melanie and Trevor sat at a round white table on the veranda at the rear of Melanie's apartment. The increasing splendor of the sunset had demanded a temporary stop to their game of Spades. Silhouetted against the darkening sky were a number of desert palms. From their vantage point on the second floor, they could almost imagine that they were seeing the sunset from the balcony of a hotel in the South Pacific.

"I love living in Phoenix because I get to see these beautiful desert sunsets," Melanie said as she sipped from her glass of ice water.

"It's a great ending to great day," Trevor said. For Trevor, it also helped that Camelback State had decimated their opponent by a score of forty-five to fourteen.

Spending the day with Melanie had been more than enjoyable.

Their conversation had covered a variety of topics, and Trevor was fascinated by Melanie. Her positive outlook on life was infectious, and her cute smile that dimpled her cheeks and lit up her eyes was irresistible. She had responded warmly when he had reached out to hold her hand or had tentatively placed his arm around her waist.

"I hope that's not a signal that you're planning on ending our day anytime soon," Melanie said. "I need to beat you again at Spades to keep you humble."

They resumed playing cards as the sunset slowly faded. It wasn't long before Melanie beat Trevor again.

"You're just too good for me." Trevor said.

"It's just a game of chance," Melanie said. "And I was just lucky tonight."

"I'd say that it's more of a case of lady luck favoring the most beautiful person here."

"I'll take that as a compliment. Thank you." She stopped and swatted an insect away from her face. "It's getting pretty dark and the lights are starting to attract bugs. Why don't we go inside?"

They collected the cards and glasses of ice water and headed through the patio door into Melanie's apartment.

"Have a seat on the couch," Melanie said to Trevor as she took his glass from his hand. Trevor obediently sat on the couch as Melanie took their glasses into the kitchen. He leaned back and stretched his arms along the back of the couch. Melanie returned moments later, and as she turned to sit next to Trevor, she caught the tip of her tennis shoe on the carpet. Off balance, she aimed for the couch, trying to end up safely on the couch without landing on Trevor. To her embarrassment, she ended up smack-dab against Trevor's side. She blushed and tried awkwardly to slide away from him.

"You don't need to move away," Trevor said gently.

Melanie smiled and looked up Trevor. "I really did catch my shoe on the carpet and..." As she was speaking, Trevor let his arm fall from the back of the couch onto her shoulders.

"I guess I'm lucky tonight as well." Trevor put his other arm around Melanie and held her close. She responded in kind by placing her free arm around Trevor. They held each other quietly and gently.

Trevor loosened his arms a little from around Melanie's back and caressed her cheek. She leaned her face into his hand and closed her eyes. Softly, Trevor lifted her chin, allowing him to look deeply into her now-open eyes. Unable to resist, and more than willing to give into the passion that was building in his chest, he bent down to kiss Melanie's lips. Melanie's eyes closed, and her lips parted a little as she waited for his kiss.

A piercing whistle of a bomb falling from the sky followed by a booming explosion emanated from Trevor's phone and shattered the moment. Melanie startled and opened her eyes. Trevor reached for the cell phone in his pocket.

Melanie said, "That's your cellphone ringtone?"

"No. I mean, not usually. My kid brother is such a joker. He must have downloaded this ringtone when I lent him my phone a few days ago." Trevor twisted so that he could see the number displayed on the phone. It was number for the emergency room at Good Hope Hospital. "It's a call from the emergency room at Good Hope," Trevor said with just a little frustration in his voice. "I need to take this one. Sorry."

"Go ahead."

With one arm still around Melanie, Trevor pushed the call button on his phone, held the phone to his ear, and then, when the ER answered, said, "Hello. This is Dr. Davis."

The conversation with the emergency room doctor took less than a minute.

"I'm so sorry, but I need to go." Trevor pocketed his phone. "A patient of mine, who is the wife of one of the obstetricians that I work with, is having chest pain. The emergency room doctor wants to admit her for observation. The obstetrician is with his wife in the ER, and he's very anxious about getting her admitted immediately."

"That sounds bad. I hope she's okay," Melanie said as she reluctantly slid forward until she was seated on the edge of the couch. Trevor reached out for Melanie's hand, and Melanie slipped her hand into his.

Trevor said, "Today was lots of fun."

"It was a great day. Thanks so much for asking me out."

Trevor stood and helped Melanie to her feet. "Thanks for accepting the invitation."

Still holding hands, they walked to the door. Trevor embraced her, and they kissed tenderly.

"I'm sorry that I have to go," Trevor said. "It seems like I only get called when I least want to be interrupted."

"That's the life of a doctor, right?"

"Yes." Trevor chuckled. "It is." He kissed her one last time and then stepped through the door. Pausing for a moment, he turned and said, "I'll call you."

"I look forward to it," Melanie answered as Trevor disappeared into the night.

CHAPTER 19

IT HAD TAKEN the rest of the day for Shannon and Jennifer to find an apartment complex that provided furnished apartments that they both liked. Since moving out of her father's home after high school, Shannon had never had a roommate before. She was rediscovering just how irritating it was to have to deal with someone else's needs beside her own. It had been years since she had been forced to mother her younger brother and alcoholic father after her mother had died.

The landlord for their chosen apartment complex had an apartment that was available for occupation the next day. After spending the night in a hotel, they moved their luggage in the next morning and then went shopping for the rest of the day. Neither of them had ever owned appropriate business attire for detailing medical providers. And with the short notice that they had gotten before shipping out for the training seminar, they definitely hadn't had time to buy anything. By the end of the day, they each had spent over two thousand dollars on new skirts, blouses, jackets, shoes, and accessories.

Since they had initially only rented one car at the airport, Shannon dropped Jennifer off at a car rental agency so that she could rent her own car. Austin had asked them to use rental cars for the first few months that they were in their new territories. They would be provided with company cars later.

After making sure that Jennifer was well into the process of renting her own car, Shannon drove straight to the closest physician's office that was on the list of providers that Austin had given her that were already prescribing weight-loss medications. As she collected marketing materials and samples of Waitnomor from the back seat of her car, she felt as nervous and jittery as she had on her first date. By the time she reached the front desk of the clinic, she felt like she was going to have a nervous breakdown. She was sure that she was going to make some terrible mistake and that the medical providers would immediately know that she was a fake. Using all of her will power, she went to the nurse's desk, introduced herself, and after a short wait, met her first doctor in the hallway. The doctor, a middle-aged bald man that was four-inches shorter than her politely thanked her for coming. While he listened patiently, she managed to spit out her memorized presentation on Waitnomor in reasonably good form.

At the end of her speech, he said, "It sounds like I should be using more Waitnomor. I have used it a little, but I have kind of been in the habit of using Reductol because it came out first. You'd better leave plenty of samples. I'm sure that I'll be needing them." He then excused himself so that he could get back to seeing his patients. The nurse showed her to the medical provider's sample cabinet, and she left ten boxes of starter packs of Waitnomor. Just like Austin had taught her, she made sure that her samples of Waitnomor were in front of and completely blocking the boxes of Reductol samples that were already in the medical provider's sample cabinet. The nurses had informed her that the physician that she had talked to was the only one that was in the clinic today. After checking with the nurses on which day would be best for her to return in order to catch all of the medical providers in the office, she had headed for her car in the parking lot.

Shannon settled into the driver's seat of her car. *That was easier than I thought it would be. He didn't even ask any questions. Medical providers don't seem to be any harder to influence than anyone else.*

Shannon was oblivious to the covert appraising glances from the nurse at the desk at East Camelback Family Practice. She was more concerned about whether she would be successful in detailing the biggest reason why Waitnomor wasn't selling in Phoenix, namely, Dr. Fife. Her plan was to talk to Dr. Davis first because Austin had indicated that he was already prescribing Waitnomor. Hopefully, she could gain Dr. Davis's confidence, which might then be helpful as she attempted to convince Dr. Fife to back off on his aggressive stance against weight-loss medications.

Although she was quite nervous about meeting with Dr. Fife, it did help that she had built up her confidence as she had mostly positive experiences with the other medical providers in the area that she had detailed over the last three days. She had visited more than a third of the clinics on her list of medical providers that were already prescribing weight-loss medications. They had all been receptive to her comments about Waitnomor and had all welcomed supplies of samples. On top of that, she had been pleased to discover that she could turn male medical-provider's heads just as easily as any of the other men she had dealt with. Her preconception that medical providers were more intelligent and more in control of their lives and therefore unreachable had been incorrect. Even the female medical providers she had met with had been pleasant to speak with and had been more than willing to try the samples of Waitnomore on their patients.

Still feeling nervous, but ready for the challenge, she had then tried detailing some of the medical providers on her list that weren't prescribing Waitnomor. There was no question that they had been more difficult. Every one of them had either resisted her suggestions that they use Waitnomor or just ignored her as she spoke about

Waitnomor. Only a few of them had been willing to sign the company tablet that would allow her to leave samples of Waitnomor. On the other hand, they had all been polite, and she could tell that most of them had been quite interested in her as a woman. None of them had told her not to come back. A slight smile curled up the corners of her mouth as she contemplated that by allowing her to return, each one of the medical providers had sealed their fate because she had never met a man yet that could resist her charms, given enough time.

One of the doors in the hallway in front of her opened, and an elderly gentleman walked through the door, assisted by a tall and attractive man wearing a white coat. Shannon recognized him from the pictures that Austin had shown her. It was Dr. Trevor Davis.

After a quick glance in Shannon's direction, Dr. Davis accompanied the older gentleman to the nurse's desk and then asked, "Laurie, could you help Mr. Williams get to his car?"

"Sure," Laurie answered as she got up from her perch behind the nurse's desk and took Mr. William's free arm. Dr. Davis relinquished the other arm as Laurie continued in a louder voice, "Come on, Mr. Williams. Let's get you out to your car." Laurie and Mr. Williams made their way slowly down the hall toward the waiting room.

CHAPTER 20

THE QUICK GLANCE that Trevor had taken at the blonde woman that was standing in front of the nurse's desk had definitely been an eye-opener. Any mental fatigue he had felt from the challenge of caring for Mr. Williams and all of his incurable medical problems evaporated in an instant. With more than a little effort, he had forced himself to look away from the woman's perfectly-proportioned body while he was assisting Mr. Williams to the nurse's desk. With Laurie now helping Mr. Williams down the hall, his pulse quickened just a little in anticipation as he turned to face the intensely beautiful woman. Looking her full on in the face, he was suddenly struck by the fact that the woman in front of him looked incredibly like his deceased wife. The resemblance was close enough that they could have been sisters! As their eyes met, he felt an intense attraction, coupled with overflowing longing and desire. Thrown off-balance, Trevor stammered, "H-Hello. Can I help you?"

"You must be Dr. Davis," the woman said in a melodious voice as she reached out her hand to shake his.

With his mouth as dry as a drought in the Sahara Desert, Trevor replied, "I am." Her hand was warm and soft, and her handshake was full of confidence.

"I'm Shannon Lowry. I'm your new Pharmplus representative. I'll be detailing you on Waitnomor."

Trevor's hand tingled pleasantly from her touch, and he found it hard to think clearly. Her eyes were so beautiful; her neck was perfect, and the neckline of her dress was so low he had to force himself look away. Embarrassed and surprised by the intense attraction that he was feeling for this woman right in the middle of his office, Trevor dropped her hand and reflexively took a half step back, hoping that the distance would help him clear his head. At the same time, he still couldn't believe how much she looked like his wife. He said, "I'm glad that you came. I have been using a lot of Waitnomor lately, and I need more samples. The previous drug rep hasn't been by for a month."

"I've got a few sample boxes with me, and I have a lot more in my car," Shannon said brightly.

Reaching down to her sample case, she pulled out a laminated information sheet as she moved to the counter that was attached to the front of the nurse's desk. "If it's okay with you, I'd like to show you some comparison data on Waitnomor and Reductol."

"Okay," Trevor agreed as he moved to join her at the counter, standing with his shoulder a comfortable two inches from hers.

"As you can see from this detail piece, patients on Waitnomor lose fifty percent more weight after six months of treatment than with Reductol. The side-effect profiles of the two medications are almost identical, as you can see from the table at the bottom of the page."

"I don't need to see this information to know that Waitnomor is superior to Reductol," Trevor stated as he turned to face her. She turned to him at the same time, putting them uncomfortably close together. Trevor couldn't breathe. Standing that close didn't seem to bother the drug rep one bit, but Trevor had no choice but to take an almost lifesaving step backward. "My patients on Waitnomor are clearly doing better than the ones on Reductol. In fact, I was wondering if I should be using Waitnomor exclusively for new weight-loss patients."

"What are you doing with patients that are already on Reductol?"

"If they are not losing weight fast enough, I am going to start switching them all to Waitnomor," Trevor replied, warming to the subject of weight loss. Focusing on the practice of medicine helped to take his mind off his intense attraction to this drug rep. His heart rate was returning to normal, and his palms were sweating a lot less.

"It sounds like there isn't anything else for me to say," Shannon said with a smile that was as dazzling as staring into the sun at midday. "Thank you for using my product."

"I use it because it really works. You're lucky to be working for a company with such a beneficial medication," Trevor said, trying really hard not to sound too complimentary. The attraction that he was still feeling for this woman left him feeling like a schoolboy that was suddenly standing face-to-face with the cutest girl in the school. Simultaneously, he felt a little guilty that he was feeling more than a little attracted to another woman when he had so recently had told Melanie how much he cared for her.

Shannon smiled. "It is nice to be detailing a successful product. I'm finished with my visits for the morning. How about if I take you to lunch?"

"Well, that was my last patient. So, I guess I'm done for the morning also."

"Great. Then I'll drive, and you pick the restaurant since I am new to the area."

Trevor was torn. He had planned to see one of his hospital patients during lunch. The patient was recovering from pneumonia. But, in reality, his patient in the hospital was stable and could wait to be seen until later that evening. "Okay," Trevor agreed with a smile as he removed the stethoscope from around his neck and took off his doctor's jacket. He set them on the nurse's desk.

Laurie came through the door that led to the waiting room and walked down the hall toward them. As she passed, Trevor said to Shannon, "I take it that you have already met my nurse, Laurie." Shannon replied that she had. Turning to Laurie, Trevor explained, "I'll be going out to lunch with Ms. Lowry. I'll be back around 1:30."

CHAPTER 21

MELANIE BRAKED HARD and then quickly turned her silver metallic Mitsubishi Mirage into the parking lot of East Camelback Family Practice. Scanning the cars in the parking lot, she was relieved to see that Dr. Davis's car was still there. She had been worried that he would leave for lunch before she arrived.

Normally, she visited East Camelback Family Practice at 9:30 a.m. every other Thursday. But, without question, today had not been a normal day. She had gotten a flat tire on the way to the physician's office that she always visited first before she made her way to East Camelback Family Practice. Not afraid to change her own tire, she had opened the trunk of her car only to find that the spare tire was also flat. It had only taken a few minutes to get through to the receptionist for her auto-club's emergency road service, but after explaining that she had a flat tire, she had been placed on hold for fifteen minutes. The receptionist had finally returned to the phone and told her that an onsite service truck was on the way. Whatever "on the way" had meant, she had waited another forty minutes for the truck to arrive. The service technician had repaired her flat tire and then had taken forever to complete the paperwork. All told, the flat tire had cost her two hours. On any other day, it wouldn't have mattered because she simply would have skipped her usual visit to the other medical office and would have gone straight to Dr. Davis's office after lunch. Today, however, she had to catch a plane for San Diego at 1:30 p.m. for a district training meeting that would last the rest of the week. Looking at the clock on the dash of her car, she saw that he only had a short fifteen minutes to spend detailing Dr. Davis before she had to head for the airport.

Sally looked up from the receptionist's desk as Melanie rushed in. Sally smiled and said, "Hi, Melanie."

Melanie returned the greeting and then hurriedly asked, "I've got a plane to catch and I only have fifteen minutes. Is it alright if I head right back to see your providers?"

"Sure, go ahead," Sally answered with a smile, but it was less cheery than usual and faded quickly.

Melanie was sure from Sally's strained smile that something wasn't right with Sally, but as much as she wanted to stop and try to cheer Sally up, there just wasn't any time to do so if she wanted to see Trevor before she left town. "Thanks, Sally," Melanie said as she headed to the door that led to the back office.

Arriving at the nurse's station, she found Laurie hard at work on her computer.

"Hi, Laurie," she said, not want to lose a second waiting for Laurie to greet her.

"Oh. Hi! I didn't see you come in." Laurie seemed pleased to see her, but her countenance also lacked its usual exuberance.

"Is everything okay?" Melanie was concerned that something had happened in the office that day that had left these two women less happy than usual.

"Everything's fine." Laurie looked away for just a moment as she spoke and then looked back at Melanie as she finished.

"Is Dr. Davis around?" Melanie wanted to be reassured at least that everything was okay with Trevor.

"He's gone to lunch," Laurie replied flatly. Melanie couldn't help but notice that Laurie was avoiding direct eye contact as much as she could. Something wasn't right.

"Come on, Laurie. I know you too well. You're not telling me everything."

"Okay," Laurie said with resignation. She took a deep breath, exhaled, and then confessed, "Dr. Davis went to lunch with another drug rep."

"I'm sorry I missed him. I had a flat tire, and it took forever to get it fixed. Dr. Davis's car was still in the parking lot, so I was hoping that he was still here. I guess I won't be able to see him before I fly to San Diego at one thirty. Would you mind telling him that I dropped by and that I'm sorry that I missed him?"

"Sure."

"Which drug rep did he go to lunch with?"

"He went to lunch with the new rep for Waitnomor."

"I can't believe that they have already replaced Becky! Did you hear what happened with Becky?"

"No. I had no idea that she was gone. What happened?"

"I thought that Dr. Davis might have told you. She left town suddenly about three weeks ago. She even left her son behind with her husband. No one has heard from her since, although her attorney did serve divorce papers on her husband a few days later."

"Becky split with her husband and left town?" Laurie said. "Dr. Davis should have told me."

"It sounds unbelievable, I know. I was her friend, or at least I thought I was. I always thought that her marriage was rock solid. On the other hand, she had been getting a lot of pressure from work. I guess she got tired and needed a change. It would have been nice, though, if she had let me know before she left." Melanie's throat had tightened as she spoke of Becky, and she paused to collect her emotions. "She always talked so proudly of her marriage. She loved her husband, and she loved her son. I would have never picked her for someone who would walk out all of a sudden like that. George, her husband, is really taking it hard." As always, when she talked about Becky's leaving, she was bordering on the verge of tears. She needed to change the subject. "What's the new rep for Waitnomor like?"

"She's tall and gorgeous," Laurie said.

Like lightening, Melanie's mind put two and two together, and she wondered if the reason that Sally and Laurie were acting differently was to protect her from the fact Trevor was in a relationship with another woman. Overwhelmed, all Melanie could answer with was a subdued, "Oh."

"Melanie, she might be pretty, but her personality can't hold a candle to yours."

Already traumatized by discussing her concerns for Becky and now filled with uncertainty about her relationship Trevor, tears began falling freely down Melanie's cheeks. Unable to converse further, she turned and rushed down the hall, waving off Laurie's request for her to stay.

CHAPTER 22

"THAT'S TERRIBLE," TREVOR said. "I'm sure that being orphaned at age eight was traumatic for you. It's such a tender time in a child's development. Who raised you after your parents died?"

"I went to live with my mother's sister for a while," Shannon said, "But that didn't work out. After bouncing from foster family to foster family for two years, I ended up with a nice couple that raised me through high-school graduation."

"Seeing you sitting here, it's hard to believe the difficult times that you've been through."

"One does what one has to do to survive."

"Well, it looks like it's time for me to head back to the office. My first patient is at one-thirty," Trevor said as he studied his watch, wondering where the hour had gone. He looked up again at Shannon's beautiful eyes that reminded him so much of his wife's eyes and smiled. Shannon was so gorgeous that in any other circumstance he would have felt totally out of his element and would have all but clammed up in self-consciousness. But the fact that she looked so much like Vanessa somehow was giving him more confidence than he usually had. He continued, "We had a wonderful time together this afternoon. I'd love to get together again and talk some more. Are you free Friday night? We could go to dinner, and then maybe we could take in a movie if there's enough time left after our conversation at dinner."

"Yes, I am free. And, I'd love to go out to dinner with you."

Trevor stood and then helped Shannon with her chair. Shannon stood and turned to him, once again standing within his personal space. He couldn't help but feel intensely attracted to her. He gallantly offered his arm to her, and she slipped her hand around his biceps. He smiled as he noticed men turning their heads as they tracked Shannon and him. There was no question that he was going to enjoy getting to know Shannon Lowry better.

CHAPTER 23

"I'M CONCERNED THAT we might have a problem here," Shane Roberts said as soon as it was his turn to speak at the Pharmplus safety committee meeting. Shane was a junior member of the committee.

Rick looked away and rolled his eyes as Shane once again used melodrama to make a point.

Shane continued, "I have received reports on eight cases of sudden deaths that have occurred in patients that were using Waitnomor. Three have occurred in our company-sponsored, double-blind, and placebo-controlled trial of Waitnomor vs. phentermine. At the time of their deaths, each of these eight patients had been on Waitnomor for nine months or more."

"But, Shane, eight deaths out of the over one million patients that have used Waitnomor in the last year is too small to be significant," Abe Wallace said. Abe was the safety director for Pharmplus and was also conducting the meeting. "Aren't you being pre-mature in bringing this matter before this committee? Aren't eight sudden deaths occurring over a one-year period in over one million patients just a natural occurrence?"

"You're right," Shane said. "It's not a large number of patient deaths. But the fact that there were no patient deaths in the first nine months that Waitnomor was on the market and that there are now eight deaths in just three months concerns me and—"

"Your concerns are important to us," Rick said smoothly as he cut Shane off. "At Pharmplus, we place a high priority on making sure that the medications that we make are safe. We present accurate and reliable information to the public about the risks of the medications. At the same time, it is critical for all of us at Pharmplus that we avoid releasing information to the public that is not known to be accurate or proven. With this in mind, I propose that Shane should continue to track cases of sudden death with the use of Waitnomor, but that this information is to be held in strict confidence until released to the public by vote of this committee." Rick allowed himself a smug smile because he was proud of his ability to find a solution that would keep everybody happy and that would also keep Shane strictly under his thumb.

"I'm sorry, but it's too late for that," Shane said. "We can't just brush this one under the carpet. I've already been in contact with Steve Jones at the FDA. If you don't remember, he chairs the committee that evaluates and tracks potentially dangerous medications. His office informed me that they will open a file on Waitnomor and that they will begin investigating all deaths that have occurred and will occur in patients that are taking Waitnomor."

"You knew that you were not to discuss any information with the FDA that was not approved by this committee," Rick said as strongly and firmly as he dared in front of the other committee members. He tried his best not to glare at the little pest that was threatening to undermine his efforts to make millions off of selling Waitnomor. Everyone present waited in silence, shocked at Shane's clear disregard of company policy. Shane stood defiantly at the head of the table. He was probably feeling protected by his association with a bigwig at the FDA.

Rick was the senior administrator at the meeting, and they all knew that his word was final. Seething inside, Rick was still the picture of calm as he spoke, "Shane, collect the information on Waitnomor as we have discussed and present it to us once a month in this meeting. Any information pertaining to this matter that you have presented here, or that you obtain in the future, is not to be discussed outside of this room, and that includes anyone at the FDA." Rick's voice had been quiet, but there had been just a hint of malice.

Shane opened his mouth to give a retort but was cut off as Rick continued in a firmer tone, "Mr. Wallace..." As he spoke, Rick turned his attention away from Shane and focused instead on Abe. "... please continue with our agenda."

As Abe droned on about a new, yet unimportant topic, Rick struggled to rein in his anger. More than a few suitably painful ways to remove Shane Roberts from his position at Pharmplus came to Rick's mind, and he relished the thoughts of Shane's suffering and death.

CHAPTER 24

"I THOUGHT THAT IT was an okay movie. I'd give it about two-and-a-half stars out of four," Trevor said to Shannon. After a pleasant dinner at one of the best French restaurant in town, they'd gone to the latest action flick. Now back at Shannon's apartment, they were seated comfortably on a plush couch in Shannon's living room. Trevor continued, "The plot was lightweight, and there was barely a spark of chemistry between the lead characters. And then there was that inappropriate love scene right after they had killed about half of the bad guys and were covered in blood."

"That part was so bad that I really had to try hard not to laugh," Shannon said.

"I don't know why most of the directors in Hollywood think that there always has to be some smutty love scene in every movie. They call it art, but I think it's just a thinly veiled excuse for voyeurism."

Shannon nodded, even though she didn't really agree with Trevor's conservative point of view. At the same time, she found his unique blend of innocence and intelligence attractive.

"Think about it. How many real-life couples have you watched while they undressed and then made love? None, right?"

Shannon nodded again with a little less intensity. Had she chosen to answer his question honestly, she would have had to say, "Quite a few, and in as many ways as you can imagine." But there was no way that she could ever let Trevor know about her past.

Trevor continued, "Repeatedly seeing love scenes like the one in this movie is damaging for many men. They begin to see women as objects of physical pleasure and not as friends and companions. For a lot of these men, sex is viewed more and more as a vehicle for self-gratification with no thought for the feelings and needs of their partner. The whole process is unnatural and destructive to human relationships. Yet Hollywood spreads it across the screen like it's the most natural thing in the world."

"I agree," Shannon said just to be agreeable. Sex and nudity in movies had never bothered her, but it obviously bothered Trevor.

"What did you think about the movie?" Trevor asked.

"I enjoyed it. I liked the part where they ended up with all the bad cop's money on the beach in Mexico. They deserved it after all they'd been through. I didn't like all of the graphic violence. When someone is killed in a movie, all I need to see is the dead body on the ground. I don't need to see the body parts flying in all directions, with blood spraying everywhere."

"To tell the truth, it was a forgettable movie. In two years, we won't even remember that we saw it."

"You're right. Most movies are that way for me. I bet I couldn't name more than thirty movies out of the hundreds that I have seen."

"I tell you what," Trevor said. "Just to get rid of the bad taste from this movie, let's go to see something that is certain to be more memorable and interesting. *Phantom of the Opera* is in town next week. I'll get us tickets for Saturday night."

Shannon was torn. She would love to see *Phantom of the Opera* on stage. But she had promised herself that she would avoid dating romantically while she was here in Phoenix so that she could concentrate on selling Waitnomor. Still, Austin had told her that she did need to spend time with her medical providers in effort to influence them to use her medication, and there was still the matter of pumping Trevor for more information about Dr. Fife. In addition, Trevor was fun to be with, and he was quite good-looking, even though he was more than ten years older than she was. She did feel happy and secure when she was with him. He hadn't even tried to hold her hand or put his arm around her at the movie, even though she was quite sure that he had wanted to do so. It was a relief to be with a man that wasn't always pawing at her and whining for sex. It wasn't that she was against having sex. If Trevor had asked for it, she probably would have given it to him. But then that would have made him just like all of the other boring men she had known. Maybe that was one of the things that was so intriguing about Trevor. He clearly was intensely attracted to her but hadn't even hinted at trying anything. She wondered how long he would last.

Shannon smiled and said, "That would be perfect. I have always loved seeing it on stage." She had only seen *Phantom of the Opera* once in her life, and that had been in a movie theater with one of her escorts, but Trevor didn't need to know how limited her experience was with the arts.

"It's a date then." Suddenly, Trevor yawned. "I guess I stayed up too late last night. I'd probably better get going." Trevor slid to the front of the couch and prepared to stand. He turned back to Shannon just in time to see her stifling a yawn of her own.

She laughed. "I guess I'm tired, too."

Trevor stood and offered his outstretched hand to help her up. She placed her hand in his and stood to join him. Hand in hand, they walked to the door. He put his free hand on the doorknob and then turned to say goodbye. As he did so, Shannon was sure to place herself within his personal space so that he ended up with his face inches from her own. She opened her eyes wide in pretend surprise at their sudden close proximity.

After only a moment's hesitation, Trevor kissed her on her lips softly. The tenderness of his kiss took her breath away. She melted into his arms as he pulled her close for an embrace. After what seemed like a long time, Trevor gently pulled away until he was holding only her hands. He squeezed them lightly and said, "Thanks for a wonderful evening. I'll call you this week to confirm our plans for Saturday."

"I'll be waiting." Shannon smiled, partly as part of her ruse and partly for real. Something about the gentle way that Trevor treated her made her feel a happiness that she hadn't felt with a man for years. He released her hands, opened the door, and stepped out onto the balcony of her apartment complex. He wished her good night and pulled the door closed. Shannon turned away, wishing Trevor hadn't left so soon. She caught herself again. As much as she was getting to know and like Trevor, it was way too soon to get over-confident in her ability to not break character. Trevor had asked her a lot of questions about her new identity's past again this evening. That scared her about him. He too smart and would notice even the slightest inconsistency in her narrative about her new life as Shannon Lowry. She promised herself to be more careful around him.

CHAPTER 25

"**T**HESE NEGATIVE REPORTS on Waitnomor are going to ruin everything," Rick said, his brows furrowed. Like a starving animal, he angrily cut off another bite of his French toast, stabbed it with his fork, shoved it into his mouth, and chewed it ferociously.

He was seated at the kitchen table in the modest home of his old friend and business associate, Candy. Candy stood with her back to Rick, putting the finishing touches on a Mexican-style omelet.

Chewing more slowly as he finished the last of the French toast, his eyes wandered aimlessly around the kitchen until his gaze landed on Candy's backside. Attired only in short shorts and a tight-fitting T-shirt, she looked as hot as ever. He'd always been a fan of her beautiful blonde hair that fell to her midback. Memories of good times with Candy helped to change his mood for the better. A sly grin stole across his face. He had spent a lot of time with many different women, most of whom were quite a bit younger than Candy's forty-something years. However, he couldn't remember many that looked as good as Candy did right now.

He had first met Candy Kane when he and Austin had been running a gang in Miami, Florida. He and Austin and been in their early twenties and were always looking for ways to increase their profits. Rick had met Candy at a stripper bar and had outbid all the others in the room for a private lap dance. He had fallen hard for her that night. Soon after, the three of them had teamed up to provide drugs and sex to high-paying customers. He had lived with her for a couple of years back then. At times like this, he wished she hadn't kicked him out for what she had called his excessive womanizing.

Candy interrupted his thoughts, "Don't you think that you're overreacting a little? The fact that a few deaths have occurred doesn't spell disaster. Over a million people have taken Waitnomor and at least a few are bound to die of something, whether they took the medication or not."

"I couldn't care less about a few deaths. What worries me is the fact that Shane Roberts is scouring the planet to find patients that have had problems while taking Waitnomor. And then he's reporting the information to the FDA. It's the FDA that I'm really worried about. The FDA has been extremely cautious with weight-loss medications since the whole fen-phen thing. If the FDA suspects that there's a problem with Waitnomor, they're going to pull it off the market in a second flat. Everything that I've worked for will be ruined."

"I can see why you're so upset." Candy placed the finished omelet in front of Rick. "However, it doesn't spell the end of the world. I'm sure that we can come up with a solution. We always do."

"We've got to come up with something soon. It's driving me crazy worrying about it." He shoveled in a bite of the omelet, chewed it only a few times, and then swallowed with a loud gulp.

"So how are the new girls doing?"

"Pretty good so far," Rick said in-between bites. "They've only been out a few days. There hasn't been time for anything to go wrong."

"Your plan to pay the girls through their bank cards is perfect. I'm impressed."

"You like that," Rick said with his mouth half full. "One good thing about the bank-card thing is that I don't have to pay payroll taxes. Pharmplus thinks the money I'm paying the girls is being spent on advertising." Rick polished off the last of the omelet.

Candy collected his plate and utensils and placed them in the sink. "Now that your stomach is full, we're ready to deal with the problem with the FDA. Let's go sit on the couch in the living room and see what we can figure out."

They stood and walked toward the living room. Rick allowed Candy to walk in front of him when they reached the door. The sexy sway of her hips left him unable to resist the desire to explore further.

"Rick!" Candy turned to face him while simultaneously moving out of his reach. "I told you none of that stuff as long as I'm not the only woman in your life."

She was trying to sound stern, but Rick knew her better than that. "Come on, you've always been the only woman in my life," Rick said, but he knew that Candy didn't believe him. She just hadn't been able to get over his need to have more than one sexual partner at a time.

"Control yourself and sit down on the couch. We have important things to talk about."

Rick obediently sat on the couch. Candy joined him at a safe distance and continued, "I think I have a few ideas on how you can neutralize any threat that might come from Shane Roberts or from the FDA."

CHAPTER 26

"I'M SO SORRY, Melanie. I only have a few seconds to talk with you," Trevor said with only a shadow of his usual smile. "I'm pretty far behind schedule."

"It's okay. Some days can be that way. If I could get a signature for some samples, I'll be out of the way in no time."

Melanie had simultaneously looked forward to and dreaded coming to see Trevor. He hadn't texted or called in a week. Although she wasn't sure if Trevor were still interested in her, her heart couldn't help but hope. The suspense of not knowing for sure had been giving her butterflies in her stomach all day.

There was another reason that she was nervous. She had also come today prepared to break the FDA's policy against drug representatives giving out any information that had not already been approved by the FDA. She had been searching the internet over the last few days for information on deaths in patients that were on Waitnomor, and she had turned up some worrisome facts. Telling Trevor about those facts would put her at risk of losing her job, if Trevor decided to report her.

"I don't need any samples of Reductol," Trevor said quietly.

He was unwilling to look Melanie in the eyes, even though she was looking right at him.

He continued, "I really haven't been using it much, and the sample cabinet is full."

"Well, at least I'll remind you that Reductol is a good choice because it has a proven track record of safety," Melanie said without missing a beat. At the same time, her heart was devastated by the cold reception she was getting from Trevor. She couldn't believe that this was the same man that had been so charming on their date just a few weeks before.

Melanie added, "I had wanted to share some information that I found on the internet about a serious side effect that is occurring with Waitnomor." Trevor had always been concerned about the safety of his patients. She hoped that her statement would get his attention and keep him from bolting to his next appointment's room. Trevor didn't answer and so she said, "I've been up late the last few nights trying to put this all together. Do you have just another minute?"

"I really don't," he replied coldly and firmly. "Information from the internet can hardly be used as a basis for changing my prescribing patterns. I need to see the results of multiple, large, well-designed studies before abandoning what I believe is a successful medication. Plus, you are trying to talk to me about information that is not FDA approved. That's not legal, and you know it. I don't think you want to go there. Thanks for coming just the same." He gave Melanie a brief, thin smile and then turned toward his patient exam rooms.

"It was good to see you," Melanie said to his back. With all hope of a continued relationship with Trevor dashed in less than sixty seconds, Melanie stood quietly in the hallway in front of the nurse's desk. She blinked her eyes quickly a few times and sighed as she stared at the space in front of her that had been occupied by Trevor just a few moments before.

"He's hopeless." Melanie was startled out of her reverie by

Laurie's voice from the nurse's desk. "He can't tell his head from a hole in the ground. You're the best thing that ever happened to him, and he has no clue." Seeing Melanie's confusion, Laurie added, "We need to sit down and talk, woman to woman. Let's go into the breakroom."

Melanie agreed numbly and allowed Laurie to lead her down the hall to the break room. Laurie motioned for Melanie to have a seat while she grabbed two diet sodas from the refrigerator. She then joined Melanie at the table.

"I'm going to cut right to the point," Laurie said as she leaned forward. "Dr. Davis thinks he has found the girl of his dreams in the new drug rep for Waitnomor. There is no hiding the fact that she is a total knockout. On a looks scale, she is truly one in a million, and I'm not joking. I can see why any man would struggle not to fall head over heels for her. However, it will never last. Dr. Davis needs someone that is kind and gentle. He needs a best friend. This girl is as cold as ice. Why is it that men can't see what is so obvious to us? Sometimes, I feel like shaking him to see if he'll wake up from the spell of infatuation that he is under." As she finished, Laurie shook her head in frustration.

"It helps a little to know that he has found another woman." Melanie was surprised at how calmly she was taking this whole thing. "I hope that he and I can still be friends."

"Oh, don't worry. This little fling isn't going to last long, or else I'm going to ring his neck." Both women laughed.

CHAPTER 27

S HANNON IS ABSOLUTELY *radiant in her burgundy evening gown*, Trevor noticed for the one hundredth time. He'd lost count of how many times he'd already told her that this evening. At risk of sounding too eager, he kept it to himself this time. Shannon's beauty had clearly upstaged that of any other woman in attendance at the theater that evening. Her presence had even made it hard for him to focus his complete attention on one of his favorite plays.

The whole evening had gone perfectly, beginning with dinner at an awesome Japanese restaurant. She had been fascinated by the experiences that he had gone through with difficult patients during his residency and now in his practice. The questions that she had asked were intelligent, and she had shown genuine concern when he discussed his fears about the future of medicine. She had even laughed at his jokes. As soon as the play had started, she had snuggled close to his shoulder and had slipped her hand into his. At intermission, she had been effusive about how much she liked the play and had wanted to know what he thought about it. The conversation on the drive back to Shannon's apartment had been delightful as she had continued to display incredible and intelligent interest in Trevor's profession, hobbies, and passions. The night had gone so well that it had left Trevor feeling even more attracted to Shannon than ever.

As Trevor had pulled into the parking lot of Shannon's apartment complex, Shannon had invited Trevor up for a drink. He had laughed and confessed that he had never been much of a drinker and now, with his weight problems, had completely given up on alcohol because it had so many calories. When she had offered to serve him a diet soda instead, he had no reason to refuse her invitation.

Once in her apartment, Trevor helped her with the shawl that she had worn to protect against the cool, desert night air. She turned to face him with a radiant smile and said, "Thank you for a lovely evening." As memories of their pleasant evening together flooded Trevor's mind, his arms found their way around her waist. She melted against his chest, and they kissed passionately for a few moments and then held each other close in a gentle embrace. "I'll take that over a glass of diet Coke anytime," Trevor said as he held her away from him a little and looked into her eyes.

"I hadn't exactly had this in mind when I invited you up for a drink. I don't want you to think that I attack every man that comes to my apartment as soon as they walk through the door."

"No need to worry there. I was one did the attacking."

"I do need to freshen up for a minute. Why don't you have a seat on the couch, and I'll be back shortly."

Trevor reluctantly let his hands slide from around her back and down to her perfect waist and hips as he said with a gallant smile, "Okay. But don't be gone too long." She turned and disappeared into the hall leading to her bedroom.

Wow, Trevor thought. *What a woman!* He couldn't believe how lucky he was to be dating someone as fun and attractive as Shannon. He sat back and enjoyed the pleasant anticipation of spending more time with his arms wrapped around her. Shannon was too good to be true.

After what seemed like forever, Shannon remerged from the hallway, and Trevor couldn't resist teasing her, "You were gone so long I grew a few more gray hairs."

"No complaining. You want me to look my best, don't you?" With that, she sat on the couch so close to Trevor that he had no choice but to let his arm fall around her shoulder. He liked how affectionate she was, although it really wasn't something that he used to. His wife had been quite shy, and they had dated for weeks before he had even kissed her.

"Now," Shannon said as she smiled innocently. "Where were we at before I had to find the bathroom?"

"About right here," Trevor replied as he gently turned her face to his and kissed her.

She kissed him back with more urgency. Feeling Shannon respond passionately to his initially gentle kisses ignited passion in Trevor, and he kissed her more eagerly in response. He felt her arms pull him closer, and he hugged her back. She was moving faster than he had planned, but with his testosterone levels soaring, he had no choice but to follow where this exciting woman would take him. He didn't struggle when she lay back on the couch and pulled him on top of her. She pressed hard against him, and he responded in return. He felt powerful, yet breathless, in control, and yet a little out of his league.

Shannon reached under his shirt, and her fingers felt warm against his back. Her tongue was hot in his mouth. Suddenly, she stopped kissing him, grabbed his hand, and moved it toward her breast. Alarms went off in Trevor's head. This was leading where he didn't want to go, at least not yet. He had been there before, but with someone that he had known and loved infinitely more than he knew and loved this woman. He wasn't about to let his resolve to be chaste until he remarried to be broken with a woman that he had barely met. With his passion barely in control, he pulled his hand away and moved away from her to the other end of the couch.

"Is something wrong?" she asked, surprised. "I'm sorry. Most men love to touch... I mean, I thought that most men wanted to feel..."

They were both silent for a moment, and then Trevor spoke, "I think I had better be going. Things were moving a little too fast just then." He got up from the couch and turned to face her. "We should take some time to get to know each other better."

Shannon sat up on the couch, straightened her dress, and then stood to face him. "I'm so sorry. I lost myself there for a minute."

Seeing the sadness in her beautiful eyes, Trevor said, "You don't have to apologize. I had a good time tonight, and I'd love to see you again." Trevor was rewarded with a smile that felt like the warmth of a ray of sun shining through scattered clouds. "I had already planned on asking you out on a picnic next Saturday afternoon. Would you like to go?"

"I'd love to," Shannon replied, back to her usual happy and confident self.

They walked to the door and said their goodbyes. Trevor kissed her lightly on the lips and promised to call to finalize their plans for the next weekend. He waved goodbye again and then walked to his car.

As he drove home, the scene from the couch in Shannon's apartment replayed itself repeatedly in his mind. She was definitely affectionate. Even though she had moved a little too fast for him, he was sure of one thing. She was too fascinating for him to even consider not continuing to date her.

CHAPTER 28

SHANNON STOOD STARING at her closed front door for a few moments. She was still in shock that Trevor had left so abruptly. Moving to her couch, she sat down slowly and stared blankly at nothing on the opposite wall. No man had ever suddenly stopped in the middle of making out with her like that before. Trevor had acted like he liked her all evening. She had thought that he was enjoying the evening as much as she was. She had even caught him in the act of checking her out multiple times, so she knew that he was attracted to her. What had she done wrong? The hardest part was that it hurt. She felt rejected physically and emotionally. Even though she knew she shouldn't, she was falling for Trevor. She hadn't felt this way about a man since her senior year in high school when she had started dating the school quarterback. She had been so in love then, at least until she discovered how possessive and self-centered he was. Trevor was so different. He was genuinely interested in what she had to say, he was so smart, and he was lots of fun. He wasn't the most handsome guy she had been out with, and he was a little overweight, but she still thought that he was cute.

She shook her head a little and got up from the couch. She still couldn't believe that he had refused her advances. The more she thought about it, the more she had to fight the anger that his rejection made her feel. Strangely, the more she thought of his rejection, the more she just wanted him to take her in his arms. She had always discarded men before that hadn't given her what she wanted. Dr. Davis couldn't be discarded because, for reasons that she didn't fully understand, she wanted him more than she had ever wanted any man in a long time.

She reminded herself that all was not lost. He had asked her out again. She would just have to be careful to not be too aggressive sexually and let him make the next moves in that department.

CHAPTER 29

MELANIE COLLECTED THE papers that she had printed from the e-mails she had received tonight about Waitnomore, put them in her open computer bag on her desk, and then closed and locked it. When she had first logged on to her private email site that evening, her inbox had contained notification of five additional cases of sudden death in patients on Waitnomor in the last three months. Her pulse had quickened at the news. She was becoming more and more concerned that Waitnomor really was a dangerous drug and that it needed to be taken off the market. It went far beyond digging up dirt on a competing product. She felt that she had to do something to help prevent more patients from dying. Why wasn't the FDA doing anything? She had called the medical department at Medicon Pharmaceuticals last week to report what she had found. The person there had reassured her that they would look into it and would get back with her. So far, she hadn't heard anything.

She was especially concerned for Trevor and for the patients that he was treating with Waitnomor. He would be so devastated if one of his patients died of complications related to Waitnomor. She just had to get this information to him. She cared too much about his patients and about him to stop trying. It didn't matter if they weren't dating anymore.

Her mind wandered to the new rep for Waitnomor that Trevor had the hots for. Her mind conjured up the image of a gorgeous woman that had every asset that she was lacking. She blinked and erased the silly image from her mind. It really didn't matter what the woman looked like. If Trevor really liked this woman and the woman liked him, then she wished them the best.

Regardless, she had to get Trevor's undivided attention for just a few minutes. She knew that he would listen once he understood just how serious the problem with Waitnomor was.

CHAPTER 30

"IT APPEARS TO have worked just as we planned," Austin said from the video chat screen on Rick's computer. "Two days after I put the R-648 in the culinary water supply for San Felix, almost everyone in town developed a severe headache. Now, we just have to wait to see if the people of San Felix start gaining weight."

"Do the townspeople suspect anything?" Rick said.

"I went into town this morning, pretending to have a headache. The pharmacist told me that he had completely sold out of every type of pain medication that he usually has in stock. The townspeople have come to the pharmacy in droves over the last few days to get relief from their headaches. He thought that the headaches were most likely due to a virus. I walked around town for a while, and everything was the same as usual. No one paid me any more attention than any other time I've gone to town. The people of San Felix have no clue about what has happened to them."

"Excellent. I'd like to move as quickly as possible in getting ready for our next target. How much R-648 are we going to need?"

"I think that we need to shoot for around 100 pounds of R-648 in order to be sure that we deliver enough of the medication to every person in Las Vegas," Austin said. "Even in the desert, most of the drinkable water isn't consumed by humans. It is used for flushing toilets, taking showers, watering lawns, and by industry and agriculture. About three hundred gallons of water is used for all purposes in desert cities in the United States for every one gallon of water that is consumed by humans. One hundred pounds should be enough to be sure that every gallon of tap water contains enough R-648 to do the job."

"It's too bad that we can't think of a more efficient way to get the R-648 into people's water. Maybe we could put it in the sugar," Rick said.

"There are too many companies with too many locations that refine and package sugar. We'd end up getting the R-648 into only a small percentage of the homes of the target population. In addition, a lot of sugar is used in cooking. Heat inactivates R-648. Also, a lot of sugar is packaged and then sits on shelves in stores and in homes for months and possibly for years. We have no idea what the shelf life is of R-648. Delivering it through the water system is the best way that we have been able to come up with."

"I guess you're probably right," Rick said. "How soon can you have one hundred pounds of R-648 ready?"

"We do have a problem there. It is going to take at least a month to produce one hundred pounds of R-648. And it's going to require a wad of cash to buy the ingredients, purchase extra equipment, and hire more technicians."

"I don't think that we can wait a whole month. Can't you do something to speed up the process?"

"Our technicians in the dungeon at the warehouse in San Felix are already working twenty-four hours a day. Anyway, it's better for us to wait a month so we can see if the R-648 has really worked in San Felix at the dose that we have given them."

"Okay. Okay. It's just that I'm anxious to move ahead and so is the other interested party that's paying for all of this. Were you able to get the information that we needed about adding the R-648 to the water at the treatment plant?"

"Our source inside the water treatment facility got the information to us last week. He says that the ideal place to add the R-648 is in the flocculation basins. That's where the water is mixed by paddles so that small particles suspended in the water will coagulate into large clumps called "floc". Most of the chemical treatments have already been added by that point so that the risk of inactivating the R-648 is minimal. There are ten flocculation basins at this facility. The water being treated flows constantly through the system throughout the day. That means that we need to design and prepare ten canisters that will release ten pounds each of R-648 into each flocculation basin over a twenty-four-hour period. The canisters will need to be about the size of a large serving platter. Our people here are working hard to have the canisters ready within the next thirty days. We are also busy testing R-648 to be sure that it won't be inactivated by any of the steps in the water treatment process. So far, everything looks good."

"I assume that this source at the water treatment facility is the same person that will help you to install the canisters?" Rick said.

"He is. He's dependable and he'll get the job done. He is a small-time dealer that my father has been supplying for years. Because of that, he owes my dad more than a few favors. We prepared a cover for him, and he was able to get a job at the water treatment facility two months ago. He works the night shift with two other guys. He will slip them something in their coffee during a coffee break that will keep them asleep while we install the canisters. He'll repeat the same process the following night when we retrieve the empty canisters."

"Excellent. I've got a problem in Phoenix that I need you to take care of for me," Rick said as he changed the subject. "There is a Dr. Erwin Fife in Phoenix that is making it very hard for us to sell Waitnomor. I told you about him a month ago when we decided to send Shannon, one of the best of our new girls, to Phoenix to try to get him to change his mind. Candy met with Shannon earlier today and, after talking with her, believes that Shannon is doing everything she can do to stop Dr. Fife. Phoenix has the worst sales record in our territory. Dr. Fife has to go. You know what to do. Get it done within the next ten days."

"Okay, boss. I take it that Candy got that Waitnomor study list to you that I lifted from the study accountant's office?"

"She did, and tomorrow morning I'm going to use it to make someone's life quite miserable."

Getting a master key for every office in the building had been simple for Rick. Soon after he had started working for Pharmplus, he had deliberately worked late one night. He had left his keys to his office on his desk, locked his office door, and then left. Finding the cleaning people, he had convinced them that he needed to borrow their master key to open his office to retrieve his keys. Back in his office, he had quickly made a wax cast of the master key and then had returned the original to the cleaning people. The next day, he had made a cast of the key from the wax cast with fast-drying gypsum cement and then had mailed the cast to Austin's father's people in Los Angeles. A perfect reproduction of the master key had arrived three days later.

The halls at the Sacramento Pharmplus office building were completely deserted at 5:30 a.m. Checking one more time to be sure that there wasn't some insomniac wandering around the building, Rick put his copy of the building's master key to use in the lock in the door to Shane Robert's office. He slipped inside the office and turned on the light. Removing the list of patients on the Waitnomor study that Austin had stolen from the accountant's office from his briefcase, he then slid it under a stack of papers on the top of Shane's desk. Moments later, with Shane's door relocked and with the light turned off, Rick walked down the hall to his own office as if nothing had happened.

Rick arrived at Shane Robert's office precisely on time for their 8:30 a.m. appointment. Rick had requested this meeting the day before to discuss any new developments in the Waitnomor vs. Phentermine trial that Shane was monitoring for Pharmplus. He knocked on the door and was rewarded moments later by Shane opening the door. Shane invited Rick into his office.

"It's good that we're meeting today. I have a lot to tell you," Shane began almost immediately.

"I'm interested in the outcome of this study, and I appreciate how hard you have been working to make this study happen," Rick lied. *Clearly*, thought Rick, *he believes that my coming here today means that I'm interested in his claims about problems with Waitnomor. Little does he know.*

"I have received report of two additional episodes of serious cardiac arrhythmia and one additional sudden death in the patients in our study," Shane stated a little too eagerly. "It's looking more and more like Waitnomor might not be a safe drug."

"I am concerned also." Rick leaned forward and rested his elbows on the front edge of Shane's desk. He glanced nonchalantly down at the stack of papers on the desk and then allowed his attention to suddenly be riveted on the list he had planted just hours previously.

"What is this?" Rick asked. He removed the papers he had planted out from under the stack and pretended to inspect them carefully for a few moments, although he already knew exactly what information the papers contained. He then continued, "This is preposterous! You shouldn't have this list."

"What list? Let me see it." Shane reached out to grab the list from Rick, but Rick held it out of his reach. Rick stood and backed toward the door as Shane came around his desk, still grabbing for the list. Rick shook the list in Shane's direction as he declared in a loud voice, "It's more than obvious that you have this blinded list of the patients in the Waitnomor study so that you can sway the outcome to meet your agenda." Rick opened the door to Shane's office and stalked out into the hallway, slamming the door behind him.

CHAPTER 31

"**N**OW WHAT IS so important that we can't discuss it in the hallway?" Trevor asked after he had closed the door to his office, offered Melanie a seat, and then sat in his chair behind his desk.

Taking a breath, Melanie replied, "I think you know me well enough to know I would never waste your time. I consider you a good friend as well as a physician that I respect highly. Please listen to what I have to say before you dismiss it as unimportant. It is important to me."

"Okay," Trevor said with resignation.

Melanie said, "I have been spending a lot of time on the internet researching problems that medical providers are having with Waitnomor. I have compiled a list of seventeen patients in the United States and forty-two patients worldwide that have died suddenly while using Waitnomor. All of these patients had been on Waitnomor for at least nine months. None of them had a history of heart disease, such as high-blood pressure or coronary arteriosclerosis. None had a history of cardiac conduction disturbances, such as Wolf-Parkinson-White syndrome or long QT syndrome. They were all completely healthy, except for their obesity."

Melanie handed a sheet of paper to Trevor that she had removed from her computer bag while she had been speaking. "Here is a list of the patients, their ages, the cause of their deaths, and their medical provider's names, addresses, and phone numbers. I have contacted my medical department about this information, but I haven't heard a thing back from them. I wrote a letter to the FDA a week ago, but I haven't heard back from them either. I am worried that Waitnomor is a dangerous drug and that we are only just beginning to see the problems that it is going to cause with people's hearts. I don't understand why no one is taking this seriously. People are dying. I don't want to see any of your patients die. I know—"

"Melanie," Trevor interrupted gently. Trevor was expecting Shannon to arrive at any moment for a lunch date. Trevor's initial irritation at being pulled aside when he was trying to hurry to get done with his charts had been softened by Melanie's sincere concern. Besides, just stopping for a moment to listen to Melanie had brought that comfortably pleasant feeling that he had always enjoyed when he talked with her. He had spent so much time lately with Shannon that he had forgotten that Melanie had been a good friend long before she had been a brief romantic interest. "I appreciate your concern for my patients. I would never want to prescribe a medication that would harm them in any way. On the other hand, Waitnomor is approved by the FDA. The FDA is aware that all stimulants, of which Waitnomor is one, can potentially cause sudden death. I'm sure that the FDA is keeping a close watch for any problems that might occur with Waitnomor and will advise medical providers of any negative trends."

Trevor stood to signal to Melanie that their discussion was over as he continued, "Thank you for providing this information." Melanie stood as Trevor walked to door and opened it for her to go through. As she walked by, he continued, "I have really missed our conversations in the hallway. I hope I'll have more time to chat with you the next time you come."

"I've missed our talks also." She smiled at him.

Trevor smiled back at the memory of how many times in the past that her cheery smile had been a ray of sunshine on a dreary day. Melanie left Trevor and walked down the hallway toward the nurse's station. He felt a sudden pang of guilt for not having called her when he had said he would. She was truly a kind and special person. He felt like rushing after her and asking her to stay and talk more. But he reminded himself resolutely, it would be unfair to Melanie and would hurt her unnecessarily if he paid her any romantic interest when he was clearly more attracted to Shannon.

CHAPTER 32

MELANIE LAUGHED OUT loud in response to the humorous story that Laurie had just told her at the nurse's station. However, her laughter faded quickly as Laurie suddenly glanced toward the lobby. Realizing that someone must be approaching the nurse's desk from the reception area, Melanie turned to see who was coming. One glance was all she needed. She immediately knew that the tall. blonde woman walking toward them was Shannon, Becky's replacement and Trevor's new flame. As Melanie averted her gaze to avoid being rude by staring, she mentally ticked off Shannon's traits: gorgeous, tall, beautiful hair, perfect figure, nice legs, great skin, brilliant blue eyes, and a radiant smile. No wonder Trevor had suddenly lost interest in her. This woman would make any other woman look like an eighty-year-old nun.

Shannon greeted Laurie in a rich, melodious voice and then asked, "Is Dr. Davis done with his patients?"

"He's in his office," Laurie replied briskly. Melanie was taken aback a little by Laurie's unusual coolness. It was clear to Melanie that Laurie wasn't happy that Shannon was here.

As Shannon thanked her and turned to walk down the hall to

Dr. Davis's office, Laurie interrupted, "Shannon, before you go, I wanted you to meet Melanie Baker, the rep for Medicon."

Shannon stopped and turned back to Melanie with a smile.

"I'm glad to finally meet my competitor," Shannon said with a gracious smile, although Melanie failed to feel any warmth in her greeting.

Laurie said, "And this is Shannon Lowry, the new rep for Pharmplus."

"I'm honored to meet my worthy opponent," Melanie said, playing along with what Shannon had started. "And may the best woman win."

"Oh, she will," Shannon replied without a change in her dazzlingly smile.

However, Melanie noticed that her smile didn't reach her eyes. In its place was a hardness that instantly troubled Melanie.

Shannon excused herself to find Dr. Davis.

Laurie and Melanie watched her walk down the hall for a moment and then looked back at each other. Laurie rolled her eyes.

"What?" Melanie asked with mock exasperation. "She's pretty much perfect. Dr. Davis is lucky to get the chance to date her."

"She might be pretty on the outside. But, as I'm sure you can easily see, she's as cold as ice on the inside. I really wish Dr. Davis weren't dating her. Any relationship he has with that woman won't last. When she gets what she wants out of him, she'll dump him flat."

CHAPTER 33

"**B**UT, SIR, I didn't put that subject list from the Waitnomor study on my desk," Shane Roberts said to the president of Pharmplus.

Rick was pleased to see the wide-eyed look of desperation in Shane's eyes.

"I have never even seen the list before," Shane continued. "You've got to believe me."

"I'm sorry," the CEO of Pharmplus said. "This irresponsible and illegal act has completely destroyed the integrity of the data from the study. I am left with no choice but to cancel the Waitnomor vs. Phentermine study. Sadly, our company will lose the forty-million dollars that it has already been spent on the study. It stands to lose hundreds of millions more by not having the positive results from the study available to our pharmaceutical representatives as they labor to sell Waitnomor. In the face of such a loss, the loss of your job is a trivial matter. You're fired. What's more, if I have my way, you'll never work in this field again. In addition, you'll be hearing from our corporate attorney in the near future. Such a criminal act will not go unpunished. Guard, please escort Mr. Roberts out of the building, and be sure that he is not allowed to return to his office or laboratory on the way out."

Rick felt no remorse as a speechless and visibly shaken Shane was taken by the arm and escorted out of the room by the security guard. With Shane's departure from the company, one more impediment to his success in selling Waitnomor was now out of the way. Shane was just an expendable pawn.

CHAPTER 34

"THIS ONE IS gorgeous," Shannon said to Trevor with her eyes sparkling. They were at a ritzy jewelry store in a mall and were casually examining the pieces that were on display. Trevor joined her in admiring a $15,000 diamond-studded necklace.

"It is stunning," Trevor said. "Although it would be even nicer if it were more reasonably priced."

"I have always dreamed of having necklace like this," Shannon said.

Trevor wasn't sure she had even heard his comment.

Shannon continued, "I almost have enough money to buy it."

"If you have that kind of money," Trevor joked, "Then I'm in the wrong profession."

"After I get paid in two weeks," Shannon continued, still glued to the necklace, "I should be able to afford it. It's worth it to me to have something so beautiful."

Trevor was surprised at the intensity of Shannon's desire for the necklace. He couldn't understand why she would want to spend so much money on a necklace. At the same time, he couldn't help but wonder how she could afford to pay for such an expensive item on a drug rep's salary.

Trevor's walk through the mall with Shannon after a picnic at a nearby park had been quite revealing. Shannon had only been interested in walking through the most expensive stores. After looking over the furnishings in a high-end furniture store, she had declared that a $28,000 dining room table was the one she would buy when she purchased her new home. Trevor had wondered how he would ever have enough money to keep up with Shannon's expensive tastes. Now, looking at the rapture that played across her face as she stared at the necklace, he wondered if any amount of income would be enough for her.

"Let's check out the bookstore next door," Trevor suggested, feeling like he needed to get her out of the store before she made him feel totally inadequate. Shannon reluctantly agreed.

They held hands as they left the furniture store and headed toward the bookstore. Just outside the bookstore, Shannon spotted one of the photobooths where people could get four pictures of themselves printed on a small strip of photographic paper in just two minutes.

"Trevor let's get our picture taken," she said.

"I'd rather not. I always look bad in pictures."

Shannon took him by the hand and pulled him toward the booth as she insisted, "Come on. It'll be fun."

Trevor finally agreed, fed the required fee into the machine, and quickly took a seat in the booth. Shannon crowded into the booth and sat on Trevor's lap. Before Shannon could finish saying, "Okay, get ready," the flash blinded them as the first picture was taken.

"Hurry. Let's be ready for the second one," Shannon said. Shannon put her arm around Trevor and positioned her head next to his. They both put on their best smiles for the picture. Just before the third picture was snapped, Shannon quickly turned her head and bit Trevor playfully on the ear. The photo caught Trevor with a shocked smile on his face. Just before the last picture, Trevor crossed his eyes and lolled his tongue out the side of his mouth while Shannon did her best Marilyn Monroe lip pucker to the camera.

They laughed as they clumsily exited the booth, and then Shannon grabbed Trevor's head and kissed him hard on the mouth. Still holding his head and with a big smile on her face, Shannon declared, "You are so much fun!"

"Right back at you. Hey, what are your plans for next week?"

"I am already committed to spend the whole week with a bunch of great guys," Shannon replied seriously, although had a sly smile on her lips.

"Oh, and who might that be?"

"I'm not telling. Why should I tell someone that is going to abandon me in Phoenix for most of the week while he gallivants around San Diego with his doctor friends?" Shannon said, obviously enjoying the little game they were playing.

"That might be true, if there was going to be any free time at the medical conference. You would be bored to death waiting for me to be done with the lectures. The lectures usually start at 7:30 a.m. and finish at about 6:00 p.m. By the time dinner is over, I'm usually too tired to do anything but relax in my hotel room before falling asleep. On top of that, you told me that you couldn't get away this week, or I would have taken you with me, bored or not."

"Okay, you're right. I do need to call on my clients. Phoenix is the slowest area in the Southwest territory for Waitnomor sales. It's too bad because it would have been fun to hang out with you in San Diego for the week."

"Do you get out to see your foster parents much?" Trevor asked, changing the subject.

"No," Shannon answered after a moment's hesitation. "It's hard to find the time to get away."

"Tell me some more about them."

"No, you tell me about your parents. We've already talked about my foster parents."

"My parents are doing well. As you know, I was there just two weeks ago. My dad has a dairy, and my mom does the books for him. They're both healthy and haven't slowed down a bit, even though they're both in their seventies."

"You're lucky to have two living parents. I mean, you're lucky to have your biological parents still alive. I've always wondered what my life would be like if I had been raised by my biological parents."

"It would have been tough to grow up in foster homes like you did. My parents were always there for me. They've helped me through some pretty tough times in my life. Even though I'm an adult, they're never too busy for a phone call or a visit. My favorite thing is to go home and go fishing with my dad. We've been fishing together since before I can remember."

The machine in front of them chimed and spat out their strip of four pictures.

Picking up the pictures and briefly looking them over, Shannon laughed and said, "You look pretty silly in the last one." She held the pictures up for Trevor to see.

After inspecting them for a moment, he laughed and said, "Not as silly as you look in the first one with your mouth half open and your eyes closed. At least we both look good in the second picture. I look bad in the rest of the pictures. So I think you should keep them."

"Thanks. I've always wanted a picture of myself looking silly. Why don't you put it in your wallet for now and I'll get it from you later?"

Trevor agreed and stuffed the strip of pictures into his wallet. Grabbing her hand, they entered the bookstore, still laughing and teasing each other about how silly they had looked in the photographs.

CHAPTER 35

SHANNON REACHED OVER and massaged the back of Trevor's neck and shoulders. He responded by arching his neck with pleasure while still keeping his eyes on the road and his hands on the wheel of the car. "Ah, that feels good," he said. "And to think that some people have to pay to get such treatment."

"I'm glad you like it," Shannon said, continuing to massage his neck. She quickly glanced at Trevor to if there was any sign that his comment had meant that he knew what she had been paid to do in the past. He was staring out the windshield with a pleased look on his face. *How would he know about my past, anyway?* She smiled as the flickering streetlights revealed his handsome profile, and then he smiled warmly as he realized that she was looking at him. She sighed. There was no doubt about it. She was falling for this guy. It was hard to believe. Just a few months ago, she had been quite certain that it would never happen to her. She had never felt much for any of the men that she had known. However, Trevor was so different than those other men. True, she reminded herself, many of them had been in better physical condition. However, none of them had ever even come close to matching Trevor's combination of a kind and selfless heart coupled with a strong intellect. Hanging out with him was so much fun. He was becoming more and more handsome to her the more time they spent together. The feeling of exhilaration that she felt from having someone to care about that cared about her was making her feel giddy and nervous like a young girl on her first date. She had even felt butterflies in her stomach for the first time in her life when Trevor had knocked on her apartment door that evening to pick her up for dinner.

Arriving at the restaurant, Trevor parked the car, got out, and then opened Shannon's door. He first offered her his hand to help her out of a car and then offered her his arm as they walked toward the entrance. Shannon snuggled up to Trevor, feeling more content that she ever remembered. The feelings that she was experiencing with Trevor were something that she could really get used to. She smiled with pleasure at the thought.

CHAPTER 36

TREVOR GLANCED AT his wristwatch as he closed the door to his hotel room in San Diego, California. It was 7:55 a.m., and he had five minutes to grab some of the free breakfast before the first lecture started. As he hurried down the hallway toward the hotel's conference center, he rationalized his tardiness by telling himself that the first lecture was usually a fifteen-minute introduction to the rest of the conference. Following a few strategically placed signs that directed him down the right hallways, he arrived at the breakfast area in the nick of time. Snagging a plate, he loaded it with eggs, bacon, hash browns, and a sweet roll. He felt a little guilty for not watching his diet like he should at these drug-company-sponsored medical lectures. However, he really didn't have a choice because the food the drug companies served to medical providers at conferences was often loaded with fat and carbohydrates. Even though it was hard for him to admit even to himself, he secretly looked forward to these conferences where he was left with no choice but to indulge in the pleasure of food that he usually did his best to avoid.

After pouring a glass of milk from an ice-chilled decanter at the end of the table, he then pushed his way through a nearby door to the lecture hall. He was relieved that the introductory lecturer still hadn't finished. Spying an empty chair at the end of a row near the front, he carefully worked his way down the side of the hall in that direction. Halfway to the chair, he suddenly heard his first name whispered loudly from behind him. Turning toward the whisperer, he was delighted to see the smiling face of Sean, one of his best buddies from medical school. His friend motioned for him to take the empty seat next to him and Trevor gladly obliged. It had been at least five years since he had last seen Sean. Trevor felt a pang of guilt for not having tried harder to stay in touch with his friend. There just hadn't been enough time with his wife's death and with his increasingly busy practice.

After carefully setting his breakfast down on the table next to Sean, Trevor greeted him with a warm handshake. "How have things been going with you?" Trevor whispered.

"Great. How have things been with you?"

"Fine."

Trevor opened his mouth to ask Sean how his practice in Albuquerque was doing, but he was cut off by an additional question from Sean, "How's that gorgeous wife of yours doing?"

"Oh, Sean. I thought you knew." Trevor had a sudden lump in his throat. "She died four years ago. When you didn't show up at the funeral, I just figured that you were too busy with your new practice."

"No way! She can't be dead. How did she die?"

With great effort to maintain his composure, Trevor whispered, "Breast cancer." He had thought that he was getting over the sadness of Vanessa's death little by little, but here was someone that Vanessa and he had known when she was still alive. The memories of times the three of them had spent together flooded his mind. Trevor turned his gaze to the lecturer, but he didn't listen to a word that the lecturer was saying.

Five minutes into the second lecture, Trevor had sufficiently recovered that he dared to try to speak past the slowly receding lump in this throat. He turned to Sean, "What are you doing for dinner tonight after the lectures?"

"Nothing."

"Why don't we go to the sports bar on the first floor of the hotel for dinner? We have a lot of catching up to do."

"Sounds great."

Finally, both men did their best to turn their attention back to the speaker, hoping to learn a few new things about treating type 2 diabetes.

The sports bar on the first floor of the hotel was a maze of billiard tables, sports memorabilia, and tightly-packed dining tables. On a busy night like this, it was all arriving patrons could do to find a spot at the bar or a billiard table for a game. In contrast to most sports bars, however, the air was clear of cigarette and cigar smoke, thanks to California's smoke-free law.

The wait for a table was over an hour. Waiting patrons stood glued to televisions placed all around the waiting area. Each screen displayed different sporting events from around the world. Loud laughter and cheering emanated periodically from the different clusters of waiting patrons.

Sean and Trevor had been waiting twenty minutes for a table when a group that had been playing pool decided to call it quits, freeing up a billiard table. Before they could finish racking up the balls, a female server dressed in a cheerleading outfit appeared to take their orders from the bar. After ordering burgers and drinks, Sean picked up his cue and started a game of eight ball by powerfully breaking up the balls. The ten ball went into a pocket immediately, and the eleven ball bounced off three bumpers and then angled off another ball toward a side pocket. Just before it lost its last shred of momentum, it dropped into the pocket.

"You lucky dog." Trevor said.

"It was skill, pure skill," Sean said playfully as he eyed the table, looking for his next shot. "I knew that the eleven ball was going to end up in that pocket before I even broke."

Trevor laughed. "Sure, just like when you knew that the brunette in our cell biology class had the hots for you, and then you found out that she was gay."

"Give me a break here. I'm trying to take my shot." After a few moments' hesitation, Sean tapped the cue ball with the cue stick, causing it to strike the nine ball. The nine ball angled toward one of the corner pockets, only to strike the bumper just before the pocket, sending the ball back to the middle of the table.

"Skill, huh?" It was great to be spending time with Sean. They had been inseparable, almost like brothers, through most of medical school. Even after Trevor had started dating Vanessa, they had found time to continue playing tennis and basketball at a local sports club. After his wedding, however, Trevor's life had started changing without him really knowing it. What little free time that he had that wasn't spent with Vanessa and her family was spent more and more with married couples that were new acquaintances. With medical school ending shortly after Trevor's marriage to Vanessa, Sean and he had gone their separate ways to different residency programs in different specialties in different states. They had exchanged Christmas cards for a few years, but neither had been particularly good at long-distance friendships.

Trevor was glad to see that time had failed to dim their friendship. Sean had been quite interested in what happened to Vanessa. They had talked of little else during free time earlier in the day. Although it was painful to recall the details of Vanessa's death, Trevor had shared every aspect of Vanessa's diagnosis, treatment, and subsequent demise.

Feeling the need to keep the topic of conversation away from Vanessa, Trevor asked, "So what about you? How's your love life?"

"Not bad," Sean said. "In fact, it's great. For the past few months, I've been dating an absolutely gorgeous brunette. It's hard to admit it, but I'm pretty smitten. After all of these years of dating but never really finding someone special, it's been like a dream come true."

"Well, good for you." They had continued to play as they had conversed, and now each had only two balls left on the table. As Trevor prepared to take his next shot, he added, "I can hardly believe that an eligible bachelor like you didn't get picked off by someone before now."

"It was certainly worth the wait. Shannon is everything that I could have hoped for."

"What a coincidence. I also met a girl named Shannon a couple of months ago. That's pretty funny that we're dating girls with the same name. Tell me more about your Shannon."

"Well, she's tall; has beautiful brown eyes; and gorgeous, long, brown hair. When I go out with her to public places, it's funny to watch all the guys falling over themselves to get just a glimpse of her."

"It sounds more like lust than love to me."

"There's more to it than that," Sean said indignantly as he sank his last striped ball, leaving only the eight ball. "She makes me laugh. When she's around, I want to be a better person. We talk about everything for hours. She's smart and has a lot of insights about life that are new and fascinating." Sean lined up the cue on the cue ball, called for the eight ball to go into the side pocket, and then sent the cue ball rolling into the eight ball, causing it to roll directly into the designated pocket. "Game," Sean said with a smile of satisfaction.

"Rack them up. You didn't know it, but we're playing best out of three."

"It won't matter whether we play one, three, or five games. I'm still going to beat you."

As they began pulling the balls out of the pockets, Trevor asked, "So what does your Shannon do?"

"She's a pharmaceutical representative for Pharmplus—"

"She's what?" Trevor demanded, pausing in his efforts to gather the balls from the pockets.

"She's a drug rep for Pharmplus. You know, the company that makes Waitnomor," Sean said.

Trevor had heard exactly what Sean had said both times, and each statement had sent a chill throughout his body. This was way too much of a coincidence. Something wasn't right. "What's her last name?" His hands were cold with apprehension.

"It's Lowry," Sean said, still retrieving the balls from the pockets.

"Where is she from?" Trevor asked, dreading, but already knowing, the next answer.

"Boston. Why do you ask? Do you already know my Shannon?"

"Just bear with me while I ask you a few more questions. What college did she graduate from? Then tell me about her family."

"She graduated from the New York College of Business. She was raised by foster parents and knows nothing about her biological family. Now, I've answered your questions. It's time for you to answer mine. Why do you want to know so much about my Shannon?"

"My Shannon is tall, blonde, and so pretty that it knocks the breath out of every male she walks by. Her last name is Lowry. She's from Boston; she graduated from the New York College of Business, and she was raised by foster parents."

"Are you trying to say is that our Shannons are the same person? I've heard of women that do that. They live double lives with different men in different cities."

"Hold on there. They're not the same person because they have different eye and hair color." He had no clue why their Shannons had so much in common, but he didn't want Sean to be worried when there was probably a simple explanation. "I do have hundreds of people in my practice with the same first and last name. And Shannon Lowry is a fairly common name."

"Do you have a picture of your Shannon?" Sean asked.

"I have a selfie that we took at a restaurant on my phone." Trevor pulled out his phone and started scrolling through his recent photos.

"Now that you mention it," Sean said as he pulled out his phone,

"I have a few selfies that my Shannon texted me." He paged through his texts from his Shannon.

After a few moments, Trevor said, "Here's what my Shannon looks like."

"And this is what my Shannon looks like."

They both looked intently at each other's phones.

Trevor instantly could see that Sean's brown-haired, dark-eyed beauty didn't look at all like his Shannon. "They definitely don't look the same, so the identical twin thing is out."

"Agreed."

"Okay. I'm sure that there's a simple explanation for all of this. It's getting late, and I need to get some shut-eye." In reality, Trevor couldn't shake a deep feeling of dread that was chilling him to the bone. He didn't feel like playing pool any longer and just wanted to get back to his room so he could try to sort this all out. "I'll call you as soon as I get back to Phoenix and have a chance to ask my Shannon her birthday. I have no clue when it is."

"My Shannon told me hers, but I've already forgotten it," Sean said. "It's sometime in the spring. Oh, and along with her birth date, could you see if you can get your Shannon's middle name and maybe even something even more identifying, like her social security number?"

"That won't be as easy. I'll see what I can do," Trevor said.

The two friends parted company after making plans to eat break-fast together in the morning and after promising to make a better effort to see each other more often in the future. Trevor headed for his room. On top of the coldness he was feeling, he also felt sick inside. Something was very wrong. Deep down inside, he had to admit that the whole thing with Shannon hadn't felt right from the start. It had just been too good to be true. On the other hand, he had wanted it to be true. She was so beautiful. Maybe it had all been lust and not love after all.

CHAPTER 37

TREVOR ARRIVED AT the door of his hotel room, barely aware of how he had gotten there. His feet had all but guided themselves because he had been lost in thought. All of the many hours that Shannon and he had spent together kept replaying in his mind as he tried to come up with clues to explain the similarities between Sean's Shannon and his Shannon. Retrieving his key card from his shirt pocket, he opened the door. Flipping on the lights, he sat on the end of the bed and then flopped backward onto the bedspread, his arms outstretched, and his eyes closed. There had to be a simple explanation. His heart wanted everything to be okay so that he could return to the thrill of their romance and the comfort of Shannon's arms. However, cold and unyielding reason repeatedly overruled his heart with the fact that something was really wrong with Shannon. She had to be living some kind of a lie.

Maybe the women were fraternal twins. But if that were true, then why would their parents have given them the same first name? Possibly, since they were orphans, they had both assumed the first name of their foster mother, foster grandmother, or even their biological mother. But from what he had learned from Sean today, both women had gone to the same college at the same time and had graduated in the same year with the same major. They worked for the same drug company and were selling the same product. They had started working for Pharmplus at the same time. There were just too many similarities for it to be just a coincidence.

Trevor rolled onto his side. He was going to have to find out what the connection was between these two women, but he didn't know quite how to proceed. Should he confront Shannon directly? He decided that such a course of action wouldn't work because if she were living a lie, she would just continue with her lies.

It did seem best to find out what he wanted to know in more subtle ways, such as trying to getting Shannon's social security number, like Sean and he had agreed. He could also call Shannon's foster parents or her college and ask a few questions to see if she was who she said she was.

Sitting up on the edge of the bed, he resolved that however he proceeded, he wouldn't let Shannon know that anything had changed in their relationship. If she suspected that he didn't trust her and that he thought she was living a lie, then she'd probably just clam up and maybe even disappear.

His cell rang. It was his partner at Camelback Family Practice, Joe Quintero. Trevor wondered why he'd be calling when Joe knew he was at an out-of-town meeting. Trevor took the call and greeted his partner, "Hello, Joe. What's up?"

"Trevor, I'm just going to come right out and say this. Dr. Fife died this morning. It looks like he had a myocardial infarction at the office and went into ventricular fibrillation. The paramedics were there within five minutes, shocked him, and gave him epinephrine. He didn't respond. He was still in full code and still flat line when they got him to the ER. The ER doctor worked him for twenty more minutes and then called it. They never got a single heartbeat." Joe paused in silence for a moment.

"Oh, you've got to be kidding."

"I'm not. The funeral is set for 1:00 p.m. tomorrow. Mrs. Fife wants the funeral done quickly. I thought you might want to be there. Plus, I needed your help to know what to do with his patients. He has a full schedule for the next six weeks, and I don't have room on my schedule to see them all. The office manager wants to know if you are going to return early to go to the funeral and maybe help see some of his patients. The office phones are going to be ringing off the hook when his patients find out."

"I'm so sorry to hear that, Joe." *What a disaster,* Trevor thought to himself, both in shock and with the understanding that he was now the senior partner at the practice. He had no other choice but to fly home first thing in the morning. He wanted to be there to console Mrs. Fife and to offer his help with the funeral arrangements. He also needed to be there to assume leadership of the clinic. Dr. Fife had been heavily involved in the management of the clinic. Trevor knew that the staff would flounder without some leadership. If they weren't careful, Dr. Fife's patients might sense the confusion and could possibly bolt to other practices. That wouldn't do since Trevor was going to need to hire another doctor to take Dr. Fife's place. That new doctor would need to see enough patients to cover their overhead.

Joe launched into even greater detail about the tragedy that had occurred that morning. Although not forgotten, Trevor's concerns about Shannon took a backseat to more urgent problems.

Trevor had reached for his pocket to pull out his phone to call Shannon three times in the last thirty minutes but had been unable to do so. He couldn't decide if he were afraid that she would immediately know that something was wrong and start crying, or if he would just blurt out his concerns and blow everything, or if he were afraid that he would be so excited upon hearing her voice that he would lose his resolve to proceed with his plan. He chided himself for the last soft-hearted thought. Trusting Shannon again was out of the question unless she somehow could come up with a plausible explanation for the similarities that existed between Sean's Shannon and her. *Shouldn't I consider her to be innocent until proven guilty?* Probably, but that wasn't going to prevent him from doing a little investigating. With new resolve, he took a deep breath and picked up his phone.

The phone rang twice, and then Shannon answered with a cheery, "Hi, Trevor."

The sound of her voice instantly sent Trevor's heartrate through the roof. At the same time, he was confused by an unexpected burst of longing for her. Doing his best to ignore the urgings of his body, he steeled himself and continued with his plan. "Hi, Shannon," he said as warmly as he could.

He was about to ask her how her day was going when she said, "Have you already heard what happened to Dr. Fife?"

"I did. Dr. Quintero called me with the unfortunate news last night. I took an early flight this morning, and I'm back in Phoenix."

"I'm glad that you're back in town. But I'm sorry that you had to return under these circumstances."

"I know what you're saying. It would be nice to see you, but I'm going to be pretty busy for the rest of the day with all of the problems that this has caused at the office and with the funeral at one. However, I should be free by about five. Maybe we could play a little tennis at your apartment complex. That would really help me to unwind."

"Are you sure you'll be up for tennis? Maybe it would be better to go out for a quiet dinner and then come back to my apartment afterward."

"That does sound nice, but the game of tennis sounds better for working off the stress of this whole thing. How about I come over after things are finished up at the funeral and graveside? Then, if we're not too tired after playing tennis, we could do dinner and maybe a movie."

"Okay, as long as you're sure. I'll reserve the court for six. That should give you plenty of time to finish and get to my place."

They said their goodbyes, and Trevor ended the call. It had been easier than he had thought. She had been pleasant on the phone and had been appropriately concerned at Dr. Fife's death. Maybe there really was a simple and innocent explanation for all this.

"Additional benefactors of Erwin Fife's humanitarianism were the Daughters of the American Revolution, the American…" the minister droned at the podium. Trevor sat in the middle of the front row of the chapel, next to Mrs. Fife.

With the stress of the last few days robbing him of sleep, Trevor now found himself fighting to stay awake. He had already caught himself nodding off a few times. He was now resorting to digging his fingernails into the wood on the underside of the front of the bench in a desperate effort to stay awake.

"Erwin Fife was a kind and gentle man, known for getting along well with everyone he met," the minister intoned as Trevor returned his attention to the eulogy. That comment brought a wry smile to Trevor's lips. He quickly suppressed it before Mrs. Fife noticed. It always amazed him that speakers at funerals made the deceased more wonderful in death then they had been in life. Dr. Fife had been a great guy, but he had not been known for his tactfulness.

Thinking of Dr. Fife, Trevor's mind wandered to the appointment that he had with Dr. Fife's attorney the next morning. He hoped that the process of buying out Dr. Fife's share of ownership in the practice would go smoothly. Right in the middle of that thought, he dozed off again.

"I really missed you," Shannon exclaimed as she held Trevor close. The warmth and sincerity of her greeting was irresistible, and he couldn't help but hug her back, despite his misgivings. A tantalizing whiff of lavender from her perfume heightened his senses. There was no denying how wonderful she felt in his arms. Trevor felt his head swimming with desire. He could scarcely resist being swept away by her charms. Using all of his willpower, he forced himself to release her from his embrace. He couldn't resist kissing her lightly on her upturned lips before he stepped back, holding her at arm's length.

Trevor said, "I feel pretty special to be missed so much when I've only been gone for two days."

"Well, it seemed like a lot longer. Are you ready to play tennis? Our reservation is in a few minutes."

"You bet, and I'm going to give you a better game than last time." They had played once before in the first few weeks that they had been dating. Neither had ever taken lessons, but Shannon had played with friends a lot more than he had. The harder he had played, the more she had responded with equal athleticism and strokes that had been better than his were. It hadn't been much of a contest.

Shannon sighed with mock sympathy and then laughed as she grabbed her tennis bag. "Wounded male egos. It's tough to get beaten by a woman, isn't it?"

Trevor laughed, feeling more comfortable in Shannon's company than he knew was prudent. He almost decided to forget his worries and simply bask in the pleasantness of her company.

"You did play pretty well," Shannon said as she wiped the sweat from her brow.

"I killed myself with stupid shots. And you were all over the place, hitting back almost every stroke I sent you."

"Thanks," Shannon said cheerily as they picked up their bags and headed back to her apartment.

"Do you still feel like going out for bite to eat?"

"Absolutely. I'm famished. But I do need to shower first. You played me hard enough that I really worked up a sweat. Did you bring any clothes to change into or do you need to go back to your apartment to change?"

"I brought clothes. I didn't sweat much so I really don't need to shower," Trevor lied, hoping that Shannon wouldn't notice that he was still moist with perspiration. "I'll change in the guest bathroom while you're showering, if you don't mind."

"Sure. I hope you don't mind waiting for me to get ready."

"I'll be fine. I'll probably just snooze on the couch. I could use some rest after the thrashing that you just gave me."

They arrived at the apartment and walked to her living room.

"You're sure that you don't want to take a shower?" Shannon asked as Trevor moved to the couch and took a seat.

"No, I'm fine," he replied as he sank into the couch and stretched out his arms and legs. "I'll just rest here until you're ready."

"I could have used some help with washing my back. But I guess you're too tired," Shannon said with a playfully seductive smile. She turned and headed for the hall that led to her bedroom. Just before she got to the hallway, she reached down to her waist and pulled her T-shirt and sports bra over her head in one fluid motion. The thought of her invitation and the sight of her exquisitely formed back made Trevor's heart race madly and his mouth go dry. She hesitated for a moment as she reached the hallway, looked over her shoulder with another smile, and added, "I'll leave the door unlocked in case you change your mind."

It was all Trevor could do not leap off the couch and do exactly as she had suggested. Forcing himself to relax, he reminded himself that he had to remain focused on his objective. Otherwise, he would never be able to resolve the doubts that were still haunting him. It helped tremendously that she had disappeared into the hallway and hadn't returned. He had no clue what would have happened if she had come back out to the living room, partially or completely undressed.

Picking up a magazine from the coffee table, he pretended to read. His eyes slipped over the words by habit, but he didn't have a clue what he was reading. His mind was wholly occupied by the inviting image of Shannon's beautiful body that was indelibly imprinted on his visual cortex. In desperation, he reminded himself that he had no choice but to ignore her less-than-subtle invitation. Shannon was more sexually forward than any woman he had ever dated. Sexuality seemed to be no different for her than breathing or taking a walk. What was it that she had experienced in her life that would cause her to act so different from most other women that he had met?

He heard the faint sound of water running and steeled himself. It was time to kick his plan into high gear. This whole snooping around thing made him nervous. He had always considered himself an honest person. Rummaging around Shannon's apartment definitely was not his idea of being honest. However, time was short, and the circumstances demanded that he contemplate the morality of the whole situation later.

He stood and glanced around the living room, looking for anything that might give him a clue about Shannon's past. Nothing jumped out right away. He quickly looked over the books and other items on the shelves in living room. No luck.

A brief search of the counters and cupboards in the kitchen was a dead-end. It was time to head into the bedroom. His palms were wet with sweat generated by fear of being caught snooping around. Swallowing hard, he walked to the open door of the bedroom. To his relief, Shannon had shut the door to the bathroom that adjoined the bedroom. He stepped as soundlessly as he could into the room. Seeing Shannon's blue purse on her dresser, he headed straight to it and began searching.

Working quickly, he found a small planner and a wallet. The wallet contained a driver's license, a Social Security card, a single major credit card, and a membership card for a local sports club. There were no other pictures, store credit cards, library cards, or anything else. There wasn't even a local bank card. Her driver's license and Social Security cards looked bona fide. He quickly jotted down Shannon's social security number and date of birth on a slip of paper that he then stuffed in his pocket.

He replaced the items back in the purse where he remembered them and then moved on with his search. He half-expected the shower to stop running at any time, at which point he was ready to bolt for the door. He glanced at the clothes in the closet. They all looked brand-new. Thinking about it, there wasn't much in the whole apartment that didn't look brand-new. Why weren't there any personal possessions that she had brought with her from her foster home or from college? There weren't any pictures from her youth or college days on the walls, no college memorabilia, and no souvenirs from other parts of United States where she might have lived. Everything was Southwestern US. It seemed strange but didn't help him in his effort to solve the mystery of the two similar Shannons in two separate cities.

The drawers in the dresser were mostly empty. Her underwear drawer caught his eye for a moment, but before his thoughts could wander, he shook his head and closed the drawer.

Feeling desperate, he looked around the room for anything that he hadn't searched. On a sudden hunch, he walked to the bed and ran his hands between the mattress and the bedsprings. His fingers found something hard! As he started to pull the object out for inspection, the shower sounds from beyond the bathroom door suddenly stopped. Panicked, he quickly removed the item from underneath the mattress. There was no time to inspect it. All his fingers told him was that it was a novel-sized book. He straightened the bedspread like lighting and then soundlessly hurried out of the room.

Sprinting to the couch, he assumed the same comfortable position that he had been in when Shannon had gone to take her shower. Realizing that the book from under the mattress was still in his hand, he quickly stuffed it behind his back. He grabbed the same magazine that he had picked up earlier, opened it, and then waited. He had no clue to what Shannon would do next. With what he had seen so far, he wouldn't have been surprised if Shannon had walked out of her bedroom in the nude. He really hoped that wasn't her plan. As much as he didn't trust her, he knew he was still vulnerable to her physical beauty. What man wouldn't be?

Moments passed, and he heard nothing. He pretended to read the magazine but still didn't comprehend a single word. The sound of a blow dryer being turned on from the direction of the bedroom put his heart somewhat at ease. He retrieved the book from behind his back and placed it inside the magazine. Inspecting it for the first time, he quickly recognized that it was a diary. It had to be Shannon's. The diary was the cheap kind with a stiff paper cover that could be bought for a couple of bucks at local supermarkets. Best of all, it looked like it had been in use for years.

Thrilled that he had finally found something helpful, he opened the diary to the first page. It was the title page where the diary's owner identified themself and entered their address and phone number. He read, "This diary along to Brittany Adams." His heart sank. It wasn't Shannon's diary. What's more, the birth date under the name would have made Brittany Adams twenty-one years old, not twenty-seven like Shannon.

Wait a minute! That didn't make any sense. Why would Shannon have someone else's diary under her bed? He flipped open the diary to the last used page, which he found easily because a pen was resting against the spine of the book on that page. "Oregon State University" was printed on the side of the pen. He scanned the page quickly and found that the last entry had been written on Saturday, October 25. The entry discussed Shannon's date with Trevor from the Saturday before.

The truth was a tremendous disappointment as well as a relief. Shannon Lowry was really Brittany Adams, and she was twenty-one years old, not twenty-seven. She was just a baby! She did look young for twenty-seven, but many twenty-seven-year-olds could have passed for twenty-one. Still, he was bothered that he had been dating a twenty-one-year-old. He was a cradle robber.

He had to find out more about who Brittany Adams was. Reading further, he came to a line on the bottom of the page that caught his eye. It read, "As I was massaging Trevor's neck tonight in the car, he remarked that he usually had to pay for something like that. Just for a second, I thought that he had found out about my past, and I about died. I'm sure that he would dump me if he ever found out. When he didn't say anything else, I realized that he was just referring to paying for a massage, not for an escort. What a relief. I've never felt this way about a guy before. I think I love him. Wow, it's been a long time since I've said that about anyone."

Trevor felt a cold chill travel up his spine. Everything was becoming less and less clear and more and more troubling. Had Shannon worked for an escort service at some point in her life? The idea that he had been dating a high-priced prostitute was repulsive, but at least it explained some of her behavior. Although he had learned a lot, he still hadn't found any explanation for the other Shannon in Albuquerque.

Hungry to learn more, he flipped back to the beginning. The first entry started eight years ago. Knowing time was short, he scanned the entries quickly. It didn't take long for him to piece together the life of a self-centered young woman that had used her looks to get what she had wanted. Her mother had died before the diary had been started. She wrote often at first about missing her mother and then later about what her mother would have done in various situations. There was also a brother and a father, but there were no foster parents.

He was shocked when he came to the entries about her forays into stripping to make ends meet. So engrossed with what he was reading, he didn't notice that the blow dryer had stopped. Reading on, he was horrifying to find that she had become a high-priced call girl for some place called Bambi's in a desperate effort to maintain her lifestyle. Fascinated, he read about encounter after encounter with an endless array of clients. At times, there were gaps of weeks and even months between entries, and he found himself feeling grateful that he didn't have to be subjected to every little detail of her sordid life.

This woman has made love to hundreds and hundreds of men, and all to pay for her expensive lifestyle. Never once in her diary did he find anything about caring for a single one of the men. She had even given up trying to graduate from college so that she could spend more time earning money through the escort service. He felt sick to his stomach. Even worse, he had already scanned through the diary to entries dating just four months ago, and she was still working as an escort in Portland. She had been busy keeping her customers happy there until right before she moved to Phoenix. *Is that all that I am, a customer? How low would Shannon go to get what she wanted?* The whole thing chilled him to the bone. Who knew what scheme she was now in the middle of that had led her to a new city with a new name and a lot of cash to spend?

He didn't even hear Shannon enter the room. She quietly approached and announced happily, "I'm ready." Trevor startled and closed his magazine too quickly. He felt like a kid that had been caught stealing cookies from the cookie jar. Doing his best to conceal his anxiety over being caught with her diary in his hands, he purposefully yawned, then stretched, and placed his hands over the magazine on his lap. Hopefully, she wouldn't notice right away that it was now quite a bit thicker than when it had come in the mail.

"That must have been an interesting article. You didn't even notice when I came into the room."

Trevor glanced casually at the closed magazine in his lap as he replied, "Oh, I'm sorry about that." With a forced smile, he continued, "I guess I was engrossed in the article that I was reading." He noticed that she was wearing a pink silk shirt and short jean skirt.

"Oh, which one was it?" Shannon asked as she sat beside him, her bare thigh pressed lightly against his. That was too close for Trevor. She was just so achingly beautiful that he could barely keep his mind from giving in completely to her charms. It was easier when she wasn't so close. Turning to face her, he moved all but his knee away from her leg. He just had to avoid as much contact with her body as possible.

Shannon looked a little hurt at his effort to distance himself from her. She apologized, "I'm sorry about my off-the-wall comment about showering with me. I offended you, didn't I?"

Trevor searched frantically for something to say that wouldn't incriminate him on so many levels but came up with nothing.

"Trevor, I can tell something is bothering you. I don't know what it is, but I want you to know that I really care about you. I believe you feel the same way about me. So, I had just thought that you might want to..."

Seeing the troubled look on her face, Trevor was relieved to realize that Shannon didn't seem to be at all worried about why he had startled when she had come into the room. Instead, she was feeling embarrassed that he had spurned her advances. Instantly, he saw his chance to extract himself from this situation. "It's not what you think it is, Shannon. I started feeling sick while you were in the shower. I don't know what's wrong with me. Maybe I'm getting the flu. I really think it's the best thing for me to say goodbye for the night and go home to rest. I don't want to get you sick either."

The expression on Shannon's face changed instantly to one of concern. "I'm sorry you don't feel well." She touched him gently on the arm and continued, "Do you want me to make you some chicken noodle soup? You might feel better with something in your stomach."

"No thanks," Trevor said. He felt guilty for deceiving her. But the more he thought about what he had read in her diary, the sicker he truly felt. He wanted to get as far away from her as soon and as fast as he could. But first, he had to get the diary back under the mattress.

"Would you mind if I used your bedroom to change into the clothes that I brought? I'm starting to feel chilled."

With worry visibly showing on her face, she agreed without hesitation. Once inside the bedroom with the door closed, Trevor didn't lose any time and slipped the diary back into place. He was aching to finish reading Shannon's diary, but he knew that the opportunity had passed. Quickly changing his clothes, he then headed back into living room. He deftly deferred giving Shannon a goodnight kiss by saying that he didn't want to get her sick. She said that she understood and promised to call later to see how he was doing. He smiled weakly as he opened the door and was finally on his way home. It wasn't a moment too soon. His mind was still reeling from what he had learned, and he was sick that he had ever liked the woman. He needed to talk to someone. As he hopped behind the wheel of his car, he decided to call Sean as soon as he got home.

"Trevor, you're putting way too much stock in this conspiracy theory of yours about the similarities between our girlfriends. I'm sure that there is a simple explanation for what's going on here," Sean said over his cell. "I've got my Shannon's social security number right here to compare to your Shannon's social security number."

"You've got to believe me. Something is not right here. I found out tonight that my Shannon never did attended New York College of Business like she told me. Instead, she went to Oregon State for a few years, but she never graduated from there or any college. And yet she's working at a job that almost always requires a college degree. And get this. Her real name isn't even Shannon Lowry. It's Brittany Adams."

"How did you find all that out? I'm sure she didn't tell you."

"Let's just say that I found out." Trevor was unwilling to tell his friend he had been snooping around in Shannon's bedroom. And he definitely was too embarrassed to tell him about his Shannon's shadier past.

"Sure, Mr. Detective. You probably gave her a roofie and coaxed it out of her under bright lights."

Trevor chuckled, but he didn't reply.

Sean said, "Okay, here's my Shannon's social security number." He read the number slowly and carefully.

Trevor picked up the paper on which he had written his Shannon's social security number and followed closely while Sean read. The numbers were identical. "Their social security numbers match."

After a moment of silence, Sean responded, "Okay, this is getting creepy. But from what you've just told me, I bet that the truth is that your Shannon is impersonating mine. You look into this, and you're going to find out that your Shannon has stolen my Shannon's identity. In fact, as soon as I hang up, I'm going to call my Shannon and ask her if she knows anything about what is going on here."

"Sean, please don't say anything yet. Think about it for a minute. Both of these women appear out of nowhere at the same time, working for the same company. Both are gorgeous and are very effective in convincing their medical providers to prescribe Waitnomor. You can bet that the people at Pharmplus that hired them know very well that they have the same name and identity. They also know that whatever they are doing isn't legal. I'm sure they don't want anyone to find out about it. Who knows what they might do to us if they find out that we know about their little scam? We really need to keep our mouths shut and sit on this one for a while."

"You're spooking me with all this. It all sounds too cloak-and-dagger to be true."

"For now, just act like nothing has happened. Keep your eyes open for anything unusual. Call me if you find out anything."

Sean agreed, and they hung up.

Trevor sat motionless at his desk in his apartment. *How could I have been so stupid as to not see her for what she is?* His thoughts raced back to the first time that he had met Shannon and then marched forward. He searched for anything that she had done or said that might have clued him into the fact that she was a fake. The more he thought about it, the more he realized that she hadn't acted differently from many of the other new female drug representatives that called on him. Of course, she certainly had been the most beautiful rep that he had ever met. However, it was true that the other pharmaceutical companies hired reps that were prettier than the average woman. It didn't take a lot of training to be a drug representative since all they did was regurgitate what they had were told in marketing meetings. And, in spite of their college degrees, some of the drug reps he met with seemed to have scarcely little in the way of marketing skills. On the other hand, some did stand out from the rest in skill and personality, like Melanie.

All of a sudden, he just knew that he had to talk to Melanie. She would understand what he was going through. Talking to her would definitely cheer him up. In actuality, he really did miss talking to her. He glanced at his watch. It was just after 10:00 p.m., but he knew that she'd understand.

Finding her number in his phone, he called her. His anxiety increased as the phone rang for the sixth time. If the phone went to voicemail, he was going to hang up in discouragement.

Just then, Melanie answered the phone. "Hello, Trevor." Her voice was like music to his ears.

"Hi, Melanie." He stopped, suddenly acutely embarrassed by the recollection that he had failed twice to call her when he had promised to do so. A moment later, the memory of how cold and rude he had been to her in the office also stung him hard. Melanie had every right to hang up on him.

"It's good to hear from you," Melanie said. "Sorry that I took so long to answer. I was brushing my teeth."

"If this is a bad time, I can call back later," Trevor said, testing the water, but hoping with all his might that she would say she didn't mind.

"Oh, no, it's just fine. I'm not doing anything. What's up?"

"Well, I have a thousand things to say, but now that I have you on the phone, I don't know where to start."

"Well, while you collect your thoughts, I'll ask you how things are going with Shannon. Is everything okay?"

Trevor was amazed at Melanie's intuition about why he had called. "You seem to know me better than I know myself."

"No, I don't." Melanie chuckled softly. "Okay, yes. I'm an expert on Trevor Davis. Just ask me anything."

Trevor didn't reply for a moment and then suddenly asked, "Can I come over? I really need your help."

"Sure. If you need to talk, I'm here for you."

"Okay," Trevor said with relief. "I'm leaving right now."

"She was what?" Melanie exclaimed. Trevor and she were seated in her living room on each end of her couch. "You've got to be joking."

"No, I'm not," Trevor said. "She was a high-priced escort until just months before she started working as a drug rep." He had planned on only sharing the highlights of his experiences from the past few days. Instead, Melanie had made him feel so comfortable that before he could help himself, he had told her everything. Trevor continued, "But what I really would like your help with is why there are two drug reps with the same name and demographics."

"Honestly, I smell a rat," Melanie said. "And that rat is Pharm-plus. Someone at a high level in the company is desperate to sell Waitnomor. Moreover, it's working. Sales of my drug, Reductol, have dropped by sixty percent in Arizona in just one month. I've been checking with other reps in the Southwest region. Sales of Reductol are down everywhere. The stories I have heard are always the same. In each area, the decline started with the arrival of absolutely stunning female drug rep from Pharmplus during the first week of September. Many of the medical providers have been so enamored by the new drug reps that they have switched completely to Waitnomor almost overnight. The question I have is where did Pharmplus find all of these women?

"Well, at least we know where they got Shannon from."

"Trevor, I hate to tell you this, but judging by how sales of Waitnomor have increased even in Phoenix since Shannon arrived, I don't think her marketing techniques have been reserved only for you."

Trevor nodded and said nothing. He was mortified by how easily he had been duped and was feeling stupid for having traded away his friendship with this wonderful and beautiful woman for a relationship with a prostitute.

"There's more to this whole story. Do you remember a couple of weeks ago when I told you about the deaths that have been occurring on Waitnomor? Well, the numbers have increased. There have now been one hundred and eighty-three deaths worldwide with sixty-eight of those deaths occurring in the United States. I found this out by leaving inquiries on the internet on medical provider and pharmaceutical representative chat lines throughout the world. The most common cause of death is a fatal arrhythmia associated with left ventricular hypertrophy. Keep in mind that most of these deaths have occurred in the last three to four months. The vast majority of people that have died had been on the drug for at least nine months. In spite of all this, the FDA is continuing say that the drug is safe. I told you that I've notified my medical department. They still haven't gotten back to me on this alarming number of deaths and what it might mean for my product, Reductol. After what you have told me, I am more worried than ever that someone at Pharmplus is paying off the FDA to suppress this information, but I have no way of finding out. I just hope that my company's medical department will be able to help, if they would just call me back."

Trevor felt even more like the world's biggest loser. "If what you're saying is true, and I'm afraid it is, then that means that I've let this woman dupe me into placing my patients in grave danger. I should have listened to you before. I feel like such a heel."

"Don't take it so hard. I know that you started using a lot of Waitnomor just two months ago. From what I can tell, you have plenty of time to take your patients off the drug before it does them any harm."

"I guess you're right. Thanks for watching out for my patients even when I was so rude to you."

"Anything for a good friend. But now I need your help. What can we do to stop Shannon and her fellow drug reps from selling more Waitnomor? This goes way beyond my concerns about sagging sales of Reductol. It has everything to do with preventing further deaths from people that are taking Waitnomor. I just can't sit idly by while people are dying."

They talked until late into the night about what could be done until they were both too tired to continue. Trevor stood to leave, and Melanie joined him at the door, standing closer to him than she had all night. Unexpectedly, a strong thrill of attraction for Melanie flooded his body to the tips of his fingers and toes, and he was barely able to resist reaching out to hug and kiss her. But, after so recently having dumped her for Shannon, he didn't want to press his luck.

Melanie broke the spell by suddenly leaning forward and kissing Trevor lightly on the cheek. Then, leaning back, she remarked, "You're a good man, Trevor Davis. I'm glad to see that your time with Shannon hasn't changed you."

"I hope it hasn't," Trevor said as he walked through the front door to the porch. Turning, he added, "It certainly has made me appreciate you more."

"I'm glad that you're feeling better," Shannon said brightly. "You were so sick at my apartment the other night." Shannon had called on Trevor at his office this morning while Trevor was seeing patients. In spite of feeling pressured to stay on schedule, Trevor had excused himself and had stepped out of a patient's room to meet with Shannon in his office. As much as he didn't want to see Shannon ever again, Melanie and he had agreed that there were a few things he needed to find out from Shannon the next time she came to his office.

"I'm glad to be better," Trevor said.

"What do you think it was?"

"It must have been a twelve-hour virus," he lied. "It's completely gone now." He paused, and then changed the subject. "Shannon, I saw a patient earlier today that thinks he might know your foster parents. He asked me what their names were, but I didn't know."

Shannon said, "Their names are Joe and Sally Williams. They live in Cambridge."

"I think that was the names of the couple that my patient knows. He gave me their address." Trevor pulled a piece of paper out of his pocket that had a random address written on it.

"My foster parents moved a few months ago to a new home a few miles away from the old one." Shannon said. "I don't have the new address with me."

"That's alright," Trevor stated, not wanting to make her suspicious by pressing too hard. "Maybe you can let me know the address the next time I see you. I can't give you my patient's name to give to your parents due to the HIPAA confidentiality law. Anyway, thanks for dropping by to check on me."

"I was worried about you. Now that I know that you're feeling better, I was wondering if you'd like to go to a Halloween party with me tomorrow night at one of my roommate's friend's house."

Trevor hesitated. On one hand, being asked to spend an evening with Shannon was about as inviting as sleeping on a bed of nails. On the other hand, like it or not, he needed to keep her thinking that nothing had changed in their relationship so that he could pump her for information if the need arose. "I'm pretty tied up right now with the arrangements for purchasing Dr. Fife's portion of the practice."

"I'm sure that's a big burden for you. Well, if you finish early, I'd like it if you could drop by." She gave Trevor the address and then said goodbye.

Dying of curiosity, Trevor used the internet on the computer in his office to look up the phone number in Cambridge, Massachusetts for Joe and Sally Williams, Shannon's foster parents. He was a little surprised when a phone number for a Joe Williams popped up on the screen. But after thinking about it, he decided that it didn't mean a thing. Joe was a common enough name that it was still probably a fake, like everything else Shannon had told him. He dialed the number. An older woman answered the phone. Trevor introduced himself and then was shocked when the woman confirmed that he was speaking to Sally Williams.

"Why are you calling?"

"I'm trying to find the foster parents of a young woman named Shannon Lowry. I was her friend in college and I am trying to get in touch with her. By any chance, is she your foster child?"

"She was." There was a silence on the phone. "She passed away two years ago in an automobile accident." There was no mistaking the angst in the woman's voice.

Improvising as he went, Trevor said, "She's dead! That's so unexpected. I told Shannon that I would get in touch with her when I finished my master's degree." It amazed Trevor that it was so easy to keep lying once he had started. "I'm so sad for your loss."

"Thank you," Sally said.

"Again, this is such a shock for me. Just so I can be sure we're talking about the same person, was Shannon kind of tall?"

"No," the woman responded with just a hint of irritation. "She was only five-foot three-inches tall."

"I'm not very tall," Trevor lied, "So Shannon always seemed taller to me. I do remember that her birthday is coming up. It's on the same day as my sister's birthday, November eleventh."

"You must have known her then, because that is her birthday."

"Again, I'm sorry to hear of Shannon's untimely death. She was so young."

Trevor quickly finished the conversation and hung up. In spite of his reluctance to keep his patients waiting, he searched for the New York College of Business on his desktop computer, found the home page, and located the main number. He called, and after a few moments of waiting, he got through to the information desk. He introduced himself and then said, "I'm considering Shannon Lowry for a position in my firm. Could you confirm for me that she graduated in marketing two years ago from your facility?" After giving the last four of Shannon's social security number and waiting a few moments longer, the person on the other end of the line confirmed that, in fact, Shannon Lowry had graduated in marketing from the New York College of Business two years previously. Trevor thanked the person and hung up.

So, he thought to himself, *Shannon Lowry was a real person that had died two years ago. Brittany Adams had illegally assumed her name.* Knowing that Sean's Shannon wasn't short either, he now knew that both women had assumed the same false identity in order to work as drug reps. Melanie had been right. Someone at Pharmplus had gone to a lot of trouble to find these irresistibly beautiful women and give them what they had thought were airtight new identities.

Now that he knew the truth, Melanie and he had to figure out how to use that truth to stop Pharmplus from selling their harmful drug. He decided that he would just have to make his patients wait a minute longer while he called Melanie to see if they could get together later that evening to go over what he had discovered. It also gave him a perfect excuse to hang out with Melanie without seeming too forward. What a bad choice dumping her for Shannon had turned out to be. He just hoped that Melanie would forgive him.

CHAPTER 38

HAPPY LAUGHTER AND mirth were once again the strange companions of witches, skeletons, and monsters. Food and beer were plentiful. As the mini kegs emptied, the quality of the jokes and funny stories told by partiers was deteriorating while listeners thought that they were increasingly hilarious. The Halloween festivities at Jennifer's friend's house were in full swing. Shannon, however, though she was stunningly dressed up as a vampire, was too frustrated to enjoy it. Trevor had never showed. She had called his cell and his office repeatedly to no avail.

Deciding that the night was ruined, she brushed off the half-drunk mummy that was trying to hit on her and thanked the host. Walking slowly to her car, her feelings of frustration and anger only deepened. Things seemed to have changed between Trevor and her since he had come back from San Diego. What had happened? She just couldn't convince herself that it was due to Trevor's grief over Dr. Fife's death and his stress over the buyout. *Maybe he had found another woman while he was in San Diego.* That thought made her heart ache, and then it made her even madder. This was the first guy that she had ever loved, and she wasn't going to give up that easily. She was going to get Trevor to like her, whatever it took. Using her best asset, which was her looks, to attract and even seduce him hadn't worked. What was his problem? Men had begged and paid dearly for the pleasures that she could give, yet Trevor wasn't interested. *Why isn't he?* she asked herself for the hundredth time.

Maybe it would be a good idea if I showed off my cooking skills. That was it. She'd invite him over for dinner. Cooking was a snap for her, although it had been years since she had cooked for her father and brother. Finally arriving at her car, she drove home a little happier, believing that Trevor would be so impressed by her cooking that he would find her irresistible.

CHAPTER 39

"THANKS FOR ALLOWING me to spend the evening with you again," Trevor said to Melanie. They were seated on Melanie's couch in her apartment. Trevor had arrived four hours previously, and they had spent most of the intervening time at the kitchen table, discussing what Trevor had found out about Shannon, as well as the latest information on Waitnomor and what they were going to do about it. At the same time, it had been a non-threatening opportunity for Melanie to get reacquainted with Trevor.

"It was my pleasure," Melanie replied with a big smile. She was trying so hard not to give her heart to Trevor like she had so easily before, but he was so much fun to talk to. The harder she resisted the urge fall for Trevor again, the closer she felt her heart coming to the edge of the brink.

"It's getting late, and I'd better get going." He stood up to leave.

Melanie stood also and accompanied him to the door. Opening the front door, she was more careful this time to give him plenty of room to pass. Any physical intimacy with Trevor was out of the question right now, but she wasn't sure she could trust her emotions if she let him get too close.

Trevor turned after walking through the front door and said,

"I know that this might sound a little forward in light of all that has happened, but would you be willing to join me for dinner next Friday?"

"Trevor, you know that I value our time together just as much as you do." Her mind screamed, *No! Don't say yes! He'll just hurt you again*. But her heart reminded her of the time-tested truth, "It is better to have loved and lost than to have never loved at all." In spite of the risk, her heart won out, and she answered, "I'd love to."

CHAPTER 40

"WOULD YOU TELL Dr. Davis that I am here to see him?" Shannon asked Laurie at the nurse's desk. She had never liked dealing with Laurie in the past, and today Laurie was acting even more cold than usual. Whatever. Shannon wasn't going to let Laurie's temperament dampen her spirits since she was sure that Trevor would be glad to see her. In line with her concern that Trevor was not impressed by overly-seductive behavior, she had gone shopping the day before and had purchased a more modest, yet still attractive, dress. Her makeup was perfect. She had the perfect dinner planned for Trevor. Nothing was going to go wrong.

"He's pretty far behind, but I guess you can wait here for him when he gets out of room five," Laurie said, still with just a hint of disdain in her voice.

Shannon turned away from the woman and let her have her space. It wasn't long before Trevor emerged from the exam room. He looked handsome in his white shirt and tie. She was excited to see him and was just a little breathless with anticipation. For just a moment, she envisioned that he would whisk her into his office and sweep her off her feet, kissing her passionately while he held her close.

Her vision of how the encounter would go was immediately

shattered by Trevor's brisk greeting, "Do you need me to sign for samples?" He had only given her a tight smile and even looked away as she smiled at him.

Determined not to give up so easily, she plunged ahead. "How have things been going with the buyout?"

"We're almost done with it. I'll be signing the papers tomorrow."

Feeling uncomfortable talking to Trevor in Laurie's presence, Shannon suggested with a demure smile, "Can we go into your office for a few minutes? I wanted to ask you a personal question."

Trevor's impatient reply took her aback, "I really don't have the time right now. Can't you ask me here?" To add insult to injury, he still wasn't looking at her as he spoke. Instead, he was busily filling out paper forms that she assumed were for his patients.

Frustrated, but still trying to be positive, she turned away from Laurie and continued in a soft voice, "I want you to come over for dinner tonight. I'm making my special lasagna."

"I'm sorry. I'm busy this evening," he answered without emotion and then returned to filling out the forms.

"How about tomorrow evening?"

"I'm busy then too."

Shannon knew he had to be lying about being busy, but she couldn't say anything in front of Laurie. This was not the Trevor she had come to know. It was obvious that he had lost any and all interest that he had ever had in her.

Stunned at the unexpected outcome of their meeting and desperate to end the conversation on a positive note, she decided that she would finish with a discussion of how successful Waitnomor had been for Trevor's patients. At least that was something that was sure to be a positive. He had been raving about it for weeks. "How are things going with Waitnomor?"

"They aren't," Trevor stated coolly as he looked up from the form he was working on. "It's true that the drug works for weight loss, but I've learned that Waitnomor causes sudden deaths from left ventricular hypertrophy, especially after longer use. I'm not waiting for the FDA to pull the drug off the market. I'm taking all of my patients off of it ASAP."

Shannon's confidence withered under his cold stare. She had never seen him like this. Maybe that was the reason for the way he was acting strangely. He blamed her for the problems that he believed were occurring with Waitnomor. *He has no right to do that.* She felt anger rising in her chest. "What is your source for this negative information that you have discovered about Waitnomor?"

"The internet."

"Just because you found some nasty little website dedicated to slamming Waitnomor doesn't prove anything. The FDA newsletter this week indicates that Waitnomor is completely safe." As she spoke, her voice was becoming louder.

"Guys," Laurie said softly, but reprovingly, from behind the nurse's desk. "The patients can hear you."

Speaking just louder than a whisper, Trevor said, "The FDA just doesn't know the truth yet." He walked directly to his next patient's exam room, leaving Shannon alone in front of the nurse's desk.

Shannon angrily snatched the unsigned company tablet off of the counter and stalked out, not even glancing in Laurie's direction.

Shannon sat fuming in her car in the parking lot of Camelback Family Practice. How could Trevor have been so mean? Whoever had given him the false information about Waitnomor was responsible for how he was acting, for ruining her plans for a nice dinner with Trevor, and for destroying their relationship. Her only hope was to get Trevor alone and find out where he was getting this information. But she also knew that he would probably hang up the phone if she called or would slam the door in her face if she showed up at his apartment.

An idea sprang into her mind that would work perfectly. Without a moment's hesitation, she picked up her phone to make arrangements.

CHAPTER 41

TREVOR RUSHED FROM his previous patient's room to the next exam room, hurrying in an effort to gain a few seconds of time. Before he entered the room, he glanced briefly at the time of the appointment on his laptop. He was sixty minutes behind. Well, at least it was the last appointment of the day. Feeling pressured to get into the room so that the patient wouldn't have to wait any longer, he didn't take any further time to read the patient's name that was scheduled in that slot.

Just as he was about to turn the doorknob to the exam room, he was interrupted by Laurie calling out from the nurse's desk, "I'm out here if you need me."

"Okay," Trevor replied, puzzled at her comment. He walked over to the nurse's desk. "Is there something that I need to know about the next patient?"

"Maybe you'd better read the name on the chart before you go in."

Trevor glanced at the name on the chart. It read, "Lowry, Shannon Marie."

That hit him as if someone had punched him in the stomach. He opened the door to the exam room and went in. Sure enough,

Shannon was seated on the exam table, clothed in a patient examination gown.

All Trevor could manage was a slightly hoarse, "Hello."

"Hello, Trevor," Shannon replied in a business-like tone. She smiled like nothing was more natural than for her to be waiting in Trevor's exam room.

A moment of silence passed as Trevor was unable to think of what to say or do.

Feeling a mixture of intense distaste for the woman and an attraction for her that he just couldn't help, he felt like running out of the room. But he stopped himself. Now that Shannon was here to be seen as a patient, he wasn't going to turn her away. She could be sick and in need of his help. Clearing his mind, he forced himself to focus the best he could on Shannon as a patient.

"Shannon, could you have a seat on this chair so we can discuss your concerns first?" He motioned for Shannon to step down from the exam table and to take a seat in a chair against the wall opposite the exam table. He then sat on a stool at a countertop that was just to the side of the chair. He asked, "What can I do for you today?"

"I have a rash that I would like you to help me with."

That must be why Shannon was already wearing a patient gown. Luckily, the gown was voluminous, and Shannon had put it on open to the back. The gown revealed nothing of her perfect figure. In spite of his distaste for the woman, he had to admit that she looked amazingly beautiful while wearing one of the most humiliating pieces clothing that a person might ever be asked to wear. "How long have you had it?"

"It started a couple of days ago on my lower back, but it's spreading up my body. It itches pretty badly." Trevor instantly felt his mouth go dry at the prospect of examining Shannon's back. An image of her perfect back flashed into his mind from the day that they had played tennis. At the same time, this wasn't the first time that Trevor had been faced with examining an extremely attractive woman. Trevor knew that it was perfectly natural to feel some physical attraction to some of his patients. It had been especially hard during his first few years in practice. He had always ignored those feelings and instead had focused on his patients as human beings that needed his help. Doing so had allowed him to get through those difficult situations without embarrassment to himself and without offending his female patients.

He exercised the same objectiveness now as he focused more intensely on Shannon's problem and ignored the strong feelings of attraction that were intensifying in his chest, making it harder and harder to breath normally. "Could you please stand up and turn around so I can take a look?"

Shannon obediently stood and turned her back toward Trevor. The back of her gown was untied, revealing Shannon's exquisitely formed backside. She wasn't wearing any underwear! Trevor struggled mightily to rein in the almost smothering waves of attraction he was experiencing. As a defense, he quickly reminded himself that it wasn't unusual for female patients complaining of rashes on the back and chest to come to the office without underwear. Wearing a bra with a rash was often too uncomfortable. And Shannon was probably one of those occasional women that he had examined in his practice that didn't wear panties. Or maybe the rash was really low on her back, and it was too uncomfortable for her to wear panties. Feeling a little better, although still lightheaded and a little short of breath, Trevor reached out with his left hand and held the gown closed over Shannon's buttocks while he commenced searching her back for a rash. The skin of her back was flawless. There was not even the slightest sign of a skin disease.

"I don't see anything. Can you show me where it itches?" Not every itching sensation in the skin was accompanied by a visible rash.

Shannon reached back with her right hand and lightly touched a spot just above her right hip. "It starts here and…" As Shannon spoke, she moved her left arm across the front of her chest to her right arm and removed her right arm from the sleeve of the gown. As she did so, she turned right to face Trevor, allowing the gown to fall off her left shoulder and onto the floor. "Then it moves to here." She finished by gesturing to her right breast.

Trevor's resolve to maintain his objectivity withered at the sight of the most perfect female body that he had ever seen. Intense physical desire coursed through him like a thousand volts of electricity, paralyzing him in place. His cheeks colored; his mouth dropped open just a little, and his tongue suddenly seemed to be too thick to function properly.

"There are little bumps on my right breast that really itch."

Trevor noted a hint of a smug smile on Shannon's lips. In spite of the overwhelming physical attraction, it only took Trevor two long seconds to realize that something wasn't quite right. There wasn't a rash anywhere on Shannon's body. His distracted brain finally reached the conclusion a few seconds later that Shannon was here instead to seduce him. With great effort, he forced himself to stand, aiming to move toward the door. However, she was between him and the door. He stopped any forward motion and hesitated as he tried to figure out how to get past her without getting any closer to her. He was about to open his mouth to ask her to please move so that he could pass when she instead closed the gap between them and threw her arms around his neck, pulling him tightly against her body.

Contact with Shannon's body was more than Trevor could take. In spite of his extreme misgivings, he knew that if he didn't leave right now, he wouldn't be leaving. Reaching up, he tried to pull Shannon's arms from around his neck as he whispered hoarsely, "No, Shannon."

Ignoring his plea, she instead held him more tightly.

Hearing his own words of protest gave Trevor newfound resolve, and he stated more loudly, "Shannon, let go."

At that very moment, the door burst open, and Laurie rushed

into the room. "Shannon, get your arms off Dr. Davis." Laurie ordered firmly. "Now," she almost yelled for emphasis.

"It's not what you think, Laurie," Shannon said. "Trevor, tell Laurie to leave us alone."

"Shannon," Trevor replied coolly and evenly as he finally succeeded in removing her arms from around his neck, "I don't want to be alone with you in this room. Please get dressed. Our visit is over." Recovering rapidly now that he had escaped from Shannon's embrace, although still feeling more than a little weak in the legs, Trevor turned and strode briskly from the room.

Trevor needed a minute to calm down. He went to his office and shut and locked the door. Less than thirty seconds later, someone knocked on the door. Fearful that it might be Shannon, Trevor didn't answer the knock. A few moments later, his desk phone rang.

He answered and Laurie said, "That was me at the door just now. Do you want to talk about it?"

"I do. Please come back to my office."

She returned to his office door, knocked again and he let her in.

"Was I ever glad to see you," Trevor said as he ushered Laurie in quickly and then shut the door.

"If I hadn't known that things were looking up with you and Melanie," Laurie said with a smile, "I wouldn't have dared to open that door."

"Did I tell you that things were looking up with Melanie?"

"No, but starting about a week ago, I noted that Melanie was looking at you during her weekly detail visits like she did before Shannon arrived on the scene. She would never have looked at you that way if she weren't beginning to trust you again as a friend."

CHAPTER 42

BARELY RECOGNIZABLE IN a loose-fitting light gray jogging suit and dark sunglasses, Shannon sat in her car waiting for Trevor to leave his apartment. Her hair was done up in a bun and was covered with a matching gray cap. She had parked across and down the street from Trevor's apartment, far enough away so that she couldn't easily be seen. It had all seemed so cloak-and-dagger when she had first arrived two hours earlier. Now she was bored and stifling yawns. She checked her watch for the twentieth time and then sighed in frustration. It was only 8:03 p.m. Time was going by so slowly, and nothing was happening. She was fairly sure that Trevor was home because the lights in his apartment were on and his car was parked in its usual place. When she had arrived two hours previously, she had figured that he would leave at least once during the evening. So far, that plan wasn't working. *Well, that doesn't matter.* She was going to follow Trevor around until she found out who or what was his source of negative information on Waitnomor.

Her mind wandered to a dress that she had put on layaway at a dress shop earlier that day. She hadn't been able to purchase the dress because she had overspent her limit on her company credit card. It was frustrating that she kept running out of money before payday each month. She hoped that the company would give her a raise soon because it was getting hard to make ends meet. Payday was tomorrow, and she could barely wait to pick up the dress.

Shannon came to attention abruptly as she saw Trevor come out of the door of his apartment building and then stop to hold the door open for another person. It was a woman. Shannon's anger grew. The woman took Trevor's arm, and they walked slowly and close together toward his car.

Shannon picked up a pair of high-power binoculars from the passenger seat and focused on the woman. She couldn't see the woman's face because they were walking away from Shannon. After waiting patiently, she was finally rewarded with a glimpse of the woman's face as she turned to wait for Trevor to open her door. Shannon instantly recognized her. It was Melanie Baker, the drug representative for Medicon! Her eyes widened with comprehension. Of course. This had to be Trevor's source of damaging information about Waitnomor. The more she thought about it, the more sense it made. Who would have more to gain by discrediting her and the drug that she detailed? Shannon's anger flared again over the injustice of the situation. The little snake. Melanie was so desperate to steal Trevor away from her that she was even willing to break the law by giving Trevor negative information about Waitnomor that the FDA hadn't approved for drug reps to give to medical providers.

She continued fuming as she watched as Trevor got into his car and then backed out of his parking spot. Putting down the binoculars, Shannon put her car in gear and then slowly pulled out into the street. She followed, but not too closely, as Trevor drove out of his apartment's parking lot and into traffic.

She has to be more than just a source of information, Shannon thought to herself as she drove. Melanie had been in Trevor's apartment for the past two hours and then had been all over him when they had walked to the car. That could only mean that Melanie was also Trevor's new girlfriend. In her current frame of mind, Shannon could hardly resist the urge to ram into the back of their car and push them off the road into a tree. In her mind's eye, she could see Trevor smiling at Melanie in the car as he caressed her leg. It made her so angry. How could Trevor do this to her? She had done everything perfectly. She was physically irresistible. What did Melanie have that she didn't?

Gripping the steering wheel so hard that her knuckles turned white, she continued following their car until it stopped in front of an apartment complex. She quickly pulled into a parking spot well away where Trevor was parking his car. Hopping out of her car, she hid behind a nearby SUV, waiting for Trevor to finish opening Melanie's door and for them to head away from her as they walked toward the apartment complex. Her goal at this point was to get a glimpse of which apartment was Melanie's. She couldn't take the chance that Melanie would have put her name on her mailbox. More than a few people didn't.

Shannon walked slowly, keeping her distance as Trevor and Melanie took their sweet time, talking and laughing as they approached one of the stairwells. Staying on the opposite side of the road until she was well past the entrance through which Trevor and Melanie had just disappeared, Shannon then crossed the street, moving quickly to the other entrance of the U-shaped building. Remaining on the ground level, she edged cautiously forward until she had a view of a landscaped courtyard and pool. She looked up and located Trevor and Melanie on the second floor of the opposite side of the apartment building. They had stopped in front of a door and were talking. She couldn't read the number on the door but knew that she could easily get the number later after Trevor was gone.

Shannon watched with a mixture of disgust and envy as Trevor and Melanie continued talking and laughing for what seemed like forever. Finally, Trevor took Melanie in his arms and kissed her for a long time. *That does it.* This girl was going to be sorry she ever even thought of stealing Trevor away from her.

Shannon was sitting in a deck chair at the pool at Melanie's apartment complex. She was wearing white shorts and a yellow top. Her hair was up, and she was wearing a straw hat and dark sun glasses. The deck chair she was sitting in was facing Melanie's apartment door. She had already been at the pool for three hours and was halfway through the rather boring book that she was reading. There was only one reason why she was wasting her time sitting by the pool: to get into Melanie Baker's apartment after she left on a date with Trevor. Since it was Saturday, and since Trevor had taken her out almost every Saturday when they had been dating, she figured that he would show up at some point and take Melanie out for a few hours. Getting into the pool area without a key to one of the apartments in the complex had been a snap. She had simply followed another tenant into the locked pool area.

Shannon glanced up at the walkway in front of Melanie's apartment. Still no sign of Trevor. She sighed and returned to her book. This private detective work was tiring, but she was determined that it was going to pay off.

Trevor arrived just minutes later and disappeared into Melanie's apartment, saving her from further waiting. Shannon tried to concentrate on her book, but now a subject that was much more interesting to her was just a short distance away. She couldn't help but seethe inside over the whole unfortunate turn of events. Maybe she'd lost Trevor for good. But if she couldn't have him, she certainly didn't want anyone else to have him either. Especially not Melanie Baker.

Trevor reappeared five minutes later with Melanie hanging on his arm. Shannon could hear faintly the sound of Trevor's happy voice, and it filled her with longing for his company. This whole thing was making her loath Melanie even more by the minute.

Melanie and Trevor took their time strolling down the balcony to the stairwell, but they finally left the complex. Shannon waited for ten minutes until she was sure that they wouldn't return for something that they had forgotten. Picking up her cell phone, she dialed a phone number and then waited briefly for the person on the other end to pick up. "Hello, Mom," she said, and then she listened for a moment. "Come over whenever you're ready." She paused again and then said, "Okay, Mom. I'll see you soon." She hung up her phone and returned to her book, still keeping an eye periodically on the second-floor walkway.

Ten minutes later, a skinny, young white male with greasy-looking blond hair entered the complex and climbed to the second floor. Fashion was not his thing, as was obvious from his black T-shirt with a large white skull and cross bones printed on the back and his low, tattered, and faded jeans. Sunglasses hid his face, and a skullcap hid most of his hair. Walking with a wide sauntering gait, he stopped at the first door he came to and placed a yellow flier on the doorknob. Shannon followed him with her eyes while she pretended to be reading her book. The young man placed a flier on each doorknob as he worked his way slowly toward Melanie's apartment. Finally arriving at Melanie's door, he seemed to struggle for a few moments with putting a flyer on the doorknob, but then he moved on, leaving a flier attached to the doorknob.

Shannon smiled. Austin had said that this guy, Mike, was resourceful. She had called Austin that morning to ask for his help. First, she had explained that she was sure that Dr. Davis's recent refusal to use Waitnomor was due to information that a drug rep from Medicon, a Melanie Baker, had been feeding him. Then she had stated that she wanted to get into Ms. Baker's apartment to see what she knew and where she was getting her information. Austin had referred her to a young man named Mike that owed him a big favor. Austin hadn't mentioned that Mike was good at breaking and entering. She had called Mike moments after hanging up with

Austin and had explained her needs. Mike had been more than willing to share with her just how good he was at picking just about any lock. They had prearranged the fake telephone call to her mother as a signal that the coast was clear.

Mike put fliers on a few more doors and then left the complex. She was impressed that he hadn't even looked around to see if he could identify her. It wouldn't have helped anyway since they had never met and probably never would.

Closing her book, Shannon picked up her purse and left the pool area. Climbing the stairs to the second floor, she casually walked to Melanie's door. Opening it, she quickly stepped inside, pulling the door closed behind her. What had seemed so difficult initially had been so easy.

After snapping on a pair of surgical gloves that she had picked up at a local drugstore, she looked around the living room. One of the walls was covered with pictures of Melanie's family. The people in the pictures were all smiling. There was more than one picture of Melanie with a woman that was certainly Melanie's mother. The two were arm in arm and all smiles in front of a geyser at Yellowstone; the Lincoln Memorial in Washington, D.C.; and on a tropical beach somewhere in the world. Shannon couldn't help but feel peeved that Melanie had what she longed for the most but had been denied by her mother's untimely death. Her father's ineptitude as a parent and his alcoholism had ruled him out as a substitute for her mother.

A needlepoint of a country farm hung on the wall behind a couch, and the couch was covered with a crocheted coverlet. Healthy houseplants were scattered around the room, and a spray of dried flowers hung over the door. Shannon's hatred for Melanie increased another notch. It was all too obvious that Melanie had domestic skills that Shannon had never even considered. Shannon felt like ripping the place apart. She refrained, knowing that she should wait for a more appropriate time in the future to exact her revenge. Sick of the living room and sure that what she wanted would be elsewhere, she located Melanie's bedroom.

The bedroom was worse than the living room. It had even more family pictures full of happy people. A laptop computer stood on a desk on the wall opposite of the bed. That was what she had been looking for. The computer was off. It didn't matter because any information she needed was password protected. If she found nothing else that was helpful in the apartment, the plan was for her to take the laptop and let Austin's men extract whatever information they could from its hard drive.

Opening the computer bag on the bed, she found page after page of information downloaded from the internet on deaths that had occurred in people that had been taking Waitnomor that had been posted to social media by grief-stricken family members or health care providers. Shannon fumed. Melanie was using this trash to discredit her product, destroy her source of income, and steal her man. She just barely resisted the urge to grab the brief case and hurl it into the nearest picture of Melanie's family, knocking it to the ground and smashing the glass covering into a thousand pieces. Instead, she quickly took photos with her cell phone of a few of the website URLs that Melanie had used to obtain the information. Replacing the papers in the briefcase, she returned it to its resting place. She no longer needed Melanie's laptop since she had what she had come for. Leaving the apartment, she locked the door behind her.

After discretely removing and stuffing the gloves in her pants, she walked along the second-floor walkway toward the stairwell. She almost wished that Melanie would suddenly come home so that she could beat the living daylights out of her. She clenched and unclenched her fists. She had never hated anyone so much in her life.

"She's ruining everything," Shannon said.

"Come on," Austin said. "It can't be that bad. One woman isn't going to make every medical provider in Phoenix stopped using Waitnomor. Especially if she's got you working against her."

"You don't know what she's done. She's found a bunch of isolated and unconfirmed stories on the internet about people dying on Waitnomor, and she's using it to turn my best prescribers of Waitnomor against me. Dr. Trevor Davis told me last week that he's taking all of his patients off Waitnomor immediately."

"I'm sure that the information that she has found is no different than what the FDA already knows. We went over what to do in this situation in our last area meeting. Didn't you tell Dr. Davis that the FDA feels that those deaths happened in sick people that shouldn't have been placed on Waitnomor in the first place?"

"I did," she lied, afraid to let Austin know that she hadn't exactly followed company protocol. Trevor had been so curt with her when she had seen him at the office that she hadn't dare say anything else. "But it didn't help. He's convinced Melanie knows more than the FDA does."

"Everything will be okay. I'll take care of Melanie Baker from this end. You just get out there and sell Waitnomor."

"What are you going to do?" She was eager to hear how her nemesis was going to get what she deserved.

"Oh, I'll think of something. You really don't like this woman, do you?"

"You don't know the half of it." She wasn't sure to what lengths Austin would go to deal with Melanie, but she really hoped that it was a lot more than his pleasant demeanor implied.

CHAPTER 43

MELANIE SMILED AT the good-looking blond man that was pumping gas. She had first noticed that he was watching her as she walked around her car as she cleaned the windows. He didn't look particularly menacing. He had smiled broadly at her when she had glanced at him again, so she had decided to smile back.

The gas pump clicked off, and she returned her attention to finishing her purchase, sure that the man was still watching her, but willing herself to ignore his stare. Needing something to keep her awake while driving, she went inside the convenience store for a diet soda. When she returned to her car, she noticed that the blond man was gone. She got into her car and locked the door, feeling glad not to be the object of the man's attention any further. He was probably a nice person, but on these trips to rural Arizona to visit her medical providers, she felt it was safest to keep to herself.

She started her car and pulled back onto Highway 60. She left the town limits of Show Low, Arizona and settled back for the forty-five-minute trip to Springerville, Arizona. Her plan was to meet with two family practice physicians in Springerville to detail them on Reductol and Posivasc.

The company required her to visit each of the rural medical providers in her area once every month. In order to accomplish this, she made three or four one-day trips each month to their offices. She could travel to any clinic in her territory within three hours so unless she had more than one day's worth of visits, which wasn't usually the case, she had no need to stay overnight. She didn't mind the long drives because it gave her time to think.

Her mind wandered to thoughts of Trevor. She could scarcely believe that she was dating him again. She had figured that once he had dropped her for Shannon, he was gone for good. He was such a nice man.

All of a sudden, Melanie perceived that her car was pulling to the left. She slowed down, and the problem seemed to go away. A quick look at the road behind her in the rearview mirror didn't reveal any evidence that the road was damaged. Thinking that the problem had been a brief crosswind and that there was no further danger, she increased her speed again. The car again began pulling to the left, only now it was definitely worse. Something had to be wrong with her vehicle. She surmised it was probably a flat tire. She felt a pang of anxiety as she contemplated the prospect of changing a tire alone in the middle of nowhere. It wasn't changing the tire that bothered her because she had done that a couple of times before. It was doing it alone and at the mercy of any rapist or murderer that happened by. She tried to calm herself by reminding herself that the odds of a rapist or murder happening on her in broad daylight in the middle of nowhere were pretty slim. The reminder didn't help much.

She brought her car to a stop on the first patch of gravel that she could find on the side of the road. She got out of the car, checked the tires on the driver's side, and found that the rear tire was flat.

"Oh, great!" Not one to be afraid of a challenge, she moved straight to the trunk of her car and removed the jack and its accessories. She unscrewed the retaining bolt on the spare tire and then grabbed one side of it in effort to pull it out of the trunk. The tire started to come but then slipped out of her grasp, leaving her hands covered with black residue. Determined, she grabbed the tire again and was just ready to lift it out of the trunk when she heard the sound of a car pulling up behind her on the gravel. Her level of anxiety heightened significantly as her fears tried to convince her that it was probably a murderous person that was going to do unspeakable acts of violence to her. She dropped the tire back into its resting place and stood up. With her heart racing, she decided that the best thing to do was to quickly get back into her car and lock the door. Without looking behind her, she ran to the driver's door, yanked it open, and hopped in. She slammed the door and locked it. Remembering that she had her cell phone with her, she pulled it out of her purse, dialed 911, and put her finger on the "Send" button, just in case the person was at all menacing.

Melanie startled. The tapping sound at the driver's window seemed a loud as a machine gun. She turned with her heart in her throat and saw, with some relief, the smiling face of the blond man from the gas station. She smiled back nervously, and then after a moment, she rolled the window down one inch.

"It looks like you've got a flat tire," he said pleasantly.

"I do," was all she could think to say at her current level of anxiety. She began feeling a little less anxious because he was someone that she had seen before, and he still looked non-threatening. She kept her cell phone in her hand, just in case she was wrong.

"Why don't I go ahead and change it for you? You can stay right there." With that, he disappeared from Melanie's view toward the back of the car. Moments later, she felt the car shudder, and she assumed that he was removing the spare tire from the trunk. He reappeared and started to jack up the car. Watching as he worked, she felt increasingly comfortable. It looked like things were going to be all right. She put her cell phone on the passenger seat. Looking in the rearview mirror, she admired the muscles of his arms as he strained against the lug nuts with the tire iron. She noticed that he had put on a pair of latex gloves that he must had have had in his car for such occasions. The man quickly removed the flat tire and then replaced it with the spare. A gust of cold wind entered through the window of the car, and Melanie felt guilty that he was doing all the work while she sat in a warm car. Wanting to show her benefactor some support, she unlocked the door and got out of the car.

"You're fast," she said, hugging her herself as the cool mountain air found ways to get through her thin jacket.

The man began twisting on the lug nuts as he said, "I have to be. I'm freezing to death out here."

"I'm so sorry. Don't you have a coat?"

"Nope," replied the man as he tightened the lug nuts.

"You can use mine," Melanie said, feeling even guiltier than before.

"No thanks." He stood after he finished tightening the lug nuts. "I'm almost done." He grabbed the spare tire with one hand with no more effort than if he had grabbed a briefcase and headed for the trunk. Melanie stood by the side of the car, feeling increasingly cold from inactivity. She was about ready to jump back into the car when she heard him say, "Where is the nut to hold the spare tire in place?"

Walking back to the trunk, Melanie replied, "I put it right there," as she gestured to one area of the trunk. She looked there and didn't see it. Sure that it had been knocked to one side by her efforts to remove the spare tired from the trunk, she leaned forward and began searching for the lost nut.

As quick as lighting, a hand holding a wet cloth was around her mouth and nose. Suddenly filled with terror, she sucked in a breath of air, but she stopped abruptly as she realized that the air smelled sickly sweet. It burned all the way down to her lungs! Realizing that her worst fears were about to come true, she began fighting madly, struggling to free herself. Panic struck her in the chest as she fought in vain against the man's powerful grip. The exertion rapidly consumed oxygen, and her need for air was becoming nearly impossible to ignore. Her chest was on fire, and she was becoming lightheaded, but she knew she couldn't breathe any more of the vapor from the liquid in the cloth that the man continued to hold clamped over her face. With little oxygen left to fuel her muscles, she began feeling profoundly weak. Her struggles lessened and she began to feel confused. The need for air from her lungs finally overwhelmed her numbed brain, and she involuntarily took a deep breath. The sickly-sweet vapor burned her lungs, but it didn't seem to be all that bad. She took another big breath, sending a big dose of the chemical to her brain. As she lost consciousness, her legs completely lost their strength, and she slumped against the man's arms, her head lolling to one side.

Melanie awoke when the plane jolted as it touched down. Feeling groggy and confused, she forced her vision to focus with some difficulty and then looked around. She numbly recognized that she was seated in the cabin of a small plane. She blinked her dry and tired eyes to be sure that she was really awake and not dreaming. It didn't make any sense that she was on an airplane. She looked around the cabin and found only empty seats. The door to the cockpit was closed. She shook her head to try to clear the dizziness that she was feeling and then went to lift her right hand to rub her tired eyes. She discovered immediately that her right hand was tied to her left hand at the wrists with a length of rope. The rope was then tied to a metal ring attached to the floor of the cabin between her feet.

She stared at the rope, too tired to be afraid. She didn't even think to check to see if her ankles were similarly bound. The more she tried to remember why her hands were tied, the more tired she became until she again succumbed to a drug-induced sleep.

Melanie awoke again with a start as hands roughly grabbed her arms and forced her to her feet. With her legs feeling like rubber, she began to sink to the floor. The tight grip on her arms increased in intensity to the point of pain. "Ow! That hurts!" she exclaimed as she looked up at her tormentor's face. Her eyes grew wide with recognition. It was the good-looking young man that had changed her tire. As her still-drugged mind tried to understand why he was here, hurting her arms, he shifted his grip from her arms to around her back, effectively preventing her from collapsing to the floor. With Melanie's arms pressed against his chest, the man lifted her feet off the floor and carried her to the door of what she recognized now as a plane.

Upon arriving at the door, the man abruptly commanded, "You need to try to walk on your own. I'll hold you up if you feel too weak to walk."

"Where are we?" she asked, sounding drunk. The man didn't answer as he propelled her through the door of the plane and into the bright sunlight. She blinked her eyes, but the man didn't give her any time to adjust to the light. Clutching her arm tightly, he led her forcibly down the stairs of the plane to the open door of a waiting car. With her reaction times slowed by whatever drug they had given her, she realized too late that she should protest about going somewhere with someone she didn't know. The car door slammed shut. The man that had changed her tire hopped in the front passenger seat, and then the driver accelerated away from the plane.

Completely confused, she turned to the man in the passenger seat and demanded, "Where are you taking me? Where is my car?"

"We're going for a ride," he replied quietly, not even glancing in her direction. "Just sit back and relax."

Confused and unable to make sense of anything that had happened since she had been standing and watching this guy tighten the lug nuts on her car, she sat slowly back into her seat. Her mind searched for answers to her questions and found none. The smooth ride of the car lulled her back to sleep.

Melanie's head flopped backward as the blonde man from the gas station picked her up from the seat of the car. She woke up again. Feeling drunk with sleep, she did her best to tighten her neck muscles to keep her head from falling back again. She put her arm around the man's neck and rested her head on her arm. She had no idea who this man was and why he was carrying her. She blinked again to clear her sleep-blurred vision and observed numbly as the man carried her up a flight of stairs, set her in a wheelchair, and then wheeled her through a set of double doors and into a long hallway. Nothing looked familiar. It didn't make any sense that she was here. She had no idea how she had gotten here in the first place.

"Where are you taking me?" she asked thickly, still too tired and feeling too drugged to struggle or to be especially afraid. The man ignored her question. They moved past rooms filled with machinery and laboratory equipment. Melanie was about to fall asleep again when suddenly the man stated bluntly and loudly, "Here's your new subject." *Subject? What did he mean?* She craned her neck around to see whom he was talking with. The man from the gas station was talking to another man that was wearing a white lab coat. She realized that she should be frightened, but strangely, she felt no fear.

"Put her in room six," the other man said. "I'll take it from there."

"Okay," replied the man from the gas station. He turned and wheeled her into a small room with a bed in its center. Without hesitation, he scooped her out of the wheelchair. "Don't have too much fun." He laughed as he dropped her roughly onto the bed. A moment later the other man came into the room.

Suddenly, Melanie did feel some fear, although it felt like someone else was experiencing it. This was not good. Being on a bed with two strange men standing nearby could only mean one thing. She attempted to sit up in an effort to get off of the bed and run from the room. The man from the gas station grabbed her by the shoulders and effortlessly flipped her back onto the bed. She was sure that he was going to rape her. She struggled futilely against his powerful grasp. He was just too strong. Exhausted, she sank back into the bed.

"Let me go," she said.

The man continued to ignore her. He turned to the other man in the white lab code and said, "I'll stay to help you get her undressed. She's a wild one."

"We like them that way," the other man said, and she immediately felt him begin to undo the buttons on her blouse. Melanie screamed in panic, sure that her worst fears were being realized. No one came to save her.

"Why am I wearing these ugly green scrubs?" Melanie asked herself out loud. She was lying on a bed in a room that was totally unfamiliar. The last thing she could remember was standing on the side of a road in a skirt and wearing a thin jacket while she waited for a blond man to finish helping her with a flat tire. Now, in what seemed to be the blink of an eye, she had awakened a few minutes ago in this bedroom, wearing oversized, light-green, surgical scrubs and nothing underneath. She couldn't remember putting them on. Something had to have gone terribly wrong back there on the side of the road.

A door opposite the bed opened, and two men entered the room. She couldn't remember having ever seen one of the men that was wearing a white lab coat and had brown hair, but she recognized the other as the blonde man that she had seen at the gas station and that had then changed her tire. Obviously, he had done a lot more than just change her tire.

"Why am I—" she tried to ask but was cut off by the male in the white lab coat.

"Now that you're awake, we need you to read this." He shoved a single sheet of paper in front of her face with one hand and then held a microphone to her mouth with the other.

"I won't do anything until you tell me where I am and why I am here," she said.

The blond man said, "Read the lines on the sheet of paper, lady, or I'm going to smack you."

"I don't have to do anything—" She stopped abruptly as the blond man lifted his open hand to strike her. His jaw was clenched, and his forehead was knitted in anger.

"Okay, okay. I'll read it." She lifted the paper and started reading. "This is Melanie Baker. Don't come looking for trouble; it will find you soon enough. I'm tired of my mother-in-law. I'm calling to tell you that I've won the lottery here in Phoenix, and I'm still me." She stopped reading and looked up at the man that had threatened her. "This doesn't make any sense at all. Why do I have to read it?"

"Keep reading," the blonde man said.

Complying reluctantly, she continued, "'Sorry things didn't work out for you,' cried Juliet to the dying Romeo. 'I'm already gone so don't cry,' Romeo replied. 'Goodbye,' wept Juliet. 'I'm calling to tell you that life is great,' Trevor said." *Why are they using Trevor's name? Why are they making me read this nonsense?*

Without any further explanation, the men shut off their equipment and moved to the door.

"What is going on?" She was more awake now but was still feeling groggy. "You can't just walk away without telling me anything."

The men opened the door and left the room without saying a word. Melanie jumped up and ran after them. "Why are you keeping me here?" she yelled, desperate to know what was going to happen to her. The door slammed in her face. She reached for the doorknob and found that there wasn't one. She pushed hard on the featureless metal door and found that she couldn't budge it even a little.

Confused and afraid, Melanie wandered to the bed and sat. She rubbed her forehead and then her face in an effort to clear the fogginess from her head. She still wasn't able to think clearly and didn't seem to be able to remember things that had happened just minutes ago. Already, she couldn't remember what the two man had said when they had first arrived in her room.

She glanced around and noticed a row of four stainless steel cabinet doors in a wall to the side of the bed. The second door from the right was labeled "COLD FOODS." Suddenly thirsty and hoping that there was a cold zero-calorie drink in that cabinet, she got up and opened that door. It contained only a tall glass of orange juice. She checked the other three cabinets that were labeled from left to right, "LAUNDRY AND SUPPLIES," "SNACKS," and "HOT FOODS", but they were empty. Still thirsty, she reopened the second door. With her brain still dulled by the drug, she was unable to perceive any threat from a simple glass of juice. She picked up the glass and drank half of it without stopping. It tasted great. She sipped the rest as she explored the rest of the room. She found a TV/DVD player combo on a desk with a supply of writing materials and DVDs. She briefly inspected the simple bathroom and found nothing unusual. And that was it. There was nothing else to explore.

Still numb from the shock and horror of what she was going through, she opened the cabinet door labeled "COLD FOODS" and placed the empty glass back in the cabinet. Closing the door of the cabinet, she suddenly yawned and realized that she was quite sleepy. She lay down on the bed, unable to resist taking a nap. She fell asleep, missing Trevor and hoping that he would be able to find her and save her.

CHAPTER 44

TREVOR WALKED OUT of his bedroom and into the living room of his apartment. He had awakened at 6:30 a.m. and had already showered, shaved, and dressed. Heading for the kitchen, he pulled out his phone and noticed he had a missed call from an unidentified number and that there was a new voicemail. Realizing that someone must have called while he was in the shower, he punched the voicemail playback button and then pushed the speaker button. "Trevor, this is Melanie," the message began. He smiled in anticipation. Although he didn't know why she was calling from an unknown number, he knew that she had been traveling all day yesterday in eastern Arizona and that she had arrived back in town late last night. "I'm calling to tell you goodbye." Trevor froze. "I'm tired of my life here in Phoenix, and I'm tired of you. I'm already gone so don't come looking for me. Sorry things didn't work out." The message ended. A silence settled over the room with such intensity that a pin drop would have sounded like a thunderclap.

Overwhelmed by what he had just heard, Trevor sat down heavily in a chair at the kitchen table. The most devastating parts of the message played back in his head repeatedly. The message just didn't make sense. He had just spoken to Melanie before she had left for her trip, and everything had been fine. She had even ended their conversation by telling him that she really cared for him. It wasn't like the Melanie that he knew to suddenly run away from her best friend.

There had to be something in the message that would help him understand. He listened to the message again. He was puzzled by the fact that there was no feeling in her words. It was like she was reading a prepared speech. The enormity of his loss began to sink in. How could he have misjudged her so much? Was Melanie really that cold?

Deciding that he couldn't let her walk out of his life without more of an explanation, he picked up his phone and texted her. She didn't text back after a few minutes, so he called her. The phone rang, but Melanie didn't answer. Each ring drove home the message that Melanie was no longer his. He hung up when the call went to voice mail. A tear formed at the corner of each of Trevor's eyes as his heart ached for the loss of his best friend.

CHAPTER 45

MELANIE AWOKE WITH a gasp. Pain from a severe headache made her screw her eyes shut. She held her hands to her head, but it didn't help. She opened her eyes. It only took seconds for her to realize that she was in a room that she had never seen before, although somehow is seemed familiar like she had seen it in a dream. Her mind reeled as she tried to remember how she had ended up in this unfamiliar place. *Where am I and why am I here?* No answers came from her now fully awake and alert mind.

CHAPTER 46

TREVOR'S APPREHENSION MOUNTED as he approached Melanie's apartment. He didn't know if he would find her at home or if she were really gone forever. He didn't know what he would say to her if she were at home. His driving need to understand why she had turned her back on him so easily pushed him onward. After listening to Melanie's message that morning, he had sat in his apartment trying to figure out what had gone wrong until he had been late for work. It had been a busy morning at the office, and he hadn't had time to think things through clearly. As his morning had ended, he had come up with idea that he would try to find her during his lunch hour and would ask for an explanation.

Reaching Melanie's door, Trevor knocked twice and then waited. A glance at her front window showed it to be completely covered by drawn curtains.

Thinking that Melanie might not have heard his knock, he tried again. There was still no answer at the door. Maybe she had already left town. On the other hand, it seemed unlikely to him that she would have been able to move all of her furniture and vacate the apartment in such a short time. On a hunch, Trevor reached up and checked to see if Melanie's spare key was in its usual place on top of the porch light. He was pleased and surprised to find that it was still there. That suggested pretty strongly that she was still in town. Otherwise, being the responsible person that he knew her to be, she would have turned the key in when she had left. His spirits picked up a little bit. He hoped that there still might be a chance for them if he could just find her and talk to her. Convinced that he couldn't leave without knowing for sure that she was still in town, Trevor unlocked her door and peered inside. The living room was completely empty and was perfectly clean. Astonished that she could have moved out and cleaned up the place so quickly, Trevor stepped inside the apartment and looked around. It was as if she had never lived there. He wondered how long ago she had moved out. It had to have been in the last two or three days because he had been here in this very apartment talking to her on her couch just five days previously.

Burning with a need to know, Trevor left the apartment, put the key back where he had found it, and walked to the manager's office. The door was open. A young woman stood behind the counter. She smiled as Trevor came through the door and then greeted him.

Trevor said, "I am a dear friend of Melanie Baker's. I'm totally surprised by her sudden move."

The manager said, "I'm just as surprised. I got a call from her this morning saying she was moving out and that friends of hers would be dropping by to clean out her things. Her friends turned in the keys just a few minutes before you got here."

"Was Melanie with them?"

"No, she wasn't. Her friends said that her new job in her new location had demanded that she start immediately."

"Did they say anything about where she moved to?"

"I'm sorry; they didn't. I asked them for a forwarding address, but they told me that Melanie would call later with that information."

"Who were the friends? Did you catch any of their names?" He was fairly sure that he had met most of her friends. If he could find out who the friends were that had helped her, then maybe he could find out from them where she had gone.

"I'm really not much help here. All I can tell you is that there were two of them and that they were young men. I didn't ask their names."

Trevor thanked the woman and left the office. He was too late. Melanie was gone. Pain erupted in his chest and simultaneously punched him hard in the pit of his stomach.

One thing doesn't fit, he thought. She hadn't turned in her spare key. He sighed as he walked back to his car. It probably didn't mean a thing. If she had needed to leave in such a hurry that she had arranged for some male friends to clear out her apartment for her, then she had probably just forgotten to tell them to take care of the spare key.

Trevor left the exam room and began walking toward the nurse's desk to get Laurie started on ordering tests that the patient in the exam room need urgently. He looked to see if Laurie was at the desk, but his eyes instead locked onto Shannon's statuesque figure standing in front of the nurse's desk. She turned and smiled at him. Their eyes met briefly, and then Trevor looked away. Clenching his jaw in frustration, he had to admit that it would be a lot easier for him to deal with this woman if she weren't so attractive. He steeled himself and walked around Shannon to the nurse's desk to inform Laurie of the urgent tests.

"Hello, Dr. Davis," Shannon said pleasantly as he finished talking to Laurie.

Trevor had absolutely no desire to talk to her. Turning to her, he stated coolly, "Hello, Shannon."

"It's been a while," Shannon said with her usual dazzling smile. "I wanted to stop by and see how things are going with Waitnomor."

Trevor hesitated as he considered what to say to this woman that clearly cared nothing for his patients' safety. He felt like telling her to get lost but couldn't bring himself to be that rude. If he criticized Waitnomor to her face, then he would have to listen while she embarked on an effort to convince him that Waitnomor was a great drug. The last thing that he wanted to do was spend time talking to Shannon.

"Are you still worried about the negative information about Waitnomor from the source you had?"

Trevor was about to open his mouth to tell Shannon that she was right, he still had concerns about Waitnomor. Then, suddenly, it hit him, and he closed his mouth with surprise. She had said the word "had" at the end of her sentence. She knew that Melanie was gone! That, coupled with the smug look on her face, spoke volumes. She knew that Melanie had been his source of information. He couldn't believe it. How could she have known?

"Had?" Trevor asked. "Why did you say 'had'? Do you know where I got the information on Waitnomor?"

Shannon's smile faded for just a brief moment but returned a second later. "It doesn't matter to me where you got the information. I just hope that you have decided to start using Waitnomor again. It's more effective than Reductol and it's just as safe."

Trevor stared at Shannon for just a moment. There was no question that she knew a lot more than she was saying about Melanie leaving town. Coupled with the suddenly empty apartment and the spare key still above the light, that meant that maybe Melanie hadn't left by her own choice and that Shannon knew what had happened. If his hunch were correct, then he didn't want Shannon to know that he suspected anything. He responded, "I'll consider it. I need to get back to my patients." He couldn't bring himself to be cordial enough to say goodbye or to thank her for coming so he turned and walked away.

Thoughts about what had really happened to Melanie had been haunting Trevor all day. It had been difficult for him to pay complete attention to his patients because his mind had kept wandering to where she might be and if she were okay. Early in the afternoon, he decided that he had to call Melanie's parents to see if they knew where Melanie was. After talking to Shannon that morning, he was more than willing to make his patients wait while he tried to call Melanie's parents. He figured that since she was close to her family, she would have called them to let them know where she was going, if she had gone voluntarily.

After a little sleuthing online, Trevor found the number for Melanie's mother in Reno, Nevada. Seconds later, he punched in the number. A pleasant, middle-aged-sounding woman answered the phone. Trevor introduced himself and was immediately greeted warmly by the woman. She identified herself as Melanie's mother, Denise Baker.

"It's so nice of you to call," Mrs. Baker said. "Melanie has told me so much about you. I'm thrilled that she has found such a good friend while she is living so far away from home."

Her comment pierced Trevor to the core, and he had to swallow a lump in his throat. He missed Melanie a lot. It thrilled him to have at least partial confirmation that what he suspected was true and that Melanie still cared for him. "Mrs. Baker, Melanie suddenly quit her job last week and left Phoenix. She left no word with me about where she was going. I'm calling to see if you know where she is. I would really like to talk to her."

"My goodness. She left town? That doesn't make any sense. She called ten days ago and told me that she was happy with her job and that she was thrilled with her relationship with you. I wish she had called me. I hope everything is all right with her."

Trevor could tell that Mrs. Baker was about to cry, and he knew that he wouldn't be far behind her if she did. "I'm sure everything is okay. Melanie is very resourceful, and she can take care of herself. I was just hoping that she would have called to let you know where she was. I bet she'll call you in the next day or two."

"Well, if she does, she's going to get a tongue lashing from her mother for running away from a good relationship and a good job and then not calling to tell her mother about it. I'll find out where she's at, and I'll call you first thing."

Trevor gave her his cellphone number and then thanked her for her help. He also promised to call if he heard anything from Melanie.

As much as he wanted to spend more time trying to put together what had happened to Melanie, he knew he had to get back to his patients. He grabbed his laptop and headed for the next patient's room.

At the conclusion of his last patient's office visit, Trevor sat at his desk in his office and stared off into space, deep in thought, as he tried to piece together exactly what had happened. He was now sure that Melanie had not left of her own free will. The more he thought about it, the more he was sure that Shannon had to have been involved with Melanie's removal from the Phoenix area. Exactly how it had been done, he wasn't sure. He was sure, however, that Shannon's superiors at Pharmplus were dishonest enough to recruit and then place her in the Phoenix area. It didn't take a leap of imagination to realize that the same people would have had no trouble removing Melanie from the picture to prevent her from adversely affecting Waitnomor sales. He realized that he might also suffer the same fate if he continued opposing the use of Waitnomor. As much as he wanted to, he now recognized that it was not safe for him to march over to Shannon's apartment and demand to know where Melanie was. He also just didn't trust himself to be alone with Shannon. Her efforts to seduce him had left him shaken and dubious of his ability to resist her if he was alone with her in her apartment. He decided that he would only approach Shannon directly as a last resort.

He considered calling the police but was sure that he didn't have enough proof that Melanie was missing to convince them to take him seriously. He would have come up with clues as to what had happened to Melanie himself.

The only leads that he had were the pen that had been stamped with Oregon State University that he had seen in Shannon's diary and the fact that Shannon had worked at a place called Bambi's in her hometown. Turning to his computer, he logged onto the internet and searched for "Oregon State University." Moments later, he saw the university's home page and discovered that it was located in Portland, Oregon. He used an internet search engine to look up "Bambi's" in Portland, Oregon and was rewarded with a phone number from a yellow pages website. Grabbing his phone, he dialed the number. The phone was answered by a friendly woman that held firm in her insistence that she would not give any information about her present or past employees over the phone. Trevor thanked her and hung up.

That settled it. He had to go to Portland to find out more about Shannon. If he could find out who had recruited Shannon and where she had gone for her training, it was possible that he could then find Melanie. She had to have been trained somewhere because she was quite knowledgeable about her products and about weight-loss medicine. The more he thought about it, the more the trip to Portland seemed like the right thing to do. He brought up his airline frequent-flier website on his computer and began making flight arrangements.

CHAPTER 47

"LOOK AT THESE numbers," Rick said as he studied an email that he had just received from the marketing department. He stopped talking and continued studying the information on the computer screen at his desk.

"What numbers?" Candy asked with mild exasperation at his failure to complete his thought.

Rick was silent for a few moments and then triumphantly stabbed the computer screen, closing the email window. Getting up from the chair in front of the computer, he walked over to the plush leather couch in his office at the Pharmplus administrative building and sat next to Candy. Putting his arm around her, he announced, "Sales of Waitnomor are up three hundred percent in the Las Vegas area in the last two weeks. Pharmacies are running out of existing supplies of Waitnomor. The distributor is rushing more to them by overnight carrier. It really worked. The R-648 that we put in the water supply for Las Vegas six weeks ago really worked. The money's going to come rolling in."

"That's wonderful. I'm so happy for you." She threw her arms around Rick and held him tight.

Rick pulled back from her embrace after returning it only briefly.

"We've got to move up the timetable for producing more R-648. We need to hit more cities right away. The profits will be endless. I need to call Austin and tell him to step up production. He'll be more than glad to do so once I tell him about these numbers from Las Vegas." He paused for a moment and then continued, "And thanks to you for convincing that Jones guy at the FDA to look the other way on these pesky reports on sudden deaths with Waitnomor."

"Everyone has a price," Candy said. "His was a little steep, but it was money well spent.

CHAPTER 48

TREVOR PARKED HIS car in a seedy-looking part of Portland. Bright signs along the street advertised massage parlors, strip clubs, and sex shops. Mixed in were a few rundown hotels, convenience stores, and shuttered buildings. This sign on the building that matched the address from the internet for Bambi's said it was a massage parlor and not an escort service. Had the escort service gone out of business? He decided that since he had made the long trip and since he was desperate to find any lead on what had happened to Melanie, he would at least go inside and ask if anyone knew anything about Bambi's escort service or Brittany Adams. He was a little nervous as he walked up to the door and opened it. Inside was a reception desk with an adjoining waiting area that looked like the waiting area for any other business. There weren't any dim lights, neon signs, or posters for salacious activities. One customer was in the waiting area playing a game on his phone.

Trevor walked up to the reception desk, and a young woman stood up to greet him. "Welcome to Bambi's Massage Parlor. How can I help you?"

"Hello," Trevor replied, still a little confused that Bambi's was a massage parlor and not an escort service. "Is Brittany Adams available?" Trevor figured that the only way he was going to avoid a flat-out refusal to give out information about a past employee was to act as if he didn't know that she were gone.

"I'm sorry. Brittany left Bambi's about three months ago. Would you like to make an appointment with one of our other masseuses?"

Just then, an attractive, tall brunette in a pale pink jogging suit walked into the reception area from a back hallway. The jogging suit only partially hid her hourglass figure. She smiled warmly as their eyes met. Trevor was struck by her youthfulness and her fresh-scrubbed appearance. Yet she worked at a massage parlor, and maybe at an escort service, if that was what Bambi's still was. Still unable to shake his misperception that escort girls looked and acted like streetwalkers, Trevor decided that the approaching young woman was probably just another receptionist.

The brunette looked away from Trevor and spoke to the receptionist, "Karrie, are there any new appointments for me today?"

"No one has called for you," Karrie replied. "Your schedule is still open for tonight, at least for now." As she finished speaking, Karrie looked up at Trevor expectantly.

Trevor blushed as he realized that Karrie was intimating that he might want to get a massage. "No, thanks. I'm not here for a massage. I'm only here to see if you can help me find Brittany Adams."

"It is hard to change when you find that special girl," Karrie said.

As Karrie spoke, the brunette walked around the receptionist desk and stopped in front of Trevor. She stuck out her hand and stated, "Hi. I'm Jessica. How do you know Brittany?"

"I've been out with her a few times in the past," Trevor said. At least that was somewhat truthful.

"I bet you miss her," Jessica said. "She's a great girl. Brittany and I have been good friends for years. I've really missed her since she got another job three months ago. I even tried to get hired on at same job so that we could be together, but they didn't want me."

"What company was that?" Trevor was suddenly excited that this might be the lead he was looking for.

"It was some pharmaceutical company," Jessica said. "I can't remember the name. I know that I had never heard of it before."

"Do you know where she went after she left Portland?"

"I'm sorry. She didn't tell me anything."

"Well, I'm sorry to hear that she's gone." Trevor was frustrated that his potential lead wasn't panning out. He decided that it wouldn't hurt to pump Jessica for more information. "I was really looking forward to spending some time with her. Do you have any idea how I can go about finding her?"

"Brittany's new job took her out of town. She got hired and left the same day. She never told me where she was going, and I haven't heard from her since."

"Maybe her father knows where she is. She did talk about her father at times," Trevor lied easily in an effort to find out how to get a hold of Shannon's father. "If I could speak with her father, maybe he would be able to tell me where I can find her."

"That sounds like a reasonable plan," Jessica said. "I'm sure that you heard Kerrie say that my schedule isn't very full today. I'd be glad to show you where he lives. Also, I really want to know where she moved to myself so I can try to get in touch with her. I'll drive if that's okay with you."

"Sure." He was taken aback by the young woman's pleasant and forthright personality. Why in the world would such a beautiful, young woman allow herself to be drawn into being a masseuse, and maybe a high-priced call girl? With her looks, she could have had most any man that she wanted. He doubted that she had chosen to be an escort for companionship, love, or eroticism. Maybe the motive was the need for money to pay her bills and to live a better lifestyle than she would have had otherwise.

As soon as they were in Jessica's car, Trevor couldn't help but ask, "Bambi's is a massage parlor. Are you a masseuse?"

"Yes, I'm officially licensed by the State of Oregon as a masseuse. However, I understand why you're asking since you've been out on dates with Brittany. Bambi's also offers a range of other services to our customers, including providing what we call 'dates with models.' That's how you met Brittany. I am also a model, and when the massage business is slow, I go on dates with paying customers. Bambi's is very careful about stating on their website that the dates with our models are just that, a night out with a beautiful model. The date does not include sexual favors of any kind."

"And the models and their customers comply with that rule?"

"They're supposed to, and Bambi's doesn't want to hear about it if they choose not to comply. Prostitution is illegal in Oregon."

"You're telling me that you go on dates with guys that have paid dearly to go out with you, and they don't expect some kind of action in return?"

"Is that much different that the regular dating world? Guys expect something in return if they just take you out for pizza and a beer."

"I see your point."

The rest of the ride to Shannon's father's house was uneventful but informative. Jessica had been working for Bambi's for two years. Before starting, she had been unable to attend college full-time as a business major because she had always been running short on money. Now she was making enough money to pay for her schooling, all of her living expenses, and even to pay the down payment for the new red Mercedes convertible that she was driving.

Jessica stopped her car in front of Shannon's father's house, and they walked to the door together. It was a single-story, cinder-block structure with a decaying wooden front porch, sagging shutters, and peeling paint. What had once been grass was a tangle of tall weeds. Jessica rang the doorbell twice but got no response. Disappointed, they were turning to leave when the door suddenly opened.

"What do you want?" an old man barked from the doorway.

A wispy mop of gray, uncombed hair fell into his gaunt, unshaven face. His bloodshot eyes swam in pools of tears, bordered by pale, swollen eyelids.

Trevor was sure that this wreck of a man couldn't be Shannon's father. He was about to turn to Jessica and tell her that they must be at the wrong house when he heard Jessica say, "Hello, Mr. Adams. Do you remember me?"

The man at the door peered intensely at Jessica for a moment and then said, "Oh. Yeah. You're one of Brittany's friends from that sleazy place where she used to work." His eyebrows rose suddenly with suspicion. "That's why you're here, isn't it? You want to ask her to come back to work for you."

"No, no!" Jessica reassured him. "We're—"

The old man continued, ignoring Jessica, "It's the best thing she ever did, getting away from that place. I'm proud of her for realizing what a horrible profession it was. She's doing well at her new job. And it's definitely a lot more respectable than where she was." He glared in Jessica's direction.

If he only knew, Trevor thought to himself. Realizing that the man's critical outburst had left Jessica struggling with what to say next, Trevor jumped in. "I'm a friend of Sha—I mean, Brittany's…" Trevor hoped that neither Shannon's father nor Jessica had noticed his blunder. He continued quickly, "And I'm here to see if you can help me find her."

The old man turned his frosty glare on Trevor and said, "Why should I tell you? If you're hanging out with one of them," he pointed to Jessica, "Then you're one of her Johns. For all I know, you've been one of Brittany's customers, too. There's no way I'm going to let you get your hands on my little girl again."

"I'm not one of her or Brittany's customers," Trevor said. At the same time, he knew that he had told Jessica that he was one of Brittany's customers. He hoped that Jessica would play along thinking that he was lying only to gain the old man's trust. "Brittany and I became friends in a class at Oregon State University three years ago. I've been away at graduate school. Before I left, I promised Brittany I would get a hold of her after I finished and let her know how things were in graduate school. Her phone number was disconnected, and I couldn't find her listed as a student at the University. I knew that she and Jessica had been friends, so I found Jessica and asked her to help me find her." He glanced at Jessica and was glad to see that she was going along with his story and not staring at him incredulously for being the liar that he was.

"I hope what you're saying is true. Otherwise, I'm going to kick your back side all the way back to your car." The old man's face relaxed somewhat, and Trevor was relieved that he seemed to have bought his story. Shannon's father continued, "Sorry about my appearance. I've been feeling kind of low ever since Brittany moved out. Having Brittany at home helped me to cope with my wife's death. Brittany is so much like her mother." The man paused for a moment, his jaw muscles tight as he suppressed his grief. "Things have been even worse since Brittany left town." He blinked slowly and stared sadly into the distance.

"I'm sorry to hear that things have been rough for you," Trevor said.

Shannon's father sighed and then looked back at Trevor. "I'm afraid that you're wasting your time. Brittany didn't tell me where she was going when she left. She has written once to tell me that she's doing fine, but she didn't put a return address or phone number in the letter. If it's any help to you, it was mailed from Phoenix, Arizona."

"Thank you for telling me what you could."

"Do you happen to remember the name of the company that she's working for?" Jessica asked.

The old man responded, "She told me that she was going to work for a company called Hughes Pharmaceuticals."

Trevor looked up sharply as the man said the name of the

company. Was the man losing it? As far as Trevor knew, there wasn't a drug company named Hughes Pharmaceuticals.

Shannon's father continued, "They really rolled out the red carpet for her. They picked her up in the company jet and flew her to a training meeting."

"Did she tell you where she was going for training?" Trevor asked.

"She didn't know herself," Shannon's father said. "And, to tell you the truth, the whole thing did bother me at first. They were in such a rush for her to leave, but they wouldn't tell her where she was going. But that's in the past now. She told me that she scored the highest marks at the training seminar and that she's now one of the company's top salespeople."

Trevor bit his tongue in an effort not to blurt out the truth about why Shannon was so successful. There was no point in causing Shannon's father any further pain. Instead, he said, "I wanted to ask one more question. Do you remember the exact day that Shannon left for the training meetings?"

"Yes, I do. It was August twenty-first, the day after my mother's birthday."

Trevor thanked Shannon's father for his help and then walked back to the car with Jessica.

When they were out of earshot, Jessica said, "He sure bought that part about you and Brittany being friends from a university. You sure think quickly on your feet. For a minute there, I thought that he was going to kick us out before we could even get started."

"I kind of feel bad for him. He seems so lonely."

"Speaking of being lonely, I don't have any plans for the evening, and I bet that you don't either. Why don't we go out and have some fun?"

"Thanks for the invitation. I'll have to take a rain check on your offer since I'm leaving town in a few hours. I need to take care of a few things before I leave."

After Jessica dropped him off at his rental car, Trevor drove directly to the airport. He returned his rental car and purchased a return ticket to Phoenix. Leaving the main terminal, he walked to the private aircraft terminal and had asked one of the clerks at the desk for help.

"I'm trying to find an old friend that I met about three months ago," Trevor explained, trying hard to make his lies sound real. "I ran into him while I was waiting for a chartered flight to Grants Pass, Oregon, on August twenty-first of this year. He gave me his business card, and I promised to give him a call, but now I've lost the business card, and I can't remember the name of his company. If I could just look at the list of flight plans for that day, I'm sure I can recognize the name of his company."

The clerk shrugged his shoulders and answered, "Sure. I don't see any problem with that." He produced the logbook within seconds. It only took Trevor a few moments to locate the name Hughes Pharmaceuticals and a company telephone number. Trevor discovered that the destination for the flight had been listed as Mexico City, with a refueling stop in Phoenix, Arizona.

Excited that he had found a lead that might help him find Melanie, Trevor jotted down the number, thanked the clerk, and then dialed the number on his cell phone. His excitement was quickly tempered by the discovery that Hughes Pharmaceuticals' phone number was disconnected. He searched for Hughes Pharmaceuticals' phone number or website on his phone but neither came up. Disappointed, but not beaten yet, he tried calling information for a listing for Hughes Pharmaceuticals, but he was told that there was no such company. He tried calling international information for Mexico and was told the same thing. Disappointed that his possible lead had evaporated, Trevor returned to the main terminal, ate lunch, and then waited at the gate for his flight. He tried to read a novel that he had picked up at an airport newsstand, but his mind kept wandering to Melanie.

He just had to find Melanie. He missed her company and her pleasant smile. Now that she was gone, he found it hard to imagine his life without her. The thought that she might have been killed by her abductors tried to force its way into his mind, but he resisted it. He knew in his heart that she was still alive.

As much as he hated to admit it, there was only one place left where he could find information about where Melanie was, and that place was Shannon. As unpleasant as the prospect was, he knew that he had to confront her. The problem was that if Shannon had something to do with Melanie's disappearance, then that meant that the people that had illegally employed her to sell Waitnomor wouldn't hesitate to commit further crimes to achieve their objectives. In that case, confronting Shannon could possibly place him in the same danger of abduction that Melanie had placed herself in when she had helped him to see his error in using Waitnomor. He forced that thought from his mind, knowing that he would risk anything to get Melanie back.

Trevor pressed Shannon's doorbell with his right index finger. His fingers felt cold with anxiety. Try has he might, he couldn't fight off the feeling of dread he was experiencing over what he had to do and what Shannon might do in response. But he was going to go ahead with his plan to confront Shannon, regardless of what happened. He had called Shannon from work and had asked if he could come over and talk. Shannon had been pleasant on the phone and had told him to come over anytime because she would be there all evening. It had taken an hour for him to build up his courage. Now that he was there, he was almost ready to leave and come back later. He was beginning to doubt the wisdom of coming to her apartment at all when he heard the doorknob turn. Too late to turn back now.

Shannon opened door. "How long have you been standing there?"

"Just a few moments," Trevor said.

"It's good to see you. Please come in."

As Trevor walked past her into the living room, a faint, yet pleasant, whiff of her perfume tantalized his nostrils. He turned to face her as she closed and locked the door. She was wearing a short cream-colored dress that showed every inch of her perfect legs. The dress was sleeveless and had a dangerously low neckline. Feeling a little lightheaded and breathless, Trevor forced himself to concentrate on her eyes. They were the least formidable part of her body.

"Please have a seat," she said. He sat on the couch. She sat just inches away from him, turned to him so that her bare knees almost touched his, and smiled warmly. "I've missed you, Trevor. It's been a while since we've spent time together."

Trevor wasn't about to say that he had missed her. "It has been a while, hasn't it." Looking around the room, he noticed that Shannon had picked up a few knickknacks to hang on the wall. It surprised him that she was interested in arts and crafts. "It looks like you've been busy shopping for a few new things for your walls. They look nice."

"Oh, they're just a few things I picked up. I'm glad you like them."

They were both silent for a moment until Shannon smiled and said, "You had said that you wanted to talk about something. Why don't I get us something to drink before we get too deep into conversation?" She was on the way to the kitchen before Trevor could protest. He wanted to be in her apartment for as short a time as possible.

Her voice carried over the sounds of preparation from the kitchen, "How have things been at the clinic with Dr. Fife gone?"

"Things are slowly getting back to normal. We interviewed a new physician this week, and we hired him the next day. He's going to be starting in three weeks."

"That's great. I'll have to come by and meet him as soon as he gets started. Is he going to be as interested in helping patients to lose weight as you are?"

"Oh, I don't know. He's as skinny as a rail. Doctors like that sometimes aren't as empathetic towards obese patients. I imagine that he'll prescribe weight-loss medications only occasionally until he learns just how helpful weight-loss medications are for his patients."

"I'll see what I can do to change his mind a little more quickly," Shannon said as she came out of the kitchen with a bottle of wine on ice and with two wineglasses. Trevor barely noticed because he was instantly afraid for his future partner. His future partner was single and would most certainly find Shannon irresistible, just as he had.

"I got your favorite wine. I thought that you would like that."

Trevor doubted that Shannon's motives were that pure, but he still said civilly, "Thanks. That was very kind of you."

Shannon picked up the wine bottle and filled the glasses. She handed one to Trevor and then took the other and settled back into the couch, again sitting just inches away from Trevor.

"Now what was it that you wanted to talk me about?" she asked as she placed her glass of wine on the table and turned toward Trevor.

Trevor had been through this scenario in his head a hundred times over the last few days. He hadn't been able to come up with questions that were guaranteed to get the answers that he wanted. One thing was certain. It wouldn't work to start by asking her directly where Melanie was. "I've been worried about something lately. It's hard to know where to begin."

"Well, I've been worried, too." She put her arm on the back of the couch just inches from Trevor's shoulder and then leaned a little bit closer to him as she continued, "Maybe we've been worried about the same thing. Perhaps it would help if I told you what I've been worried about first."

Feeling threatened by her closeness and at the same time bothered that he couldn't completely shake his attraction to her, Trevor was at a loss for how to continue. All he could think of to say was, "Okay, why don't you go ahead."

Shannon smiled sweetly. "I've been worried that I did something that offended you, and that's why you haven't been calling or coming to see me. I've been at a loss as to what it might have been. If there was something that I said or did, please forgive me." As she spoke, Shannon's smile had been replaced by a genuine look of sadness. As she finished speaking, she allowed her arm to slip around Trevor's shoulder.

Alarms went off in Trevor's head. She was trying to use her physical charms to come on to him again. This time, he had already decided what he would do. With some difficulty, he pulled away from her a little and then gently placed his left hand on her right shoulder, holding her at arm's length. "Shannon, I didn't come tonight to kiss and make up. I don't think that our relationship can ever again be the way it was." Trevor removed his hand from her shoulder and slid farther away from her on the couch. Shannon sat quietly and emotionlessly, staring at him with her beautiful eyes.

Trevor decided that it was time to get to the point. "A few weeks ago, a dear friend of mine left the Phoenix area suddenly. I have been worried about what happened to her and was hoping that you would be able to help me to find out. I'm talking about Melanie Baker, the rep for Medicon."

Shannon spoke with more than a little indignation in her voice, "How would I know anything about what happened to her? I heard that she left town because she was tired of her job. She could have gone anywhere."

"I don't think she left Phoenix on her own accord. I think she was abducted."

"And why in the world do you think that I would have any clue about where she is or what has happened to her?"

Her happy smile was gone, and her eyes were narrowed in anger. Trevor continued, "I think that she was removed from the Phoenix area because she had discovered information that would hurt sales of Waitnomor. I think that someone in your company had something to do with it."

"You've got to be joking. My company has no need to do something like that. Use of Waitnomor is increasing while use of Reductol is declining. There is no incentive for us to do something that terrible or illegal."

"I just want you to tell me if you know anything about where she is." He searched Shannon's face for any sign that she knew more than she was willing to let on.

Shannon stared at Trevor icily for a moment and then suddenly her face softened. "I really don't know anything about why she left Phoenix or where she is. I'll ask some of the other drug representatives from Pharmplus if they have heard anything. I'll let you know if I find out anything."

"If that's the case, then I'd best be going," Trevor said as he got off the couch and headed toward the door. As he opened the door, he turned back toward Shannon to say goodbye.

"I had really hoped that we'd have a more pleasant evening together," Shannon said.

"Thanks for letting me have a minute of your time," Trevor said in a businesslike manner. He knew that Shannon was lying, but he had no way to prove it and he couldn't think of any other way to way to get any more information out of her. There was no point in staying any longer. He opened the door and walked out into the hallway.

As he walked away, he heard Shannon say, "Call me sometime. I'd really like to talk some more."

Trevor pretended that he hadn't heard her and kept on walking. He had nowhere else to turn to find out where Melanie was. The thought that he might never find her crashed down on him. He tried to fight despair, but with no avenue left to give him hope, it overwhelmed him.

CHAPTER 49

TREVOR'S DAY AT the office had been long and stressful. In addition to being worried sick to the point of distraction about Melanie, he also felt burdened by the difficult challenges facing the patients that he had taken care of that afternoon. He really needed the weekend to come sooner than later. The phone in Trevor's pocket began ringing and Trevor pulled his phone out to see who it was. It was an unknown number. Reflexively, he went to hang up on the call. Suddenly remembering that he was on call for all of the medical providers in his practice, he instead hurriedly swiped his phone to pick up the call. He was too late. The display on the phone indicated that he had missed the call. Trevor's stress level moved up one notch at the thought of being on call for the rest of the week and the weekend. *So much for the restful weekend idea.* After a minute, he checked to see if the caller that he had missed had left a voicemail. They had. He pushed the play button.

"Dr. Davis, this is Jennifer, Shannon's roommate. I'm sorry to call you, but I really need to talk to you about Shannon. Meet me tonight at the Green Gecko Bar at nine-thirty. Tell the bartender that you're with the Anderson party of two, and he'll lead you to me. I'll know that you can't make it if you're not there by nine forty-five.

I know that you are a busy man, but the information that I have will be of great interest to you. No matter what you do, don't call our apartment. Shannon is at home tonight. She thinks that I'm out to dinner with one of my medical providers. I'll see you at nine thirty."

Trevor was amazed that Jennifer had the guts to call him and pretend that she had something important to tell him. It was probably all just another ploy by Shannon to get her hooks into him. Since Jennifer worked for Pharmplus selling Waitnomore, Jennifer was most likely in cahoots with Shannon. Her invitation to meet him at the bar was probably an invitation to get him kidnapped, just like Melanie. But, as he thought about it for a moment, Trevor realized that getting kidnapped and being taken to where Melanie was being held might be the opportunity that he had been looking for. At least he would get to see her again. He might even be able to help her escape.

If Shannon had asked Jennifer to meet with him in an effort to convince him to resume dating her, then the meeting would be very short. *There is one more possibility,* he reasoned. It was possible that Jennifer actually had information on where Melanie was and wanted to share it with him. That possibility seemed remote since what little he knew about Jennifer indicated that she was as conniving and dishonest as Shannon.

After a moment's hesitation, Trevor decided that he had nothing to lose and everything to gain by meeting Jennifer. He grabbed his keys and headed for the door, suddenly anxious to get to the Green Gecko Bar on time.

The Green Gecko Bar was a seedy, one-room, smoke-filled haven for hard-bitten alcoholics. It stood on a deserted road on the outskirts of the city. A country western song that Trevor didn't recognize blared from a beat-up jukebox that a sat against one wall. The solitary occupants at the scattered tables sat nursing their latest drink of hard liquor as they stared wordlessly at nothing. The light in the room was so dim that Trevor could barely discern the expressions on the patron's faces. A few soused individuals sat at a bar that stood against the wall that was opposite the jukebox. An overweight bartender stood guard behind the counter. He was cleaning the glassware with a stained cloth. The outline of a gecko rendered in green neon lights hung on the wall behind the bar. The tail was only partially visible because some of the neon tubing was not working.

The atmosphere in the bar added to the bad feeling that Trevor already had before he had walked through the door. He couldn't stop feeling like the same people that had kidnapped Melanie were probably waiting somewhere in the bar to kidnap him. After carefully checking around the room and not finding a single woman, Trevor approached the bar and addressed the bartender. "I'm with the Anderson party of two."

"We don't take reservations here, nor do we ask our patrons who they are," the bartender said gruffly. "Take a seat and I'll get you something to drink."

"I was supposed to meet a woman here," Trevor said more loudly, sure that bartender hadn't heard him correctly. "She told me that I was to ask for the Anderson party of two."

"Well, why didn't you say so?" The bear-like bartender growled. He threw the stained cloth over his shoulder and walked out from behind the bar. "Follow me," he said.

He followed the bartender across the room to a side door. The bartender opened the door and motioned for Trevor to walk through the door. Jennifer was seated at a card table in a small, bedroom-sized room that was attached to the back of the bar. Shelves with bottles of alcohol, napkins and peanuts lined the walls of the room. A single, bare light bulb illuminated the space. Jennifer looked very much out of place in a light blue, sequined party dress. Her makeup and hair were perfect. The room was otherwise empty. A set of double doors on one wall that most likely led to a delivery dock were held shut by a steel bar.

"Hello, Dr. Davis," Jennifer said in a pleasant voice. "I'm glad that you decided to come."

"I'm not exactly sure what could be so important that we have to meet in this dive, Jennifer. However, here I am, as you requested." As he spoke, Trevor pulled out a folding chair from the card table and sat down. He regretted the abrupt, business-like tone of his voice, but he was just a little irritated with the whole situation.

"I tried to think of the most unlikely place in town where we could meet. I wanted to minimize the possibility that Shannon or anyone else connected to Pharmplus would find out about our meeting."

"You're right, then. This is about the last place where I would expect to be found on a Friday night." Trevor definitely didn't feel safe or comfortable in this bar or in this part of town. And he didn't feel safe as long as he was around anyone connected to Pharmplus. Leaving as soon as possible was a top priority. "So, what did you want to talk to me about?"

Jennifer leaned forward and began speaking more softly, "I know that you're going to find this hard to believe, but I know that Shannon had something to do with Melanie Baker's disappearance." She stopped and looked at Trevor, waiting for his reaction.

"Okay. Why do you think that?" Trevor asked coolly, pretending to be only marginally interested. He didn't trust this woman enough to let her know just how interested he really was. At the same time, he couldn't help but notice that Jennifer was physically every bit as attractive as Shannon. Her large and dark brown eyes were perfectly set in her flawless face, and her thick and flowing dark brown hair shone lustrously in spite of the harsh light. He hadn't paid her much attention in the past because when he had seen her at Shannon's apartment, he had only had eyes for Shannon. Where had Pharmplus gotten these gorgeous women? Were they all using fake identities, like Shannon? Had all of them been escorts before working for Pharmplus? There were so many questions that he could ask, but he doubted that he would get the truth from Jennifer.

He

"Well, she never came right out and admitted it, but she has said some things over the last month that have made me suspicious. Shannon was madder than a hornet when you dumped her and started dating Melanie again. She couldn't stop talking about how mad she was at you and about how much she hated Melanie. It was depressing to live with her for a while. Then, a few days before Melanie disappeared, she suddenly cheered up and started talking about how you and she were going to get back together again. I didn't think much of it at the time and figured that it was just wishful thinking. On the night that Melanie disappeared, I overheard Shannon talking to our boss, Austin, on the phone about how thrilled she was that someone was gone. They were talking about a woman, but Shannon didn't mention her name. Shannon asked him what he was going to do with the woman, and she had seemed pleased with his reply. At the time, I didn't know that Melanie was gone and so the conversation that she was having with Austin didn't mean much to me. I lost interest and returned to the novel that I was reading. Just before she hung up, I heard her say, 'Sure, that sounds like fun. I'll have to arrange for a few more of these disappearances so that you and John will have a good reason to fly back into town. I'm sure that we won't have any trouble convincing John and Jennifer to double date with us.'"

"Did she say anything else?"

"She hung up right after that."

"Who's John?"

"He's the pilot for our company's jet. I've been dating him since I started working in Phoenix. Every time that John flies Austin into town for something, John calls and we go out. The reasons for some of their visits have been obvious, such as business meetings. However, they have come twice in the last two months without any obvious reason. When I asked John what had brought them to town on those two occasions, he told me that he didn't know and that it was best that I didn't ask. I thought that it was strange for him to be so secretive."

"What happened after the telephone conversation?"

"The next morning, Shannon told me that she was elated that the rep for Medicon, Melanie Baker, had suddenly quit her job and left town. She said that the time was perfect to push sales of Waitnomor when there wasn't a rep around for our competition. When I asked why Melanie had quit her job, she replied that she guessed that Melanie had left because she had realized that Reductol was a worthless drug. I thought that was strange because I had run into Melanie just days before at another medical provider's office. We had talked for a while, and she had told me that she was happy with her job and her life. I had even teased her a little about stealing you away from Shannon, and she had mentioned how pleased she was to be spending more time with you.

"The reason that I am here talking with you is that I can't stand to think that Shannon and Austin have done something to hurt Melanie. She's such a sweet person. When I signed up for this company, I had no idea of what I was getting into. They are doing a lot of unusual and even illegal things. At first, I talked myself into going along with what was happening because of the excitement of getting a new job and the money that they were paying me. However, I can't believe that they would turn to kidnapping in an effort to achieve their goals. There is a limit to how low I'm willing to go to get what I want, and they just passed it. That's why I just had to talk to you. I can't live with myself any longer, knowing that I'm part of such a horrible organization that would do something so terrible to Melanie." Jennifer began crying. Her tears left lines on her cheeks as they disturbed her carefully-applied makeup.

Trevor looked around the room, found a box of tissues on a shelf, and offered them to Jennifer. He had so many questions to ask, but he'd need to give Jennifer time to collect herself. Any reservations that he had about meeting with Jennifer were gone now that it was clear that she was sincerely interested in helping Melanie.

Jennifer dabbed her tears and continued, "I got home a few minutes after you left on Tuesday. Shannon was angrier than I had ever seen before. She had even thrown a vase of flowers against the wall, and it had shattered into hundreds of pieces. Ranting and raving, she told me about how selfish and rude you were. At one point, she even said that if getting rid of Melanie wasn't enough to convince you to use Waitnomor, then she would make you pay even more than Melanie had. That was when I knew for sure that Melanie had been kidnapped and that Shannon had been part of it."

"I had a pretty strong feeling that Shannon had some part in Melanie's disappearance, Trevor said. "But I couldn't prove it. Now that I know for sure that Melanie has been kidnapped, I have to find her as soon as possible before they do something even more terrible to her. I just hope that I'm not too late."

"I'm so worried about her. What if they have hurt her or even killed her? I would feel so bad that I was ever part of this whole…" Jennifer stopped, and tears streamed down her face again.

"I'm sure that she is still alive. I just know she is." Trevor didn't really know if Melanie were alive or not, but there was no way he was going to allow himself to consider the possibility that she was dead. "We have got to find her soon. Do you have any idea where they might have taken her?"

"I don't," Jennifer said as she blinked back tears.

"You've got to try. Where are your bosses' main offices located?"

"It is possible that they took her to the place in Mexico where we did our training."

"Where was that?"

"I don't know. They picked me up in a private jet in New Orleans. We stopped for fuel in Phoenix. They shut all of the windows in the airplane before we took off, and they asked me not to open them while the plane was in the air. We landed at a small airport a few hours later. I didn't see much at the airport because they rushed me off the plane and into a waiting car. I did notice that the traffic signs at the airport were in Spanish and so I was fairly certain that we were in Mexico. I looked for the name of the airport, but I didn't see it. That's probably because I don't speak Spanish."

"You must have seen an address somewhere at the training meeting. Think carefully. Did you see an address on a letterhead or on a napkin? Was there an address on the mail that you received?"

"I don't remember ever seeing an address. They didn't let us send or receive mail and we couldn't use telephones, computers with internet access, or cell phones. They kept us very busy, and we weren't able to leave the grounds of the training center for the whole month that we were there. At the end of the training seminar, they rushed us back to the airport and flew us to our destinations with the windows closed on the airplane again. I'm sorry I can't be of more help."

"There has got to be some way that we can find where they have taken Melanie. What about the pilot? I'm sure he knows where Melanie is because he certainly must have flown her there."

"I wouldn't dare ask him. He would tell Austin that I was asking about things that were none of my business. Who knows what Austin would do then? And even if I did ask, I'm sure that John wouldn't tell me anything."

"I don't think that you're going to need to ask him," Trevor said, beginning to formulate a plan in his head. "Are you willing to help me find Melanie?"

"Yes, I am."

"All I need you to do is to call me when your pilot friend is coming back into town. I bet that we can put something on the plane, something like a homing beacon, that will tell us where it is going. If we can find out where your bosses' headquarters are in Mexico, I have a feeling that we will find Melanie there also."

"Okay. The next time John calls to say he's flying to Phoenix, I'll call you immediately."

"There's just one more thing that I want to know. I hope that I don't offend you by asking this question. Did you work for an escort service before you hired on as a drug rep?"

"I did. All of the girls at the training meeting, including Shannon, were working as escorts at the time they were hired."

"And, your real name isn't Jennifer, is it?"

"No, it's not. However, I've grown attached to it and would prefer that you called me Jennifer, at least for now. Who knows what the future will bring? At the same time, I don't think that Pharmplus can keep this sales force a secret forever."

"Laurie, do you remember the name of the patient that was seen last week for the severe pain in his left shoulder?" Trevor asked. "I have been seeing him for high blood pressure for years, and yet I still can't remember his name. I can see his face in my mind's eye, but I can't think of his name. He is about six-feet tall and has dark curly hair. His hair is thinning a little on top, and he is a little calorie challenged. He's about thirty years old and works as a private investigator."

"I do remember him." It always amazed Trevor that Laurie was able to conjure up names for patients that he hadn't seen for months. "He's the guy that drives a Harley and goes to Sturgis, South Dakota, every summer for the Harley convention. His name is Max Johnson."

"You're amazing." Trevor jotted down the patient's name on a sticky note and shoved it in his shirt pocket.

Before Trevor could scoot off to his office to call Max Johnson, Laurie said, "I'm glad that you're going to get some help in trying to locate Melanie. If you can find her, I bet that you'll be able to convince her come back to Phoenix. She really didn't seem like type that would just run away and never come back."

Laurie is definitely astute, thought Trevor. Still, it was best that she was not privy to everything. Trevor thanked her for her help and then headed to his office to make the call. It really helped to have patients from all walks of life in his practice so that he could request their services in times of need. Right now, he was definitely in need.

Trevor entered through and closed the outside door to the office of Max Johnson, private investigator. In spite of his efforts to close the door softly, the seemingly paper-thin door suddenly slammed shut and then rattled loudly in its frame, threatening to shatter the pane of opaque glass that occupied its upper half. Trevor initially winced and then slowly relaxed when he realized that the pane of glass had survived. A draft must have blown the door shut harder than he had planned.

Trevor hadn't known what to expect as he had driven to Max Johnson's office. The building that housed Max's office was an old warehouse and was nestled amongst other unused warehouse buildings. The hallways in the building were dirty and sorely in need of paint.

The interior of the investigator's office wasn't much different. Max was the only occupant of the single-room office. He was seated at a desk in the center of the room and was talking on the phone. He looked up suddenly as the door slammed. Recognizing Trevor, he waved and then signaled that it would be just a moment. He pointed to a beat-up vinyl chair that was in front of the desk. Trevor took a seat and waited.

"No, Mrs. Price," Max said emphatically into the phone. "He's lying. No one is trying to frame him with false information. I followed him myself from your house to her apartment. He was never out of my sight. There is no doubt that it is him in those pictures." Max stopped talking and listened for moment. He looked at Trevor and rolled his eyes. Max continued, "Of course he's going to try and deny it. He'll lose everything if you divorce him over this." Max paused to listen again and then continued, "He owns nothing. All his talk about money here and property there is lies. He was a bum when you found him and let him live off your fortune. He'll be a bum again when you kick him out. He's a user and abuser. If you let him stay, he's going to keep using you until he uses you up." Max listened again for a moment and then suddenly held the phone away from his ear a little. Trevor could easily hear a woman's sobbing.

As Max finished the call, Trevor looked around the office. A rusting fluorescent light fixture with two naked bulbs hung from the ceiling over the desk. An old bookshelf stood against one wall. It contained a few books and a lot of disorderly stacks of paper and magazines. A couple more vinyl chairs stood against the opposite wall, along with an unused coat tree. The office décor didn't inspire a lot of confidence, but Max was young, and Trevor figured that he was probably just starting out. Trevor hadn't known anyone else that was in private investigation and had jumped at the chance to get help from someone he knew.

"Doc, it's good to see you when I'm not in pain or sick," Max exclaimed loudly after finishing his call. He stood and shook Trevor's hand warmly. "I feel like we're on more even ground here. At least I don't have to worry about bending over." Max laughed at his own joke, and Trevor smiled.

"I appreciate your seeing me at such short notice," Trevor said.

"Anything you need, Doc. You've always been there when I've needed you."

Trevor had admitted Max to the hospital in the middle of the night a year earlier for a bad case of pneumonia. The pneumonia had been missed a few days earlier at a local urgent care clinic. By the time Trevor had admitted him, the right side of his chest had been half full of thick pus. Surgery had been required to remove it. Since then, Max had reminded Trevor at every visit that Trevor had saved his life.

"So, what can I do for you?" Max asked.

Trevor started at the beginning and told Max everything. It felt good to share the whole thing with someone.

Max listened patiently and asked a few clarifying questions while taking down pages of notes. When Trevor had finished, Max sat back in his chair and let out a deep breath. "You've got a big problem here. My biggest concern is that your girlfriend…" He searched his notes for Melanie's name and was still searching when Trevor reminded him. "… Melanie is already dead. The guys that you're up against are professionals. These kinds of guys waste people without a second thought."

"I have this strong feeling that she isn't dead. I can't quit looking until I know for sure. I need your help to figure out where she is."

"Okay. Then let's assume she still alive. Where do you think they took her?"

"I suspect that they have taken her to somewhere near Mexico City. That's what the flight plan said for the flight that took Shannon to her training meeting. Shannon's roommate was pretty sure that their pharmaceutical representative training took place in Mexico and that it was a two-hour flight south of Phoenix. I was thinking that I could stow away on the company's plane the next time it comes into town. I was hoping that you could help me get onto the plane."

"Stowing away on a plane is a lot more easily said than done. What kind of plane is it?"

"She only told me that it was a private jet with seats for eight passengers."

"Then I really doubt that there is going to be room for you to stow away, even if I could get you inside. Baggage areas often aren't pressurized, and small jets fly high enough that you wouldn't survive the trip. It would be a lot easier to put a GPS tracker in the plane. That way, we can track him to anywhere he lands. Hopefully, that will be the place that you are looking for."

"That sounds great."

"I'm sure that the private jet can do five hundred miles per hour. If what you're saying is true, then we are going to be looking for a city that is two hours, or one thousand miles, south of Phoenix and in a direct line from Phoenix to Mexico City."

As Max spoke, he pulled an internet map program up on his computer and then motioned for Trevor to stand up and look over his shoulder. Max zoomed in until Phoenix and Mexico City were at the top and bottom corners of his screen. He placed his thumb over the bracket that indicated a distance of one hundred miles in the map legend, and then he used his thumb to count ten thumb widths from Phoenix in a straight line toward Mexico City on the screen. He put his index finger at the roughly one-thousand-mile mark he had determined.

"There. That's where he is going to land. It's somewhere in the desert, three hundred miles north of Mexico City." Max zoomed in to the area he had been pointing to.

"From this map, it could be any one of a number of cities," Trevor said.

"He has to be landing in an area that doesn't have radar coverage or else air traffic control would get on his case for not sticking to his flight plan. It wouldn't work for him to turn off his transponder either."

"What's a transponder?"

"A small jet can fly higher than eighteen thousand feet and therefore is required to carry a device called a transponder to tell the air traffic control system his position and altitude. He couldn't just turn off his transponder if he were within radar coverage because that would make it look like he had crashed. It would bring major scrutiny by the Mexican aviation administration. These guys don't want that to happen. However, air traffic control radar only works within line of sight on a clear day or about one hundred miles. There are many remote places in Mexico that aren't covered by radar. When a plane that is flying above eighteen thousand feet is out of radar range, the pilot has to report his position and altitude by radio every half an hour when flying over land and every hour when flying over water. Our man probably touches down for just a few minutes, just enough time to either drop off and pick up whatever he needs to. He then takes off and heads for Mexico City, just as he said he would in his flight plan. He then lies about his airspeed the next time he reports in by radio so that air traffic control never finds out that he stopped in route.

"With all that in mind, it makes sense that he is landing at a small airport that isn't covered by the Mexican air traffic control radar. It can't be too close to Durango, Mexico, because there is an international airport there. We'll fly to Durango after we plant the GPS tracker, and we'll wait to see if he stops or at least flies by. When is the plane going to be coming to town next?"

Trevor explained his arrangement with Jennifer.

Max sat back in his chair. "Doctor Davis, what you've told me is right down my alley. I want to help you find Melanie."

"Thank you so much. How much is your fee?" Trevor grabbed his wallet and went to pull out a credit card.

"Doc, this one is going to be on me. I owe it to you for taking such good care of me. Plus, I make plenty of money by helping rich ladies track down their cheating husbands. It would be nice, however, if you could pay for the gas for the plane."

"I'd be glad to. How soon will you be ready with the GPS tracker?"

"I can borrow it from my buddy anytime. I'll get it tomorrow and put it in my van. Text me when the plane comes into town. We'll get right over to the airport and put the device onto the plane. We'll have to leave immediately afterward for Durango in my Cessna in order to get there before the jet catches up with us. In the meantime, I'd like to make a few phone calls to try and find out just how widespread the use of escorts as drug representatives is at Pharmplus. I doubt that the entire company is corrupt. Most likely what we are seeing is the work of a greedy district or area manager that has ties to one of the local crime organizations."

Trevor's phone began ringing while he was working out on the stair stepper in his bedroom. Looking down, he could see it was from Jennifer. He hopped off the stair stepper, accepted the call, and breathlessly said hello.

"Dr. Davis. John just called. He'll be here in two hours. He wants to go out to dinner with me and then spend the evening together. I'm not sure, but I think that he's going to be leaving first thing in the morning."

Trevor thanked her and hung up. He immediately texted Max that the plane was coming. Trevor couldn't believe that the opportunity that he had been waiting for was finally here. If things went well, he would have Melanie back in just a few days. He missed her tremendously. If Melanie would have him, he was going to ask her if he could become a much more permanent part of her life.

His phone rang and Trevor picked it up before the second ring. It was Max. After exchanging greetings, Trevor said, "The plane is going to be here in just under two hours. Is everything ready on your end?"

"Everything is ready. I have the GPS tracker in the back of my van. My Cessna has been serviced and is full of gas. What size coat do you wear?"

"What does that matter?"

"Oh, never mind. It doesn't matter. I'll just bring what I have, and we'll make do. I'll meet you at your house in thirty minutes."

As promised, Max arrived at Trevor's house a half an hour later. Max was wearing a white jumpsuit with the name "KELLY" embroidered over the left shirt pocket.

"What's the get up for?" Trevor asked.

"You didn't think that we could just walk into a major airport and plant our GPS device on the airplane without someone noticing us, did you?" Max smiled.

"I guess I hadn't thought about it."

"We're going to act like we are repair men on a service call. Check out the name of our company." As he spoke, he turned his back toward Trevor. A colorful design containing the title "WHITE GLOVE AIRCRAFT REPAIR" was stenciled on the back of the jumpsuit.

"You're amazing. I suppose that you have one for me, too?"

"You bet I do." Max removed a matching jumpsuit from a bag that he was carrying. "I hope this one fits you. I had to guess your size."

Trevor slipped the white jumpsuit over his clothes. It was a little long in the legs but otherwise was a good fit. The name "LYNN" was embroidered over the left shirt pocket.

The two men left Trevor's house and walked toward Max's van. The van was white and had a logo on its side that matched the one on the back of their jumpsuits.

"Well, look at that," Trevor said. "You've really done your home-work. Where did you get the van?"

"It's one of my vehicles. I bought it so that I could have a non-descript vehicle from which to carry out my surveillance work. It's amazing how people tend to ignore unattractive, unmarked white vehicles."

The two men entered the van and then pulled away from the curb with Max at the wheel. As they drove to the airport, Max reviewed the plan that they had outlined at their first meeting.

"What are we going to do if someone doesn't buy our story?" Trevor asked.

"The rule in this type of work is to act like you have every right to be where you are and then to deny everything that you are accused of. It's kind of like being a politician. Most people will fall for that kind of a bluff."

"You make it sounds so easy. If anyone comes along, I'm going to let you do all of the talking."

The men continued discussing their plan until they arrived at the private aircraft terminal. Trevor waited in the van while Max went inside to convince the attendant to open the gate to the tarmac where the private aircraft were parked.

"How did it go?" Trevor asked upon Max's return.

"They were concerned at first about why we are here so late in the afternoon. I told them that the pilot of the plane himself had called for an urgent assessment and possible repair of the plane's front landing gear. They relaxed after I told them that we refused until he had promised a lot of extra cash for our work. I explained that the pilot, John, is wanting to get the job done right away so that the plane will be ready to leave first thing in the morning."

Max drove the van up to the gate that led to the tarmac where the private planes were parked. He honked once and waited for moment. The gate slowly opened, and they drove through. Max stopped the van in front of one of the small jets. "This one has got to be it," he said. "It's the only eight-seat, unmarked, private jet here."

The two men exited van. Max opened the rear doors and removed a small sports bag. He told Trevor to grab the toolkit and the battery-powered lantern that were also in the rear of the van. Trevor followed Max to the front landing gear of the airplane. After assisting Trevor with setting up and turning on the lantern, Max ducked down and peered into the landing gear bay.

"The transmitter is about the size of a pack of cigarettes. There are a half a dozen places that it will fit into nicely." Max rummaged around in the sports bag until he extracted a small, gray, plastic box and a tube of epoxy. "This is the GPS tracker," Max said as he switched the device on. "It's battery is good for about twenty-four hours at its current settings. It has a magnet on the back to hold it in place, but I'm not taking any chances." He uncapped the tube of epoxy and applied it liberally to the back of the transmitter. He then placed transmitter inside the landing gear bay and held it in place for thirty seconds. While he was waiting for the epoxy to harden, he continued, "Just in case you're wondering, this epoxy is designed to withstand the cold associated with high altitudes."

Feeling nervous about what they were doing, Trevor glanced around the tarmac and then at the private aircraft terminal. A door in the terminal building opened, and two men in matching white shirts and black pants began walking quickly toward where they were working.

"Max," Trevor said quietly but sharply, "I think that you weren't quite as convincing as you thought you were with the attendants. Two of them are coming this way fast."

"Oh, great. Let me do the talking on this one."

Max turned and shut off the lantern. He and Trevor picked up their equipment and had just started walking toward their van when they were intercepted by the attendants.

"We tried to look up your company to confirm that you are who you say that you are," one of the attendants said. "There is no such company listed on the internet. We're going to have to ask you to leave the premises immediately unless you can produce proof that you are a real aircraft repair business."

As the men had been speaking, Max had opened the rear doors of his van, and he and Trevor had placed their gear in the back of the van. Max said, "We're a brand-new company, and we just opened our doors this week. We don't have a website, yet. Anyway, we are done checking out the landing gear of the plane. No repairs were needed. We were just about to leave."

Max's calm and cheerful demeanor seemed to put the attendants at ease for the moment. Without waiting for further questions, Max and Trevor hopped into the van and took off for the exit. The gate opened automatically, and they quickly merged with the traffic that was exiting the airport.

"Well, that was close," Trevor said.

"Take my word for it. In this line of work, that was nothing."

Suddenly struck by the thought that they would have to pass by the same attendants in order to get to Max's plane, Trevor asked, "How are we going to get past those guys to get your plane? They can't help but recognize us and then ask more questions."

"I anticipated that something like this would happen. I moved my airplane to a private field in Mesa. That's where we're headed now."

The ride to the private airfield in Mesa went by quickly. Thirty minutes after arriving, they were accelerating down the runway into the cloudless night. The small, single-engine Cessna quickly gained altitude to five thousand feet. Leveling off, Max headed south toward Durango, Mexico.

Trevor shifted to a new position in the passenger seat of the Cessna and tried to get comfortable. The seat wasn't padded enough to be comfortable after twelve hours. It had taken them ten hours to fly to Durango. They had stopped once for fuel. Upon arriving in Durango at 7:30 a.m., they had refueled and had eaten breakfast. Since they weren't exactly sure when the private jet would be coming and since Max was so tired that he could barely stay awake, Trevor had volunteered to let Max sleep while he kept an eye on the software on Max's laptop that was tracking the GPS tracker on the jet. They wanted to be ready to take off as soon as the private jet was a hundred miles from Durango. Trevor hadn't awakened Max when Trevor has seen on the laptop that the jet had left the Phoenix Airport at 9:00 a.m.

The temperature at the Durango airport had been rather cool when they have arrived. Now, with the sun beating down on the black asphalt of the airport tarmac through a cloudless sky, it was getting hot inside the plane.

Trevor wiped the sweat from the back of his neck, opened the small window on his side of the plane, and then looked at his watch. The jet had been in the air for almost two hours. A glance at the laptop screen indicated that the plane would be overhead in less than ten minutes. It was time to wake Max.

"Max, wake up. The jet is almost here."

"Okay." Max yawned long and hard and then immediately sat up. He reached for his laptop and studied it for a few moments. "He's slowing down, dropping in altitude, and getting ready to land." He reached out and started the Cessna's engine. In spite of not getting much sleep, he seemed to wake up quickly as he went through the checklist for takeoff. He checked the laptop once again when they were ready to take off and announced, "He has landed in a small town called San Felix." Max immediately opened a search window on his laptop and searched for San Felix. He clicked on the first hit, read for a moment, and then announced. "San Felix is a small town of about five-thousand people that is just over one hundred miles from here. It doesn't have an airport so the pilot must have landed the jet on a private airstrip."

Just minutes away from the city of San Felix, Max said, "I see him. He's just lifting off."

"I just hope this is where they have taken Melanie," Trevor said.

"I hope so, too. The pilot is heading toward Mexico City. He's trying hard to make it look like he never landed. That's all the more evidence that something fishy is going on here."

Max then flew within view of the airport that the jet had taken off from. "That is clearly a private airstrip that probably belongs to the same bad people that have been causing all your problems. It's best that we don't land there and let them know immediately that you're in town." After searching the aviation maps on his laptop, Max found a small public airstrip that was close to a nearby city. Soon they had landed and slowed to a stop at the end of the runway. There were a couple of rusty airplane hangars next to the runway, but their doors were chained shut. The place was deserted. Max shut down the engine, and the men exited the airplane.

"Now that we know where the plane is landing, what's the next step in your plan?" Max asked. "How are you going to find Melanie, assuming that she's even here and alive?"

"Well, besides getting to San Felix, I figured that I would check into a hotel and then would snoop around and ask a few questions."

"I hope that you speak at least a little Spanish. Are you sure that you don't want me to stay and help you find her? I'm pretty fluent at Spanish, and I have a better feel for how guys like these operate."

"My Spanish is rusty, but I think it will do. And I really need you to return to Phoenix and try to find out who hired the escorts as drug reps and how they got their false identities. I also want to know how this place is connected to Pharmplus."

"Well, if you insist, then I'll be on my way back to Phoenix. Be careful. I hope you understand the danger your placing yourself in." Max reached behind his back and pulled out a leather holster containing a pistol. The holster had a plastic clip that allowed it to be carried concealed between a person's belt and the small of their back. He reached out to hand it to Trevor.

"I don't want that."

Max said, "This is just in case things go badly. Get online as soon as you get a hotel room and learn how to use and take care of it. Call me immediately if you have any problems."

Trevor stood back as Max hopped back in the plane and taxied to the end of the runway. Soon the Cessna was airborne. Max tipped the wings in a goodbye gesture and then headed north. After waving goodbye, Trevor slung his luggage bag over his shoulder and started walking in the direction of San Felix.

The road to San Felix was a narrow, dusty, dirt road. It didn't take long to discover that even in the middle of winter, it could get pretty hot in the deserts of Mexico. He was damp with sweat and covered with a fine blanket of dust within thirty minutes. A few vehicles passed him and but didn't stop to see if he needed a ride. He decided that he would try to flag down the next vehicle. Finally, he heard an approaching vehicle. It was a truck, and there were already other people sitting in the back. He used the only signal he knew, his thumb sticking out from his fist, and they stopped. He told the driver he was heading for San Felix and handed him ten U.S. dollars. The driver indicated he should get in the bed of the truck with a toss of his head. Trevor hopped in the back of the truck, and they were on their way. With the wind blowing as they drove, there was no chance to talk to any of his fellow riders.

Trevor got off when the truck stopped in the center of San Felix. He asked the driver in Spanish if there were a hotel in the town, and the driver gave him directions. After a short walk, he arrived at the hotel.

The hotel was a long, one-story building with a dark-red tile roof and whitewashed adobe walls. The closely-spaced doors to each room shared a common covered walkway that faced the street. The door on the far right of the building was labeled as the office. Trevor opened the door to the office and stepped inside. As soon as his eyes adjusted to the darker interior of the room, they instantly met those of a chubby young girl that looked to be three years old. Her eyes were big and brown, and she had straight black hair. She stood quietly in the center of the room, staring at him.

"Hello. How are you?" Trevor asked in Spanish.

The girl stared at him for a few seconds longer, then suddenly turned and ran into a back room. He heard her from the back of the house as she called out loudly, "Dad, a man is here."

Trevor smiled. Children were the same all over the world. A few moments later, a short, overweight, middle-aged man walked into the office from the same door that had swallowed the little girl.

"Good afternoon," the proprietor greeted in Spanish.

Trevor returned the greeting and then asked, "I need a room for a couple of days. Do you have one that is available?"

"Yes, sir. I have a room for you."

As Trevor filled out the hotel registration card, he was glad that he had taken Spanish in high school and college. He had also had a lot of practice talking with Spanish-speaking patients at his medical office.

"I noticed that you have a private airport outside of town," Trevor said, hoping to pump the proprietor for information. "I saw a private jet land there earlier today and then take off ten minutes later. It seemed strange that a private jet would land at such a small airport and then take off again so quickly. I was wondering if you knew anything about that jet."

"That jet belongs to Morales Trucking. The company has a big warehouse just north of the city," the man said as he ran Trevor's credit card. "That jet has been landing here once or twice a week for some time now. The runway belongs to the company."

It didn't make any sense to Trevor that a trucking company needed a private jet. "Isn't there a pharmaceutical company that has a warehouse or a factory in this city?"

"Not that I know of. The only warehouse around is the one that belongs to the trucking company."

"What else can you tell me about Morales Trucking?" Trevor hoped that maybe the trucking company had some connection to Shannon and Melanie, but also, he was starting to wonder if Jennifer had sent him on a wild-goose chase.

"I don't know much more about the place." The man grabbed a room key off the wall behind him and then gave it to Trevor. "I stick to my job here at the hotel and try not to get involved in other people's lives and business. However, my son knows quite a bit about Morales Trucking. He will return from work at 5:00 p.m. today. I'm sure he would be glad to talk to you since he likes to practice his English."

Trevor thanked the proprietor and then headed for his hotel room. The room was tiny, and the bed was small and hard, but at least it was clean. Trevor put his suitcase in the closet and then sat down on the bed to think through what his next move would be.

Within moments, he was overcome by a feeling of extreme sleepiness. His long night in the cockpit of Max's Cessna was catching up to him. He lay back on the pillow to rest for a moment and instead fell asleep with a vague smile on his face, dreaming that he had found Melanie and that they were back together again.

Trevor was in the middle of a dream in which Shannon had Melanie and him pinned down behind a rock outside of San Felix. Every time he or Melanie tried to move from behind the rock, they were forced by blistering salvos from Shannon's machine gun to dive back behind the rock for cover.

"Dr. Davis!" Shannon yelled from somewhere in front of the rock. She then fired three more bursts from the machine gun in rapid succession. "Dr. Davis!" Shannon yelled again in a deeper voice and with a Spanish accent. "Wake up!"

Suddenly, Trevor was wide-awake and knew that he had been dreaming. He sat up abruptly in bed as he heard three more loud knocks at the door of his hotel room. The fear he had felt faded rapidly as his mind began to come out from under the shadow of his dream. A moment later, his head cleared enough for him to realize where he was and why, and the memory of the dream with Melanie and Shannon was all but gone. He quickly sprang out of bed and began dressing with haste as he responded back to the person at the door, "Just a moment." He was still tucking in his shirt as he got to the door.

Trevor left the security chain attached and opened the door just a crack. A young man stood just outside the door. He was three inches shorter than Trevor and had a handsome face that was unmarred except for a few pimples. The young man smiled, revealing a set of perfectly-spaced, white teeth. "You're awake," the young man said in English.

"Sorry about not answering when you first knocked."

"My dad told me that you wanted some information about Morales Trucking. I'm here to answer your questions."

Trevor told him to wait just a minute. He undid the security chain and opened the door. After inviting the young man in, he said, "I'm Trevor."

"I'm Marco," the young man replied.

"Thanks for taking a minute to help me. And I'm glad that you speak English. My Spanish is kind of weak. Where did you learn to speak so well?"

"I took English in high school and then I worked as a migrant worker for a couple of years in Southern California. I tried to hang around people that spoke English and studied some books that I bought."

"Well, it really paid off." Trevor motioned for Marco to sit in the only chair in the room and then he sat on the edge of the bed. "I guess your dad already told you that I was asking about Morales Trucking."

"He thinks that you're from the CIA and that you're here to bust the company for the illegal things that they are doing," Marco said.

Trevor smiled. Marco didn't. It seemed to Trevor that Marco might agree with his father. "No, I'm not from the CIA. I'm not a spy or even a private investigator. I'm just a guy that lost his girlfriend and hopes that he can find her." Trevor wondered if he was convincing enough. If he couldn't convince this young man that he wasn't with the CIA, he wasn't going to get his help.

Marco didn't say anything.

"So, Marco, can you tell me what illegal things have been going on at Morales Trucking?"

"It doesn't matter whether you're from the CIA or not," Marco said, ignoring Trevor's question. "Morales Trucking is not what it seems, and sooner or later, they're going to get caught. Our town doesn't need that kind of a company here. I would do anything to get rid of it. This town hasn't been the same since those people moved here."

"So what is it that they are doing that is so wrong?"

Marco still refused to answer Trevor's questions. "First, I need to be sure that you're not one of their men that is here to snatch me away from my family and then leave me dead in the desert if I say the slightest thing against the company. So tell me why you're here and why you're interested in Morales."

"I don't know anything about Morales Trucking," Trevor answered as sincerely as possible. "I'm here because someone kidnapped my girlfriend in Phoenix, Arizona. She was a pharmaceutical representative and was considered to be a threat by a competing pharmaceutical company. Someone from the competing company kidnapped her to shut her up. I got a tip that she was flown here to San Felix, and so here I am. I'm not even certain that my girlfriend is here. If she is here, I don't know where to look for her, except to try to find any place here that has anything to do with pharmaceutical industry. I have no idea how this trucking company, Morales, is connected to all this, but your father did tell me that he was fairly sure that the jet that I followed here earlier today belongs to Morales. That's why I need you to tell me what you know about Morales so that I can find my girlfriend."

The young man stared at Trevor for a few moments and then broke into a smile. "Okay, I'm convinced that you're the real thing. The thugs from Morales aren't bright enough to come up with a story like that. Also, your story jives with the fact that there have also been a number of people from San Felix that have disappeared without a trace over the last six months. One was a good friend of mine. Sometimes a person has to go with their gut feelings. I feel that you're a person I can trust."

"I won't let you down."

"I'll tell you what I know about Morales. About five years ago, a Mr. Vernon and his son, Austin Vernon, came to town looking for a place for a warehouse for their trucking company. They said they had decided on this location since our town is close to the main route from Southern and Eastern Mexico to the Southwest United States. The leaders of the town were excited about the jobs that the construction and staffing of the warehouse would bring to our area. The leaders let them purchase a large parcel of land about five miles from the city for next to nothing. They gave them tax breaks and promised them help with roads and utilities. The leader's excitement was short-lived. Soon after the sale of the land had been completed, the Vernon's announced that crews from the United States would construct the facility.

"The Vernon's built a big wall topped by razor wire around the whole place and wouldn't allow anyone from the city inside. The people from town grumbled about the unfairness of it and tried their best to guess what was going on inside the wall. I was a little more curious and a lot more determined than the rest. Working at night, I tunneled under the wall. I hid the entrances to my tunnel with camouflaged trap doors. Using the tunnel as an access, I spent many nights hiding in patches of sagebrush, watching the construction of a huge underground facility. I couldn't believe how much dirt they moved out of the area. No one in town had any idea about what was going on inside the fence. I didn't dare tell anyone because it might have gotten back to the company that I had tunneled under the wall. I didn't want to disgrace my father by getting caught, and I was worried about what they would do to me for trespassing.

"The crews worked around the clock, and within three months, they had finished an underground building that was about two stories high and about as long and wide as a soccer field. They buried the building under six feet of dirt and then proceeded to build the above-ground structures. The tallest of the above-ground buildings stands over one end of the underground building and houses the elevator shafts and stairs that lead to the underground building. As far as I know, no one else in town knows about the underground building. I have no clue as to what they're doing in it.

"After the construction was finished, the Vernon's tore down the wall and opened the warehouse for business. It didn't take long for trucks to start arriving, loading and unloading goods that were bound for the United States. They hired a few individuals from town to work at the warehouse. Everything went smoothly until about six months ago when people started disappearing. Like I already said, one of the people that suddenly disappeared was a good friend of mine. I have this feeling that she is still alive in that underground building. Who knows what they have done to her over the last six months."

"Why haven't you gotten inside and tried to find her?"

"That place is guarded better than your Fort Knox. There are always two or three North American guards walking around with automatic weapons. However, that hasn't kept me from keeping an eye on the place and learning a few things. One thing is for certain: Morales Trucking is a front for drug smuggling. The company ships legitimate Mexican goods of all types to the Southwestern United States. That makes it easy for them to hide drugs inside of about anything. I've been able to get close enough to hear the guards bragging about hiding drugs inside of all kinds of things. They have some dogs that sniff out every shipment before it leaves the ware-house to be sure that there is no scent of the drugs. These guys don't make mistakes."

"Yes, you can say that again." Trevor considered how easily and thoroughly they had engineered Melanie's removal from Phoenix.

"I've also discovered that they probably have the local police-men in their pocket. I've seen our town's police officers show up at the warehouse late at night and meet with Austin Vernon. They are just too friendly to not be working together. It seems that whenever anything doesn't go the way that the company wants it to, the lead-ers of our city let them go ahead and do whatever they want. When one of their thugs got drunk and raped one of our women a few months ago, he spent only one night in jail and then was released to the custody of the company. He was back at his post the next night. I heard him laugh at how easily he had gotten off. The whole thing stinks, and I would love to get rid of these people. But I feel powerless to do anything about it. If I tell anyone and it gets back to the wrong person in town, I'll probably disappear just like the others have. At the same time, I'd do anything that would work to find my missing friend. I just haven't been able to come up with a plan that has even a remote chance of success." Marco stared sadly at the floor.

"From what you're telling me, it sounds like I probably have found the place I'm looking for. I don't know exactly how this trucking firm is connected to the pharmaceutical company that engineered my girlfriend's disappearance, but I just know that it is. I bet that I can find what I am looking for in that underground building and maybe even help you to find your friend. The question is: how can I get inside?"

"I've thought about it a million times. Digging a tunnel to the underground wall of the building and then drilling through the concrete wall would never work because they would hear us before we ever broke through. Getting into the building that houses the elevators is just as impossible. The warehouse and the other build-ings are always in operation. There are always people coming and going. The guards are on duty all the time. I've asked some of the people from town that work in the warehouse if they have ever been inside the building that houses the elevators. They have all said that they haven't been near it and that they have been told that they would be severely disciplined if they tried. None of them suspects that there is anything unusual going on at the facility, or at least they are too afraid to tell me about it."

"Even if we could get inside the building, I'm sure that we'd have to have a code or a key to use the elevators. Is there any other way that you can think of?"

"There are the two large air vents about a hundred meters away from the building."

"What do you know about them? Do they lead to the underground building?"

"They do. I watched while they were being built. It's just that they're virtually impossible to get through. They have covered the vents with grates made of thick steel bars. I tried to cut through the bars one night with a hacksaw blade. It took over a half an hour to cut through just one of the them. Moments after I started on the next bar, I saw a light shining up the airshaft and then I heard the sound of someone climbing. I ran as fast as I could and hid in the desert. They looked for me for hours. They must have had some type of alarm that sounded when I cut the bar. I definitely don't recommend that approach. The problem is that besides the elevator and the air vents, there just isn't any other way inside."

"I know that you watched them build that building and that you know better than anyone else that there isn't any other way in or out. It doesn't make sense, that a structure that big would only have one exit. There has to be an emergency exit somewhere." Trevor thought for a moment and then asked, "Can you take me to the air vents?"

"Sure, if you think it will help. I can take you tonight if you want."

"The sooner that I find my girlfriend, the better."

CHAPTER 50

"WE'LL BE FINISHED with the new batch of canisters of R-648 by tomorrow morning," Austin said to Rick over the video link on Rick's laptop.

"Great. I want to pick them up right away. Everything needs to be in place so that we can be ready to dose LA within the week. I'm thinking that the night before Christmas Eve would be a good time. The R-648-laden water will just be arriving at water faucets throughout the city just as businesses close for Christmas Eve. Then, with the reduced usage of water by businesses because of the holiday, a greater percentage of the R-648-dosed water will be used in homes. The water system will probably remain contaminated for all of Christmas day. In addition, during a holiday like Christmas, more people than usual are going to have some intake of city water, either in ice cubes, holiday punch, or at restaurants, ensuring that most of the population will get a dose of R-648. In a few months, sales of Waitnomor will be in the hundreds of millions of dollars when people in LA start getting worried that they can't stop gaining weight. Oh, and that reminds me."

"About what?"

"We've got a problem in Phoenix.

"I know. Sales are really poor in Phoenix."

"That's true, but this problem is a lot bigger. We've got a leak in Phoenix."

"Oh, great."

"Someone has contacted a private investigator in Phoenix named Max Johnson. Mr. Johnson has been making phone calls to some of the other regional managers for Pharmplus across the country. I have no idea how he got their numbers. He's been asking them if they are bothered by how well the Southwest is doing in sales of Waitnomor in comparison to their areas. Of course, each one of them is insanely jealous of how successful my area is. He then told each of them that he has inside information indicating that we are using escort-service girls as drug reps to seduce medical providers into using Waitnomor. I'm sure each of the area supervisors called the CEO of Pharmplus within two seconds of hanging up with Mr. Johnson. So, naturally, the CEO immediately called me and grilled me about the techniques that I have been using in my area to sell Waitnomor. That really ticks me off. Just last week, he couldn't quit telling me how great I was. Anyway, he told me about the calls that he had received and asked if they were true. I asked him for his source and that's how I got Max Johnson's name. Obviously, I didn't tell the CEO anything about our operation. I think that he bought the yarn that I spun him about how we are doing so well because we are working hard and because we have made every effort to hire good quality reps. Of course, I denied vehemently that we have hired escort girls. He seemed even more comfortable when I shared my projection for growth in sales of Waitnomor in my area. That's why it's critical for us to get the R-648 into LA's water supply. I need to wow him with massive increases in sales of Waitnomor so that he'll be too excited to pay any attention to the whining from the other regional managers."

"That doesn't solve the problem of the leak in Phoenix. Do you have any idea of where the Johnson guy is getting his information?"

"No, I don't. I need you to get up there as soon as you can and find out more about this Max Johnson and who the leak is."

"Okay, I'll get started on it as soon as the plane gets back from making your delivery of the R-648. Do you want me to personally fly the R-648 up to you in Sacramento?"

"No, I want to deliver it directly to our people in LA myself. Have John bring the plane here to Sacramento at 7:00 a.m. tomorrow. I'll then fly to San Felix and pick up the canisters of R-648. I should arrive just after noon."

"John isn't going to be happy. He just flew in this morning and is chilling at a hotel in Mexico City."

"That's just too bad. If he complains, tell him that he doesn't have a choice and that he'd better not be late."

CHAPTER 51

CLAD IN A black T-shirt that Marco had found for him and his own black jeans, Trevor crouched by a clump of sage brush and waited while Marco went ahead to make sure that the coast was clear. Marco had insisted that Trevor dress in dark clothing so as not to stand out in the bright lights that surrounded the warehouse area and lit up the desert for hundreds of yards in all directions. As he waited for Marco to return, he glanced in the direction of the four-story glass office building that Marco had told him housed the offices for the trucking firm and the elevators to the underground building. He could also see the huge warehouse building that was just past the office building. On one side of the warehouse stood a row of about twenty identical white trailer homes. He reasoned that the staff must be housed there. He figured that the extra staff must be manufacturing illegal drugs in the underground building that Marco had told him about.

Trevor took a quick look up at the cloudless skies. The lights from the warehouse area were so bright that the Milky Way was only barely visible. Suddenly, Marco was back. Trevor was amazed by how quietly Marco moved. Marco's skills must have come from years of sneaking around this facility. Marco waved for Trevor to follow him.

Trevor stuck close behind Marco so that he wouldn't lose him in the dark. Seconds later, Marco stopped in front of a low-slung, dark, square building that vibrated with a faint hum. Trevor reached out and touched the building. It was made of metal. Marco signaled for him to follow and then led him around one side of the building. Instantly, Trevor felt a flow of air that was coming from inside the building. He reached out and found the steel grate that Marco had told him about. Peering through the grate with only the help of starlight, Trevor could dimly make out the inside of the metal air vent.

"This is it," Marco said quietly. "There is no way in except through the bars. You can feel how thick they are."

"Cutting through these bars would take forever. It seems silly that they even went to the trouble of alarming them." Trevor continued around to the other side of the building. Pulling a small flashlight from his pocket, he began searching the wall of the building. To reduce the chance of detection, he limited the glare of the bulb by holding his cupped hand above the beam.

Marco joined him and watched in silence. After a few moments, Marco said, "I'm sure that there isn't any other way in. I've already searched multiple times in the past."

Trevor answered Marco's comment with the sound of a click and then the slight squeal of the hinges of a door being opened. "Persistence pays off in the end. I just knew that there had to be a door somewhere here. The fact that it isn't locked is a little peculiar."

"Good work."

"There's no sense in risking your life by going in with me. Stay here while I go in and check things out."

"No way. My friend is probably down there. I'm coming with you."

Deciding that further discussion wasn't going to prevent Marco from following him as soon as he was out of sight, Trevor shrugged his shoulders and stepped through the door. Trevor wondered who Marco's friend was that would inspire him to put his life in danger.

Marco's friend was probably a girlfriend. Trevor himself was here, a thousand miles from home and risking his neck, just to save Melanie. Love made men do the strangest things.

Wordlessly, the two men moved to the vertical portion of the air vent, keeping an eye out for security cameras and stopping frequently to spray water into the air from a spray bottle that Marco had suggested they use to detect laser trip wires. So far, they hadn't found any. Trevor shone his light downward and immediately found a steel ladder that was welded to the side of the shaft that led down to a concrete floor. Descending the ladder first, Trevor held the flashlight facing downward so that he could see where he was going. Once Marco had joined him, Trevor discovered another door in the metal wall of the small chamber at the bottom of the ladder. Air flowed from a mesh grating on the wall opposite the door. Trevor opened the door cautiously and shone his light into what appeared to be a long hallway leading to another similar door. The coast was clear. Trevor advanced slowly into the hallway. He heard a strange rustle to his right and turned quickly to see what it was. He never saw the blow that sent pain from the back of his head down to his toes. The hallway seemed to spin, and his field of vision blurred. Unable to maintain his balance, he fell. Mercifully, he lost consciousness before hitting the ground with sufficient force to split his forehead open just above his eyebrows.

CHAPTER 52

"I CAN'T BELIEVE THAT she stabbed us in the back like this after all that we've done for her," Rick said to Austin over the phone. "She was one of our best."

"We only thought that she was one of our best."

"If she really betrayed us, and it looks like she did, we're going to have to waste her. After John picks me up tomorrow morning, I'll have him swing by Phoenix and pick her up. Call and tell her to be ready at the airport's private aircraft terminal at ten in the morning for a mandatory business meeting."

"We need to make sure that she didn't talk to anyone else before we dispose of her."

"You're right. We need to make her talk. We'll take care of that as soon as I get there tomorrow at about noon. And one more thing, I need a case of those R-648-laced fruit drinks to take with me back to Sacramento. There are a few people at Pharmplus that I'd love to get even with by watching them turn into massive tubs of lard."

"I'll put a box in the back of the car when you are ready to fly out tomorrow afternoon."

CHAPTER 53

THE BACK OF Trevor's head hurt like a baseball bat in full swing had hit him squarely on the back of his head. His probing fingers had confirmed that there was a huge lump where something had contacted his skull. He had no recollection of how he had gotten the lump, but he was fairly sure that he had been cold-cocked in the ventilation tunnel by the trucking company's security guards. He had awakened a few minutes before and had been initially confused and disoriented by his unfamiliar surroundings. The small room that he had found himself in had only a toilet, a small sink without a mirror, and a cot with a thin mattress. He knew that he wasn't in a local hospital because of the lack of any medical equipment and because hospitals didn't lock their patients in. The featureless steel door in the wall opposite the bed didn't have visible hinges or a doorknob. Trevor had reached for his wallet to find a plastic card that could be used to slip between the door and its frame in effort to force the door open, but to his chagrin, he had found that his pockets were completely empty. A search of the room for an instrument to help him in opening the door had been fruitless.

Frustrated by his inability to escape from the room and still feeling lightheaded from the stabbing pain emanating from the back of his head, Trevor sat on the cot and buried his face in his hands. As soon as his hands touched his forehead, he was startled by the discovery of a new pain lancinating from his forehead. He winced as his fingers discovered what felt like a deep laceration on the right side of his forehead. The wound felt moist. Inspection of the fluid on his fingertips revealed it to be a mixture of new and old blood. He wished for a mirror so that he could inspect the damage. Someone had really done a number on his head. He hoped that Marco hadn't suffered the same fate. He should have made more of an effort to keep Marco from entering the air vent with him.

Things had been going so well, and he had felt so sure that he would soon be united with Melanie. Now his search had come to an abrupt halt, and he had no idea what was going to happen to him next. The people that had captured him had probably killed before, and he was sure that they wouldn't think twice about killing again. In fact, he was surprised that he was even still alive. He tried to remain positive in spite of his bleak surroundings and helpless situation. He wasn't dead yet, and until he was, he had to believe that he would get another chance to find the woman that he loved.

CHAPTER 54

"**H**ELLO, SHANNON. YOU'RE looking bright and cheerful today," Rick stated as his eyes cast an approving glance at the light tan business jacket that Shannon was wearing over a low-cut salmon blouse. Then his gaze lingered too long on her slightly-exposed breasts. *Typical man,* she thought to herself.

Shannon thanked him as she looked into his eyes, hoping to discover his intent in calling this sudden business meeting. She was surprised that he hadn't invited Jennifer. Usually Austin, not Rick, came to Phoenix to meet with the reps. She had only met Rick once in person at a Pharmplus training meeting and twice when he had been a presenter at webinars. It seemed almost certain that she was being singled out for doing something wrong and was being transferred or worse, being fired. Whatever his agenda was, right now his face revealed nothing other than the same look of admiration that she had seen on countless men's faces before.

They left the terminal and walked across the tarmac to the waiting company jet. Rick showed her to an upholstered seat by a small coffee table in the rear of the passenger compartment of the otherwise unoccupied plane, closed the cabin door, and then took a seat across the table from her. They chatted briefly about the weather in Phoenix and then fell silent for a moment. Shannon was almost certain that Rick wasn't taking her to a company business meeting, seeing that she was the only other passenger on the plane. Desperate for relief from the dread that was weighing heavily on her chest, Shannon asked, "Can you tell me what our meeting is going to be about?"

"Austin and I are interested in improving sagging sales in some of our slower areas," Rick said. "You're the best that we have in the Phoenix area. We have some new sales strategies that we would like to discuss with you."

Shannon stared into Rick's eyes, but he wasn't willing to look her in the eyes. She suspected that he was lying. She sat back into her chair, fighting to maintain her composure. How could he be unhappy with her work? She had been killing herself to sell Waitnomor, and it wasn't her fault that sales were slow. They had sent her to a difficult area. She took a deep breath and then let it out slowly and quietly in effort to calm herself. She knew that any further effort to discover why she was being flown to this sham business meeting would be met with more lies. Putting on a forced smile, she turned back to Rick and engaged in superficial conversation for the rest of the flight.

Looking out of the windshield of the car, Shannon recognized the large warehouse and the office building where she had undergone her training as a drug rep. Seeing the buildings reminded her of how hard the training had been and of how proud she had been to finish at the top of the class. She just hoped that her being here again wasn't the end of everything she had worked for.

Rick was sitting in the front passenger seat of the car. He had been pleasant enough during the flight but wasn't saying much now.

The car approached and then passed the road that led to the office building that she was familiar with. Shannon was surprised and asked, "Where is the meeting going to be held?"

"Just sit back for a minute, and you'll see," Rick answered.

In answer to her question, the car turned into a broad paved road that led to the loading docks for the warehouse that was next to the office building. This side of the warehouse contained a row of dark, square openings that were spaced along the side of the building. She could see a few semi-trailers backed up against some of the openings, and she assumed that they must be unloading or loading goods. The car slowed in front of a large roll-up steel door that opened slowly as they approached. When the door had opened enough to let them pass, they drove into the building. Inside, palates of merchandise of all kinds were stacked on tall metal shelves that stretched the length of the building. The rows of shelves were broken periodically by aisles that crossed the rows perpendicularly. As Shannon watched, forklifts moved down the rows and aisles carrying palates of merchandise to and from the waiting semi-trailers.

The car took a sharp left down one of the aisles and then drove down a ramp that descended to another floor of the warehouse. The same rows of heavy metal shelving were everywhere. The car drove down one of the perpendicular aisles until it approached a blank brick wall and stopped. It didn't seem to be a likely place for a business meeting. Shannon didn't have a good feeling about this place, and she shifted uncomfortably in her seat. She couldn't help but wonder if the reason they had brought her here alone was to kill her and then drop her body in the desert somewhere. That thought gave her a shiver of fear and made her mouth go dry. The more she got to know Austin and Rick, the more she suspected that the men had a much more sinister side that they hadn't yet revealed.

Neither Rick nor the driver moved or spoke. With a faint rumble, the brick wall in front of the car suddenly began receding away from the front of the car. A split appeared in the center of the wall and then rapidly widened as the two halves of the wall slid sideways out of sight. Beyond the brick wall stood an underground loading dock. It didn't look like anything special and didn't seem to be worth the secrecy provided by the false brick wall. A single garage-door-sized, steel, roll-up door stood in the center of the loading dock and a set of double doors were located on each side of the roll-up door. The doors were closed and revealed nothing about the need for such secrecy.

The driver stopped the car at the right end of the dock next to a set of stairs that led up to the loading dock. Rick opened Shannon's door, didn't wait for her to get out, and then led the way up the stairs. As Shannon climbed the stairs, she noted that the brick walls that had opened to let their car pass were now moving back to their original position. Rick opened one of the double doors and let Shannon pass through. He followed and then led her to an office just past the entrance.

"Have a seat, and we'll be with you in a few minutes," Rick said as he motioned for Shannon to sit in one of the two chairs that stood in front of a small metal desk. He left the office and closed the door behind him. Shannon sat as she had been instructed and looked around the office. Besides chairs, it contained only a steel desk that was painted black and a black filing cabinet that stood against a wall behind the desk. The desktop was devoid of papers, and a thin layer of dust on everything suggested that the office hadn't been used for some time. With nothing to hold her attention in the featureless office, Shannon simply sat, legs crossed, and stared straight ahead, deep in thought as she considered her present predicament. She dreaded what was going to happen next but had no clue about what it was going to be. Her mind raced in a million directions at once. Peering out a window that looked out on the loading dock, she wondered if she could escape out the doors, find an exit, and then make it out of the warehouse undetected.

The door opened suddenly, causing Shannon to startle. Austin stepped into the room. "Good afternoon, Shannon."

Shannon stood and returned the greeting as naturally as she

could, given the uncomfortable situation that she was in. "Hi, Austin."

"I trust that your flight here was pleasant?" Austin asked as he took a seat behind the desk.

"It was a little long, especially without an in-flight movie." She could play this game of making small talk like everything was fine. However, Shannon was even more concerned as she sensed that he was more aloof and colder than usual.

Austin smiled at her attempt at a joke. "You're probably wondering why I called you in the middle of the night to ask you come to a business meeting."

Shannon nodded.

"I'm not going to beat around the bush. There isn't going to be a business meeting. You were brought here because we need your help with an important matter. Dr. Trevor Davis tried to break into this facility last night."

"What?" Shannon was shocked beyond belief. *What is Trevor doing here in Mexico and how in the world did he find this place?*

"We have no clue as to how he discovered this place or as to why he felt the need to travel here from Phoenix. We need you to help us find answers to these two questions."

"Dr. Davis was here last night?"

"In full, living color."

"He must have come looking for Melanie," she said as she thought out loud. Her eyes widened as she realized why she had been summoned in middle of the night. "And you think I told him how to get here. That's why you woke me up and flew me down here in such a rush this morning."

"You're very perceptive."

"Austin, you have to believe me." Now that Shannon knew the stakes, she had no trouble realizing just how dangerous of a situation she was in and how critical it was that she convince Austin that she had played no part in Trevor's being here at the warehouse. "I didn't tell him about this place. I have no idea where in Mexico we are right now. I could never have told him how to get here when I have no idea of how to get here myself."

"So I'm curious. Why did you say that he came looking for Melanie?"

"Dr. Davis and Melanie, the drug rep for Reductol that conveniently left town with your help, were more than friends. He told me that he wondered where she had gone."

Austin said nothing.

"So what happened? Did you catch him?"

"Dr. Davis is locked up right here in our facility. We met with a little resistance when we tried to apprehend him, and he did get roughed up a little."

Her face showed immediate concern as she exclaimed, "Let me see him." Immediately, however, she knew that she had betrayed an overabundance of concern for Trevor. She didn't want Austin to know how much she still cared for Trevor, but she was afraid that it was now too late. She had no idea what that knowledge would do to her credibility. Making her voice more casual, she continued, "I'm sure that I can persuade him to tell me how he found this place."

"Okay, I'll let you see him. It should be interesting to see the two of you interact."

"What do you mean by that?" Shannon asked with a carefully measured amount of indignation in her voice. "I really didn't have anything to do with Dr. Davis being here."

"Don't get so worked up." He got up from the desk and asked Shannon to follow him. "You know that we can't let him leave here alive after what he has done?" Austin asked at the door to the office.

She nodded her head gravely, unsure of what to say to his comment. She had no desire to see Trevor killed. But, at this point, she was too worried that she was going to meet the same fate if she couldn't convince Austin that she was innocent. Trevor would have to fend for himself.

As she followed Austin, Shannon couldn't help but notice the vast array of equipment that was in each room that they passed. There were machine shops, chemical labs, and animal labs. There was a small army of men, some in white lab coats, scattered around the various rooms. Most were heavily tattooed and had straggly long hair. The more she looked around, the more she realized that this hidden building could only be one thing: a giant illegal drug lab. That would explain where Austin and Rick got their seemingly never-ending source of cash.

Austin and Shannon arrived at a long hallway that had a number of heavy steel doors. Each door was closed. Next to each door was a rectangular window, and on the other side of each door was a narrow hallway that ended in a dead-end. Austin stopped in from of one of the windows, and Shannon could see Trevor lying on a cot in the otherwise empty room. Pressing a button between the steel door and the window, Austin said, "Dr. Davis, you have a visitor. Stay seated on the cot as the door opens. Any attempt to storm the door will result in a bullet to the head." Keeping an eye on the window, Austin pulled a key from his pocket and opened the steel door. Shannon noticed that Austin didn't have the gun in his hands that he had promised he would use. She was sure, however, that he had one on his person and that he was very skilled in its use.

"Go ahead." Austin indicated for Shannon to enter the room with a nod of his head. "I'm going to lock you in with him." That statement brought a sharp look in his direction from Shannon. He explained with a laugh, "I'll be back in fifteen minutes to let you out."

Shannon stepped into the small room, took one look at Trevor, and was instantly overcome by concern as she noticed the huge, gaping gash on his forehead. She paid no attention to the door as it clicked shut behind her. "Trevor, what happened? Are you all right?" She walked over to Trevor and reached out her hand to touch him gently on the forehead next to the wound.

"Don't touch me." Trevor said angrily as he put his hand up to block hers. "I don't need any more of your pretend care and concern. You must want something from me, although I can't imagine what it is this time."

Hurt by Trevor's angry words, but desperate to win his support, she protested, "I don't want anything from you. I've always cared for you, and I'm only trying to express my concern about how roughly they have treated you."

"Oh, come on. The very fact that you're here tells me that you're in cahoots with them. I can't trust a single thing that you say."

"It's true that I work for these guys, but I had no idea about this place, whatever it is. How did you find out where this place is anyway? I don't even know where it is. I flew here with the plane's passenger windows closed."

"With as much security as you have around this place, it's obvious that you have something to hide. I'm sure that you'd love to find out my source of information so that you can have them killed to cover up your tracks."

"Trevor, you're not listening. I really have no idea where this place is or what it is. They flew me down here this morning to chew me out for the poor sales of Waitnomor in Phoenix. I had no idea that you were going to be here or that you were even trying to find this place. I need you to believe me because we're going to have to work together if either of us is ever going to leave here alive. Your only hope is to convince them that you're on their side and that you're more than glad to return to Phoenix, say nothing about this place, and then go on practicing medicine like you have in the past. It wouldn't hurt to also agree to prescribe Waitnomor on a regular basis."

"I'd rather die than prescribe that medication to another patient. I can't believe you've sunk so low that money is more important than people's lives." Trevor turned away from Shannon with a look of disgust on his face and then loudly said, "I am done speaking to Ms. Lowry. I would like her to leave now."

"Trevor, you can't just dismiss me like that, not after all we've been through together. We really do need each other to get through this."

"I'd rather spend the rest of my days in a pit of vipers than spend another minute with you." Trevor turned toward Shannon and looked her in the eyes for moment, his brow furrowed and his lips thin with anger, and then he turned away again.

"You're going to regret this," Shannon said. "I could have saved you. We could have had everything together. And now you'll have nothing, not even your life." She turned toward the one-way mirror and said angrily, "I'm ready to leave." The door opened, and she stalked from the room, leaving Trevor alone.

"If you'd like, I can arrange for that pit of vipers," Austin said to Shannon and then laughed. Shannon and Austin had left the hallway where Trevor was imprisoned and walked back to the hallway outside the office where Austin had first questioned Shannon.

"You were listening," Shannon said as her cheeks colored slightly. She was so anxious that she felt like her stomach was being twisted in knots. "I thought that you were going to leave us alone for fifteen minutes. Now I'm really embarrassed."

"It's good to know that you thought that I wasn't listening. You've almost convinced me that it wasn't you that told Dr. Davis about the location of this facility."

"Besides pharmaceutical detailing at his office, I have barely seen Dr. Davis since Melanie left Phoenix. I don't know when I would have had an opportunity to tell him anything."

"Well, if you didn't tell him, then who did?"

"There is only one other person in Phoenix who knows anything about this place."

"And who might that be?"

"Jennifer. She has been acting really funny lately. I don't think that she has been visiting her medical providers like she's supposed to. A few weeks ago, she asked me if I had anything to do with Melanie's leaving Phoenix. I told her that I hadn't. She said that she was glad to hear that because she wasn't willing to work for a company that would sink to kidnapping as a way to eliminate the competition. However, I don't think that she believed me because she's been a little cold to me ever since. I bet that she got John to tell her the location of this place on one of their dates, and then she told Trevor." Shannon wasn't absolutely sure of Jennifer's guilt, but she was going to do everything she could to avoid taking the blame for Trevor's presence.

"I doubt that John told her anything. He's been loyal to us for years. Besides, I doubt that Jennifer means any more to him than any of the other four or five women that he sleeps with on a regular basis across the United States. Still, I think I agree with you that Jennifer is the most likely source of the leak. The only thing I'm not sure of is how she knew where this place is."

"So that means that you believe me?"

"I guess that you're mostly off the hook. Jennifer, on the other hand, will have to be dealt with. I'm afraid it won't be pretty. Are you going to be okay with that?"

It was obvious to Shannon that there wasn't anything that she could say that would save Jennifer. After all, why should she try? Even though they were roommates, Jennifer couldn't be trusted. Telling Trevor the location of this place had put Shannon's job and even her life in jeopardy. On top of that, she had never really liked Jennifer that much anyway. "Sure. She knows too much and can't be trusted. You don't have a choice."

"You're right about that." He paused for a moment. "You might be interested to know that Melanie is right here in this facility. Ever since she left Phoenix, with our help of course, she's been part of a little experiment on obesity that we've been conducting. You'll be happy to know that she's not looking quite like her beautiful self. She's gained a lot of weight."

"Good. I want her to suffer for all the trouble she's caused me."

"She'll suffer plenty by the time we get done with her. We also need to talk about Dr. Davis. I told you that he can't leave here alive now that he knows the location of this facility."

Still seething from her conversation with Trevor and certain that Austin was watching to see how she would react, Shannon didn't bat an eyelid as she answered icily, "It doesn't matter to me. As far as I'm concerned, you can tear him apart piece by piece and feed him to the dogs. Make Melanie watch while you do it. It would be entertaining to watch them both suffer as he dies slowly and painfully."

Rick walked up to Shannon and Austin. Rick asked, "Austin, I take it that you're sure that Shannon didn't have anything to do with Dr. Davis being here?"

"I'm sure."

Rick said, "Well then, let's give the lady the entertainment that she's asking for." As he finished speaking, Rick looked at Shannon and smiled wickedly.

Shannon smiled back with an equally devilish smile.

CHAPTER 55

THE BURLY GUARD shoved Trevor headfirst into the open rear door of the car. With his hands tied behind his back, Trevor had no choice but to land face-first on the back seat. He struggled to sit up in the middle seat just as the guard sat down next to him and closed the car door. Unable to speak because he had been gagged with a rolled-up cloth bandanna, Trevor had no choice but to sit and stare at the road ahead. It seemed pretty clear that he was being taken to some remote location where they were going to kill him and then dump his body.

Less than a minute later, the other rear passenger door of the car was jerked open, and another bound and gagged figure was shoved headfirst into the rear seat on top of Trevor. The woman landed unceremoniously face-first in Trevor's lap. The woman's jaw smacked Trevor's thigh with such force that he was sure that it was going to cause a bruise. *At least,* he reasoned as he winced in pain, *my thigh has saved her jaw from a harder impact elsewhere in the car.* The woman's legs were shoved into the car, and the car door was slammed shut almost immediately.

Trevor couldn't see the woman's face since her long brown hair covering and obscuring her features. She was wearing green scrubs and was overweight. Her hands were fastened behind her back with a zip tie in a similar fashion to his. The woman struggled to remove her face from Trevor's lap and right herself, but she was barely able to do so in the cramped space. Unable to assist the woman, Trevor could only watch as she slowly turned away from him toward the passenger door and then struggled to a sitting position in the passenger seat. He turned to look at her face, but he was still unable to discern any of her features because her disheveled hair completely covered her face. The woman repeatedly flipped her hair forward and then back over the top of her head, trying to get her hair out of her face. Not wanting to stare at his fellow prisoner, Trevor looked out the front window, wondering what was going to happen next. Another burly guard got into the front passenger seat, and the car drove toward a brick wall. The woman's movements at his side finally stopped, and Trevor figured that she had succeeded in getting her hair out of her face.

Trevor turned to look at the woman again to see who his fellow prisoner was. Her eyes and features were now only partially obscured by her hair. She simultaneously turned to look at Trevor. Almost immediately, the woman's eyes widened in recognition, and then the corners of her eyes crinkled as if she were smiling. The gag hid the corners of her mouth, but Trevor perceived that her upper lip was flattened a little. She was smiling at him. *She knows me*, Trevor thought to himself. Tears began forming at the corners of her eyes. He looked again at the woman's eyes. There was something familiar about them. The woman mumbled an unintelligible word that was muffled by her gag. Something in the timber of the woman's muffled voice was all Trevor's brain needed. In an instant, he knew it was Melanie! Her face was so swollen, and she looked so tired, but he now knew that the eyes were Melanie's.

He did his best to communicate with his eyes all of his pent-up feelings of happiness at seeing her again and his concern for her wellbeing. Their eyes were still locked firmly on each other's as the car passed through the false brick wall. The guard sitting next to Trevor jabbed him hard in the back with his elbow and growled. "Quit that lovey-dovey stuff. You're making me sick."

Trevor winced from the pain of the blow. The only way that Melanie could console him was to lean forward and touch her head to his shoulder. Trevor sat back and allowed Melanie's head to rest on his shoulder as the car moved past a steel roll-up door and into the bright sunlight. Trevor stared blankly ahead, lost in thoughts of happiness about being reunited with Melanie and of sadness as he contemplated that they would soon be separated by death.

The guard drove the car around the side of the warehouse building and moments later pulled up to a sleek, black, seven-passenger Bell 429 helicopter that was sitting on a concrete pad at the edge of the warehouse compound. Trevor could see that Shannon was sitting next to the blonde pilot in the copilot's seat and looked thoroughly bored.

Another man with dark hair stepped out of the passenger door of the helicopter as the car came to a stop. He opened Melanie's door just as Austin started the engine of the helicopter. The giant blades began rotating menacingly over their heads. The man jerked Melanie out of her seat and roughly pushed her to helicopter. He shoved her into the passenger compartment, banging her knees on the threshold. The man returned to the car and helped the guard manhandle Trevor out of the car and over to the passenger door of the helicopter. They shoved Trevor into the passenger compartment, causing him to strike his head hard on the first seat. Dazed, Trevor moaned and fell to his knees. He was sure that the gash in his forehead was bleeding again. The guard kicked him squarely in the buttocks. Trevor forced himself to his feet and then crumpled into the seat next to Melanie.

The whine of the engines was increasing in volume. The dark haired man hopped into the passenger compartment and put on a headset with a built-in microphone. He took a seat opposite Trevor and Melanie and said into the microphone of the headset, "Austin, we're ready back here to take off."

Trevor watched the guard first close the passenger compartment door of the helicopter and then back away from the whirling blades.

The whine of the engines increased, and the helicopter lifted off the ground. Unable to hear anything except the painfully loud whine of the engines, Trevor leaned against the wall behind him. Melanie leaned her head against his shoulder. Trevor looked down at her messy mop of hair. She looked up at him, and her eyes squinted a little in a smile. Trevor smiled back. In spite of their hopeless situation, just being with her made him happy.

Austin guided helicopter to a particularly flat spot in a desert canyon and then set the chopper down gently. He killed the engines and then hopped out of the pilot's door as the rotating blades slowed to a stop. Walking to the copilot's door, he helped Shannon get her door open and then helped her down to the canyon floor. Shannon followed Austin to the passenger door of the helicopter just as the dark haired man opened the door.

Austin spoke to the dark haired man, "Rick, did these two behave themselves?"

"They were model prisoners," Rick replied. Rick turned and jerked Melanie out of her seat, propelling her towards the door. He sent her sailing out of the door with a violent push. She crashed down hard on the sand. Without stopping to observe the results of his violent act, Rick repeated the same procedure with Trevor. Then he stood in the doorway of the helicopter and laughed as Trevor and Melanie slowly rolled onto their sides and sat up. Their faces were covered with sand and yet, with their hands tied, they were unable to do anything but shake their heads and blink hard in effort to remove the sand from their eyes. A drop of blood ran slowly down Melanie's upper lip from her left nostril.

Shannon watched the proceedings with a cold stare.

Austin, on the other hand, laughed along with Rick. "Oops," Austin said. "You guys shouldn't be in such a hurry. People get hurt that way."

As Austin was speaking, Trevor got onto his knees and struggled to get to his feet when Austin caught sight of his effort and shoved him roughly with his foot, throwing him completely off balance. Unable to break his fall with his arms tied behind his back, Trevor hit the sand hard.

"See, I told you not to be in such a hurry." Austin laughed cruelly.

"Stake him to the ground," Rick said as he watched Trevor try to get up again. "I'll keep an eye on him while you get the stakes and the hammer from the luggage compartment." He turned to Shannon and continued, "Shannon, keep an eye on Melanie. Tell me if she moves. I'll shoot her in the head right now if she does." Rick walked over to Trevor and placed his boot firmly in the small Trevor's back, immediately stopping Trevor in his efforts to get up. "You'd just as well stop struggling," Rick said to Trevor. "There's nowhere for you to go. We're miles from the nearest city.

"You don't know me. Let me introduce myself. I'm Rick, and I'm the brains behind the organization that you thought that you could mess with. That was a brilliant move that you pulled last night. Why did you think that you had a chance of success by barging straight into our headquarters? Your plan, if you can call it that, was doomed from the start. You'd have been a lot better off if you had stayed in Phoenix and prescribed Waitnomor like you were supposed to."

Austin returned with the hammer and stakes. While the others watched, he picked a flat spot in the sand about ten yards from the helicopter and then drove the four stakes deeply into the sand.

After warning Trevor that Rick would shoot him in the head if he tried to escape, Austin helped Trevor up and led him to the center of the four stakes. He pushed Trevor down to a seated position on the sand, removed the zip-ties from Trevor's wrists and then shoved him onto his back. Working quickly and efficiently, Austin tied a length of rope around one of Trevor's wrists and then secured the other end to one of the stakes. He repeated the same procedure with the remaining wrist and with Trevor's ankles, leaving Trevor lying face up in a spread-eagle position on the sand.

As Austin stood and brushed the sand off his hands and legs, Rick stated, "Go ahead and take off his gag. We need to ask him a few questions." While Austin was removing Trevor's gag, Rick walked over to Shannon. Pointing at Melanie, he ordered, "Untie her hands and take her gag off. She's not going anywhere in this desert without her precious Trevor. Besides, it will be entertaining to hear her beg for Trevor's life."

"Leave her out of this," Trevor said as soon as his gag was off. "I'm the person that you want. She didn't have anything to do with my being here."

Austin gave Trevor a sharp kicked in the ribs and said, "Quiet. You're in no position to be giving us orders."

Melanie, her hands now free, suddenly bolted past Shannon and rushed to Trevor's side. Trevor turned and looked into her eyes. She asked him quietly, "Are you okay?" as she began wiping the sand from his face. Although still in pain from the blow to his ribs, Trevor smiled wanly and nodded.

Shannon walked over to Rick and tried to explain, "She's pretty fast when her arms untied. I tried to stop her, but—."

"It's okay," Rick interrupted. He turned back to Trevor and demanded, "How did you find our warehouse?"

Trevor ignored Rick's question and continued gazing at Melanie's face. It didn't bother him that her face was caked with sand and that her hair was in complete disarray. She looked like she had gained a lot of weight. He had thought that her face was swollen, but he could see that her neck and hands were heavier also. That didn't matter even a little. He was so glad to have found her.

Without warning, Austin landed another sharp kick on Trevor's ribs, causing Trevor to wince in pain. He strained against the ropes that held his arms to no avail. "You'll answer Rick if you know what's good for you."

Trying to hide the pain, Trevor smiled and said to Austin, "I was down here on vacation and just happened to stumble onto your facility. I'm sorry for having inconvenienced you. So if you'll just untie these ropes, Melanie and I will be on our way." The comment resulted in another swift kick to Trevor's ribs from Austin. As the pain seared through his chest wall, Trevor reminded himself that he had to hang on and not tell these guys about Jennifer, Max, or Marco. He was sure that they would kill them all if they found out what they had done. He decided to try a half-truth. He grimaced in pain and said, "Okay. Fine. I tracked down the flight plan for the plane that brought Shannon to her training meetings here. Once in town, it was easy to figure out that the warehouse was your base of operations. While snooping around last night, I found the air vent. You know the rest of the story." That had sounded pretty convincing to Trevor, and he hoped that they would buy it.

"That flight plan listed Mexico City as the destination in Mexico," Rick said. "San Felix is only one of hundreds of small towns along the flight path from Phoenix to Mexico City. There is no way that you could have known that the plane would stop here. You found this place because someone told you how to get here. So why don't save yourself some pain and tell us who it was?"

"I found this place on my own," Trevor said, trying to sound as convincing as he could. "No one told me anything."

"I'll save us all some time then," Rick said. "Jennifer, Shannon's roommate, told you how to get here. Isn't that correct?"

Trevor hesitated for a moment and then knew instantly that he had blown it. By hesitating, he had already answered Rick's question.

Rick said, "Your lack of a response has told me much more than anything you've said so far. It's too bad that Jennifer will have to pay with her life for what she's done."

"Leave Jennifer alone, you homicidal maniac," Trevor said. An especially hard kick from Austin cooled his anger quickly. As Austin prepared to kick him again, Melanie launched herself off the ground toward Austin in an effort to stop him from torturing Trevor. Effortlessly, Austin turned, grasped Melanie by her shoulders, and flung her to the ground. Austin laughed as Melanie righted herself and assumed a sitting position on the sand, spitting sand out of her mouth and wiping blood from her nose. She glared silently at Austin.

After gasping painfully for air, Trevor said in a weak voice, "It accomplishes nothing to kill Jennifer. Just let her go back to her old life as an escort. That's punishment enough for anyone."

"The fact that you know that she's an escort means that she must have talked to you," Austin said.

"No, it doesn't," Trevor said. "I know that Shannon was an escort until just a few months ago, and I didn't find that out from Shannon. I also know that there is another Shannon Lowry working for you in Albuquerque that has the same birthday, parents, and social security number as our Shannon."

"How did you find that out?" Rick said with his brows furrowing. He looked over at Austin and said, "The fact that he knows so much makes me question the security of this whole business."

"Hey, I told you that it was a mistake to use the same dead girl's identity for two of our drug reps," Austin said. "Someone was bound to find out, and they did."

Trevor was desperate not to reveal his other sources. Jennifer was already going to die for her involvement. "It took a lot of work to figure it out," he said to Rick. Trying to change the subject, he continued, "What I really want to know, however, is why you're so desperate to sell Waitnomor. You're willing to seduce medical providers with prostitutes, kidnap your competition, and kill anyone that gets in your way, all to sell a drug that kills people while it helps them lose weight."

Rick smiled wickedly. "My. My. Those are pretty big words for a man who is staked to the ground in the desert. However, since you know too much about my operation for me to let you live, I don't mind satisfying your curiosity before you die." Rick looked over at Austin. Austin shrugged noncommittally. Rick continued, "You're right, I am very interested in selling Waitnomor. I expect to become quite rich from doing so."

"You're just an area manager," Melanie said. She had moved back to her position kneeling at Trevor's side. "Drug companies don't pay their managers enough for them to get rich."

"You're right. I wasn't willing to settle for a manager's salary. I convinced the CEO of Pharmplus that I could sell more Waitnomor than he could ever dream of. He was excited enough about the possibility that he was willing, at my insistence, to include a generous bonus plan in my contract. The contract states that I am to receive ten percent of the profits from sales of Waitnomor in my area if I can double sales from last year. If I can quadruple sales, then I get twenty-five percent of the profits. Increasing profits by more than eight hundred percent would give me fifty percent of all the profits. I'm sure that he thought that I would never achieve such outlandish increases in sales. However, I'm already receiving ten percent of the profits from the Southwest region because I've more than doubled sales, thanks to the efforts of my new and irresistible sales force." Rick stopped, turned to Shannon, and smiled. Shannon smiled back faintly for just a second and then the smile faded from her face.

"You're never going to be able to increase profits of Waitnomor enough to get rich," Trevor said. "The drug has too many problems and is probably going to get yanked off the market by the FDA. Plus, most medical providers don't believe that weight-loss medications are necessary."

"You're wrong again, doctor," Rick said with a smile. "You just can't see the big picture. The best way to increase sales of a product is to increase the need for that product, whether perceived or real. I have discovered a way to increase people's need for Waitnomor." Rick paused again, allowing the weight of his words to sink in.

"Most people are thin enough that you're never going to convince them to take Waitnomor," Trevor stated.

"But they're not going to be thin for long," Rick said like a patient schoolteacher. "Sales of Waitnomor have increased four hundred percent in Las Vegas in the last month. Over eighty percent of the population of Las Vegas suddenly started gaining weight six weeks ago. Grocery sales are up by thirty percent. Even pet food sales are up. People's cats and dogs are getting fatter. It all started after we added a special little chemical named R-648 to their water supply six weeks ago."

"You fiend," Melanie said with a sudden understanding of what had been happening to her for the last months that she had been a prisoner. "You did the same thing to me when I first got here, and now I'm getting fatter and fatter. Who gave you the right to ruin innocent people's lives?"

"No one did," Rick said. "But how could I resist such a marvelous opportunity to get rich quick? The R-648 was accidentally discovered at Pharmplus and was quickly shelved as having no medical value. However, I recognized its value the moment I heard about it. With Austin's and his dad's help at first, and now with almost unlimited cash from an outside party that is very interested in what we are doing, we have begun manufacturing the drug in large quantities. We conducted tests here at our facility on human subjects to be certain that the R-648 worked. We recruited you, Melanie, into the study when one of the original subjects committed suicide. We found that the R-648 worked marvelously. We then tested the R-648 in the water supply for the city of San Felix where our warehouse is. The results were impressive. More of the R-648 was produced and we introduced it into the water supply for Las Vegas. I am here today to pick up the next batch of the R-648 to take back to California. I have a city in mind that is extremely weight conscious. After they receive the R-648 in their water supply, I expect sales of Waitnomor in my territory to go through the roof."

"You can't do that," Melanie said. "You just can't poison people like that for your own selfish desires."

"And who's going to stop me?" Rick said. "With the help of Austin's father and his connections in the various communities in the Southwestern United States, we can take out any opposing force before it gathers strength. Even the police are afraid of us or are on our side. You saw what we did to Dr. Fife."

"What! What did you do to Dr. Fife?" Trevor asked.

"My father has a wonderful laboratory here in San Felix," Austin said. "We are experts in manufacturing drugs and devices to bump people off and make it look like a natural death. I used a device in Dr. Fife's stethoscope that squirted venom from the Australian blue octopus into his ear canal. What looked like a natural death from a cardiac arrest was really a successful use of one of our devices to remove a man who was hurting sales of Waitnomor."

Trevor was stunned. He looked into Melanie's eyes in silence.

Shannon said, "Not bad. I had no idea how resourceful you guys are. If you would just treat the water supply in Phoenix, I'm sure that we would see an increase in use of Waitnomor in my area."

"Soon," Rick said to Shannon. "Soon. Phoenix will probably be next after Los Angeles."

"Los Angeles. So you're going to hit Los Angeles," Shannon said admiringly. "I can't think of a better place. All of those arrogant Californians won't feel so proud when they all weigh three hundred pounds."

"With your looks," Austin said to Shannon, "You'll be able to land a part in a movie when all the actresses in Hollywood are porked out."

Rick laughed. Shannon struck a sexy, Marilyn-Monroe-like pose and said, "I like that idea." Rick stared at her sexy pose with a little too much hunger in his eyes.

Austin turned to Rick and said, "We need to be going. I told the guards that we'd be back in less than two hours."

"Let's not be in such a big hurry," Rick said with a smile as he tore his eyes away from Shannon and looked at Austin. "We still need to find out how much Dr. Davis knows about our operation and who his other sources are." Turning to Trevor, Rick said, "Tell us what else you know about our operation." Trevor stared blankly at Rick and didn't answer his question. Trevor's silence caused Rick to say, "Tell us what else you know, or Austin is going to start kicking you in the ribs again."

"Okay, fine." Trevor said. "It wasn't hard to find out that you are covering up the fact that Waitnomor kills people. In spite of increasing deaths worldwide, the FDA is continuing to say that Waitnomor is a safe drug. I'm sure that you're paying off someone on the inside at the FDA. Also, it was easy to figure out that you are manufacturing illegal drugs here in San Felix. You are hiding the drugs inside of innocent-looking goods that are being shipped to United States by your trucking firm. Sales of the illegal drugs have been financing part your operation with Waitnomor. Your success in selling Waitnomor has made the other area managers at Pharmplus intensely jealous. They would love to see you fail."

"And who told you all these things?" Austin asked.

"I ask a lot of questions and keep my eyes open," Trevor replied. Trevor stared unflinchingly at Austin and Rick while they glared back at him for what seem like an eternity. Trevor was sure that Austin was going to kick him in the ribs again at any moment.

Austin turned suddenly to Rick and said, "We're wasting our time. Let's finish with him and be on our way."

Rick thought for a moment and then said, "I guess that's okay with me. As far as I can tell, his only sources of information have been Jennifer and that private investigator in Phoenix. We can take care of both of them."

Trevor was aghast to realize that they knew about Max. However, he didn't dare to say a word because he was certain that would only make things worse for Max.

Turning to Trevor, Rick said, "Austin and I have a little surprise for you. We brought some of the venom of the blue-ringed octopus with us, and we thought we'd let you sample it for us. It will give you a real firsthand view of what your irksome colleague Dr. Fife suffered through."

"Why don't you save yourself the effort and just shoot me?" Trevor said. His mind had gone into high gear as soon as Rick had mentioned the venom of the blue-ringed octopus from Australia. Trevor had done a paper years previously on the blue-ringed octopus and challenges faced by emergency medical technicians in providing first aid to its victims. If they used the venom in a small enough quantity, he might have a chance of surviving.

"Oh, I think you'll find this method of dying to be a lot more interesting," Austin remarked as he removed a small pocketknife from his fanny pack and moved toward Trevor. Austin knelt by Trevor's outstretched left arm and then opened the blade of the pocketknife as he continued with a sneer, "Now be a good patient and hold still. This won't hurt too much." He reached out with the pocketknife and drew it quickly across Trevor's wrist, leaving rivulets of blood that ran down his wrist and dripped onto the sand.

Trevor glanced quickly over at his wrist and was relieved to see that the cut was minor.

Austin said, "I know that it doesn't look like a very serious wound. But let me assure you, it's more than enough to allow for a toxic dose of the venom applied to the wound to enter your bloodstream." As he spoke, he had reached into his fanny pack and had produced an amber vial. He smiled menacingly at Trevor as he gently shook the bottle.

"Leave him alone," Melanie shouted in desperation. "Just leave us alone in the desert and go. From what you say, we won't survive anyway. The end result will be the same."

"I'm sorry, my dear," Rick said with his voice dripping fake sincerity. "After all of the trouble that you and Dr. Davis have caused us, a quick death is too kind. We think that you should suffer first by watching the man that you love die slowly before your eyes. It won't be pretty. Then you will die even more slowly of heat exhaustion and dehydration."

Melanie burst into tears and seemed to bow her head in defeat. She suddenly lunged at Austin in an effort to knock the vial from his hands. Anticipating her desperate move, Rick had already positioned himself closer to Austin. He easily pushed Melanie off-balance and sent her sprawling harmlessly onto the sand. Rick moved quickly to Melanie before she could get up and pinned her to the ground. "Sit on her legs and take off her shoes," he barked in Shannon's direction. Shannon complied hastily. As she worked, Rick said to Austin, "Take off Dr. Davis's shoes, also. We don't want them wandering too far just in case the venom doesn't work." After removing Trevor's shoes, Austin collected Melanie's shoes from Shannon and tossed both pairs into the passenger compartment of the helicopter.

Returning to Trevor's side, Austin again removed the amber vial from his fanny pack. He turned to Rick and asked, "Are we ready?"

Rick thought for a moment and then replied, "Not yet. I'd like to hear what Shannon has to say on this momentous occasion. After all, you are doing away with her competition and her old boyfriend all at once. She must be feeling some sense of loss."

CHAPTER 56

SHANNON HAD REMAINED mostly silent since leaving the helicopter. She had been feeling an intense need to reach out and hold Trevor in her arms, protecting him from Austin and Rick. She realized at the same time that doing so would put her at risk of being executed along with Trevor and Melanie. Trevor would probably have rejected her anyway. She also was experiencing intense hatred for Melanie for having taken Trevor away from her. She had felt like kicking Melanie in the ribs every time that Austin had kicked Trevor.

At the same time, she was strongly attracted to the idea of teaming up with Rick and Austin. It seemed to her like they had already accepted her into their circle of confidence by letting her be a witness to their operations in San Felix. Joining them would mean that she would have all the money that she had ever wanted. It would be more exciting than selling Waitnomor to recalcitrant medical providers in Phoenix.

She also felt some fear by being an accomplice to murder. She wasn't nearly as worried about the act of murder itself as she was worried about getting caught and losing everything. A few years ago, she had heard of a survey that had asked anonymously if the respondents would commit a murder with no risk of being caught, if by doing so they would receive one million dollars. Five percent of the respondents had answered that they would commit murder under those circumstances. Although she hadn't been surveyed, Shannon knew that if she had needed money badly enough, she would have been in the five percent that would have murdered to get it. It was a fairly easy decision to make when the reward was so high and carried no risk.

Shannon looked at Trevor, looking so pathetically helpless on the sand. There wasn't any hope for him. In addition, there wasn't anything to be gained by maintaining any feelings for him. Looking away from Trevor, she willed any feelings that she still had for him from her heart. She didn't need to look at Melanie's face again to be reminded of how she felt about her. Shannon turned back to Rick and replied in quiet, yet piercing, voice, "They mean nothing to me. Kill them both." She then looked into Rick's eyes and finished, "The sooner the better."

CHAPTER 57

TURNING TO TREVOR, Rick said, "You shouldn't have made her so mad. Now I have no choice but do what the lady asks." He looked at Austin and signaled for him to apply the venom to Trevor's left wrist wound. As Austin donned a pair of latex gloves in preparation for removing the cap from the vial, Rick moved into position behind where Melanie was kneeling at Trevor's side and clamped his fingers painfully onto her shoulders to remind her not to try anything.

Melanie turned and said, "Get your hands off me, you disgusting man."

"And how are you going to make me, little fat girl?" Rick said and then laughed.

"You might have messed with my brain so that I'm always hungry," Melanie replied angrily as she began struggling to free herself from Rick's painful grip. "But that's nothing compared to how intense your hunger is for wealth and power. You've grown fat off of other people's suffering as you go to the extreme to satisfy your selfish needs. You and your henchmen are no more than a bunch of juvenile bullies that are unable to rise above your genetic tendencies."

Austin said, "Rick. I don't want her to talk to you like that. Knock her silly."

"No. I think that her comments, no matter how rude, are thought-provoking," Rick said as he squeezed Melanie's shoulders a little tighter in retaliation. Melanie squirmed in pain, still trying to free herself. "Just like Melanie here said, we are much more influenced by our genes than most of us would like to admit. Scientists say that our behavior is sixty to eighty percent determined by our genetics. I guess that's why I grew up to be like my old man. He was a drug user and dealer in the nineteen seventies. He died of a drug overdose just a few years after I graduated from high school. Austin, you are turning out just like your father in spite of your high-class upbringing. Your dad told me that he had sent you to Harvard to give you a chance to make it in life away from the crime industry. He was hoping that you wouldn't follow him in his dangerous profession. It's obvious that his plan didn't work. That's because the genes that you inherited from him are determining your behavior more than anything else."

"Thanks," Austin said. "And I thought that I had decided on my own that a life of crime pays better than wearing a suit."

"The beauty of it is that we can make millions off of this very concept," Rick said. "All we have to do is to come up with ways to enhance the genetically-coded tendencies of the general population. We're already going to make a fortune off of manipulating the appetite centers in people's brains. Next, we could find a way to enhance people's appetite for alcohol. Only five percent of humans are genetically at risk for becoming alcoholics. If we could alter people's appetite centers so that everyone had an increased tendency toward alcoholism, then we could profit immensely from the resulting rapid increase in sales of alcoholic beverages. We could make even more money if we could develop an effective prescription-drug treatment for alcoholism, like we have with Waitnomor and obesity. The profits would be immense, both on the supply and treatment sides. We could then apply the same principals to cocaine, gambling, pornography, and sexual addictions."

"You're insane," Trevor said.

Rick smiled. "No, Dr. Davis. The proper term is rich. Stinking rich."

"Enough of this self-indulging prater," Austin said. "I need to get back if we're going to get that drug shipment out this evening."

"Okay. Fine," Rick agreed with irritation in his voice at being interrupted. "Let's have a little fun watching Dr. Davis take his last breath, and then we will be on our way."

All eyes watched as Austin turned and carefully removed the cap from the vial.

"How did you get the venom?" Trevor asked nonchalantly. Inside, he was a ball of extreme anxiety and fear, but he wasn't going to give these men the privilege of seeing how he felt.

"My father has connections all over the world," Austin said as he placed the cap from the vial on a small rock on the sand and then put his left foot on Trevor's forearm near the elbow to keep Trevor from moving. He positioned the vial just inches above Trevor's wrist and then paused as he finished answering Trevor's question. "I'm not exactly sure how he got it." With that, he tipped the vial toward the laceration on Trevor's wrist. Trevor turned away and looked at Melanie with a brave smile.

"No!" Melanie cried in horror as a small stream of clear liquid poured onto Trevor's wrist. She looked away and began sobbing.

Austin quickly retrieved the cap from the rock, tightened it on the vial, and then returned it to his fanny pack. He stood and took a few steps backward toward the helicopter. Rick let go of Melanie's shoulders and walked over to join Austin. Shannon stared expressionlessly without moving.

Ignoring the others, Melanie moved back to Trevor's side, knelt, and then hugged him around the neck. "Trevor, I'm so sorry." She held him close to her for a moment longer and then straightened a little as she asked, "Are you okay?"

Trevor smiled and replied, "I'm fine for now. Make sure that you don't touch the venom on my wrist. It will affect you, too, even through your skin."

"How touching," Austin said to Rick, loud enough that Trevor and Melanie could easily hear what he was saying. "However, he probably doesn't realize that it would be better for her to die with him from the venom. Instead, she's going to die slowly over the next seventy-two hours from dehydration and from exposure."

"Melanie. I need you to listen to me," Trevor said with urgency in his voice but softy enough that Rick and Austin couldn't hear him.

"What?" Melanie asked.

"We only have a few moments before the venom starts to take effect. I know about this venom. I did a paper on poisonous animals from around the world in medical school. This toxin will paralyze my body and I won't be able to breathe on my own for about two hours. However, the toxin won't stop my heart. If you can breathe for me with artificial respiration, then I might be able to survive. Do you know how to do mouth-to-mouth resuscitation?"

"I took a CPR course a number of years ago and practiced on the dummies. I've never tried it on a real person."

"I need you to breathe for me about ten times a minute. Remember to pinch my nose closed with your fingers."

"But I don't have a watch. They took my watch when I first arrived here."

"Just count by thousands to six thousand after each breath and then give me another."

"Oh, Trevor. What if I can't do it? What if I do it wrong or what if I can't do it for long enough? You'll die and I'll lose you forever!" She began to sob.

In spite of being in pain and in spite of being tied spread eagle on the sand, Trevor attempted to give her strength with his words.

"You've got to try. I want to live. I want to marry you and have kids with you. I want to grow old with you. Please, don't give up on me now."

"I want to grow old with you, too, Trevor." She took a deep breath and then exhaled. "Okay. I can do this. I'm not going to let you to break your promise to marry me."

Trevor opened his mouth to reply, but nothing came out at first. The venom had started working so quickly. He finally said with a weak whisper, "I'm glad to hear that." He paused for a moment, swallowed with difficulty and then continued, "Sorry. I feel so weak. Everything's numb…"

Walking over to join Austin and Rick, Shannon asked, "How long does it take for the venom to take effect?"

"It should be just a few minutes," Austin answered.

"In that case, I'd rather wait for you in the helicopter," Shannon said. "I'd like to leave as soon as possible." She turned and walked toward the copilot's door. Austin followed Shannon.

"I guess we'll watch your last moments from the helicopter," Rick said. "Goodbye, Dr. Davis. Goodbye, Miss Baker." Rick turned and entered the passenger door of the helicopter. He closed the door behind him and then posted himself at the window to watch.

Austin hopped into the pilot's seat and closed his door.

Trevor suddenly felt short of breath. He took as deep a breath as he could, but it wasn't enough. He still felt short of breath. He began panting for air.

Melanie asked, "Trevor, are you okay?"

Waves of nausea abruptly surfaced from Trevor's stomach. Trevor was sure that he would have thrown up if there had been any food in his stomach. He hadn't eaten since dinner the night before. The chance that the water in his cell might have been poisoned had kept him from drinking it. Trying to think clearly, he remembered that some victims had survived when the dose of venom was small.

With this in mind, and with extreme effort, he opened his eyes and whispered, "Use sand to wipe… venom… off…" and then he could say no more.

Melanie quickly perceived what he meant. Using her body to block the view of the others in the helicopter, she rubbed sand onto the laceration on his arm. Going one step further than Trevor had asked, she quickly tore off a piece of her scrub top and wiped his wrist clean. She threw the piece of her scrub top on the sand and buried it. Turning back to Trevor, her eyes widened to see that he was struggling desperately to breathe. "I did it," she said. "I hope that helps. Is there anything else I can do?"

He stared at her with eyes wide with fear but was unable to reply as he struggled for each breath. She touched his shoulder lightly with her other hand and cried, "Trevor, I love you. Don't leave me." She began sobbing in frustration. "Breathe!" she yelled. Those were the last words Trevor heard as he lost consciousness.

CHAPTER 58

A S THE HELICOPTER lifted off the desert floor and turned toward San Felix, Shannon stared mutely out the window at Trevor's barely-perceptible, sand-shrouded body. She could see Melanie crouching over Trevor's head. Shannon assumed that Melanie was protecting him from the sandstorm created by the helicopter. The helicopter moved rapidly away from the valley, and soon Trevor was mercifully lost to view. She sighed and sat back into her seat, staring glumly out the front window at the featureless landscape rushing beneath her. Trevor had been the only man that she had ever really loved. Sure, she had told a lot of men that she loved them to get what she wanted, but she had never felt anything. Loving Trevor had showed her what real love felt like and had put all of her past relationships to shame. Now Trevor was gone, leaving her feeling emptier and colder inside then she had ever felt before.

"Cat got your tongue?" Austin asked via the headphones.

"Sorry," Shannon said as she glanced briefly at Austin. "I've got a lot on my mind."

"Come on. Dr. Davis is dead. That should take a huge load off your mind."

"Oh, and why is that?" Shannon said with irritation.

"He dumped you for the other woman. I figured you'd be happy to see him get his due."

"You're disgusting," Shannon said as she undid her seat belt and got up. She stalked through the door to the passenger compartment, ignoring Austin's apologies and pleas for her to stay.

Rick looked up from a magazine that he was reading. He smiled and said smoothly in the headphones, "You've decided to come and keep me company. I was getting pretty lonely back here." He patted the seat next to him. "Have a seat."

Shannon smiled back and sat next to Rick. She leaned back, closed her eyes, and rubbed her temples with her fingers.

"What's wrong?" Rick asked. Shannon didn't reply, and after a few moments, Rick continued, "You've been through a lot in the last twenty-four hours. I'm sure you feel like you have the weight of the world on your shoulders."

Shannon couldn't agree more. The love of her life had just died. She had been yanked out of her territory at a moment's notice and had been scared to death that she was going to lose her job and possibly her life. Her convincing defense of her own innocence had implicated her roommate and would probably result in her death. Tears began to fill her eyes. How could so many things have gone wrong so quickly? She had been working so hard to get ahead.

Shannon felt Rick's arm around her shoulder. Looking through tear-blurred eyes, she saw genuine concern on his face. That opened the floodgates, and the tears flowed even more copiously. Rick guided her head to his shoulder and held her gently as she cried. He offered a Kleenex, which she gladly took. His closeness was calming. Little by little, the intense emptiness she felt inside over having lost Trevor began to dissipate.

CHAPTER 59

PINCHING TREVOR'S NOSE closed with the thumb and index finger of one hand while simultaneously lifting his chin and keeping his mouth open with the other, Melanie pressed her lips tightly against his lips and blew air into his mouth. She was gratified to see Trevor's chest rise out of the corner of her eye. She removed her lips from his and turned her head a little to see Trevor's chest fall back to its previous position as he exhaled. She was instantly relieved.

Melanie had been so afraid that she wouldn't be able to perform the artificial respiration correctly, but now that she had given Trevor a few breaths, she was feeling a little more comfortable with the whole thing. She leaned down and gave him another breath of air. In her anxiety to save Trevor, she blew too much air into Trevor's mouth. The extra air from that breath and the previous breaths had nowhere to go except for his stomach. As she stopped breathing out and removed her lips from his, air mixed with fluid from Trevor's overdistended stomach shot out of his mouth and into hers. Instantly, she began retching. Her stomach convulsed severely and tried to throw up everything it could find. However, she hadn't eaten since the night before, and her dry heaves only managed to bring up bitter-tasting bile. Her mouth watered copiously with the unrelenting waves of nausea. Her eyes filled with tears, and she could barely see Trevor through the sheets of liquid that were pouring from her eyes. She sat back on her heels and then shook her head slowly back and forth in despair and disgust over the thought of resuming mouth-to-mouth for even a moment. As much as she loved Trevor, she knew that she couldn't do it anymore.

The waves of nausea slowly ebbed, leaving Melanie feeling exhausted. Melanie shook her head in disbelief that she had ever thought, for even a moment, that she wouldn't continue. "I can do this," she said out loud. "I love you too much to let you go." Moving back to Trevor's side, she briefly checked his chest and confirmed that he still wasn't breathing spontaneously. Steeling herself, she wiped the sheen of vomit from Trevor's face and then cleared any residual vomit from his throat and mouth by turning his head to one side and allowing the liquid in his mouth to flow out on to the sand. She pinched off his nostrils and then gave him a quick breath.

The queasiness in her stomach increased again as she smelled the odor of vomit on his face and then tasted it on his lips. She willed herself to continue with all the strength she had. The next breath went in easily, much to her relief. She then removed her mouth quickly from Trevor's mouth in an effort to avoid getting vomit in her mouth again. It wasn't necessary, however, as he didn't vomit. Melanie remembered suddenly that her instructor in CPR years ago had warned her not to breathe out into the patient's mouth with too much force or it would fill the stomach with air, making it harder to fill the lungs with each breath and also causing vomiting. Her efforts to be sure that Trevor got enough air had worked against her! With that knowledge, Melanie backed off a little on the force of her exhalations and was rewarded with no further vomiting. Her queasy stomach slowly calmed down, and she settled down into a rhythm of one breath every five seconds. Besides a dry mouth, she felt good and was sure that she could keep up the CPR for a couple of hours until Trevor could breathe on his own.

After a while, she stopped rescue breathing for a moment and checked Trevor's pulse at his neck. It was steady and strong. "Keep it up, Trevor. You're going to make it," she said to his unheeding body. As she resumed rescue breathing, she thought to herself, *Trevor, you could show a little more enthusiasm. I'm doing all the work here!* She smiled in-between breaths at her attempt at humor and tried not to think about what she would do if this didn't work. The smile didn't last long as it drowned in a sea of worry.

Melanie glanced over her shoulder at the sun that still burned brightly in the clear blue sky. Its rays beat oppressively on her back and made her sweat. Her sweat-drenched shirt clung to her chest. It seemed that the sun hadn't moved much in the sky from where it had been the last time she had glanced at it. She wondered how long she'd been performing artificial respiration. Her mouth was becoming so dry, and she was feeling really lightheaded. She turned back and looked at Trevor, lying completely motionless on the sand. If she hadn't been checking his pulse, she would have thought for sure that he was dead. She repositioned his arms at his side. Earlier, she had stopped rescue breathing for a few seconds every minute to untie Trevor's hands and feet from the stakes.

She brushed a few grains of sand away from around Trevor's mouth. Trevor's mouth was dry, and it was becoming more difficult to make a good seal with her mouth against his in order to success-fully fill his lungs with air. Initially, it had been easy to blow air into Trevor's lungs. At the time, she had figured that she would be able to continue for hours, if necessary. Now, as she had begun to get tired, she knew that there was a limit to how long she could perform artificial respiration before she collapsed out of sheer exhaustion and dehydration. Her heart ached with fear that she wouldn't be able to keep going long enough to save Trevor's life. She had fought to stay sane and alive in her prison cell so that she could have a future with Trevor. Now she just had to keep going to ensure that she wouldn't lose what she had struggled so hard for.

A shadow passed momentarily over the desert floor where Trevor lay, startling Melanie and making her heart race. She glanced upward sharply and was both frightened and chagrined to see a vulture swooping down to make a landing on the desert floor ten yards away. The frighteningly ugly bird swooped to a halt with a few flaps of its wings and then turned its baleful eyes toward Trevor.

"Shoo!" Melanie shouted as loudly as she could with her dry throat. The bird startled a little, and then upon perceiving that she wasn't going to get up to chase it away, it made no effort to leave. "Go away!" she yelled louder as she waved both arms in the air. "He's not dead yet. You can't have him." She resumed artificial respiration while periodically keeping an eye on the necrophagic beast. It made no effort to move closer. Melanie had a hunch that it would wait patiently until they both were dead and rotting in the sun, no matter how long that took. Her initial fear faded and was replaced by loathing for the bird and what its presence represented. She couldn't imagine how things could get worse.

The cycles of blowing out into Trevor's mouth and then breathing in to fill her own lungs seemed to go on forever. Her fingers were starting to go cold. She ignored that, thinking that it was only due to anxiety over Trevor. The lightheadedness that she had noticed previously was getting worse. It was making it hard for her to think. She was surprised that she didn't feel hungry after going so long without anything to eat or drink. She had long since lost track of time. The sun had been inching closer to the horizon and so she knew that she had been keeping Trevor alive for at least a few hours. All the same, it seemed like forever.

She stopped for a moment and sat back on the sand. "Come on, Trevor. Breathe!" She paused and looked carefully at his chest. She couldn't see any movement at all. She yelled, "You've got to breathe!

I can't go on forever." She paused in exhaustion for a moment. "You said it would only be a few hours. It's been a few hours, and you're still not breathing." Trevor's chest hadn't moved a bit during her tirade, and it wasn't going to. As exhausted as she was, she forced herself back onto her knees to resume the endless cycles of breathing.

Suddenly, everything got strangely quiet. Trevor, the sand, and the sun became distant. She knew that she was fainting and fought it the best she could for Trevor's sake. Her eyes rolled back into their sockets, and she fell with a thud onto the sand, her head just missing Trevor's head.

Melanie's eyes shot wide open at someone's touch on her shoulder. Sucking in a quick deep breath, she sat bolt upright with her eyes open wide with fright. Looking around frantically for who had touched her shoulder, she saw a young man standing a few feet from her. She didn't recognize him. "You're here to finish us off, aren't you?" she said. Struggling to her knees, she clenched her fists and continued defiantly, "Well, we don't die easy." She shouted the last few words as she got to her feet with her arms up, ready to fight.

"Miss, I mean you no harm," the young man said.

"Yeah, sure. You'd be surprised at how much evil can hide behind a friendly face. But then, if you work with Rick and his goons, you already know what I mean."

The young man opened his mouth and started to protest, but she cut him off. "Just leave us alone. Please. He needs me now, or he's going to die." Without a further glance at the young man, she dropped to her knees at Trevor's side and gave him a rescue breath. She continued breathing for Trevor without looking up.

"Miss," the young man said. "I drove all this way to try to help you."

She didn't look up.

"Mr. Davis stayed at my father's hotel last night. I am the one that helped him to break into the underground building. He was captured. I was barely able to escape. I stayed up all night waiting to see what would happen next. I watched them put you and Mr. Davis in the helicopter. I overheard them talking about where they were taking you. I knew that they were probably going to kill you. I drove up here in my father's truck to see if you might still be alive and if you needed my help."

In-between breaths, Melanie looked up at the young man's face. From the scant stubble on his chin and the unwrinkled skin of his face, she recognized that he was nothing more than a kid, still in his late teens. She gave Trevor another breath and then sneaked another look at the boy. He did look sincere. Her initial bravura, fueled by a sudden rush of adrenaline from being startled into a wakeful state, was fading. She was physically exhausted and was weakening rapidly. She was starting to feel faint again and knew that she needed someone's help. She leaned over and gave Trevor another breath.

"I know CPR," the young man said. "Can I take over for you? I completed basic CPR training in a health class at school last year."

The young man's sincere offer melted all of Melanie's resistance. He wouldn't be offering to help with CPR if he had been sent to kill them. "Yes," she gasped weakly. "I'm too tired to keep going."

The young man moved quickly to her side. Melanie scooted slowly around Trevor's head until she was opposite the young man and then sat on the sand while he wiped off Trevor's mouth, positioned Trevor's head, and pinched Trevor's nostrils closed. Inhaling deeply, he covered Trevor's mouth with his and gave him a big breath of air.

"Don't blow too much or too hard, or he'll vomit back in your mouth."

"Okay," the young man replied with a nod. He took another less voluminous breath and gave it with less force to Trevor. He asked Melanie a few quick questions in-between breaths. "Have you checked his pulse?"

"He's got a pulse."

"Have you checked to see if he's breathing on his own?"

"A few times, but I can't tell if he's breathing or not."

The young man stopped breathing for Trevor and both of them stared at Trevor's chest. His chest didn't seem to be moving at all.

The young man turned his cheek and ear toward Trevor's mouth and listened carefully. "I think I hear some faint crackling, and I think I might feel his breath against my cheek." He paused for ten seconds more and then said, "Never mind. I don't think he's breathing." The young man resumed breathing for Trevor. He asked in-between breaths, "Miss... I can't help but think... that Mr. Davis is already dead. Have you considered that?"

"He has a pulse. Check it."

The young man reached down and checked for a pulse. He looked up and said, "He's got a pulse. He's still alive."

Just at that moment, Trevor coughed weakly.

"Did you hear that?" Melanie said. "He's breathing." She reached out and gently shook Trevor. "Trevor, can you hear me? Are you okay?" There was no response. She glanced at his chest for a few moments and said, "He's breathing weakly but regularly. But why isn't he waking up? Maybe he suffered permanent brain damage when I fainted and stopped rescue breathing. It seemed like I was only out for a moment."

Trevor's eyelids began fluttering intermittently like he was trying to open them.

"Trevor. Trevor! Wake up." Again, Melanie shook his shoulders gently, hoping that she could help him regain consciousness. His eyelids stopped fluttering after a few moments, and he seemed to slide back into a comatose state. Melanie just sat there with nothing to do. Trevor was breathing again, but he just wouldn't wake up. She was so worried that he had suffered brain damage.

"Miss, he's not waking up. We need to get him to a doctor as soon as possible. Can you help me get him into my truck?"

"You bet," Melanie replied as she quickly got up on her feet.

Within seconds, she felt the blood rushing out of her head. She plopped down hard on the sand on her hands and knees with her head hanging down. Trying hard to fight impending unconsciousness, she allowed herself to sink slowly to the sand until she was lying flat on the ground. Her vision, that had gone almost black within moments of her standing up, now began to slowly clear. She looked at the young man as she corrected herself, "I guess I'm not going to be able to help you after all."

"I've got juice and sports drinks in the truck. I'll be right back."

"Wait. Before you go. What is your name?"

"Marco."

"Mine is Melanie. And I'll take the sports drink."

"It's nice to meet you, miss," he said as he turned and hurried to his truck.

Moments later, Marco returned with the sports drink. As Melanie sat up and then drank slowly, she watched as Marco skillfully maneuvered Trevor into a sitting position. Marco then positioned himself with his back to Trevor and placed Trevor's arms over his shoulders. The young man stood and lifted Trevor onto his back like Trevor was a backpack and Trevor's arms were the straps. She wanted to help, but she needed just a little more time to get the electrolytes, sugar, and water from the sports drink into her system.

When Marco returned, Melanie was kneeling, ready for him to help her to the truck.

"Are you feeling better?" Marco asked.

"I think so. I'm ready to try again. I need to stand up a little slower this time." Melanie got to her feet with the help of Marco's outstretched hand.

"He's breathing better now," Marco said. "He opened his eyes for a few moments just after I laid him down in the truck. He's still not responding to questions. Also, he's burning up with fever. We've got to get him to a doctor soon."

Sensing the urgency of the situation, Melanie forced herself to start walking toward the truck. "I can get Dr. Alvarez to see him at my house once we get him there," Marco said. He stopped suddenly and peered at Melanie's face with concern. "You still look pale. Are you okay?"

"I'm feeling a lot better. I'll be even happier when I know that Trevor is okay."

CHAPTER 60

"YOU REMEMBER ASHLEY, don't you, from the training seminar?" Rick said.

"I do," Shannon said. "She was the one of the three that quit and went home."

"She never returned home," Rick said. "She had been doing poorly at the seminar, so we removed her from the training and instead used her as a test subject for R-648. She gained a ton of weight and then hung herself with her bedsheets."

"That's horrible," Shannon said with more than a little anxiety. Being fat, like the women that Rick had just shown her in basement of the warehouse that were test subjects for R-648, was about as awful of a fate as Shannon could imagine. "It's just as well, though," she said with a detached tone that was contrived to please Rick. "She wasn't bright enough to make it as a drug rep."

It amazed her how coldhearted Rick and Austin were. It was beginning to look like anyone that got in their way or didn't perform up to their expectations was just eliminated, as had happened to Dr. Fife, Melanie, and Trevor. Jennifer was most certainly the next target, along with the private investigator that Trevor had hired. She herself had barely escaped with her life that very morning. For now, she was pleased that her fortunes had completely turned so she was on Rick's good side. Nevertheless, she was coming to realize that being on Rick's good side could be short-lived and with deadly consequences.

"It's good to see that you're capable of appreciating this whole operation for what it really is," Rick said. "You understand that this is a business and that the bottom line is profit. You know, the more I think about it, you've got the brains, beauty, and savvy that I have been looking for. You would be perfect as my personal assistant."

"Thanks," Shannon said with just the right touch of self-assurance and an alluring smile. She knew that she was walking a thin line by throwing her fortunes in with Rick. They had just finished touring the dungeon, which was what they called the hidden basement of the warehouse. After walking through the illegal drug production facilities, he had shown her the R-648 study subjects, including the now quite-obese Becky. Rick had told her that after Becky had been kidnapped, she had taken Ashley's place in the study. He had informed Shannon that the study subjects would be terminated once the study ended in a few more weeks. Shannon had acted like that hadn't bothered her at all.

They ended up back in the hallway that led to the secret underground loading dock. Austin joined them in the hallway.

"Hey, Austin. I've hired Shannon as my new personal assistant," Rick said as he put his arm around Shannon's waist and gave her a squeeze.

Shannon smiled and played along with Rick's flirting. Shannon observed that Austin fell quiet as he watched Rick and her flirting. She could see that Austin's brow was knitted and his lips were thinned in anger. Shannon had little sympathy for Austin. She had made her decision, and the guy with the most power and the deepest pockets had won.

Checking his watch, Rick said, "The plane is scheduled to leave in two hours to get me back to Sacramento. I can drop Shannon off in Phoenix on the way." Turning to Shannon, he explained, "I'd like to leave you in Phoenix for another week or two so that we can have the time to find a replacement for you, especially since you will soon be the only rep in the Phoenix area. Also, that will give you the time to pack up your personal belongings and make any final arrangements." Turning back to Austin, he continued, "Also, why don't you pick her up on your way to LA next week? I'd really like her to be there with us for the R-648 delivery. With everything that will be going on, I'm sure that we will be able to use her help."

Austin hesitated and then said, "That's okay with me."

Completely oblivious to Austin's ill-disguised anger, Rick turned back to Shannon and said, "It has been a long and tiring day for you. I'm sure that a few hours to rest and freshen up would be welcome before we leave. How about I show you to one of our guest rooms?"

"That would be nice," Shannon said with a dazzling smile. "Can we stop by the car and get my bag first?"

"Your bag is already in the room," Rick said. "Take my arm, and I'll lead the way."

Shannon latched gracefully onto Rick's arm, and they were off in the direction of the guest sleeping quarters. Austin followed behind them. Rick told a few crude jokes along the way, and Shannon laughed at each one.

Arriving at the door, Rick asked Austin to check to be sure the room was presentable for their guest. As Austin passed by them and opened the door, Rick moved smoothly behind Shannon and began massaging her neck.

As Austin disappeared into the room, Shannon arched her neck with pleasure and leaned back against Rick's probing fingers. "Ah. Please don't stop," she purred. "You really know what I like."

"Pleasing you is my pleasure. And who knows? I might even have a few more pleasant surprises up my sleeve."

"Sounds intriguing," Shannon lied while maintaining just the right amount of contrived pleasure in her voice. It wasn't that she didn't enjoy his touch or didn't think that he was attractive. It was just that it was all too obvious where all this was heading. She'd been through this routine a thousand times before, and it was hard to get too excited about it. It did give her a smug sense of satisfaction to know that however powerful this man might be, she now had him under her sway. She had no doubt that he would do anything she asked.

Austin stepped out of the room and announced that the room was ready. His eyes flitted back and forth from Shannon and Rick a few times and then he looked away, clearly unhappy.

"Thanks, Austin," Rick said. He slid his hands slowly down Shannon's back to her hips and then put his arm around her waist as he propelled her gently into the room. "I hope this is nice enough for you."

"It's just perfect," Shannon said demurely. She turned toward Rick, put her arms on his shoulders, and smiled with just a touch of naughtiness. "Now what were these pleasant surprises that you said you had up your sleeve?"

Without a reply, Rick took her in his arms and kissed her passionately as he simultaneously kicked the door shut in Austin's face.

CHAPTER 61

MELANIE SAT IN the passenger seat of Marco's truck, worried sick about Trevor but unable to do anything to help him. All she could do was watch the endless parade of rocks and desert plants as they rushed by the bouncing truck. Lines of dirt streaked her face, making her skin look old and leathery. Her windblown hair lay in a disorganized tangle atop her head and across her upper face.

Trevor lay in the back of the truck, stretched out on two disheveled blankets. A third blanket had been folded into a makeshift pillow for his head, but it kept moving to one side due to the thousands of bumps that had jolted the truck's bed since leaving the desert canyon where Austin had poisoned Trevor with the toxin. Marco had told her that the canyon was called Devil's Canyon, which fit the horrible place well in Melanie's mind.

The last time she had asked Marco to stop the truck so she could check on Trevor, Trevor's eyes had been closed and the only movements that he had been making had been his shallow rapid breathing. Each exhalation through his partially open mouth had made a gurgling sound. Dirty, pale and with sunken eyes and cheeks, he had looked like he already had one foot in the grave with the other close behind.

It was nearly dark when the truck finally approached a small city. Marco slowed the truck to a stop in the driveway of a house. Melanie turned to check on Trevor through the dirty rear window of the cab. He was still unconscious.

Marco leaned on the truck's horn for three extended honks. After getting no response, he jumped out of the cab and went to walk toward the door of the house.

"Marco!" An older man appeared from the front door of the house and rushed to meet Marco at the side of the truck. "Why were you honking the horn so loudly? The neighbors…" He stopped suddenly as he saw Trevor's dimly lit figure lying motionless in the bed of truck. "What is this, Marco?" he said. "Why do you have a dead man in the back of my truck? What have you…?"

"Dad. He's the American that stayed at our hotel last night. The gangsters from the warehouse that I have been telling you about left him for dead in Devil's Canyon. I overheard their plan and went to Devil's Canyon to help him. He's still alive, but he's very sick. We need to get Dr. Alvarez over here right away."

"What am I going to do with you?" Marco's father said. "You insist on making lies about the men at the warehouse. They have done so much for our community. They are not criminals. It is you that have done something terrible and you are making these lies to cover up…"

"No, sir," Melanie said in Spanish from the cab of the truck. "Marco is right." As she was speaking, Melanie got out of the passenger door of the truck and stood by the other side of the bed of the truck. "The men from the warehouse are criminals of the worst kind."

"Who are you?" Marco's father said. "Why should I believe anything that you say? For all I know, you are just using my son to help hide your own criminal activities."

"You've got it all wrong," Melanie said. "Please listen. I'm Melanie Baker. I work for a pharmaceutical company in Phoenix,

Arizona. I was kidnapped three months ago, and I have been a prisoner in a secret underground laboratory under the warehouse since that time. Those men in there have done horrible things to me. Today, two men named Rick and Austin took my friend here in the truck and me in a helicopter to Devil's Canyon. They poisoned my friend, took my shoes so that I couldn't go far, and then left us to die. Your son saved us." She paused to smile at Marco but noted that Marco's father was opening his mouth to speak. Melanie hurriedly continued, "Let me finish. Since they were sure that they were leaving us to die, they bragged to us about things that they have done and the terrible things that they are going to do in the future. They have experimented on the people of your city by putting a drug in your water supply that makes people gain weight. Marco tells me that most the people here have gained a lot of weight over just a short period of time. I'm sure that you remember a few months ago when the whole town got headaches. That was when you were first drugged by these villains."

Marco's father's furrowed brows and pursed lips had softened by the time Melanie had finished speaking. Since he didn't comment, she continued, "The warehouse is just a front for shipments of illegal drugs to the United States. Thousands of people's lives are being destroyed by that evil alone. They have paid off your policemen to keep them quiet about their illegal activities. With your policemen looking the other way, they have kidnapped young people from your town and are doing the same things to them right now that they did to me." Melanie's voice broke, her upper lip began quivering and her eyes filled with tears at the memories of her terrible experiences in the dungeon.

"Father, you see, I was right," Marco said. "You and the town's leaders were just trying to do a good thing for our city when you let them build the warehouse here. But those men have lied to you and they are hurting our people. It's got to stop. Also, father, I just know that they have my girlfriend, Alicia, is in their underground laboratory." Tears began filling Marco's eyes as well. "We have got to go in there and get her out."

Marco's father stood silently between the two tearful figures for a long a moment. He sucked in a deep breath, held it for a few seconds and let it out. He put his hand on Marco's shoulder and said, "My son, I'm sorry that I didn't believe you earlier when you tried to tell me that something was wrong at the warehouse. I hope you and the people that have been hurt can forgive me. But now, we can't let our sorrows delay us any further from acting quickly to end this terrible wrong."

Marco looked into his father's eyes and smiled.

His father smiled back.

Marco gestured toward his dad as he spoke, "Melanie, this is my father, Luiz."

Luiz said, "It's nice to meet you. Now, let's get your friend inside. Then, we'll call Dr. Alvarez. Marco, I'm going to need your help in calling an emergency town council meeting."

Anxiety tied Melanie's stomach in painful knots for the umpteenth time that day as she forced herself to wait patiently while Dr. Alvarez examined Trevor. The doctor had listened for what seemed like forever to Trevor's lungs and abdomen. For the lung exam, she and Marco had helped to hold Trevor in a sitting position by his shoulders. Trevor had half opened his eyes and had moaned like he was in pain. Elated that he might be coming to, she had tried to talk to him. However, she hadn't been able to get him to respond to any of her questions. When they had laid him back down on Marco's bed, his head had fallen heavily onto the pillow. He looked terrible, and Melanie was worried about him. She just couldn't let him die after all they had gone through, especially now that they were together and out of danger. She felt like reaching out and shaking the doctor in desperation, pleading for him to do something. Instead, she waited with her stomach churning.

Finally, the elderly man straightened as much as his back would allow him, looked her in the eyes and said, "He most certainly has pneumonia. He's severely dehydrated. I don't see any sign of appendicitis or bowel obstruction. His liver and pancreas seem to be okay, but I can't be sure without lab tests. I'm concerned that he might have meningitis. He really needs to have an ambulance take him to the hospital."

"I've already told you that going to a hospital is out of the question," Melanie said. As much as she absolutely wanted the best medical care for Trevor, she didn't want him to end up dead at some local hospital because one of Rick's informants had found that he was there. She was sure that any American in a hospital in this area would definitely attract unwanted attention from the wrong people.

The doctor shook his head. "It's not the right choice. He could easily die without proper medical care. Are you willing to take that risk?"

"Yes," Melanie said in a voice that was supposed to sound strong and firm, but instead cracked because of anxiety and the dryness in her throat that she hadn't been able to get rid of, even after drinking tons of water.

"Okay," the doctor said as he turned and walked to the table where he had placed his medical bag. "I'm not going to abandon you because you won't do as I have requested. I often am forced to provide marginal medical care to the villagers around here because of their unwillingness to go to the hospital. I said the part about making the wrong choice that could result in a bad outcome because I do that every time I take care of potentially sue-happy U.S. citizen."

"I would never sue you."

The doctor pulled IV bags, tubing, syringes, and vials of medication out of his bag as they spoke. He turned to Trevor as he said, "That's what they all say. I left my practice in San Diego fifteen years ago because of a nasty lawsuit that a patient's family won against me. I was sued even though the alleged malpractice occurred when the patient was under the care of an excellent cardiologist that I had referred her to. The cardiologist had tried his best to help her with her heart disease but hadn't succeeded. Through the efforts of a greedy attorney, the case went to a jury trial and the sympathetic jury sided with the grieving family." The physician deftly started an IV, placed the IV bag on top of a tall bookshelf, and filled a syringe with a yellow liquid as he spoke. Melanie's eyes were drawn to the working end of the needle as he held it up and squirted out the air bubbles along with a little bit of the medicine that had been in the syringe.

"I'm sorry to hear that."

"I'm not. It was the answer I was looking for. My malpractice insurance covered the damages, but I didn't have the heart to continue practicing medicine in the U.S. I sold my practice the week after the judgment and moved here. I have never looked back." Gesturing at Melanie and Marco, he added, "Help me roll him onto his side and pull his pants down so that I can give him this injection."

Melanie and Marco complied, and the physician gave the shot while he continued, "The folks here are grateful for whatever I do and would never sue. I left the U.S. with a good retirement and don't need to make money. They pay me if they can, and I get a small amount from the government. I spend all of my spare time rockhounding. This place is a rockhounding paradise."

He finished by putting a small round adhesive bandage over the injection site. With Melanie's help, they pulled Trevor's pants back up, and then they rolled him onto his back once again.

"Well, that's about all I can do. I left you two more bags of IV fluid. Marco knows how to change them. He worked with me for a couple of days last year as part of a health class." Turning to Marco, he said, "Give him two bags of intravenous fluid as fast as you can, then turn the drip rate of the intravenous fluid down to one drop every two seconds. That will keep him going until morning. I'll be back in the morning to check on him."

"Thank you, doctor," Melanie said. "I have nothing to pay you with right now. Can I mail a check to you for your services?"

"This one is free," the doctor said with a smile. "From what Marco's father has told me, this town owes you a big debt of gratitude. I have always had a bad feeling about those guys at the warehouse." He grabbed his bag and left the room.

Melanie turned back to Trevor and watched his breathing while Marco fiddled with the IV. Neither spoke. Melanie thoughts were dominated by worry for Trevor's well-being.

Marco's father walked quietly into the room. "The town council is meeting with me in the kitchen. I'd like both of you to join us. The council needs to hear what you told me."

CHAPTER 62

RELENTLESS AND SEARING pain radiated like lightening from deep inside Shannon's forehead toward the top of her head. It seemed that at any moment her head would explode. Never had she experienced pain like this before, and she could barely keep from screaming. Fear that she was dying from a ruptured aneurysm in her brain caused mounting fear. In extreme discomfort and in abject terror, she subconsciously began breathing in short rapid cycles, causing lightheadedness, numbness and tingling in her lips and fingers, mental confusion and increasing nausea.

"What's wrong?" Rick asked. They were seated side by side in the company jet. "Just a few minutes ago, you couldn't get enough of me. Now you're acting like you're sick and all you want me for is a pillow."

Rick's tone of voice told Shannon that he clearly cared more for his own needs than for her well-being. Angry because of his insensitivity and wanting to cope with the pain and nausea without having to listen to the irritating whining of a wounded male ego, she went to lift her head off of his shoulder so that she could sit back into her own seat on the airplane. However, the pain in her skull tripled the instant that she moved her head. Intense nausea emanated from her upper abdomen and roiled toward her mouth. She fought down the bile in the back of her throat and continued to return her head to her own seat, although much more slowly and carefully. Sweat beaded on her forehead, and her face paled to the color of white marble.

"No, you don't," Rick said as soon as he perceived that Shannon was trying to move away from him. "I want you close." As he spoke, he tightened his grip around her shoulders and tried to pull her back. The added strain on her already tensed stomach was too much. Her hand arrived too late at her mouth to keep her vomit from spraying all over Rick's chest and lap.

"Oh, sick," Rick exclaimed in disgust as he forcefully pushed Shannon away from him while he jumped up to escape being splattered even more. Glancing down at his vomit-covered suit, he said, "This is what I get for letting you live." He wheeled and stalked back to the plane's single restroom to clean up, leaving Shannon with her mouth over a paper bag, dry heaving almost incessantly.

CHAPTER 63

"I HAVE TO ADMIT that there were a few moments there where I thought I'd never see another sunset," Trevor said in a weak voice that betrayed the fact that he was still far from well.

"Well, I'll admit that there were more than a few moments at Devil's Canyon when I didn't think that either of us would ever see another sunset, especially one as beautiful as this," Melanie said as she gazed out of the window next to Trevor's bed. The sky over the mountains to the west was an incandescent orange-red. Turning back to Trevor, she said, "And then after Marco rescued us and brought us to his house, I still have been worried sick that you wouldn't make it because of your pneumonia. I'm so glad that you're feeling better."

"If this is feeling better, then why do I feel like I've been dipped in boiling acid and then run over by a convoy of a hundred dump trucks? I guess I should be glad that I don't remember what worse felt like." He smiled weakly as he finished speaking and then groaned in pain as he tried to shift his position in the bed.

Concerned, Melanie immediately came to his assistance and helped him pull himself up in the bed. The worry in her eyes faded when she felt Trevor's right hand come to rest lightly on her forearm. She looked down at Trevor's tired face and saw a silly grin.

Trevor said. "I'm going to be fine. Tough birds like me don't die that easy, especially when they know there's a Mrs. Bird waiting for them if they can hang on."

Seeing a hint of the usual sparkle in Trevor's eyes made Melanie's heart soar. He was going to be all right. "That's Miss Bird to you. We're not married yet. What would people think to hear you talk like that?" Melanie smiled couldn't resist a quick kiss. As she moved to pull away, she felt the grip on her arm unexpectedly tighten as Trevor held her close for a longer and more passionate kiss. Melanie sighed dreamily as she slowly moved away from Trevor. His hand slid loosely down her arm until the precise moment when their fingers touched. On cue, they gave each other's hand a gentle squeeze as they continued gazing tenderly into each other's eyes.

Trevor said, "I should be feeling well enough by tomorrow morning to leave for the States."

"You are in no condition to travel tomorrow, Trevor." Melanie shook her head in exasperation. "Why is it that doctors make the worse patients?"

"Can't you see how quickly I'm improving? All I had was a little pneumonia. Most patients improve dramatically in the first twenty-four hours on antibiotics."

"It's not happening. Nurse's orders."

"All right, we'll see how I feel in the morning. If I feel up to it at all, maybe then we can leave for Phoenix. After that, once we're home, we need to come up with a plan to stop Rick from poisoning Los Angeles. I will feel terrible if he carries out his plan while I stand by and do nothing."

"You look very handsome when you're being heroic," Melanie said as she reached out and gently pinched Trevor's cheek. She wasn't going to let Trevor's obvious attempt to persuade her to let him leave for Phoenix get very far. She smiled as she said, "On the other hand, it won't do all the people you're going to save any good if their knight in shining armor is too weak to even put on his underwear."

"Do you mean that I haven't been putting on my own underwear?"

"Don't get any ideas, buckaroo. Just because I've seen you naked doesn't mean that I'm now putty in your hands. Like it or not, we're not leaving here until you get better, and there's nothing that you or your cute little cheeks can do to persuade me otherwise."

CHAPTER 64

THE NARROW SHAFT of sunlight stabbed across Shannon's bedroom like a laser beam. The unrelentingly bright light easily penetrated her closed eyelids, illuminated her retina, and caused the pain in her head to increase exponentially. It seemed like she couldn't escape the tortuous beam of light no matter which way she turned. Her suffering intensified to the point that she had no choice but to force herself to get out of bed and close the curtains.

Ever so slowly, Shannon swung her legs over the side of her bed while simultaneously bringing her body to a sitting position. In spite of her best efforts to move cautiously and carefully, the intensity of the headache in her forehead increased incrementally. She griped the edge of the mattress hard with her fingers for a moment to try to steady herself. The more she moved, the worse the headache got, and the more it increased her disequilibrium and nausea. She was beginning to doubt whether she could even get out of bed without collapsing. Nevertheless, the thought of the continued discomfort caused by the inescapable beam of light from the window was even less tolerable. She launched herself onto her feet and staggered to the window. Feeling that she might faint at any moment, she clutched heavily at the fabric curtains on the right side of the window to support herself. Ignoring the tearing sounds coming from the fabric at the top of the curtain, she roughly yanked the curtain closed while continuing to use it for support. With great effort, she repeated the process for the curtain on the left side on the window. Mercifully, neither curtain tore from its rod. Her herculean effort was rewarded with a significant reduction in the intensity of the light in the room. Almost immediately, the pounding in her head lessened a degree. However, the reduction in light didn't do anything for the waves of nausea that were building in her stomach.

Relinquishing her hold on the curtains, she staggered toward the bed. She didn't make it more than two paces when she suddenly and involuntarily bent over at the waist and began retching nonstop onto the floor. The almost continuous vomiting sapped what little strength she had left. She pitched unceremoniously onto the floor, barely managing to break her fall with outstretched arms. Her head came to rest in a puddle of her own vomit. Too weak to even notice the sticky, foul-smelling liquid that covered her face and clothing, Shannon crawled back into her bed and curled up in a fetal position. She couldn't help but wonder, through the waves of pain, what she had done that would have caused such a terrible headache. She wondered if she had picked up an infection in Mexico that was causing this headache. She had drunk that fruit drink that had been in the back of the company car while she had been waiting for Rick to take her back to the airport. Otherwise, all the food she had eaten had been on the plane there and back.

Her nausea slowly receded to a more tolerable level. She snuggled into her pillow wanting to sleep to escape the intense pain. Her mind wandered to her roommate, Jennifer. Shannon had been back for almost twenty-four hours, and Jennifer was nowhere to be seen. All of Jennifer's personal belongings were undisturbed. There hadn't been any sign of a struggle in the apartment when she had arrived. At the same time, there was no question in her mind that Jennifer was no longer alive. Rick and Austin's people were efficient at what they did. Anyhow, Jennifer had gotten what she deserved for getting her falsely accused of being the snitch and nearly getting her killed.

CHAPTER 65

"WE'LL BE THERE in just a few minutes," Marco stated without taking his eyes off the road. Trevor glanced over at Marco. The young man's face was barely visible in the light that was glowing from the dashboard of the truck. Marco turned, met Trevor's gaze, smiled thinly, and then returned his attention to his driving. Trevor, likewise, turned his attention to the poorly-marked, narrow road ahead. The two men had spoken little since they had left Interstate 15 in northern Mexico an hour ago and had taken Highway 2 east to Agua Prieta. Trevor was sure that Marco's silence was born of the intense need to concentrate on the barely visible road ahead in order prevent an accident. On the other hand, Trevor, in spite of his rapid recovery from his pneumonia, felt more ill now than he had all day. He couldn't shake a gnawing anxiety in his upper stomach over their upcoming attempt to illegally cross the U.S.-Mexican border without papers.

Trevor's health had been better than ever upon awakening that morning. Rising before Melanie, he had showered, shaved, and dressed without assistance and then had helped Marco's mother with breakfast. He had served Melanie breakfast in bed in an effort to show her he was healthy enough to travel. With a little additional persuasion from a homesick Becky, who had joined them after being rescued from the dungeon by the townspeople, Melanie had been left with no choice but to agree. They had been ready to leave within the hour. Just as they were leaving, Becky had casually remarked to the group that she didn't have any form of identification and wondered if they'd have any trouble at the border. Trevor and Melanie had immediately expressed the same concern. Trevor's billfold was somewhere in the burned-out warehouse. Both women had been brought illegally across the border in Rick's airplane, sans identification. And since there was a chance that Austin's dad's people would be looking for them in retaliation for the warehouse being destroyed by an explosion during the rescue, a commotion at one of the legal border crossing points would only serve to attract their attention.

Gratefully, Marco had come to their rescue. Within minutes, he had reached Alfonso, a distant cousin that lived near the U.S. border and had made arrangements for help with crossing the border without papers.

The border crossing had seemed like a simple matter that morning, but now that they were nearing the border town of Vinateria where they were to meet Alfonso, Trevor was becoming concerned that it was anything but a straightforward matter. "Are you sure that we can trust your cousin?" Trevor asked.

"Yes. I'm sure, Mr. Davis." Marco said. "I know that people in the US think that 'coyotes,' the name we call people that help others cross the border for a fee, are nothing more than reckless and dangerous criminals. However, the majority of the 'coyotes,' including my cousin, are good people. I promise you that everything will be all right."

"I certainly hope so. The three of us have been through enough trouble this past few weeks to last a lifetime."

Marco nodded. Trevor took a quick peek through the rear window. The pale light cast by the moon was just enough to make out the shapes of Melanie and Becky, huddled close on the bed of the truck, underneath a blanket. He had insisted that they ride in the cab, but they had overruled him vehemently, insisting that he would get sicker and possibly die if exposed to the cool night air.

Returning to look out the windshield, Trevor was greeted by the faint lights of an approaching city. Moments later, Marco pulled off of the highway onto a bumpy side road and then parked in front of a house. The truck's headlights revealed the house to be in a poor state of repair with deep pockmarks scattered across the dust-stained adobe walls. The dirt yard in front of the house was strewn with trash and car parts, and the light from the truck cast eerie shadows, born of those objects, against the house. A beat-up Ford truck was parked in front of a narrow, single-panel door. A light shone dimly through a translucent, yellowing curtain that covered the only window in the front of the house. Marco killed the engine and snapped off headlights of the truck, immediately plunging all but the dimly-lit window into deep darkness. The absence of light only heightened Trevor's anxiety.

Fighting back his intense misgivings, Trevor followed Marco's lead as he exited the truck. Carefully testing the invisible driveway for debris, Marco and Trevor collected Melanie and Becky from the back of the truck. Then, using the window as a beacon, they inched their way to the door and knocked softly.

After a long moment of silence, the door opened wide, revealing a short man with a cherubic face. "Marco, my dear cousin," the man said as his arms opened wide. Giving Marco a fierce hug, the man continued, "It's so good to see you." Looking past Marco at the others, he added, "Come in. Come in. Welcome to my humble abode."

"It's good to see you, Alfonso. It's been too long." The two men moved into the front room of the house, followed by Trevor, Melanie, and Becky.

"These are my American friends that I told you about," Marco said.

"Well, any friend of yours is a friend of mine," Alfonso said with a broad grin, and the Americans couldn't help but smile in return. Before Trevor could return the greeting, Alfonso continued, "Are you hungry? Can I get you something to eat?"

"Alfonso, we need to get them across the border as soon as possible. They had a little run-in a few days ago with some pretty dangerous characters, and I'm sure those same people are going to be looking for them. They have spies everywhere. The longer we're here, the greater the chance that they will happen on us. I'm very concerned about my friend's safety."

After a moment's thought, Alfonso said, "In that case, let's leave right now. I've got water and extra coats in my truck. We'll have you across the border in no time."

Just minutes later, wearing ill-fitting, cheap coats and clutching one-liter bottles of water, they were bouncing along Highway 2 in the back of Alfonso's truck. The rough ride and rushing cold air made all but the simplest conversation impossible. After a few minutes, the truck slowed to a crawl, turned north, and then went through the desert without headlights and running lights. Alfonso even turned off the dashboard lights. The road they were following was invisible to all but Alfonso. Tire tracks crossed their path at all angles on a frequent basis, giving the impression that this area of the desert was a busy place. Although the ride was still bumpy, their slow rate of progress across the desert was almost soundless.

Feeling Melanie's touch on his arm, Trevor turned to her barely-perceptible, moonlit face as she spoke quietly, "Trevor, this whole thing gives me the creeps. I can't help but feel that something is going to go wrong."

Trevor hesitated, not sure of what to say without increasing her anxiety.

"I feel the same way," Becky said. "I've heard the stories about these border crossings. It seems like all too often that the Mexicans crossing the border end up dead at the hands of criminals or arrested by the border guards."

"Well, I'm just as afraid as you are, but I do know that the majority of Mexicans that try to cross into United States are successful," Trevor said, trying to sound reassuring.

The conversation ended in a nervous silence as Alfonso suddenly shut off the engine. The truck rolled to a stop at the base of a low bluff that had appeared out of the darkness just moments before. The light emanating from the moon and from a brilliant canopy of stars was adequate to see that they were alone, except for occasional clumps of sagebrush and islands of desert grass that seemed to float on an expanse of gray sand. The serene desert scene was marred in this location, however, by an even greater number of deep tire tracks and by an oppressively large amount of trash that was strewn across the desert. Without question, this was a popular place for border crossings.

Alfonso and Marco exited the cab of the truck and were joined by the others moments later. Alfonso spoke first, "The U.S. border is only one mile north of this bluff. As long as you follow the North Star, you can't miss it." Alfonso reached in his pocket and pulled out a cell phone. He handed it to Trevor as he continued, "Once you pass the border, use this burner phone to call the only number on its contact list. Tell the person that answers that you made it across and that you'll need to be picked up. Then continue north for another mile, and you'll run into a rural road. Wait there out of sight until a minivan stops on the side of the road and flashes their lights on and off two short times followed by two long times. If the coast looks clear, then head to the car and tell them I sent you."

"That's too far for Trevor to walk," Melanie said. "He's just getting over pneumonia, and I don't think he'll make it. Can't you drop us off closer to a town?"

Marco interrupted Trevor just as he was about to protest by explaining, "The border guards are as thick as flies on rotten meat the closer you get to the cities. You'd never make it across the border. It's even worse now that the National Guard is helping the border patrol."

"I can make it just fine," Trevor said. "It's only two miles. We'll just go slowly if I get tired."

"This really is the best place to cross the border," Alfonso said. "The sagebrush is taller at this part of the border than at any other. If you're careful, the border patrol will never see you. Even if you do get caught, just tell them that you are American citizens that got lost on a night hike. With your accents and skin color, most likely they'll let you go after they chew you out for not bring your IDs."

"It sounds like our options are limited at this point. I guess we'd better just go for it," Melanie said.

"If you see or hear any other groups of people," Alfonso continued with his instructions, "Stay clear of them. Some of the 'coyotes' out here carry guns and aren't afraid to use them. Who knows what they might do if they see your skin color and suspect that you're working for the border patrol?" After pausing, he continued, "Are there any other questions?"

Everyone shook their head no.

After briefly thanking Marco for saving their lives one last time, the trio bid Marco and Alfonso goodbye and then followed a steep, but well-worn, path up the side of the bluff and then into the desert. The cloud cover was scant, and the North Star was easily visible just above the horizon. It didn't come as a surprise to Trevor that there was a well-worn trail that led in the direction of the North Star. With Melanie on his right and Becky on his left, Trevor set out at a brisk pace, determined to put an end to his unpleasant trip to Mexico and also in an effort to stay warm in the cold night air. The sides of the path were strewn with used diapers, trash, and discarded personal belongings. They even came upon what was almost certainly a human hand and wrist protruding from the sand at the side of the path. Any desire to report the unmarked grave to authorities was quelled by the knowledge that they had to get to the border without being detected. They spoke little because of the briskness of the pace that Trevor had set and because they were afraid of giving themselves away by being too noisy.

After walking for ten minutes, they heard the unmistakable sounds of another group of people moving north on the trail just ahead of them. Trevor cut around the unseen group to the east and then set a new course toward the North Star. They found themselves in a much-less-traveled area of the desert with a lot less trash. However, the trail was more difficult to follow, which slowed their progress because of the need to backtrack frequently to get around thick sagebrush growth and small ravines. Soon after starting on their new path, the noises from the group that had been ahead of them disappeared to the west.

After walking through the desert for thirty minutes, they finally arrived at a simple, five-foot tall fence that supported regularly-placed signs stating in Spanish that this was the border between Mexico and the United States of America. The signs said that any person crossing the border illegally would be apprehended and prosecuted to the fullest extent of the law. Trevor hesitated and then had the women wait with him behind a clump of sagebrush, wanting to be sure that the coast was clear before proceeding. Motioning for Melanie and Becky to stay put while he checked out the border, he turned and took two steps toward the fence.

Suddenly, a voice barked in Spanish, "Freeze and put your hands over your heads. This is the U.S. border patrol. You're under arrest."

Obediently, Trevor raised his hands over his head and froze, his heart sinking with fear and despair. What was he going to say to the guards? How was he going to get out of this predicament? Suddenly, the sound of the retort of a distant rifle crackled through the air, making Trevor flinch involuntarily. *Are they shooting at me? Why? I haven't moved at all. Could it be that this isn't the border patrol after all and that it is really Rick's men who have tracked us down and are now going to kill us?* The night air was again rent by more distant gunshots. Trevor was now sure that the gun shots were too far away to be coming from any nearby border patrol unit.

"Stay where you are," the same amplified voice said.

Trevor heard an engine start on the other side of the fence to the west. The sound of the engine faded in the distance. Trevor began to relax, feeling lucky to have escaped capture by the border patrol.

However, Trevor all but jumped out of his skin as a hand touched him on his shoulder.

"Move it." It was Becky, and not one of Rick's henchmen. "This is our best chance to get across while the border patrol is involved with that group we passed."

"Why'd you have to scare me like that?" Trevor asked. He was still shaking like a leaf from the surge of adrenaline.

"You looked so cute standing there with your arms up that we couldn't resist," Melanie said in-between breaths of exertion as she followed Becky to the fence and quickly scrambled over it. She turned and motioned to Trevor. "Hurry up. Before you get caught."

Trevor sped into action, all but vaulted over the fence, and joined the two still-panting women in three seconds flat.

Without a word, the trio turned and sped away from the fence on the adrenaline high of being back in United States and out of danger. As they half-walked and half-ran, Melanie couldn't resist teasing Trevor in-between breaths. "You looked pretty cute jumping over that fence. It was like you'd seen a ghost. It's a miracle that you didn't split out your pants."

"It's amazing what a man will do to follow the woman he loves," Trevor said.

Becky grimaced and exclaimed, "Oh no! Here comes the mushy stuff. Where's my husband when—"

An ear-shattering retort of a shotgun blast right in front of them brought them to dead stop. The flame from the muzzle of the shotgun drew their eyes like bugs to a night light and then instantly blinded their night-adjusted vision with its brightness.

"On the ground with hands behind your heads, or you're dead," a deep, bodiless voice boomed from right in front of them in Spanish with a heavy English accent. Temporarily blinded and confused by the brain-numbing loudness of the shotgun blast, the three simultaneously dove for the dust like swimmers in a syncopated water ballet, sure that they had just jumped from the frying pan into the fire.

"Hands behind your heads," the man's voice boomed. He spoke at first in Spanish and then finished in English. Trevor, Melanie, and Becky rushed to comply.

In their haste, Melanie and Becky smacked their elbows together, and Becky exclaimed, "Ow!"

"Quiet!" the man commanded in Spanish. Then, in English again and under his breath, he said to himself, "I should shoot 'em in the back of their heads and put 'em out of their misery. But, well, that would be murder, wouldn't it? Can't have none of that, I guess."

A beam from a flashlight in the man's hand suddenly washed over their bodies as the man switched it on with his thumb. He returned to addressing them in terrible Spanish, "I am sick of you stealing across the border and then murdering my cattle for a few pieces of meat. I'm so sick of it that—"

"Sir, we are Americans," Becky interrupted as soon as she realized that the man was only a frustrated rancher and not a renegade officer with the border patrol.

"What? You think that because you know a little English that you can fool me into thinking that you're Americans that got lost in the desert?"

"We are Americans," Becky said. "They are white. I'm Latino, but I'm American born. And we have a hard time understanding Spanish, especially the kind that you're speaking. It would help if you spoke to us in English."

Aghast at Becky's impertinence and sure that they were in for it now, Trevor let his head fall limply against the sand as he muttered softly and sarcastically, "Way to go, Becky."

"So you're the spokesman for this little group," the man said as he centered the beam of light on Becky. "Sorry that my Spanish isn't very good. The class that I took at the community college didn't help much. So why don't you sit up so that I can see you better?" As Becky removed her hands from behind her head in preparation to push herself up from the ground, the man boomed an additional warning to Trevor and Melanie, "You other two need to stay where you are. For all I know, you're Mexicans that have paid this American woman to smuggle you across the border."

"We're all Americans," Becky emphasized as she got up and sat cross-legged on ground. "We're all from Phoenix, and we are down here hiking along the border—"

"I've heard that line a thousand times," the man said. "If you're Americans, then show me your identification."

"We don't have our passports, driver's licenses, social security cards, or birth certificates with us," Trevor said, figuring that it wouldn't hurt to try honesty with what he perceived was probably just a frustrated, but decent guy. "We have been stranded in Mexico, and we're trying to cross the border without them. My wallet was lost in a fire in San Felix three days ago."

"The other woman and I were kidnapped and flown across the border without identification," Becky added. "We escaped during the same fire."

The man thought for moment and then stated, "Your story sounds even more far-fetched than all the rest I've heard. At the same time, I'm beginning to believe that you might be Americans after all. It does help that you all have no accent to your English. Why don't the other two of you sit up and then let me ask you a few questions? Don't think that just because you can't see my gun that it isn't still aimed right at you." The man waited patiently for

Melanie and Trevor to get to a seated position on the sand. Pointing to Melanie, he requested, "What work do you do in Phoenix?"

"I'm a pharmaceutical representative for Medicon Pharmaceuticals, or at least I was," Melanie said. She glanced quickly at Trevor and then back to the man as she explained, "I recently found out firsthand just how competitive the pharmaceutical industry can be. At this point, I'm not sure that it's the right career for me anymore."

"What's your address in Phoenix?"

"I live at 14345 North Honey Bird Lane in Scottsdale."

Appearing to be satisfied with her answers, the man turned his attention to Trevor and asked, "And what's your profession?"

"I'm a doctor."

"Oh, really? What kind of a doctor?"

"I'm a family doctor."

"What's your name?" the man asked with a little more warmth in his voice.

"Trevor Davis."

"Well, I'll be a monkey's uncle," the man exclaimed as he slapped his knee. "You're my mother's doctor. What a small world."

"What's your mother's name?" Trevor asked.

"Lorna Fairbanks," the man said. "Do you remember her?"

"Sure, I do," Trevor said. "She's been coming to see me for over ten years. She's a great lady."

"She sure is," the man replied, now sounding warm and friendly. "But she's going to be madder than a hornet when she finds out that I've been holding her doctor at gunpoint." The man put his gun down and hurried over to Trevor. He extended his right hand to Trevor and helped him to his feet as he introduced itself, "I'm Grant Fairbanks. I'm Lorna's third son. And who might these young ladies be?" Grant helped Becky and Melanie up as Trevor introduced them. Grant continued, "I've had nothing but trouble with these illegal border-crossers killing my cattle for food. The border patrol just isn't doing a good enough job and so recently I've been taking matters into my own hands. That's why I was out here tonight. How was I to know that I was going to run into my mother's doctor?"

"Don't worry about it," Trevor said. "There's no harm done."

"Well, the least I can do is offer you a ride to town. In fact, seeing the situation that you're in, I'd be more than glad to drive you up to Phoenix first thing in the morning. I need to stop by mom's place and see how she's doing, anyway."

Trevor looked at Melanie and then Becky. Seeing no protests, he replied, "Normally, I'd object to putting you out that much. However, with no money and no vehicle, we aren't going to get far. Plus, it's getting pretty cold, and I'm worried about the girls getting hypothermia."

"And we're worried about Dr. Davis," Melanie said. "He's recovering from a case of pneumonia from just three days ago."

"It's settled then," Grant said jovially. "I've got a warm bed waiting for each of you at my house. We'll get up early, have a good breakfast, and then leave for Phoenix."

"I can't believe I still have room for dessert after that big steak," Melanie said. "I've eaten at this restaurant at least ten times, and I've never been able to finish my meal. Even though I intellectually understand the damage that was done to my appetite center in San Felix, it's still so hard to cope with my roaring appetite. It feels like I'm going to starve to death if I don't keep eating. And then, when I do eat something, the hunger only goes away for five minutes at a time."

"Take it from someone who has struggled with this very problem all of his life," Trevor said as he finished the last bite of his filet mignon. "I've never felt full in the middle of a plate of food like some people do."

"It's been that way for all of my life until now," Melanie said. "I've always wondered how my overweight friends could keep on eating even though they had clearly had enough for their activity level. Now I know how it feels to never get full. I'm going to weigh a ton if I don't stop eating." Melanie grimaced in mock horror as she finished.

As Melanie loaded her fork with another bite of the garlic mashed potatoes, Trevor couldn't help but smile at the pleasure of being with Melanie. When he was with her, he felt such incredible peace and contentment. It felt as good as or better than it had felt with his first wife, like he had come home from a very long, cold, and tough day to a warm and love-filled home.

Grant Fairbanks, the rancher that had stopped them just north of the border, had been incredibly helpful. They had spent a restful night in bedrooms that had belonged to Grant's adult children. Breakfast had been a tasty. Grant had driven them all the way to Phoenix and then had even offered to buy them lunch. After the group had politely declined, Grant had dropped Becky off at her house. Becky had insisted on going to the door alone and had pretend that she had come back from the dead. The look on George's face had been priceless, even though it hadn't taken him more than a few seconds to realize that he wasn't seeing a ghost after all. Melanie and Trevor had joined Becky at the front door after George had finally stopped hugging her. Melanie hadn't been able to resist ribbing George that he should have known that Becky wasn't a ghost because ghosts don't need to ring the doorbell to get into the house. The tender, yet joyful, reunion had brought them all to tears.

Since Trevor's apartment had been on the way to Grant's mother's house, they had parted ways with Grant at Trevor's apartment. Following a quick change of clothes, Trevor and Melanie had been off to the airport via a ridesharing service since Trevor's car was still at the airport. Once they had Trevor's car, they had gone to Melanie's apartment for her to change. The next few hours had been spent getting replacement driver's licenses, bank cards, and new cell phones. Trevor had tried to call Max to tell him about the events of the last few days. All he had reached were the voicemail systems on Max's cell and office phone. They had then decided that they were starving for some good old-fashioned American cooking.

Seeing that Melanie had finished with her last bite of food, Trevor asked, "I was surprised to hear you say to Grant that you weren't sure that you wanted to be a drug rep anymore. Are you serious about that?"

"After what has happened to me in the past month, I don't think anybody would blame me for wanting to find a new profession. I am utterly amazed at the length that Shannon and Rick are willing go to in order to get what they want. I am aware that what they did is unusual for the industry, to say the least, but at the same time, the pharmaceutical market is becoming so fiercely competitive and companies are becoming so desperate to sell their drugs that I'm not sure that I want to work under that kind of pressure. I was thinking…" Melanie glanced to the left while she paused to think and then suddenly and quickly covered the left side of her face with her hand while she simultaneously turned her face to the right. "Speaking of the devil, she's walking past our table. Don't—"

The warning came too late to prevent Trevor from reflexively turning to his right to see whom Melanie was talking about. Shock and fear registered visibly on his face as his eyes immediately locked onto Shannon Lowry. Upon seeing Trevor, Shannon came to an abrupt stop three feet from where they were sitting with a similar degree of shock displayed on her face. It seemed like forever until Trevor could tear his eyes away from Shannon and turn to Melanie with an expression that begged for help. Melanie shook her head imperceptibly to indicate that she too was clueless.

"You're supposed to be dead," Shannon said in a voice that was shrill enough to turn the heads of nearby diners. The young man that had been walking just behind Shannon stopped abruptly in his tracks, barely avoiding running into Shannon.

"Sorry to disappoint you," Trevor said, exerting extreme effort to act as nonchalantly as he could as he turned back to Shannon and her male companion. "Hello, Alex," Trevor said to the doctor that was with Shannon. Alex was new to the area, and although Trevor had met him previously, he didn't know him very well. "You'd better watch out for this one. Believe me, she'll stop at nothing to push her pills on you."

With eyes narrowed and with a hint of color in her cheeks, Shannon said, "And how would you know, Dr. Davis?"

After a moment of silence that dripped with tension, Trevor said, "I did die out there in the desert, you know." Trevor paused for effect. Poor Alex looked frantically from Trevor to Shannon in an effort to understand what was going on. Trevor was relieved to see that Shannon didn't have her hooks in Alex too deeply yet. Trevor continued with a just a hint of smugness in his voice, "It seems that I just can't resist coming back from the dead to haunt you." Trevor ended with a brave smile, but inside, he was experiencing a mix of revulsion, anger, and fear. To his relief, he wasn't feeling even a hint of attraction. A sudden sharp pain in his left shin from a kick under the table from Melanie got his attention, although he tried hard not to let the pain show.

Looking malevolently back and forth from Melanie to Trevor, Shannon collected her thoughts for a moment and then replied in a quiet, yet piercing, tone, "Oh, I don't think your visit from the land of the dead will last long. You'll be back where you belong in no time." Abruptly taking Alex's arm, she continued, "Come on, Alex. I've got to get going. I've got a very important telephone call to make to someone that will find Dr. Davis and his friend's presence here quite interesting."

After Shannon's exit, neither Trevor nor Melanie was able to speak for a few moments as each contemplated the enormity of what had just occurred. Finally, Trevor said, "You know, in the back of my mind, I was afraid that this was going to happen. I think that I have been so relieved to be back in the U.S. that I just haven't let myself think about this possibility."

"Yeah, me too. But now it's painfully obvious that we're in big trouble. Rick and Austin are good at what they do. We're no match for them."

"Only if they find us. And that's not going to happen as long as we're smart."

CHAPTER 66

THE INSIDE OF the private air terminal in Phoenix looked no different than any other air terminal that Shannon had ever been in. However, just the fact that she was in a private air terminal waiting for Austin to pick her up inescapably drew her back to the private air terminal in Portland, where she had met up with Austin and had flown off in his company jet on this wild adventure. A lot had happened since then. She had passed her training with flying colors, started her new job, and then had made more money than she ever could have if she had stayed in Oregon. However, the biggest thing that had happened had also ended up being the most negative for her. She had been utterly taken off-guard when she had fallen in love with Trevor. She had never been happier. Then Melanie had come along and ruined everything. In the end, her relationship with Trevor had been such a disaster that she hadn't been surprised when it hadn't bothered her much to leave him and Melanie to die in Devil's Canyon. Then, to her utter astonishment, she had run into Trevor and Melanie at the restaurant earlier that day. How had the two of them gotten out of that canyon alive? Rick had been totally ticked when she told him the bad news as soon as she had been able to get rid of Alex.

Looking out the windows of the terminal, she was less than thrilled to see Austin come down the ladder from the company plane and then head toward the terminal. She had really hoped that Rick would have changed his plans and would have come himself to pick her up. Austin was becoming more and more irritating with his poorly concealed jealousy of her relationship with Rick. Any respect that she had felt for Austin as her boss had vanished weeks before.

Rick, on the other hand, was a lot more interesting. There was no question that he was volatile. But Shannon felt up to the task of keeping him just so close, but not too close, so that the possibility of a deeper and more exciting relationship with her in the near future would keep him interested.

Suddenly intensely hungry, Shannon reached into her bag and pulled out a caramel nut bar. She'd had a big breakfast and was surprised to be hungry again so soon. She quickly removed the wrapper and then took a big bite. The concentrated sweetness of the caramel and the fulfilling crunchiness of the fresh peanuts tasted delicious. *Wow!* she thought to herself. *I've never had a candy bar that tasted this good.* Unable to help herself, she took another quick bite.

As Austin approached the door to the terminal, she was struck with the realization that since Austin and Rick's friendship went back for years, completely isolating Rick from Austin could easily backfire. Austin would either retaliate against Rick, or Austin and Rick would unite against her for trying to break up their friendship. That settled it. She would have to keep both men interested, but still at arm's length, no matter how much she was irked by Austin. She couldn't risk her future earning potential as Rick's assistant by damaging his relationship with Austin.

As Austin approached, she put on her best smile and greeted him with a quick hug.

"My, aren't you the pretty one today," Austin said. "How's that headache?"

"It's a lot better, and not a moment too soon. If I ever thought that I was in pain before this headache, then I was a wimp. The headache that I had was so bad that I can't even imagine feeling worse without instantly dropping dead on the floor. Near the end, I was beginning to think that if the pain didn't end soon, that I wouldn't be able to go on living. I had even planned how I was going to go to a gun dealer, buy the biggest handgun he had, and then blow the whole top of my head off to escape the pain."

"It was that bad? Have you ever had a headache like that one before?"

"I've never had any more than a mild headache in my life. I wonder where that one came from."

"Well, I'm glad that you're feeling well enough to fly to LA. Rick told me that you had run into Dr. Davis and Melanie. I can't believe that they're still alive. This has necessitated a change to our plans. After we plant the R-648 in LA's water treatment plant, I'm going to have to come back to deal with Dr. Davis." He grabbed Shannon's bag. "We're on a tight schedule, so let's get going."

She grabbed his arm, and they were off to the plane, but not until after Shannon had stuffed the rest of the candy bar in her mouth. Flavor that good just couldn't be wasted.

CHAPTER 67

"MR. AND MRS. John Smith? Couldn't you have been a little more original than that?" Melanie said as Trevor shut the motel room door behind them.

"I'm sorry. I was nervous. I couldn't come up with anything else. And besides, I wanted to make it as hard as possible for Rick and his men to find us. I couldn't use our names and using an unusual name would probably attract suspicion." Trevor felt he had done everything he knew to make them impossible to find. After leaving the restaurant, they hadn't dared to go to either of their apartments to avoid being seen. They had taken a ride share across town and had used their bank cards to take out as much money as they could out of their bank accounts. Then they had taken three more ride shares before stopping at a mall. They had bought a single burner phone and then watched a movie. They had used cash to pay for everything to avoid being tracked by their bank card transactions. Taking three additional ride shares, they had finally found this uncharacteristically drab motel and had paid for their room with cash.

Melanie grinned mischievously as she walked to the queen-size bed in the cramped motel room and patted the olive-green, threadbare bedspread, "You really outdid yourself in finding this luxurious honeymoon suite for our first night together as a married couple."

Trevor looked around the room. It was a sorry sight, to say the least. The walls were painted in a pale yellow that screamed for a new coat of paint. Dust streaked the walls, and there were a few cobwebs in the corners. A chest of drawers sat at the foot of the bed. Its pale violet laminate finish clashed so heavily with the olive-green bedspread that Trevor had to look away. A small LCD TV stood on the chest of drawers. A rickety table and two squeaky wooden chairs rounded out the room's furniture.

"Well, it could be worse," Trevor said. "We could still be in the dungeon in San Felix with our friends Austin and Rick."

"Oh, I think I'd rather live in a sewer and eat rats and bugs three meals a day than hang out with them." Melanie approached Trevor and touched him lightly on the arm. "I can't begin to express how grateful I am that you came for me. You were so brave."

Trevor didn't need any further coaxing as he tenderly took Melanie in his arms. She melted against his chest and shoulder. They held each other tightly, basking in the warmth of the moment.

Trevor said softly, "I'm just glad that I found you and that you were still alive." As he finished speaking, he relaxed his arms a little and let them fall to the small of Melanie's back. Melanie settled back against his arms, still keeping her arms around his neck. Smiling as she looked up at his face, she said, "Whew, you really take my breath away."

Without a word, Trevor leaned forward and kissed her lightly on the lips. She took his head in her hands and pulled him closer. She kissed him back with increasing ardor while he matched her every move with increasing passion. Finally, feeling weak in the knees from the heat of the moment, Trevor gently guided their entwined bodies to the side of the bed. They sank slowly to a seated position while remaining momentarily attached at the lips. When their lips finally separated, Melanie rested her head on Trevor's shoulder as he continued to hold her close in his arms.

"Not only do you take my breath away, but you also make me feel like I'm going to pass out," she said dreamily.

With his heart swelling with almost overwhelming attraction and admiration for the dear person he held in his arms, Trevor couldn't keep himself from expressing how he felt. "Melanie?" he began.

"Yes?"

"I really…" He paused.

Melanie looked up at Trevor's eyes and smiled, totally disarming him. "You really what?"

"I really love you."

"I love you, too!" They embraced again.

Suddenly, without warning, Melanie yawned, surprising both of them. The passion that had been building between them was immediately dampened.

"I'm so sorry. I didn't realize that you were so tired."

"I guess I am more tired than I thought."

"You didn't get much sleep last night, and I'm sure that constant worry about Rick and his henchmen has only increased your fatigue." Trevor suddenly covered his own mouth to stifle a yawn and then chuckled. "I guess I'm feeling pretty worn out, too."

"So," Melanie asked casually, "Do we share the bed?"

Without question, there was nothing in the world that Trevor wanted more right now than to hold Melanie close in bed for the rest of the night. However, the practiced restraint that had kept him celibate for the years since his wife's death won out instead. "Melanie, that was not what I was thinking when I suggested we find an obscure motel room to hide out in."

"Sure, you weren't." Melanie smiled.

Trevor couldn't help but try to defend himself further. "Honest. How was I to know that they would only have one room and that it would have only one bed?"

Melanie just kept on smiling without saying a word.

"Okay. Fine. I am thoroughly and completely attracted to you. It's true. However, in my opinion, it's just not the right time for us to…"

"It's alright, Trevor," Melanie said. "I was just asking if you had a plan for our sleeping arrangement and nothing more." As she finished, she reached out and touched Trevor affectionately on the nose with her index finger.

"Aren't you the funny one," Trevor said as he gave her a quick tickle on her exposed armpit.

They both laughed and then gave each other a quick kiss.

"Let's not start that again, or you'll never get any sleep," Trevor said. "I'll sleep on the floor and you can sleep on the bed."

"That's not fair for you. Why don't you sleep on top of the bed-spread with the spare blanket from the closet on one side of the bed, and I'll sleep under the bedspread on the other? We need a good night's sleep so that we're awake and alert tomorrow when we try to get on our way without Rick and his men finding us."

"Are you sure that you can control yourself in bed with such a handsome guy?"

"You nut." Melanie giggled like a schoolgirl.

They brushed their teeth with the rudimentary toiletries that had been provided by the motel and then Melanie hopped into one side of the bed. She promptly popped the blanket over her head and began wiggling around underneath it.

"What kind of bizarre bedtime ritual is this?" Trevor asked.

"Did you think I was going to sleep in my clothes? I'd never get to sleep." Moments later, her head reappeared, followed by her left arm that was holding her pants, shirt, and bra. "Could you put these on the table for me?"

"Things are getting pretty personal here," Trevor joked as he looked down at the still-warm bra in his hands. He moved to the table and hung her clothing over the back of one of the chairs.

After a moment of indecision, he quickly and strategically hid the bra under her shirt. It took all of his strength to stop himself from becoming overly focused on the fact that the woman that he found more attractive than any other was lying mostly unclothed in a bed just a few feet away. Handling her clothing had made his resolve of self-control a little more difficult.

Melanie smiled and added, "Well, at least I kept my panties on."

Trevor smiled and shook his head as he turned back to her. "Too much information."

As Trevor moved to the other side of the bed, Melanie asked casually, "Can I borrow your T-shirt?"

"Sure," he answered. But after thinking about her unusual request for a minute, he asked, "How did you know that I was even going to get undressed? Guys aren't all that adverse to sleeping in their clothes, you know."

"Well, I do feel kind of naked under here. I've always slept in a night shirt."

Trevor unbuttoned his shirt and hung it next to Melanie's on the chair. He stared at the articles of clothing for a moment, realizing how natural it felt to see them hanging together. It reaffirmed just how comfortable he felt with Melanie. He tucked that thought away for future consideration.

Turning back to Melanie, he pulled his T-shirt over his head while simultaneously sucking in his belly to make it look smaller. He hoped that she wouldn't think he looked fat.

"Oh baby! What a handsome chest," Melanie exclaimed mischievously.

Trevor dropped his arms in embarrassment and blushed. He handed his T-shirt to Melanie, not daring to take a breath, since it would cause his tummy to stick out. He quickly got under the spare blanket and turned to find that Melanie was completely under the blanket again, donning his T-shirt. She popped her head out a moment later and smiled mischievously. She looked so beautiful that

Trevor couldn't help but steal a kiss. Of course, that one kiss felt so good that he closed his eyes and moved in for another.

"That's enough for you. If you keep this up, I don't know if I'll be able to trust myself, either."

"Okay," Trevor said with a sigh of resignation. "I'll be good."

They both giggled.

"Melanie, we forgot. You need to call your parents. They are sick with worry about you."

"Oh, my gosh! I can't believe I didn't even think of them. See what you do to me."

Trevor reached for the burner phone on the tiny nightstand on his side of the bed and passed it to Melanie.

Melanie dialed her parents. She sat up in anticipation and waited for an answer. Trevor watched in pleasure as her face lit up as her mom came on the line. He got tears in his eyes as Melanie broke down and cried as she told her mother first that she was okay and then what had happened. Seeing Melanie sitting there, looking so cute in his T-shirt and so animated as she talked to her mom, he couldn't believe that there so much that was wonderful about Melanie.

CHAPTER 68

AUSTIN SURFACED, PULLED the regulator out of his mouth and said, "That was too easy. If it's always going to be this easy, then we need to hurry up and hit more cities."

"All in due time, my friend," Rick said. "It did take longer to produce enough R-648 to treat a big city like LA. The next cities won't be as big."

As Rick had been speaking, Austin had unlatched the belt on the diving vest that he was wearing and had slipped the vest and attached air tank off his shoulders. Rick grabbed the tank by its regulator, lifted it out of the flocculation tank, and then set it safely back from the edge. Austin heaved himself onto the side of the tank and took off his mask and flippers. Shannon, trying to be helpful, took his mask and flippers and set them by the vest and air tank. There hadn't been much for her to do while Austin and Rick had been working in tandem to place the R-648 dispensers in the flocculation tanks at the Los Angeles Aqueduct Filtration Plant, and she was feeling very much like a fifth wheel. She had brought along a bag of chocolate chip cookies to share with Rick and Austin, but in her boredom had ended up eating most of the bag of cookies herself.

Austin stood and turned to Shannon and Rick, water dripping

off his wet suit. As he removed the hood of the wet suit, he said, "Now all we have to do is wait until tomorrow night, and the people of Los Angeles will start having the worst headaches of their lives."

Shannon stuffed the last chocolate chip cookie in her mouth, finished chewing, and then asked, "How do you know that there is enough of the R-648 in your dispensing devices to treat all of the people in the Los Angeles area?"

"That's a good question," Rick answered. "I had my lab guys do the math for me. The eleven pounds of R-648 that is in each of the ten dispensers will be enough to treat everyone in the LA area that drinks water or drinks anything made with water. We have set the dispensers to start pumping out the R-648 at 5:00 a.m. instead of starting immediately. We did that because it takes about twelve hours for the water to get from here to the end users. We want the water with R-648 to be getting to people's houses at about the time they get home to cook dinner."

Austin added, "We're quite sure that our plan will work. We did the same thing in Vegas, and sales of Waitnomor have gone through the roof."

"We've got to get going," Rick said as he checked his watch. "The night shift is going to be waking up soon from their roofie-induced nap, and we need to be as far from here as possible."

Rick's cell phone began ringing softly. Rick grabbed it, silenced its ring, and then answered it. Austin grabbed his tank, vest, and gear and headed for their truck that was parked at the opposite end of the flocculation tanks.

Since Rick was occupied, Shannon decided to make herself useful. Using the control for the overhead crane, she raised the now-empty rack that had held the R-648 dispensers and moved it along the crane's overhead track toward the truck. She got the rack to a position just over the bed of the truck and then stopped it, not wanting to risk setting it down incorrectly on the truck.

As she stood waiting for Austin to put his gear in the truck, Rick walked up to her and said, "We found them. Melanie just called her mother from a hotel in Phoenix, and one of my men traced the call back from her mother's house to the hotel."

"Did I hear you say you found them?" Austin asked as he came up the stairs leading from the road where their truck was parked on the platform. Seeing the look of relief on Rick's face was all the confirmation he needed. With chilling malevolence in his voice, he said, "I want to personally take them out. This time there won't be any chance that they will slip away. "

CHAPTER 68

TREVOR AWOKE WITH a start but needed only a moment to get oriented to where he was. Sunlight was streaming into the room through a gap in the curtains, giving him more than enough light to discover that Melanie was still peacefully asleep on her side of the bed. The morning light gently lit her beautiful and peaceful face. He wondered how long she had talked to her mother. It could have been hours. Not wanting to wake her, but feeling very much awake himself, he slipped out of bed, pulled on his shirt, and grabbed the room key. Hoping to find a vending machine for a diet soda, he quietly padded over to the door of the room, opened it, and stepped out onto the balcony that fronted the motel rooms on the second floor.

He headed for the stairs that led from the balcony down to the office. The sky was clear and pale blue. The cool of the desert morning was invigorating. As he reached the end of the balcony and was about to turn to head down the stairs, movement in the parking lot caught his eye. He watched for a moment until he realized that it was just some guy walking toward the office. Trevor thought nothing more of it until the man turned to open the door of the office, giving Trevor a brief glimpse of his profile. Trevor froze. It was Austin!

Immediately recognizing that there was absolutely no time to lose, Trevor sprang into action. As soon as Austin was out of sight in the office, he tore back to the room, quietly opened the door, and then sprang to Melanie's side as he almost hysterically exclaimed, "Get up now! Austin's outside, and he'll be here any second."

Melanie woke with a start and sat bolt upright in bed. "What?"

Trevor grabbing her by the shoulder and propelling her to her feet. With no time for further questions, he headed for his side of the bed to get his shoes. "Grab your shoes and follow me." Melanie now seemed to be awake, and her eyes were wide with fear. Trevor sprinted back around the bed, grabbed her shoes, and then caught her by the arm on the way to the door as he urged, "There's no time to get dressed. I've got your shoes. Grab your pants, and let's go."

Melanie snatched her pants off the chair and then ran out the door behind Trevor. They hurried down the other side of balcony away from the office in their bare feet, making almost no sound as they ran. Melanie tried to hold Trevor's T-shirt down over her underwear as she ran, but quickly gave up as she realized that it was just too short to keep her covered. Like it or not, modesty was the last thing that she needed to worry about at this point.

Trevor looked back down the balcony to be sure the coast was clear and then turned and flew down the stairs with Melanie close behind. Reaching the bottom of the stairs, he signaled for her to stop, and then he carefully peered around the edge of the corner that led to the walkway in front of the first-floor rooms. There was no sign of Austin. Pulling back from the corner, he whispered, "Hurry and put on your shoes." Trevor did the same as he continued, "I can't see him, but that doesn't mean much with these guys. We need to get out of here fast."

Trevor turned to see if she were ready when suddenly he heard footsteps running down the second-story balcony toward them. They simultaneously turned and sprinted around the side of the motel and down a street that ran just next to the motel. Trevor led Melanie by just one stride as they approached an alley that ran behind the back fence of the motel. He turned into the alley with Melanie close behind. Trevor was amazed at her speed and was elated that she wasn't going to slow them down.

The alley was unpaved, but its tightly packed gravel gave them a good running surface. They made good time in spite of having to dodge the occasional garbage can and pile of debris that belonged to the houses that lay beyond the alley. Most of the owners kept their portion of the alley behind their houses clean and the weeds cleared.

Trevor chanced a look back and was terrified to see Austin was just fifty yards behind them. To make matters worse, he turned around too late to keep from tripping on the end of an exhaust pipe of an old muffler that was partially hidden in the weeds behind one of the houses. Teetering forward severely, he tried to catch himself for the next five steps and would have landed face-first on the ground if it hadn't been for Melanie's steadying hand.

"Follow me," she said in-between gasps for air. Spying a nearby wooden gate that was ajar that led into the back yard of one of the houses, she ran to it and flung it open. A woman in her fifties was on the third rung of a ladder, picking oranges from a tree that stood just to the side of the wooden gate. Melanie narrowly missed running into the ladder and only muttered, "Sorry," as she sped past the startled woman. Trevor followed, but he paused momentarily to slam the gate shut. As he turned to follow Melanie, he ran right into the ladder, sending the woman tumbling to the ground with a high-pitched scream and scattering oranges all over the ground. She sat up quickly as Trevor lurched to his feet and screamed at Trevor, "Get out of my yard. You almost killed me."

"Sorry," Trevor gasped, but then he didn't wait around to hear the rest of her diatribe. Melanie had already crossed the well-manicured backyard and was just scrambling over the fence that led to the front yard, although she dropped her pants as she did so. There was no time to grab them for her. Trevor hit the same fence running and was over it in moments, but not before he heard a crash as the back gate flung open from the force of the impact from Austin's body. Trevor rushed to the street in front of the house. He quickly spotted Melanie about thirty yards away on his right. She was sprinting down the middle of the street. He hoped that she had a plan, or Austin was going to pick them both off with a few shots from his revolver. The screams from the woman that he knocked off the ladder faded as he turned down the street and followed Melanie. Seconds later, he heard Austin hit the same fence that he had just scaled. That meant that he wasn't more than thirty yards behind. The impact with the ladder had really cost him some of his lead on Austin, and if Melanie didn't come up with something soon, maybe it would cost him his life.

CHAPTER 69

DESPERATE TO FIND somewhere to hide from their pursuer, Melanie scanned the street in front of her. A man to her right was checking his mailbox. *He has probably left his front door open.* Without hesitating, she fixed herself on the front door of the man's house, praying that Trevor would follow her and that the door would be open.

To her relief, the front door was only partially closed, and she pushed past it with ease. She didn't expect the front room to be filled with five children snuggled in a blanket and watching morning cartoons. With ten saucer-sized eyes fixed on her, she slowed to a stop. *What is going to happen to these kids?* She wished with all her might that she hadn't chosen this house and put these kids in danger. But what other choice had she had? Frantically looking around the room for a way to block the door once Trevor came in, she yelled, "Lie down, and cover your heads with your blankets." Four of the five heads disappeared. She spied a cabinet beyond the other side of the door and was just passing the open door when Trevor burst in.

Melanie slammed the door shut and locked it. She sprang to the cabinet, and with adrenaline-accentuated strength, she pushed it partway to the door. Instantly, Trevor joined her, and they tipped it over in front of the door just as Austin smashed into the door with his body and splintered the doorjamb. The door opened only two inches and then struck the fallen cabinet. Melanie grabbed Trevor and flung them both to the floor. Austin unleashed a salvo of shots through the door, heralded by moderately loud sounds of a gun firing and by the bullets tearing through the door and into the opposite wall above their heads. Glancing at the couch, Melanie was grateful to see the oldest and last remaining child abruptly pull his blanket over his head in terror as the shooting began. Maybe now Austin wouldn't see the kids as he ran through the house after Trevor and her.

"My kids are in there. Don't shoot." they heard a man yell hysterically from beyond the door. Not waiting a second longer to see if Austin would get through the door, Melanie tore through the house at a crouch with Trevor right behind her and out the back door, gratefully not running into any other family members. They ran hard across the back lawn and around a swimming pool to get to the back gate. Finding themselves in another alley and desperate to lose Austin, they vaulted a nearby three-foot, chain-link fence into the backyard of another house on the opposite side of the alley. Dodging numerous orange trees loaded with fruit as they ran, they headed for the carport, only to run into a barking and snapping Terrier. The sound of a gate banging open behind them, barely audible above the yapping of the dog, warned them that Austin was still close behind. Ignoring the small dog, they ran through the home's open carport and into the street in front of the house. They slowed as they frantically looked around for options. A car was idling in a driveway two doors down the street. Melanie couldn't believe their luck.

"Follow me," Trevor said as he sprinted to the driver's door. Mercifully, the door was unlocked, and Trevor hopped into the car. Melanie jumped into the passenger seat next to him a split second later. Trevor rammed the car into reverse and hit the gas. The car roared backwards into the street. Just as the car came to a stop in the middle of the road, Austin came running out of the carport of the same house two doors down the street that they had come from. Simultaneously, the presumed owner of the car they were stealing came running out of his carport directly toward them and he didn't look happy. Trevor hit the gas, popped the clutch, and the car sped forward with a squeal of tires.

"Get down," Trevor yelled. Melanie and Trevor hunched down just as she heard five clinking sounds from the windshield. Keeping his head down and the pedal to the metal, Trevor roared down the road and out of Austin's range. They both sat up and were greeted by five holes in the windshield, each surrounded by a halo of fractures in the safety glass. They looked at each other in silence. Melanie was amazed that they were still alive. One thought pervaded her mind: *When is this going to end?*

CHAPTER 70

"YOU'RE STILL SHAKING," Trevor consoled Melanie. He held her in his arms in the men's bathroom of the big-box department store, trying to help her to get warmed up and calmed down.

"What do you expect after what we just went through? I can't believe that Austin is still alive after we left him in the burning warehouse in San Felix. I figured that if the rampaging townspeople hadn't killed him, that the fire and explosions that followed would have. And how did Austin find us at the hotel? What's to keep him from finding us here? These guys are so good that I expect them to barge through that door at any second and fill us full of holes."

Trevor reached down and took her by her cold and still-shaking hands. Her eyes were full of fear and threatening to overflow with tears. She had been so brave through all of this. He didn't know how much more she could take. "I'm sure they can't find us here," he said without being absolutely sure that what he was saying was true.

They had dumped the stolen car a mile away from their motel in a parking lot near the downtown area. Trying to act as casually as they could with Melanie wearing only Trevor's T-shirt and her panties, they had hiked to the nearest large hotel that they could find and had caught a cab. By that time, Melanie was shivering, due to her sweat-dampened and skimpy clothing. They had switched cabs two more times and had been careful to pay with cash each time. Desperately needing to find clothing for Melanie, they had then requested to be dropped off at a big-box department store on the west side of Phoenix. The store had just opened and was almost deserted. Melanie had grabbed a pair of sweatpants, a matching warm top and a bra, while Trevor had found her a brush. Not willing to be alone in the women's restroom, she had convinced Trevor to stand guard over an empty restroom for employees that they had discovered in the back of the store. After changing in one of the stalls, she had rushed to Trevor's arms for comfort and warmth.

"The only thing we did was call my mother," Melanie said. "That has got to be the way found us."

"Then that's how they found us. I can't believe how stupid I was for letting you use the phone to call your mother," Trevor said as he pulled the burner cellphone out of his pants pocket. He popped the phone open, removed the battery and then chucked them in a nearby trash can. Melanie had trusted him to keep them safe, and he had failed her miserably. "Well, at least we know that we can't call anyone we know, or they'll trace our calls. Let's get another burner phone before we leave the store. We'll be more careful in the future."

"How can we get away from these guys?" Melanie said. "They are in control of the illegal drug market here, and they probably have hundreds of dealers and thousands of users under their thumb. I feel like anywhere we go, we'll run into one of their people, and then they'll try to kill us again. It all seems so hopeless. I don't even want to leave this restroom."

"There is someone that can help us. Max. We need to try to get him on the phone again." With more enthusiasm in his voice, he let go of Melanie's slightly warmed-up hands and added, "He's the private investigator that helped me find you in San Felix. He'll know what to do."

Once they were outside the store and walking away from the front door, Trevor dialed Max's business phone number. An answering machine came on, and Max's recorded voice announced that the office was closed until 10:00 a.m. Trevor hung up. Fighting back concern that his good idea was going to fail, Trevor tried Max's cell number. Max didn't answer. Trevor left a plea for help on the voice mail and told Max to call them on the number on the caller ID.

"What are we going to do?" he exclaimed as he slumped against the outside wall of the store.

"We don't want to go to the bus station, train station, or airport. Someone will spot us."

Trevor sighed. "Well, the only thing I can think of is to either wait for Max to get to his office or go to Max's house and see if he's home but just not answering the phone. Maybe his cell phone is on silent."

Not able to come up with a better plan and too afraid to wait out in the open for fear that one of Austin and Rick's henchmen might spot them, Trevor called for a ride service. Thirty minutes later, they exited the car in front of Max's home in Paradise Valley. The neighborhood was quiet and almost completely devoid of people. With every house having desert landscaping that required virtually no maintenance, there was no reason for the inhabitants to be outside. Any kids that were awake would still be inside watching cartoons.

Max's house was no exception and showed no external sign of life. A knock at the door went unanswered. Desperately focused on finding Max as an answer to their predicament, Trevor looked around to be sure that no one was watching and then unlatched the gate that led to the backyard. They quickly stepped inside and closed the gate.

The backyard was as quiet as the front. A pool sporting an insulating cover was in the middle of the back yard. Instead of a lawn, sand covered the back yard and was interrupted asymmetrically with large, oddly-shaped reddish rocks interspersed with strategically-placed beds of desert plants and cacti. A covered hot tub was on a wooden deck to the side of the back door.

Trevor led Melanie to the back door where he first rang the doorbell and then knocked again. Once again, there was no answer. Thoroughly defeated, Trevor sat down on edge of the small porch and let out a sigh. "This isn't getting us anywhere. I guess we could knock on a few neighbor's doors to see if they know where Max has gone to."

Melanie sat next to Trevor. Gazing at Max's tranquil backyard, she said, "It's so nice and peaceful here. No one knows that we're here. Let's just stay here for a while. Maybe Max will come home in the next little bit, and everything will be fine."

"We can't stay here forever." Trevor stood and stretched. "Besides, I have this feeling that Max isn't going to be coming back very—" The last word ended in a higher pitch as Trevor had leaned against the back door and had been shocked that the door abruptly pushed open under his weight. Totally off balance, Trevor fell heavily onto the floor just past the door. The door swung into the room and banged loudly against a wall.

"Trevor. Are you okay?" Melanie jumped up and rushed to Trevor as he pushed himself to a sitting position. However, seeing that he wasn't badly hurt, she stopped suddenly at the doorstep.

"I'm fine. It's odd that Max didn't push the door all the way shut and didn't lock it when he left." Standing, Trevor brushed some dust off his clothes that he'd gathered from the floor during his fall. Trevor turned and surveyed the interior of the house. He had fallen into the kitchen.

"Trevor, we shouldn't go in. What if someone sees us and calls the police?"

Trevor was surprised that Melanie would allow such a minor thing to bother her at a time like this and after all they had been through. "Melanie, it's not like we're going to steal anything. Besides,

Max is a friend, and I owe it to him to check on him to make sure everything is okay."

The look on Melanie's face made it plain that she wasn't convinced. "It doesn't seem right to go into someone's house when they aren't home."

"We are in a desperate situation here, and we seriously need help to stay alive. I'm going to go and see if I can find anything that will help me reach Max. You're welcome to wait here and keep an eye out for trouble if you want."

"There's no way I'm going to wait outside alone. I'm coming with you." Melanie crossed the threshold into the kitchen.

Trevor closed and locked the door behind Melanie and then turned back to the kitchen. It was a mess. Dirty dishes were strewn across the kitchen counter, and the sink was full. The air was tainted with the faint, but unmistakable, odor of rotting food. Bowls and plates still containing the residue of past meals sat on the kitchen table, their contents in various stages of desiccation. The floor hadn't been swept in weeks. "Oh my," Trevor exclaimed. Max obviously wasn't a tidy person.

Melanie wrinkled up her nose at the sight of the disastrous mess. "I take it that your friend lives alone?"

"I'm pretty sure that he does. His wife left him a few years ago."

"Maybe she got tired of cleaning up after him."

Seeing nothing in the kitchen that would help them locate Max, Trevor said, "Let's check out the rest of the house. He's got to have an office here somewhere."

They moved into a hall that led to the front of the house. The first door on the right led to a small office. Loose papers, books, magazines, and maps lay in unruly piles strewn across any and all available surfaces, including the floor. Layers of dust of varying thickness coated most of the items in the room. At least a dozen empty microwave popcorn bags sporting yellow, translucent, oily patches overflowed a garbage can at the side of the desk, explaining the faint smell of rancid oil and burnt popcorn that assailed their noses. Bookshelves lining the walls of the office were crammed full of additional stacks of paper and books, without any obvious effort at organization. Food-stained, mostly-empty, paper bowls, plates, and cups encircled the small, dust-free area in the center of the desk. "Whew," Trevor said. "I'd say that Max really needs a housekeeper."

"How can he live this way?"

Trevor approached the desk, not sure that he'd be able to find anything helpful in all the clutter. He shuffled around a few dust-free sheets of paper, hoping that they might contain some useful information. All he found were bills. Upon shifting one of the bills aside, his eyes were immediately attracted to the flashing red light of an answering machine that had been hidden under the clutter. Without a second thought, Trevor reached out to punch the button marked "New Messages."

"Trevor. Those are his personal messages. You shouldn't be listening to them."

"It won't hurt anything."

The machine announced a message from that morning and then played back Trevor's call. The next message was announced as having been left two days previously at 11:14 p.m. Max's voice boomed out of the machine's speaker, surprising them both. "This message is for Trevor Davis, just in case you came to my house to try to find me. I left this same message on your cell phone when you didn't answer. Trevor, since you are listening to this message, then I'm a goner. No, don't go crying for me. I knew that this was a dangerous profession when I got into it. Besides, since I'm dead, at least I won't be feeling any pain. Just remember me every once in a while. That's all that I ask." Trevor and Melanie locked eyes initially in disbelief and then their eyes widened in concern as they simultaneously perceived the enormity of what Max's message portended.

Max's voice continued, "Trevor, old boy, our snooping has stirred up something bigger than we ever imagined. The guys that kidnapped your friend Melanie are just a small part of one of the biggest crime rings in the Southwestern United States. I must have asked too many questions of the wrong people because now their hit men are after me. I'm hiding out, but I don't know if I'm smart enough to elude these thugs. If you get this message and if they're after you, call a friend of mine, Von Black." Max stated the phone number twice. "Tell him that I sent you and tell him the code phrase, 'Armageddon waits for no one.' That will get his attention. If you have any chance of escaping these goons, it will be with Von. Good luck. Oh no!" Max's voice suddenly increased in pitch and intensity. "They found me. How did…" There was a pause, and then Max continued in an angry whisper, "It's my stupid cell phone. I'm a PI. I'm supposed to be smarter than this. Don't use your cell phone." A click signaled the end of the call. Trevor and Melanie stood in shocked silence. The answering machine began playing the next message.

Trevor pushed the stop button on the machine and then said, "That's why we can't find him. They got him."

"You can't be sure. He could still be hiding somewhere."

"That's possible. However, it's not a particularly good sign that we found his message two days after he left it. I'm sure he planned on returning here before now and erasing it."

"He's probably with his friend, Von. We really should call this Von guy right now. We need help."

Trevor nodded. He replayed Max's message so that he could write down the phone number. Pulling out the prepaid phone, he dialed the number and waited for an answer.

Trevor hadn't given it much thought when Von had hurriedly announced that he'd pick them up in a black military vehicle at the end of their phone call. Now that the monstrous vehicle had turned the corner and was bearing down on them, he was in awe at its size. The sound of the tires on the road increased in pitch as the driver accelerated toward them. It appeared that the ungainly vehicle would pass them by in a cloud of dust when suddenly it came to a rapid stop directly in front of where Trevor stood with Melanie at the side of the road. The heavily-tinted glass made the driver difficult to see and completely shrouded the passenger compartment, creating an air of mystery.

Suddenly, Trevor was struck with the thought that the vehicle could just as well be full of Rick and Austin's thugs, hiding in the back behind the tinted glass. He barely suppressed an almost undeniable urge to run. For all Trevor knew, Rick could have bugged Max's home and then, upon learning they were there, sent his people to gun them down.

The driver's window suddenly and soundlessly glided down into the door. With his heart beating wildly, Trevor stepped in front of Melanie. He tried to quell his raging anxiety by telling himself that everything was okay and that it was too late to run, even if his worst fears were confirmed. He focused on protecting Melanie, no matter the cost.

The figure behind the wheel turned toward them, and the man's mirrored sunglasses reflected back two tiny images of Trevor standing in front of Melanie. Unable to see the man's eyes, Trevor was clueless as to whether the person was friend or foe. Even worse, the man wasn't smiling. With his neck muscles as tense as steel cables, Trevor cursed himself that he had ever agreed to wait to be picked up outside Max's house. They were sitting ducks.

The man reached up and snatched the shades away from his eyes. A wry grin lit up his face. "Are you going to stand there all day, or are you going to get in?"

Reluctant to trust anyone completely, but clearly relieved by the appearance of the man's friendly smile, Trevor relaxed a little. His mouth dry, he stammered, "Who are you?"

"Von, at your service," the man said, still grinning. "Who'd you think I was?"

"I was almost sure that you were someone I really didn't want to see again," Trevor replied. *How do I know for certain that this guy really is Von?* "Reassure me that you are Von by answering a question about Max that only Von would know. What nickname did Max's ex-wife call him?"

"Maxibear," the man replied without a moment's hesitation. His brown eyes remained calmly fixed on Trevor as he waited for Trevor to make up his mind.

The man's correct answer was good enough for Trevor. Besides, he had gone too long feeling his way blindly through this whole thing. He was more than ready to turn the mess that they were in over to an expert. He turned to Melanie to see if she were okay with the situation. An affirmative shake of her head was all the reassurance that he needed. He quickly stepped around the vehicle, climbed up the rungs to the passenger door, and opened it. The front of the vehicle only had two captain chairs and the middle console was large enough that he couldn't get around it to the rear seat. There wasn't a rear passenger door.

"You'll have to let your lady friend in from the back," Von said from the driver's seat. "These Paramount Marauders aren't very family friendly."

Trevor climbed back down to the ground, walked to the rear of the Marauder and opened the back door. He stood aside as Melanie climbed up and in. She moved forward to sit in another captain's chair behind the front passenger seat. Trevor closed the back door, made his way back to the front passenger seat, and shut the door.

"It's good to meet you folks," Von said warmly as he pulled away from Max's house. "I have to admit that you guys gave me a bit of a surprise when you gave me that code phrase over the phone. I'm even more surprised that Max isn't with you. Where is he?"

"We don't know where he is," Trevor answered truthfully. "We thought that maybe you'd know."

"I don't have any idea where he is and, frankly, that worries me.

Very few people know that code phrase that you gave me. The few people that do know it have been told that it's only to be used in case of a..." Max hesitated momentarily. "... major emergency. I have to assume that Max told you the code because something serious is about to happen. However, there hasn't been even a whisper from any of my contacts about any major problems brewing in this area. There hasn't been any mention of a problem in the news. To tell the truth, I'm a little confused about why I'm even here, and I'm curious as all get out to hear what your important problem is."

"It's hard to know where to begin," Trevor said. He paused, not exactly sure of how much to tell the man.

"I know that we're being evasive," Melanie said. "It's just that we're so shell-shocked from the trauma of the last few months that it's hard for us to trust anyone." She glanced at Trevor, and after getting a nod of approval, she continued, "Just what is it that you do and how are you going to help us?"

"Okay," Von replied resignedly as he took his hands off the wheel for a moment and raised them in a mock plea to heaven. "I guess I'm going to have to be the one that spills the beans first." As they had been talking, Von had directed the vehicle onto the freeway and was traveling south toward downtown Phoenix. "I'm the leader of a secret paramilitary group. My colleagues and I feel strongly that the United States government isn't capable of adequately protecting its citizens from every single terrorist attack. We are prepared to intercept and terminate terrorist attacks if and when we perceive the U.S. government is failing to do so. Unlike other militias in this country, and there are many, we are not anti-government, anti-establishment, or prejudiced against any race or ethnicity. Our sole purpose is to protect American citizens when they are threatened on our soil. Most of the militias in the U.S. are loosely-organized bands of would-be vigilantes. Our group, on the other hand, is highly organized and outfitted with the latest in military technology, thanks to the generous contributions of a number of concerned citizens that are both in and outside of our group.

"Now, it's your turn." Max's voice suddenly lost just enough of its congeniality that it was clear to his passengers that he was now all business. "I'm certain that you are good people and that your cause is just. However, I do need to know exactly what the problem is, right now, before I reveal any more about my organization and before we go any further." To emphasize just how serious he was, Von pulled to the side of the freeway, turned off the Marauder's motor, and turned to face Melanie and Trevor. The smile was gone.

"Okay," Trevor said. "I'm Trevor Davis and my friend is Melanie Baker." Trevor carefully summarized Rick's plan to poison Los Angeles' drinking water with R-648.

After Trevor finished, Von reached over to a keyboard in the center console and punched a button. The middle of three flat screen TVs sprang to life, displaying a menu system. As Von's fingers danced through various screens of information, he said softly to himself, "I always told Max that he shouldn't work alone." After just a few moments, he achieved his desired result, blanked the screen, started the engine, and then hit the gas pedal. The massive vehicle's tires spun a little in the gravel on the side of the freeway as he accelerated quickly and then joined the flow of traffic.

"I'm beginning to get the picture," Von said, still without a hint of his initial joviality in his voice. "From what you have told me, we have little time to lose. I'm going to take you to our base of operations. The rest of my group will be joining us there shortly. On the way, I want you to start over at the beginning and tell me everything. Don't leave anything out, because any detail, no matter how trivial it may seem, could be the key to stopping these guys."

"It's amazing to see how organized their group is," Trevor said to Melanie. Moments after Von had finished briefing the members of his group on their plans to try to stop Rick and Austin from poisoning Los Angeles, the basement floor of the building that they had been meeting in had turned into a hive of activity. All around the room, automatic steel doors had rolled into the ceiling, revealing bank after bank of military weapons neatly mounted on wall displays.

Without much fanfare, each member of the group had got up from their chairs at the end of the briefing, quickly visited their assigned sections, and picked out the items that they would need for the mission. Twenty minutes later, they were back in Von's Marauder and rolled out of the secure parking garage. Two of Von's men, Tyler and Hank, had joined them in their vehicle. Tyler sat in the front with Von, and Hank joined Trevor and Melanie in the back. Three additional Marauders, each carrying five men and their equipment, left the base close behind them.

"Von, you weren't kidding when you said that you were prepared for anything," Trevor said with admiration.

"You only saw part of it," Von said as he looked at Tyler in the front passenger seat and grinned knowingly. "With the number of men in the opposing group being relatively small and since they are armed only with handheld weapons, we didn't need any of our tanks, armored personnel carriers, helicopters, and jump jets."

"You store those in that same building, too?" Melanie asked.

"No. Military toys that large are a little too hard to hide in a building like this in a populated area. We keep those hidden at a secret base," Von replied with his usual jovial smile. It was now clear to Trevor that the smile was a camouflage for a mind that was as sharp as a tack. Von had been a model of efficiency and organization at the planning session that had ensued as soon as they had arrived at the group's base of operations.

"How did you ever find a group of men that were so well trained?" Melanie asked.

Von looked at Tyler. "Why don't you tell them?"

"Most of us are founders of, or are high-ranking executives in, high-tech companies," said Tyler as he stopped fiddling with the computer in front of him. "Each of us has had military experience and quite a few of our group saw action in the Gulf wars. After serving Uncle Sam, most of us used the GI Bill to obtain degrees in engineering, electrical engineering, and computer science. We then set up companies, or joined companies, that specialize in designing and manufacturing high-tech military equipment. It doesn't take long in the high-tech military equipment industry to realize that the government only wants what it thinks it wants, even if that doesn't represent the best that is available. Our mutual concern that our enemies would soon have better technology than the United States military brought us together. Our collective companies make most of the equipment that you've seen. Knowing that, you can understand that assembling the equipment at our base was as simple picking up items from off of shelves at our warehouses. To avoid jeopardizing national security and to avoid being arrested for the same, we are very careful to be sure that the equipment that we use employs technology that is not currently in use by the U.S. military."

"But I thought that it was illegal for private citizens to own tanks and explosives," Trevor said.

"You're right. It is illegal," Hank answered. "However, we do have permits for the design and testing of the equipment that we make."

Von took over. "When our group has seen action in the past years, it has involved mostly infiltration and neutralization of dangerous individuals or groups of three or four people at the most. We've used non-traceable weapons and have covered our tracks so well that no governmental agency has ever suspected that we were involved."

"Would I know about any of the incidents that you were involved in?" Trevor asked.

"It's best that we keep that information to ourselves," Von said.

"Otherwise, we'd have to kill you," Tyler quipped from the front seat.

"Ignore him. He still thinks that he's in Iraq," Von said with a smirk. "The reason that you haven't heard about any of the incidents that we've been involved in is because they were taken care of so quickly and definitively that there was no news to report."

"Wouldn't it be nice if that were the case with Austin and Rick," Melanie said.

"Communications has found something interesting, guys," Tyler said, staring at the computer screen in front of him.

"Put it on the center screen," Von said.

Seconds later, the center screen sprang to life, displaying the newsroom of a Los Angeles television station. A blond female with the standard A-line haircut and a nothing-but-business tone of voice was anchoring a special news flash. "We've just received news that a pair of dangerous criminals has escaped from a prison in New Mexico and is heading towards Los Angeles. Reports indicate that a Trevor Davis and Melanie Baker were being held without bail at the county jail in Santa Fe, New Mexico." Melanie gasped as first Trevor's picture and then her picture appeared on the screen above the newscaster's head. The anchor continued, "The suspects were awaiting sentencing for multiple charges of sexual assault and murder connected to the rape and murder of nine young girls that have occurred in the Santa Fe area over last two years. The girls that the suspects are charged with assaulting and murdering range in age from twelve to fifteen years old. The police in Santa Fe allege that the couple lured the girls to their home with promises that they would find them high-paying modeling jobs and then help them to get emancipated from their parents. Once in the home, police allege that the couple bound, tortured, raped, and then murdered the girls. Their bodies were buried in the home's unfinished basement.

"Davis and Baker are to be considered armed and very dangerous. Any information that would help law-enforcement officials capture these two criminals should be reported immediately to the LAPD. Do not attempt to apprehend these individuals yourself."

The camera's view backed away from the anchor's head. A male anchor came into view on the right of the screen just as he began speaking, "I think that I can speak for myself as well as for any parent of a young woman. We'll all sleep better at night as soon as we know that this terrible duo has been captured and returned to jail where they belong."

Tyler punched a button on the keyboard, and the screen went blank. A silence filled the interior of the Marauder. Trevor and Melanie stared straight ahead, eyes focused on nothing.

"I guess that these people that we're up against—" Von said.

"They're lying," Melanie almost screamed in exasperation. "We didn't do any of those things." Tears welled up in her eyes.

"Melanie," Von said. "We know that you didn't murder anyone. The people that we're after are fairly sure that you're heading to Los Angeles to try to thwart their efforts to poison the residents of the area. Clearly, they have inside connections at this television station and probably at the police department. They're trying to neutralize any threat that you might be to them. After this news broadcast, they figure that you'll be too afraid to contact anyone with information about the city's tainted water supply. I can see that these guys are going to be a formidable foe."

CHAPTER 71

PULLING OFF INTERSTATE 10 just outside of Los Angeles in La Verne, California, Von took a right turn and pointed the Marauder north. He said, "We should be at Brackett Airfield in just a few minutes." He jabbed away at the nearest computer screen on the center console for a few seconds and then added with satisfaction, "The two-engine Cessna will be arriving at the airfield just about the time we get there."

Melanie said, "I just hope the LA police don't catch on to what we're doing and force us out of the sky before we even get started." She couldn't keep from feeling a little discouraged now that thousands of policemen, countless private citizens, and Rick's men were on the lookout for Trevor and her.

At least, she had the consolation of knowing that the back of the Marauder was stacked with boxes of fliers warning people of the consequences of drinking the city water in LA. Von's plan to try and save as many people as possible in LA from the R-648 was simple enough. His group had sent out messages on social media about not drinking the city water. Then, to reach all those that didn't use social media regularly, they were going to fly around in a small airplane and drop the fliers out the windows. The three Marauders had split up as soon as they had arrived in the LA area and gone to three copy shops each in order to get the one hundred thousand fliers copied in as little time as possible. Melanie just hoped that the people of LA would heed their warning and that the police or the Air National Guard, or something like it, wouldn't try to force their plane down.

The Marauder turned onto a road that passed by the end of a runway just as a two-engine Cessna with its engines purring passed over the Marauder and then touched down behind them. Moments later, they were parked at Bracket Field and were each carrying a box of ten-thousand fliers across the tarmac to the same Cessna that had flown over them seconds before. The plane's engines were still humming as the group reached the plane and began loading the cases of fliers into the rear. Back blast from the propellers blew their hair fiercely back from their faces and made speech near impossible. Just as they finished stowing their load of fliers, Von's men from the other Marauders arrived with the rest of the fliers.

Faster than Melanie had thought was possible, Trevor and she were securely buckled in the seats behind Keith, the plane's pilot, and the plane was taxing down the runway to the west. Melanie had been astounded and chagrined when Von had suddenly hopped out of the plane after making sure that Trevor and she were safely in their seats. He had only smiled and given them a big thumbs up in response to the concerned and quizzical looks on their faces. Unable to make themselves heard above the engines, all Melanie and Trevor could do was return the thumbs up signal as their erstwhile savior was left in their dust on the side of the taxiway. Once again, it was just the two of them, along with their pilot, against Rick and his seemingly invincible allies.

As the plane leveled off above the city, Keith asked, "Is everything okay?"

Trevor glanced at Melanie, shrugged and replied, "I guess so. I just wish that Von had given us a clue that he wasn't coming with us."

"Don't worry so much. I've got things covered here, and Von is only as far away as my radio headset." Keith paused. "We're burning daylight. Let's get those fliers out and start dropping them before someone shows up and tries to stop us."

Trevor grabbed a box of fliers that was just behind his seat. Opening it with Melanie's help, they each pulled out a handful of bright-red, half-page fliers with a skull and cross bones splashed across the top. Underneath the skull and cross bones was printed the warning "DON'T DRINK THE WATER" in bold block letters. Smaller print below the warning explained that the LA County water supply had been maliciously poisoned on December 24th with a chemical that wouldn't kill immediately, but it would cause serious damage to the central nervous system. The warning explained that the water in LA County would remain unsafe for days. It detailed that the first symptoms of being poisoned with this chemical would be a severe headache. The flier then explained that water bottled locally before Sunday, December 24th would be safe to drink, as well as water from northern California and other states. Last, the flier exhorted the reader to warn everyone they knew about this serious act of domestic bioterrorism.

Trevor looked at Melanie and asked, "Are you ready?"

"You bet I am," Melanie said. "I wouldn't be able to live with myself if I didn't do something to save people from the same thing that happened to me."

Melanie turned to her window and opened it. She was met by an immediate blast of air. The effect caused Melanie to startle and freeze, not sure how to pass the fliers out the window against the blowing air. She looked over at Trevor to see how he was faring. Trevor was folding twenty or thirty fliers in half and then pushing the fold successfully against the rushing air and out the window. He glanced over at Melanie and gave her a thumbs-up. She gave him a thumbs-up in return and then smiled.

She decided that without a doubt, she knew she loved Trevor. Nothing would make her happier than to live with him for the rest of her life. The joy of the moment was so intense that she wanted to immediately blurt it all out to him in a gush of words, and she opened his mouth to do so. But she closed her mouth again reluctantly as she realized that the noise caused by the open windows would drown out anything she said. Also, she couldn't let selfish desires win out over the greater need to get these fliers out to the people below. As she turned her attention back to the fliers held tightly between her legs, she suddenly thought of a way to tell him how she felt about him. It was something that she and her mom had done when she was young. Looking at Trevor again, she used her right hand to first touch her right eye, then her heart. and then she pointed at Trevor. The action instantly brought a look of confusion to Trevor's face. He mouthed the word, "What?" as he turned a free palm up quizzically. Melanie repeated the sequence again, sure that he would know what it meant. Instead, Trevor just smiled and shook his head. He didn't get it.

She smiled again, mouthed the word, "Sorry," and then grabbed the fliers between her legs and began shoving them out the window. She looked back at Trevor and saw that he was doing the same. The moment was gone, and the warm glow faded slowly from her body, but not completely.

Working as fast as they could, they continued shoving the fliers out the windows into the rushing air. Case after case of fliers were sent on their way, and with each passing minute, Melanie felt the satisfaction they were finally succeeding to a small degree in turning the tide against Rick and his nefarious plans.

"That takes care of Santa Monica," Keith announced.

They had been in the air for about a half an hour and Trevor and she been steadily shoving fliers out the windows over the suburbs of Covina, Pasadena, Glendale, Burbank, Hollywood and Santa Monica.

"I'm going to head back toward Brackett Field. Keep dropping the fliers."

Without warning, the plane suddenly lost altitude and lurched to the right, throwing Melanie hard against her seatbelt. Red fliers emblazoned with skulls and crossbones fluttered around the cabin.

"What was that?" Melanie cried out.

Keith said, "I don't know." He paused as he looked in all directions around the plane. "I can't see any other plane that might have passed over us."

Keith gestured in Trevor's direction. Melanie looked over at Trevor. He was unconscious, but still in his seat thanks to his seatbelt. He must have hit his head on the side of the plane during the turbulence.

Keith yelled, "Is he okay?"

Melanie opened her mouth in reply, but at that very moment she noticed a sleek, black and very large looking helicopter coming into view alongside their Cessna on their left side. There were no identifying markings on the helicopter and its tinted windows gave no clue as to the identity of the pilot or passengers.

"That's what caused the turbulence," Keith said. "It has to be the drug cartel guys."

Almost in answer to Keith's statement, one of the side windows of the helicopter opened and a machine gun barrel protruded menacingly out of the black opening.

Keith yelled, "Hold on." He immediately moved the stick away from the helicopter.

The little plane responded, but too slowly.

"I feel like we're sitting ducks."

Melanie saw the gun barrel start to recoil repeatedly. A split second later, as the staccato like sound of splintering fiberglass emanated from behind her, Keith jammed the stick forward and sent the plane into a desperate dive in an effort to escape the deadly hail of bullets.

With Keith pulling back hard on the diving Cessna's stick, the engine strained and the fuselage groaned as the plane responded by pulling out of the forced dive, leveling off just above the back yards, streets and homes of Covina.

"Did we lose them?" Trevor shouted, now conscious, but still groggy from his bump on the head.

"Don't count on it," Keith replied. "I'm sure our dive surprised them, but they won't be far behind. I'm kind of hoping that they won't be willing to fire on us when we're this close to the homes."

"That's not going to stop these guys," Melanie yelled. "Isn't there anything else we can do?"

Almost in answer to her question, slugs from the machine gun suddenly began ripping into the fuselage just behind Melanie. She screamed in fear and lurched forward in her seat, head down and with her arms over her head, just in time to miss being struck by four or five rounds that pierced the upper part of her seat back. The impact shredded the material and splattered pieces of foam padding into Melanie's hair.

Keith put the plane into a tight turn to the right. The sound of bullets ripping through fiberglass mercifully stopped.

Melanie looked up at Trevor from under the protection of her arms. His face looked pale and his expression grim.

He asked, "Are you okay?"

Feeling numb to her own close call with death, but sick with worry for Trevor's safety, Melanie nodded bravely that she was okay, just as Keith guided the plane out of the sharp turn and into a steep ascent. The sudden change in centrifugal force caught Melanie totally by surprise and she fell hard against her shredded seat back. *When will this stop?* Frustration over the non-stop violence coming from Rick and his men brought tears to her eyes.

"Sorry about the rough ride," Keith yelled over the roar of the engine and the whistling of air through the many holes in the fiber-glass body of the aircraft. "Is everyone okay?"

"Besides a splitting headache from a bump on the head, I'm

fine," Trevor answered. He looked at Melanie. "I'm not sure if Melanie is okay or not."

"I'm fine," Melanie said. "Sorry about the tears. I'm just so frustrated with these horrible people. Why can't they just leave us alone?"

"They're not going to leave us alone until either we're dead, or they're dead," Keith said.

Melanie glanced out her window and was frustrated to see the helicopter rising quickly to match their ascent.

Keith shouted, "They're sticking to us like glue. Hold on tight for this next part." Keith flipped the plane over backwards in a barrel roll and then put the plane into a falling spin away from the chopper, leaving Melanie feeling like her stomach was in her mouth. Keith leveled out the plane after three revolutions.

Melanie glanced over her left shoulder out the window. The copter was still right behind them.

Keith said, "I just can't outmaneuver these guys in this plane no matter what I do. Our only hope is to get back to Bracket Field as fast as we can."

The helicopter easily caught up to the plane on its left side. The ominous machine gun barrel again protruded from the open window in the side of the helicopter. In desperation, Keith banked the plane away from the chopper again, but their tormentors simply executed a banking turn just above the Cessna. The deadly stinger emanating from the black messenger of death began to recoil again, tearing away chunks of the Cessna's fuselage behind Melanie.

"They're just playing with us," Trevor cried in exasperation.

"Yes, they are," Keith said, "But, for how much longer?"

The machine gun paused for a moment, but then began again. The rounds pierced the cabin of the Cessna, with one of them striking Keith in the chest. His hands instantly fell from the steering wheel and his head slumped over to his chest.

Almost simultaneously, another round found Melanie's left thigh. Melanie immediately clutched her thigh and bent over in pain.

CHAPTER 72

"**M**Y LEG," MELANIE groaned in intense pain from her seat in the Cessna. As Trevor tore his eyes away from the shock of Keith's suddenly lifeless body and prepared himself for the worst, he saw that Melanie was grasping her left thigh with both hands. Blood was oozing between her fingers.

"Melanie," Trevor cried with concern as leaned toward her. Her head was down, and her shoulders were hunched, making it hard for him to see how badly she was hurt. Touching her lightly on her right shoulder, he asked, "How bad is it?"

She turned her face to Trevor, and he was shocked by her paleness and by the pain that clearly etched in her face. Her eyes were full of tears as she gasped, "I don't know. It just hurts so bad."

In spite of his concern for Melanie, another matter needed his immediate attention. With Keith dead, there was no one flying the plane. Trevor's stomach churned and his chest tightened as he realized that no matter how bad Melanie's wound was, it wouldn't matter if he didn't take the stick immediately. The only problem was that he had never flown an airplane. Galvanized by a vision that they might already be heading for the ground, Trevor tore off his seat belt and leaped forward to the cockpit. Keith was slumped forward against his seatbelt, and his head lolled unnaturally to the side. One look out the windshield told Trevor that they were indeed heading straight down toward a residential area. He reached across Keith's lifeless body, grabbed the stick, and pulled back as hard as he could. Instantly, the engine growled, and the plane shuddered as it struggled to obey Trevor's command. After a few moments, the plane came out of its dive just above the trees in the neighborhood and started climbing He looked back out the windshield and was horrified to see a radio tower directly in front of him and coming up fast.

Trevor turned the steering wheel sharply to the right. He watched out the windshield of the plane as the radio tower rushed toward the plane. Little by little, the aircraft finally began moving away from its collision course with the radio tower. Trevor braced himself in case the plane didn't clear the guy wires that were attached to the tower. Finally, the plane passed the radio tower and seemed to Trevor to be traveling on a level plane. Trevor moved Keith's body to the passenger seat and secured Keith's body with the seatbelt so that it wouldn't go flying around the cockpit if Trevor had to make any sharp maneuvers. He then sat in the pilot's seat. Glancing out the left side of the plane, he was greeted with a view of the all-too-familiar black helicopter. The machine gun barrel was again sticking out the window, and seconds later, the roof of the cockpit began shattering from the impact of the slugs. *They're playing with me. They could have killed me instantly if they had wanted to.* Unable to do anything to evade the helicopter, Trevor held the stick at neutral and ducked his head to avoid being hit by the flying debris. All he could do was hope that the killers in the chopper would keep playing with him for just a little longer until he could figure out how to get out of this disastrous predicament. However, the situation appeared to be hopeless.

"Trevor," Melanie asked wearily from behind him. "What happened to the helicopter?"

Trevor looked to his left. The helicopter was gone. He blinked in surprise. "I don't know. It's gone."

"I can't believe that they didn't stay to finish us off after they played with us for so long," Melanie said with frequent pauses to catch her breath.

To Trevor's surprise, Melanie suddenly appeared at his elbow. She was perched on her left leg and leaning heavily on both the front seats. She looked pale and weary and was breathing heavily. Congealed, maroon blood covered the wound in her thigh.

"Melanie, what are you doing? You shouldn't be up."

"The bleeding has slowed down quite a bit, and besides, with you at the wheel, my life is probably in greater danger."

"Hey, didn't you see how I pulled us out of that dive and then I saved us from crashing into the radio tower?"

"You were wonderful, but do you think that you can land this plane safely?"

"You've got me on that one, but inexperienced or not, I'm the only pilot that you've got right now." Suddenly, the fact that Melanie was aware that he didn't know the first thing about flying struck him. "Hey, how did you know that I've never flown a plane?"

"There's a lot you don't know about me," Melanie said with a sweet smile. "I just happen to have over six hundred hours of experience in small aircraft, mostly dusting local farmers' crops and orchards."

"That's why you're standing there. You're here to relieve me from my command."

"No, I'm here to save your precious life. Now hop out of that seat before I faint cold on the floor."

Trevor obeyed instantly and helped Melanie ease herself, as best as he could, into the pilots' chair. Even with great care, she grimaced in pain.

"I'm okay," she said. "I need to focus on getting us back to

Bracket Field before this severely damaged aircraft quits on us. I'm surprised it's still flying after all that it has been through."

"Trevor," Melanie cried from her position in the pilot's seat, "There's another helicopter just off our port side."

"What in the world?" Trevor said as he searched out the right side of the aircraft for the new threat. "I don't see anything."

"Port is the left side when you're facing forward," Melanie said.

"Oh," Trevor said as he quickly shifted seats and peered out the other side of the plane. There was a helicopter there all right, and with their recent encounter fresh in his mind, things didn't look good. "It looks like Rick has sent another helicopter to finish us off."

"I'm not so sure of that," Melanie said. "This one has the letters 'LAPD' painted on its side. The pilot is signaling for us to land immediately."

"Can we outrun them?" Trevor asked.

"This poor plane is ready to fall apart at any second. Every time I move the stick, I wonder if it's still connected to the rudder. I'm already trying my best to do what he is asking." She paused for a moment as she surveyed the terrain ahead and then continued, "There is a small airstrip just ahead and to the right of us. I'm going to land there."

"Trevor, I need you take over," Melanie requested weakly as she allowed the plane to roll to a stop before the end of the runway at El Monte airport. Beads of sweat dotted her forehead, and Trevor had never seen her look so pale. In spite of her discomfort, she smiled weakly at him and then turned her head to look out the front of the aircraft. As he unbuckled his seatbelt, Trevor couldn't help but admire this wonderful woman. It was amazing that she had been able to guide the aircraft into a near-perfect landing when she was in so much pain.

Melanie suddenly half-leaned and half-fell forward onto the

stick. Trevor quickly sprang to Melanie's side, unbuckled her seat-belt, and then carried her back to the rear passenger seat. She was out cold. He secured her in place with the seat belt and then returned to the pilot's seat. Gripping the stick, he gave the propellor some gas and guided the Cessna to the end of the runway. He quickly realized that he couldn't steer the airplane on the ground with the steering wheel. After a moment of panic, he discovered that he could steer the plane by applying pressure to one of the two brake pedals on the floor. To his embarrassment, he was still unable to keep the plane from seesawing back and forth from one side of the side runway to the other. He felt like a three-year-old riding the bumper cars at an amusement park for the first time.

He was just getting the hang of driving the plane when he was surprised by the appearance of the flashing lights of a police cruiser coming up alongside the airplane from his left. The squad car sped past the plane, and then the driver caused the car to skid sideways to a screeching stop in front of Trevor so that the taxiway was completely blocked. The problem was that the cops had no idea that a non-pilot was guiding the plane. Trevor let up on the gas and then stomped on the brakes. Immediately, he looked back through the windshield at the squad car that the plane was rushing toward, sure that the plane wouldn't stop in time to keep from ramming it.

As the plane got closer and closer to the passenger side of the squad car, the officer that was sitting in the passenger seat became wide-eyed and his mouth opened in a silent scream. The cop suddenly tried to unbuckle his seatbelt but was unsuccessful. Trevor knew from the look on the cop's face that he was sure that the spinning blades of the propeller were going to slice through his door and make like a giant food processor on his upper torso. Relief showed on both their faces as the plane miraculously slowed to a stop with the propeller still spinning just inches from the side of the cruiser.

The driver of the police car pulled forward a little, allowing the officer in the passenger seat enough room to safely exit the car.

Carefully eying the still-spinning propeller with concern, the officer drew his gun, skirted the propeller, and then walked over to Trevor's side of the Cessna. The man signaled Trevor to open the window.

The officer waited patiently as Trevor fumbled with the mechanism on the window. Trevor finally got it to open, and then the officer said in a deep and commanding tone, "I'm going to have to ask you to turn off the engine and exit your vehicle."

"Is there something the matter, officer?" Trevor asked, trying to appear calm, while he was really scared to death and trembling inside.

"You have violated a city ordinance that prohibits dropping anything out of aircraft, except in designated areas and with a permit," the cop recited. "Now just turn off the engine and then exit the aircraft slowly with your hands in the air."

Trevor soon located and turned off the ignition. The idling engine sputtered to complete stop moments later. Trevor looked back to the officer and stated, "I've got an injured passenger, sir. She needs immediate medical attention."

"You just need to exit the aircraft as instructed, and then we'll assess your passenger's condition," the officer said, his tone leaving little room for further discussion.

As Trevor dutifully followed the officer's instructions, a second officer got out of the driver's side of the squad car and joined the first officer. Together, the two policemen, guns in their hands, hurried around the rear of the plane and met Trevor on the starboard side of the aircraft. The first officer, whose badge read Walter Swallow, raised his gun to point straight at Trevor's chest as Trevor opened the door of the Cessna and stepped down onto the tarmac. The sight of the gun caused even greater fear to well up in Trevor's chest. He couldn't help but wonder if and when his life would get back to normal. In spite of his intense anxiety, Trevor had sufficient presence of mind to stand completely still at the side of the aircraft with his arms over his head.

The second officer quickly spun Trevor around and, in an

obviously well-rehearsed maneuver, forced Trevor against the side of the Cessna. Trevor barely had time to get his arms in front of him to keep from smashing his face against the fuselage. "Spread your legs," the second officer said.

"You have the right to remain silent," the officer said coldly as he recited Trevor his Miranda rights while he simultaneously patted Trevor down for a weapon. At the end of the thorough body search and the rapid-fire recitation of Trevor's rights, the officer fluidly flipped Trevor's outstretched right arm behind his back and then snatched a pair of handcuffs from off his belt. The policeman snapped one end of the cuffs on Trevor's right wrist and then, after retrieving Trevor's left arm, he placed the other end on Trevor's left wrist. The officer reached out and unceremoniously spun Trevor around to face him, causing Trevor to nearly lose his balance.

"You're in bigger trouble then we thought," the second officer said. Trevor could see from the man's name badge that his name was Scott Finlayson. The second officer continued, "I recognize you from the news. You and your friend are Baker and Davis from Santa Fe. You tortured and murdered all those young girls. Besides the kidnapping and murder charges from Santa Fe, it seems that you had a little altercation with a helicopter, and the helicopter lost. People died in that crash, mister." The officer hesitated momentarily and stared hard into Trevor's eyes.

"Officer," Trevor stated, hardly able to even believe his ears. "I didn't have anything to do with—"

Not seeing or hearing what he wanted, the policeman interrupted, "Don't you get it? It's murder. You've committed murder. How'd you do it? How'd you shoot down the helicopter? Or are you going to make me guess?" Trevor stood there dumbfounded, unable to think of any answers that would satisfy the officer's ridiculous questions.

"Okay, let me try to guess. You used a gun to shoot them out of sky, right?" Still in shock, Trevor remained silent. The office continued, "Where's the gun?" Without waiting for Trevor to answer, the second officer moved to the open door of the plane and looked inside. He took in a sharp breath as he took in the horrendous scene inside the plane. "What have you done?" the officer asked. "It looks like you went crazy and shot up the plane and everyone in it. It had to have been you because the others are all dead." A soft moan from Melanie interrupted his tirade. The office got into the plane and moved to where Melanie was seated. A moment later, he called to his partner and stated, "Walter, call an ambulance. We've got one here that's still alive."

Walter pulled a radiophone off his belt and got to work.

"She has a gunshot wound to her right thigh," Trevor said, "It's not bleeding much right now, but she's lost quite a lot of blood. The pilot is dead."

"Shut up," the second cop said from inside the plane. "I'll decide if he's dead or not." The officer moved to the front of the plane, reached out, and touched his index and middle fingers to Keith's neck. After a moment, he announced, "He's dead. But then that's pretty much the way things go for people when you and your buddy here are around, isn't it?"

"I didn't kill anyone."

"Sure, you didn't," the cop said.

"You've got to believe me," Trevor said, trying not to shout. "That whole news story is a lie. I'm a doctor from Phoenix. I've never hurt anyone in my life. The helicopter was shooting—"

"Scott," Walter interrupted as he returned from the squad car. "The ambulance is on the way. I've also got more news from dispatch on the chopper wreck. There are no apparent survivors. The helicopter is registered to a private citizen. From what dispatch can gather, the poor sucker was trying to force our friends here to stop dropping the fliers and land when they opened fire on him and knocked his chopper out of sky. What's worse, they're pretty sure that two kids were playing at the playground where the chopper went down. They're dead too."

"You're no doctor." Scott snarled as he got out of the plane. "You're just a freakin' baby killer," he yelled and then accentuated his statement with a roundhouse punch to Trevor's right jaw. Caught completely unaware, Trevor's head snapped back, and then he collapsed to the tarmac. The cop didn't hesitate for even a second as he fiercely kicked Trevor in the ribs on his exposed side.

"Stop it," Trevor heard Melanie yell in horror through his pain. "You're hurting him."

"Scott," Walter stated firmly, his gun still aimed steadily at Trevor. Scott ignored Walter and also ignored Melanie's shrill and continuous pleas. He landed a second kick in Trevor's unprotected abdomen. "Scott, stop it," Walter yelled loudly. Walter quickly pushed his way protectively between Scott and Trevor.

"Scott. Cool off, buddy," Walter said. "This isn't helping anything and is only going to get us all in big trouble."

Trembling with barely repressed rage, Scott growled. "Scum like this doesn't deserve to live."

"That might be true," Walter said. "But not by our hands. If you injure this guy, you're going to prison along with him. Just calm down, and we'll get this guy to jail where he belongs. After the horrible things that he's done to those young girls, the guys in prison will rip him to pieces."

After a moment's deliberation, Scott's angry stance relaxed, and his balled-up fists loosened at his side. He glanced at Trevor where he lay moaning softly on the tarmac in pain. Hesitantly, Scott continued, "You're right. Thanks for stopping me. I can't help but go nuts when I think of young kids being hurt by animals like these two."

Hearing the sound of an ambulance approaching, the two policemen quickly glanced at the road leading up to the airport's small terminal. Walter turned to Scott and said, "Let's get the woman out of the plane. The ambulance is for her." Scott took Melanie by the shoulders and pulled her to a stand. She gasped in pain. Walter holstered his gun and lent Scott a hand in getting Melanie down to the runway, all the while keeping an eye on Trevor.

As the officers helped Melanie to the tarmac, she let out a sharp cry of pain. Her face went an even lighter shade of pale. At the sound of Melanie's cry, Trevor forgot the pain and nausea Scott's kicks had caused and struggled to sit up to see what was happening. In intense pain, Melanie leaned heavily against Walter, and then suddenly, all the strength went out of her arms, and her head fell against Walter's shoulder. It was clear to Trevor that she was out cold again. Melanie's dead weight was more than Walter had been prepared for, and he was barely able to keep her from slipping out of his arms and on to the cement.

A tall, muscular paramedic suddenly appeared behind Melanie and effortlessly lifted her off the ground and into his arms. "I've got her," the paramedic reassured, and then he turned to carry the unconscious woman to the waiting ambulance with its overhead lights still flashing. With help from his partner, the paramedic put Melanie onto a waiting gurney, placed a blanket over her still form, and then secured her to the gurney with straps from underneath the stretcher. Office Scott finished the job by cuffing her right wrist to the gurney.

"I'm not certain how badly she's hurt," Walter reported from the foot of the gurney. "It appears that she was shot in the right leg by the male suspect that's over by the plane." Walter gestured at Trevor, who was now sitting up. Scott stood just behind Trevor with his gun drawn, watching his prisoner closely.

"What about the other passenger in the plane?" the burly paramedic asked.

"Half his chest is ripped out from multiple gunshot wounds. He didn't make it," Scott stated grimly from his position by the plane. Disgust oozed from his voice as he spoke. "From what we can see, our friend here went wild with some type of automatic weapon and shot up the plane, these two victims, and a helicopter. What's even stranger is the woman on the gurney there is his partner. He shot his own partner. They're both wanted for torturing, raping, and killing multiple young girls in New Mexico, as well as for armed robbery and who knows how many other crimes."

The two paramedics looked uneasily at each other across the gurney. After a moment's hesitation, the paramedics easily hoisted the gurney into the back of the ambulance. One of the paramedics got into the back of ambulance with the gurney. The other paramedic asked, "Is there anything else you need to tell us before we head to the hospital?"

"No," Walter replied, but then, on second thought, he added, "But, for your safety and for security reasons, I'm going to have to send Officer Finlayson with you."

"Fine," Scott said with indignation. After glaring at Walter for a moment, during which time Trevor wasn't sure whether Scott was going to lose his temper again or not, Scott shook his head and then headed for the cab of the ambulance. The ambulance was soon on its way out of the airport.

Walter unholstered his gun and turned to Trevor where he was still seated on the tarmac. "On your feet. It's time to get you to your new home." Holding his gun ready in his right hand, Walter reached down with his left hand and lifted Trevor up by the arm.

"Officer, would you wait just a minute and give me a chance to explain what really happened here?" Trevor asked as respectfully as he could.

Walter took Trevor by the arm and began propelling him toward the police car. "You're the only person that survived the incident without a serious injury. You're a wanted killer. Anything you tell me will be wasting your breath."

Trevor said, "If I had really shot my partner, don't you think she would have turned against me and told you that I was the one that pulled the trigger?"

Walter stopped walking but kept his gun pointed at Trevor's chest. "No. I've seen female companions defend their male partner in crime, even though they themselves were being beat up. You've got to do better than that."

"Okay, what about the pilot. Why would I have shot the pilot in the back while he was flying the plane, placing myself in danger? On top of that, I don't even know how to fly a plane. Why would I kill the pilot?" As Trevor finished speaking, he noticed a line of three familiar Marauders approaching the airfield's terminal. Even though his heart leaped in his chest at the sight of the Marauders, he managed to look away and pretend that he hadn't seen anything. At the same time, his confidence rebounded as Trevor was sure that Von would find some way to get him out of this.

"The plane was probably on autopilot when you shot him from behind through the seat," stated Officer Swallow. "That would have given you plenty of time to get him out of the pilot's seat and into the front passenger's seat without losing control of the aircraft. And even if you say you aren't a pilot, given the circumstances, I can't trust you to tell the truth."

"You saw how I was barely able to stop the plane before I ran in to you. And I'm sure you saw me struggling to keep the plane on the runway just before you passed me." Trevor was beginning to feel a little exasperated, and he was sure that it was showing in his voice.

"That's no good at all. You could have easily been faking the whole thing."

Trevor paused for a moment to think of another argument and to stall while he waited for Von to arrive. Walter waited impatiently for about three seconds and then asked, "Well, is that it? Was that supposed to convince me? You're wasting your time and mine..." Walter 's voice trailed off as he heard the rumbling coming from the three rapidly approaching Marauders. "What's going on here?" he exclaimed as he turned to face the vehicles. For the first time, the barrel of his gun drifted away from Trevor's chest as his whole attention was diverted to the new arrivals.

The Marauders abruptly fanned out into a rough semicircle around the plane and then simultaneously ground to a screeching halt. Almost immediately, the driver's side door of the middle vehicle flew open and a black hooded figure, sporting mirrored sunglasses, jumped down to the tarmac. Trevor knew that it had to be one of Von's team or even Von himself, but the mask and hood prevented him from identifying the figure.

As soon as the masked figure appeared, Walter instinctively pulled Trevor in front of him and jammed the barrel of his service revolver into Trevor's back. Using his free arm, Walter began dragging Trevor forcibly toward his squad car.

"Hold it right there, officer," the hooded figure said in a booming voice. Trevor instantly recognized Von's voice. Walter stopped dragging Trevor for a moment.

"You have no idea what you're up against here," Von said as he sauntered into full view from the other side of his Marauder, revealing a sinister-looking, black sub-machine gun cradled in his right arm. "Now put your gun down, and let's talk."

Walter remained frozen, clearly clueless as to what to do next.

"Oh, by the way, there are eleven more of these H&K MP5 pea shooters aimed right at your head at this very moment," Von said. "So what do you say? How about you just put your gun away and then we can explain what's really going on with our boy, Dr. Trevor Davis."

"Okay," Walter said as he lowered his revolver. "You've got a lot more fire power than I do. But you'll never get away with this. My backup will be here at any minute."

"What backup, Walter?" Von asked. "We've been monitoring all of your calls to dispatch, and you haven't called for backup."

"You caught me, even though I have no clue how you are monitoring our encrypted calls. So now that you've overwhelmed and embarrassed me, please tell your guys to aim their guns some-where else. Then please be so kind as to tell me what in the world is going on."

"Never thought you'd ask," Von said as he made a brief signal with his left palm open and rotating side to side in full view of the three Marauders. "Your prisoner is Trevor Davis, a family doctor from Phoenix. He is as harmless as a fly. The story that he's a mur-derer from New Mexico is completely false and has been planted at your news agencies and at your police department by moles working for a local drug lord. I know it sounds farfetched, but the culinary water supply for Los Angeles really was poisoned last night with a permanently mind-altering drug by men working for the same drug lord. The drug initially causes severe headaches and then causes victims to quickly gain massive amounts of weight. The drug lord will then profit fantastically from interests he has in a company that makes a well-known weight-loss drug. When Dr. Davis and his friend tried to warn LA of the poisoning by dropping leaflets out of this plane, the drug lord sent some of his thugs in his personal chopper to shoot them down."

"What you're telling me is too far-fetched to believe," Walter said. "And, how do you explain that witnesses say that the occupants of the Cessna shot the helicopter out of the sky?"

"That's easy," Von explained as he walked toward the Cessna. "Look at these bullet holes in the fuselage. By the inward pucker of each hole in the plane's skin, you can see that the gun that fired the shells was always on the outside, not the inside."

After a moment's inspection, Walter replied, "You've got a very good point there. But then how did the helicopter suddenly fall out of the sky?"

Von said nothing.

"You did it," Walter exclaimed incredulously. "How did you do it? There were no reports of another aircraft in the sky at the time."

There was still no reply.

"Whether you or my prisoner shot the helicopter out of the sky, it was still cold-blooded murder of the occupants of the helicopter, and especially of the two kids that were killed on the ground."

"I was waiting for you to get to that part," Von said patiently, sounding very much like he was instructing a group of eager seventh graders. He removed a black cellphone from his fatigues. "Listen to this. It's a recording of a cell phone call from the helicopter to a home in Newport Beach." Von punched one of the buttons, and instantly the three men heard the unmistakable sounds of a helicopter in flight, along with a small amount of background static.

"We're alongside the plane, again," Trevor heard a voice say that he didn't recognize. Suddenly, the sound of a sub-machine gun firing assailed their ears, and Trevor shuddered with terror as he realized that this was a recording from the black helicopter as it was shooting at Melanie and him in the Cessna. The machine gun was fired in three short bursts and then fell silent. The voice on the phone continued, "Mike just slaughtered the pilot. The guy's guts are all over the windows." There was another pause and then the voice continued, "The plane looks like it's beginning to lose altitude."

"That's not good enough," a new voice exclaimed angrily. Trevor immediately recognized the voice as Rick's. "Tell Mike to keep shooting until the plane blows up or hits the ground."

"He's having too much fun watching them die slowly," the first man answered.

"Tell him that I'll tear him apart piece by piece if he doesn't finish off the doctor and his girlfriend now," Rick yelled.

"Okay. Hang on a minute," the first man said, and then the sound of the chopper cut to silence as Von stopped the recorder.

Trevor's mind continued to replay the horror of the experience that he had just been through in the Cessna while Walter asked incredulously, "Where did you get that recording? How do I know it's real?"

"Believe me, intercepting and recording phone conversations

is child's play," Von said. "I had my men begin monitoring all cell phone communications in and out of the area where the helicopter was accosting our Cessna as soon as our pilot, Keith, radioed us that he was having problems. We recorded a much longer segment and then downloaded the best parts as MP3 files to my phone." Von held up the player briefly. "By the way, did you like the speakers?"

Trevor and Walter looked puzzled, and Trevor asked, "What speakers? I thought the sound came from your cell phone."

"The speakers are built into my suit. My phone communicates with them by Bluetooth. Pretty cool, huh?"

Trevor and Walter nodded.

"As for if the recording is real, you'll have to be the judge of that. At the same time, from the evidence here, I think you already know that it's real."

Walter said, "Maybe, maybe not. Why don't you tell me how you got involved with my prisoner?"

"Trevor was referred to my team by a friend." Von said.

"Who do you think you are? It looks to me like you're just a bunch of vigilantes out for a joyride with your toys. The only problem is that by taking the law into your own hands, you're breaking the law. Once this thing is over, I'm going to track you down and have you arrested."

"I understand your confusion about which side of the law that we are on. I can assure you that we are only here to help. Listen to this next clip and see what you think then. We picked up this cell phone transmission just before we got here. It's from the same residence in Newport Beach that was talking to the helicopter."

"Hello, this is Tony Jensen," a new voice spoke from phone. Trevor didn't recognize the voice. Walter, on the other hand, startled a little at the name.

"Walter, why don't you tell Dr. Davis who Tony Jensen is?" Von asked as he paused the recording.

"There is a Tony Jensen that is the deputy chief of police for LA County, if that is who we are really listening to."

Von punched the play button.

"Hey, Tony. This is Carl Vernon."

"I can't believe you're calling me here," Tony said in a lower tone. "If anyone ever finds out—"

"You worry too much. You're going to get an ulcer."

"What do you mean, going to? I've already got one. So, what's up?"

"I need you to put a little spin on a helicopter that just crashed out in Covina. Have you heard anything about the crash?"

"No, I haven't."

"Well, it's one of my helicopters, and I need you to make sure that no one connects it to me. Also, I need to be sure that the police and the public are made to believe that it was that pesky doctor and his friend that I called you about yesterday that shot down the helicopter. Make it look really bad, like some good citizen was trying to save LA from these two, and that when his chopper crashed, some kids were killed on the ground."

"Sure thing, Carl. I'll get the word out as soon as we're off the phone. Say, about that shipment you promised me yesterday. When do I get it?"

"You just take care of this little problem for me, and then I'll make sure that your shipment gets to you as soon as possible. Just to be sure, tell me again what you wanted."

"I need one hundred of sniff and one hundred 'X.'"

"That right. I'll get it to you soon. Now get to work on this right away, all right?"

"I'm on it," Tony said. Von stopped the recording and stuck his phone back in his pocket. He looked at Walter for his response.

Walter ran his hand through his hair and then shook his head in disbelief. "I can hardly believe what I've just heard. I've suspected a number of guys on the force were selling, but I'd never have picked Jensen for a pusher. What's this world coming to?"

"We'll talk about that later." Von chuckled. "So what do you think? Now do you agree that Dr. Davis is innocent?"

"Okay, okay. You've convinced me," Walter said with a sigh.

"Then, could you please take these cuffs off?" Trevor asked. "They're hurting my wrists."

"Sure," Walter said. He removed his keys from his pants pocket and went to work on the locks on the cuffs. Seconds later, Trevor's arms were free. Trevor immediately grasped his wrists where the cuffs had bitten into his skin and rubbed them.

"So, now what am I going to do with you?" Walter asked Trevor as he attached the cuffs to his belt. "Dispatch knows that I've got you. If I don't show up with you at the jail in the next few hours, they're going suspect that something is up and come looking for us. If I take you in, Carl's men on the inside will make sure you never leave prison alive."

"Given those choices, I'm all for staying with Von," Trevor said hastily.

"Trevor, Walter 's right," Von said. "We don't want to take any chances with anyone's life here, including Walter 's. If he doesn't convince dispatch that he's in route to jail with you, it will alert moles in the police force that Walter is on to them. Then Walter 's life will be in danger. Trevor, go with Walter. Walter can call dispatch and tell them that you are complaining of belly pain and that he's taking you to the nearest hospital for evaluation. Then head for whatever hospital Melanie went to and pick her up. By that time, I'll have a plan for getting us all out of town while at the same time keeping Walter above suspicion."

"I'd feel a lot more comfortable with Dr. Davis staying with me for the time being," Walter said. "By the way, do you have any idea who this Carl is?"

"We've traced the calls to his home in Newport Beach. Initial background checks are telling us that he's been arrested in the distant past for possession, dealing, assault, and armed robbery. There's been nothing in recent years."

"Yeah, that's because he's got other people carrying out his dirty work, and then they take the heat if things go bad," Walter said. "That's why it's so hard to take down leaders of criminal organizations. The only way to pin a charge on them is to get one of their own people to rat them out for conspiracy to commit crimes."

Von added, "Yes, and they're usually too scared for their own lives to cooperate."

"There's no question that this whole thing has certainly put me in a difficult position," Walter said. "If I'm not careful, I'm going to lose my job or even wind up dead. The problem is I don't even know who I can trust anymore."

"You just lay low and be patient," Von said. "I have a hunch that things are going to work out just fine."

"You're confident, and you have a lot of amazing gadgets, but you'd better not underestimate these guys that you're up against. I have a hunch that they'll swat you like a fly if you get in their way."

"Do I really have to wear these?" Trevor asked about the handcuffs that Walter had just put back on his wrists. "They're so uncomfortable."

"Yes, you do," Walter answered. "To the public, you're a wanted criminal, and your face has been all over the news for the last twenty-four hours. If anyone sees you with me without the handcuffs, they will immediately begin asking questions."

"What are you going to say to your partner?" Trevor asked.

As he was speaking, Walter began guiding Trevor from his squad car to the sidewalk that led to the emergency room entrance of Greater El Monte General Hospital. "I'm not sure yet. I'll come up with something."

To Trevor, the one-story, white stucco building with its dark red, ceramic-tile roof seemed peaceful compared to some of the large and overcrowded hospitals in Phoenix. Even though it was a weekday, the parking lot wasn't completely full. As the automatic doors responded to their approach, Trevor noted that the glass in the entry was clear of fingerprints, and that the floor was clean and freshly waxed. Attractive, dust-free plants lined the hallway to the ER check-in desk. The desk was manned by two clerks that greeted Walter with a smile. It was obvious to Trevor that this hospital was privately owned and was serving a largely middle-class, non-Medi-care, and non-Medicaid population.

"We're here to check on a Melanie Baker," Walter announced to the clerk at the desk. "She came in about thirty minutes ago with a gunshot wound to the right thigh."

The clerk looked at the white board on the wall behind the check-in desk, scanned it for a moment, and then frowned, "I don't see her on the board. Are you sure it's Melanie Baker?"

After getting a nod from Trevor, Walter answered, "Yes, I'm sure."

"Well, there isn't a Melanie Baker here right now," the clerk said as she shook her head. After a moment of contemplation, her eyes widened as she thought of another possibility. "I just came back from a doctor's appointment. Maybe Janessa knows something about your friend." The clerk turned to her fellow employee and asked if there had been a Melanie Baker in the ER in the last hour.

After finishing with the patient she was helping, Janessa turned to Walter and clarified, "She came in about a half an hour ago with another cop. I think his name was Scott. Yes, that's right. She was in a lot of pain, so the nurses took her right back to a treat-ment room. The doctor was about ready to see her when two more officers showed up with paperwork ordering her to be transferred immediately to the LA County Central Jail Hospital. Officer Scott seemed to be fine with it and so was our doctor. The three of them left here about ten minutes ago. Officer Scott pushed the woman out in a wheelchair."

"Did you catch the names of the two policemen?" Walter asked.

After rustling through some papers on the desk in front of her, Janessa read from the signed authorization to transfer, "Officers Derek Alcott and Samuel Oliver."

Walter thanked the clerks and quickly guided Trevor to a distant corner of the waiting room before speaking in a hushed tone, "I don't know Derek Alcott, but I do know Sam Oliver. I've long suspected that he is into some shady things around here. There was even a time about a year ago that I busted a chronic cocaine and ecstasy user that identified Sam as the supplier. I was naïve enough at the time to believe that cops didn't do that kind of stuff."

"I'm worried sick about Melanie," Trevor said. "How are we going to get her out of jail? And how do I know she's safe where they've taken her? You said yourself that the guys in prison would kill me. Won't the women do the same to Melanie if they think she's killed children?"

"I don't know. I was sure that she'd be here, but now that she's not, I don't know quite what to do. The truth is that if she is in jail, it's going to take an attorney and a lot of bail to get her out. The most important thing is to find out where she is right now." He grabbed his radiophone from his belt and asked for dispatch.

Trevor waited anxiously for Walter to find where Melanie was while his thoughts raced ahead, all the while trying to figure out some way to make the whole thing turn out right. But he kept running into roadblocks and dead-ends. He knew that he had to get Melanie out of the jail as soon as possible, but he had no legal contacts in Los Angeles. It was possible that Von might have some. Regardless, Melanie would still be in the jail overnight. He was sure that if that happened, Rick's inside contacts would find her. She might not last the night.

"This is Officer Walter Swallow." Walter listened for moment and then replied, "I'm fine, thanks. How are those kids?" He paused again. "Say, Maggie, could you confirm for me the status and location of Melanie Baker, the woman involved with the helicopter crash this afternoon?" Again, Walter waited for Maggie's reply, and then he said, "Are you sure? I'm at El Monte right now. The clerk here says that two of our officers picked her up about ten minutes ago to transfer her to the County Jail Hospital." Walter listened for moment longer, then thanked Maggie, and hung up his phone. The baffled look on his face told Trevor exactly what had happened to Melanie.

"Rick's men have her, don't they?" Trevor asked.

"That's what it looks like. There was no order for her to be transferred to the County Jail Hospital. And now we have no idea where they've taken her."

"We need to call Von right now." He could hardly bear the thought that she might already have been be hurt. His pulse quickened in response, and his hands became cold and clammy. His chest felt like an elephant was sitting on it. "If anyone can find where they have taken her, Von can."

CHAPTER 73

IT WASN'T HARD for Melanie to surmise that they had reached their destination. It would have been easier for her to just look out the car's window and see for herself, except that a cloth hood had been unceremoniously placed over her head minutes after she had left El Monte Hospital. Although initially surprised at the strange actions of the new set of officers that had said they were transferring her to the county jail, it hadn't taken her more than a second to realize that cops or not, with these men, she was once again in Rick's clutches.

A few seconds ago, the car she was riding in had come to a complete stop in a place where she couldn't hear other traffic. After a short interval, she had heard a faint rumbling sound like that of an electric gate opening, and then the car had had proceeded at a much slower speed. The new surface that the car was on was much smoother than the roads that they had just traveled. The tires squealed on the surface even when the car made the slightest of turn. Melanie figured that they had arrived at someone's private dwelling. *Do Tom or Rick have a home in LA?* That thought made her nervous.

As the car came to a stop, both front doors opened almost simultaneously; the car rocked a little. and then the front doors shut resoundingly. A short time later, the door on her left opened, and one of the policemen announced from outside the car, "We're here. Get out, and we'll take you to your new accommodations."

Melanie slid over to the open door carefully as so not to cause too much pain in her injured left leg and then clumsily got to her feet. She felt a firm grip of take a hold of her right biceps, and she allowed herself to be propelled forward. After twenty steps, the hand on her right arm firmly jerked her to a stop as she heard a doorbell ring in the distance. She heard the sound of a door opening.

"Hi, Sam," Melanie heard Shannon say flirtatiously.

Melanie couldn't suppress a deep chill as she heard the voice that she had hoped to never hear again.

Shannon said, "Who's your new partner? He's cute."

Melanie felt even sicker listening to the way that Shannon was playing her two captors like they were toys. Who knew what kind of upheaval she was causing with Rick and his men as they fell over themselves in an effort to get her attention.

"This is Mark," one of the policemen announced.

"It's nice to meet you, Mark," Shannon said with a sultry tone in her voice that said, "I'm available, maybe." Melanie rolled her eyes at the woman's audacity.

As one of the cops guided Melanie blindly across the threshold, Melanie caught the heel of her good right leg on the doorsill. She tried to support her weight with her injured left leg, but she couldn't because of the pain. She would have fallen to the floor if it hadn't been for the strong grip on her arm. Melanie did her best to regain her composure in spite of the pain she felt in her wounded leg. She felt a desperate need to not show any weakness in front of this loathsome woman.

"And Melanie, it's so nice to see you again," Shannon said in a sickly-sweet voice. Shannon punched Melanie as hard as she could in the middle of her stomach and then exclaimed, "Not."

The sudden and unexpected explosion of pain that erupted in

her abdomen caused Melanie's knees to buckle, and she would have collapsed to the floor if it had not been for the policeman's firm grip on her arm.

One of the officers roughly yanked the bag from Melanie's head. Melanie's could feel that her hair was matted around her sweaty face. With her eyes closed, she sucked in huge breaths of air.

After a cruel laugh, Shannon said, "Oh, Melanie, dear, you really aren't looking your best, are you? What a shame." To the officers, she said, "Take her to the breakfast nook."

Since she was still unable to walk, the policemen mostly dragged Melanie by her arms through a magnificently-designed kitchen and into the breakfast area. They parked her with a jolt on the floor against a blank wall.

Feeling too nauseated to even remain seated, Melanie slowly slide to the floor and curled up in a ball.

CHAPTER 74

"**V**ON, THEY'VE GOT Melanie," Trevor said as soon as he got Von on Walter 's phone.

"I'm way ahead of you," Von said calmly. "My men have been tracing all calls in and out of the home in Newport Beach, either by cell phone or by land line. They let me know just minutes after you left the airfield with Officer Swallow that the cops were on their way to get Melanie from the hospital."

"Then why didn't you hurry over there and stop them?"

"I think you already know the answer to that one. We can't afford to carry out our operations in public."

"I guess I understand. If you're monitoring their phone calls, you must already know where Melanie is. What are we going to do now?"

"We're going to get her back."

"Just like that? You're going to walk in and just take her away from Rick and all of his henchmen?" He knew Von and his men were good, but were they that good?

"Yes, it will be something like that. At least, I hope it will."

Even though the neighborhood surrounding the Newport Beach house where Melanie was a prisoner was mostly dark and quiet, the sidewalk next to the Marauder was a hive of activity at the moment. Von's men were exiting the three Marauders in organized haste, each carrying a different piece of equipment. Some of the men disappeared wraith-like into the night while others were quietly attaching devices to the top of the Marauders or pieces to devices that were already on the ground.

"Trevor," Von stated quietly as the two men approached each other on the sidewalk on the passenger side of Von's Marauder. "You're going to see things tonight that most likely are going to amaze you. We're truly glad to be of help. However, many of the devices that you're going to see in action involve trade secrets that belong to the various military supply companies that my men own. I need you to agree to keep everything that you see tonight absolutely secret."

"Sure," Trevor answered, more than willing at this point to place his all his trust in Von and to have Von trust him in return.

Von nodded and then continued, "Also, I want you to be absolutely clear on a few points. You are to stay by my side at all times. You are to follow my orders without question. You are not to get involved in or even get close to any of the action tonight. Is that clear?"

"Yes, it's clear," Trevor said. He wanted Von to get on with the rescue.

"Okay. Let's get to work." Von quickly stepped over to two of his men that were removing a tarp from a large flat object that was lying in the middle of the road. In the dim light of the nearest streetlight, the newly-uncovered object looked like an extra-large fan. The outer rim of the housing was encrusted with a number of protruding boxes, at least one of which held a camera. A few others contained smaller fans on what looked like swivels. As Trevor watched, one of the men flipped up two antennae on the outer rim of the housing while the other man leaned over and pressed a button on one side of the device. The button lit up, flashed on and off for ten seconds, and then shut off just as the fan blade began to spin in the housing. Within moments, the fan blade accelerated to the point that it began blowing dust in Trevor's eyes. Suddenly, the whole housing lifted off the ground and soared rapidly and soundlessly into the night sky, steered by the smaller fans that were attached to the side of the housing.

"That was Ernie," Von said. "He's our eye in the sky. It's always amazes me how Ernie lifts off without a whisper when he weighs close to three hundred pounds. His hybrid fuel-cell batteries alone weigh one hundred pounds." Von stopped and looked at Trevor for his reaction.

Awestruck by Von and his never-ending array of toys, all Trevor could muster was, "Wow."

Von continued, "Come with me and I'll show you what Ernie can do."

Trevor followed Von to his Marauder and climbed through the back door and on to the rear passenger seat. Von got into the driver's seat and began fiddling with the controls for the middle screen. Moments later, the other two screens came on. The middle screen began showing an overhead view of a residential area at twilight.

Before Trevor had time to ask any of the questions that were racing through his mind, Von said, "The videos are from Ernie. The one in the middle is a color-enhanced view of the terrain beneath Ernie, taken by a night-vision camera. The image on the right is a highly-sensitive infrared view of the same area." As Von spoke, Trevor could see pastel blotches of orange-red superimposed over a vague overhead image of the houses in the neighborhood. Trevor quickly grasped that the orange-red images had to be human figures. Some of the images were circular and were moving around in the homes. *That must be people walking.* He noticed that the majority of the orange-red images were oblong in shape and were unmoving. At this time of night, those were probably people sleeping in bed. A few moments later, the images on the screen stopped moving over the houses of the neighborhood and came to rest on one home. This home was different than the others because it was quite a bit larger and because there were about twenty infrared images inside and around the home.

Von turned to Trevor again and handed him a set of headphones. "Here, put these on. You might find our dialogue interesting."

"I'm sure I will," Trevor said as he donned the light-as-a-feather wireless headphones. Just as he finished putting the headphones comfortably on his head, the left most screen changed from black to blurry shapes that were flying by the central point of view. Before Von had a chance to explain, Trevor asked, "What's the window on the left for?"

"Good. It's up and on its way," Von said with just a bit of relief in his voice. "We're trying a new technology out tonight. The result is what you see in the left window." The image in the left window was mostly a chaotic blur of dark images. After a moment's inspection, Trevor became aware that he was seeing a camera's view of a dimly-lit garden area from about six feet above the ground. The problem was that there was too little light coming into the camera's lens to make out much, and the man holding the camera was moving extremely fast through the garden, avoiding dimly-lit branches and trellises with almost inhuman deftness. The more he watched, Trevor began to doubt that anyone, even with night vision glasses, could move so quickly through a garden.

"There is not much to see yet," Von said. "Just watch for a minute or two and then tell me what you think we're seeing here." The two men watched as the dancing images on the screen suddenly came to a screeching halt. A view of the side of a house came into sharp focus. In the center of the video, there was a door with an overhead light. A curtained window flanked each side of the door. Trevor stared at the completely motionless screen, wondering what would happen next. The image seemed even more unreal now that it was so still, and yet moments before it had been moving wildly through the garden.

"Come on, Rick," Shannon's voice said over the headphones. Trevor about popped an aneurysm on the spot at the sound of Shannon's voice. Shannon's voice continued, "You were the one that wanted to play strip poker. At least be a good sport when you lose."

"Fine then." Trevor heard Rick say angrily over the headphones. Rick continued, "I'll take my shirt off, but I'm not taking my pants off unless one of the two of you does it first."

Trevor heard Austin say, "Oh, come on, Rick. Just because you lost the last three hands in a row doesn't mean you're going to lose every time. Let's just get on with the game."

"Amazing, isn't it?" Von asked. Von fiddled with a volume control on the dashboard, and the sound of the three card players faded. "One of my men is aiming a special laser at the window nearest to these three card-playing clowns. Part of the beam reflects off of the glass and back to a receiver in the same instrument. As the sound of their voices causes the pane of glass to vibrate ever so slightly, the receiver detects the minute differences in the distance the laser beam has traveled and converts it into digital sound waves."

"I didn't hear Melanie's voice," Trevor said. "I hope that she's all right."

"I hope that she is, too," Von said. "Let's keep an eye on this left monitor. I think we'll get chance to find out how she's doing very soon."

Two minutes later, the door in the center of the left image opened, and a man that Trevor didn't recognize stepped outside. As soon as the door cracked open, the view of the door shifted down a few inches and began swaying. Why the guy was bobbing back and forth made no sense. All Trevor could figure was that the guy was on speed or meth because no human in his or her right mind could bob like that and not get dizzy. The man at the door hesitated and then reached back to pull the door closed. Without any warning,

Von's man rushed the open door. The man didn't even look up at the threat that was approaching him at breakneck speed. Their man with the camera blew past Rick's guard and whipped through the door into a richly-furnished study. The guard at the door hadn't even reacted. *What in the world?* He opened his mouth to ask Von who was holding the camera and how he had gotten inside without being seen when the scene on the screen rapidly changed as Von's man approached a kitchen area.

The cameraman blew into the kitchen. The camera started circling around the room. A brief flash of Melanie crumpled against a wall sent Trevor's heart into a burst of rapid heartbeats. He felt like yelling for Von to bring the image back so that he could see if she were okay, but he was too fascinated by the images on the screen. How was this guy sprinting around the room in clear sight without someone seeing him? The only explanation was that the cameraman was invisible, yet that was too incredible and unnerving to believe. Suddenly, as the cameraman passed by the kitchen refrigerator, he or she jumped on top of the refrigerator without breaking their stride and came to a stop.

"What in the world?" Trevor said. "How can the cameraman do that?" As he spoke, the camera's view rotated toward and zoomed onto Rick, Shannon and Austin playing cards at the kitchen table.

"That," Von said, sounding every bit like a dad bragging about his child's latest accomplishment, "Is our newest and latest invention. And you are right. The camera isn't being carried by a human."

"You've trained a monkey to carry the camera?"

"No, it's a creature that's much more fascinating. That camera is a marvel of miniaturization in itself. It's half the size of a button from a man's shirt, and that includes the microphone and the transmitter. Its battery is about the same size. Believe it or not, all that is mounted on the back of a common dragonfly."

"How do you get the dragonfly to do exactly what you want it to do?" Trevor asked, even more amazed.

"There's where the real breakthrough comes in. One of my colleagues has discovered a way to control the dragonfly's rather rudimentary nervous system by computer. Without going into all the details, he surgically detaches the nerves from the dragonfly's brain and then he coaxes them with nerve-growth hormone to attach to tiny, energized wires on a miniature circuit board implanted at the base of the dragonfly's brain. He can then program the computer on the circuit board to control the dragonfly's body."

"I wouldn't believe it if I hadn't seen it," Trevor said with wonder dripping from his voice. As eager as he was to learn more about Von's toys, he was still more worried about Melanie. "But, Von, I would really like to know how Melanie is doing. Can you move the dragonfly's camera back to her for a minute?"

"Sure thing," Von said as he pushed a button on the left most screen and then spoke into his microphone.

In response, the image on the screen shifted abruptly back to Melanie. The two men fell silent as they studied Melanie's form. The bruises on her legs and the limpness in her body as she lay slumped against the wall worried Trevor. There were tracks of tears on her checks. They had been hurting her! He felt like running over there to save her but knew he would have no chance of ever getting past the guards.

After a few more moments of tense study of the image on the screen, Trevor relaxed a little with the knowledge that for the moment, Melanie otherwise appeared to be okay. And there was no visible blood. Turning back to Von, he said, "We've got to get in there and save her as soon as we can. I'm afraid that if we leave her there any longer, who knows what else they'll do to her."

"And, who knows what horrible things she's already been through," Von said. "Just hang on. It won't be long."

Rick yelled off the screen, "You cheated."

The image on the screen shifted back to the kitchen table. Rick was on his feet and was leaning on the table with his hands, glaring at Shannon.

"Oh, come on, Rick." Austin said.

Rick's eyebrows knitted in anger. Like lightning, he whipped out a revolver and pointed it between Austin's eyes. "You'd better watch your mouth."

"When are you going to figure out that you can't get everyone to do what you want by being a bully?" Melanie said from off the screen.

The players all turned toward her.

"Maybe you didn't get Shannon's message earlier," Rick as he turned his gun toward Melanie.

Melanie said, "I won't cower in front of you and agree to every little thing you want me to say or do, like everyone else around you does just because you're a big part of their lunch ticket…"

As Melanie spoke, Rick's lips curled into a snarl. He crossed the room to Melanie, raised his gun and smashed it into the side of her head. The force of the blow caused Melanie's head to crash against the wall behind her with a hollow thud. Her eyes rolled up into her head and she crumpled sideways onto the floor. Not satisfied, Rick reached down, grabbed the front of her shirt and jerked her upright. He jammed the barrel of his gun into her mouth and yelled, "Keep your stinking mouth shut or I'm going to blow your brains out."

As soon as Von saw Rick pistol whip Melanie, he was galvanized into action.

"We have to move in now," he said to Tyler, who was seated in the front passenger seat. "Take out the guards and hit Rick at the same time. Have your men ready to move in on my command."

Tyler immediately began barking orders into his headset microphone while he reached over and punched a switch on the console.

Trevor paid him little attention as his eyes were riveted on the screen where Rick was still holding his gun in Melanie's mouth. As much as he trusted Von, it seemed to him that there wasn't anything that Von was going to be able to do to keep Rick from killing Melanie right then and there.

Trevor watched as Tyler brought up in rapid succession an image of each of the guards that were stationed around the house. He only hesitated on each image long enough to see each of the guards suddenly grab their stomach and fall to the ground, writhing in pain. Trevor turned back to the image of Melanie and Rick, and then watched in morbid fascination as Rick suddenly let go of Melanie's shirt and fell to the ground clutching his abdomen and grimacing in horrible pain. Melanie also crumpled straight to the floor like a lead weight. Almost immediately, Rick began to vomit uncontrollably. The sound of chairs falling over was heard off screen. The image shifted to Shannon and Austin. They were doubled over on the floor in severe pain and were vomiting.

On the other screen, Von's men, completely dressed in black and wearing night vision goggles, trussed up each of the incapacitated guards around the yard and house with plastic zip-ties.

"Turn out the lights," Von said. Tyler pushed another button on the console and then spoke briefly into his microphone. Even before Tyler began speaking, Trevor heard a soft hissing sound emanating from the direction of Austin's house. Looking out the front window of the Marauder, he got a glimpse of a something large and black that suddenly enveloped Austin's entire house. Trevor decided that it must be some kind of a smoke cloud, but he never got to find out because in next instant, all the lights the house and in all the neighbor's houses went out. Plunged into darkness, Trevor could see next to nothing outside the window of the Marauder. He looked back at the screen that had been showing the guards on the ground, but the screen was now completely dark. He wondered what surprise Von would have for him next and hoped that whatever happened, Melanie would be okay.

The scene in the left screen was in a completely different color, because he was now watching a light-amplified view of the kitchen where Rick had been holding Melanie hostage. Almost immediately, three of Von's men entered the image on the screen. They were recognizable due to their light-amplification goggles. They had Rick, Austin, and Shannon trussed up with their arms behind their backs in seconds.

"Is everything clear?" Von asked, still businesslike in his tone, but with much less urgency in his voice.

"All guards are accounted for, and the three kitchen perpetrators are subdued," Tyler replied. "We also have subdued all other individuals from around the house."

"What in the world did you just do?" Rick asked. "Why didn't you do that when we first got here?" What had seemed to be a disaster for Melanie just moments before was now completely and one hundred percent over.

Ignoring Trevor's question, Von gave Tyler one more order, "Turn the power back on before the neighbors wake up, get worried, and start calling the power company. Get all the guards and all the other perpetrators into the kitchen, and I'll meet you there in just a moment."

Turning to Trevor, he said, "So you liked that?"

"That was awesome," Trevor said. "But how did you do it? I can tell from the grin on your face that you're dying to tell me."

"That, my friend, is a firsthand demonstration of what highly-amplified, low-frequency sound can do to the human body. It can completely nullify a potentially lethal situation. It works instantly and has no long-term toxic effects on the human body. My only regret is that Melanie had to experience it firsthand because we can't focus the beam accurately enough through a window. Hopefully, she'll forgive me." Von started for the house as he added, "Let's go check on our prisoners and see how Melanie is doing."

Scurrying after Von, Trevor asked, "But what was that black thing that covered the house in seconds?"

"That was an ultra-lightweight, carbon-fiber, light-obscuring blanket. It was ejected by pressurized air from Ernie and was weighted to the ground by hundreds of small lead weights. I used it in this situation just to be sure that there was no light whatsoever in the kitchen. I didn't want Rick firing away at shadows. However, since the low frequency sound waves had the desired effect, I'm not sure if the light-obscuring blanket was necessary. What you thought were light-amplifying goggles and cameras were actually the latest high-resolution, infrared goggles and cameras that can see perfectly fine even in the complete absence of light."

They were arriving at the back door of Rick's house. Von's men were quickly pulling the carbon fiber blanket from off the roof. They stepped aside to let the two men enter the house.

"The technological marvels that you have at your fingertips amaze me," Trevor said.

"It seems so commonplace to us because we use them so often in our lines of work," Von said. "I think that I forget that the public has no idea about the tools that we use and about how amazing they are."

"It's probably best that the public doesn't know about what you've got because we'd rather have the crooks be completely clueless about your capabilities until the moment you nab them."

At that moment, Trevor entered the kitchen and saw Melanie curled up in a ball against the wall. She lay still, and he couldn't tell if she were breathing or not. He rushed to her side, afraid to touch her in case she might be hurt, but he was unable to resist the need to reassure himself that she was alive. He touched her on the arm. and her skin felt warm. She took a shallow breath, and his heart leaped for joy. He leaned over her back and tried to peer at her face without touching or moving her. Her eyes fluttered, and she let out a whimper of pain. He asked, "Melanie, are you okay?"

She took in a deeper breath and then let out a sigh. She opened her eyes just a little and managed the weakest of smiles. "I don't dare move, for fear that I will vomit again." She swallowed hard. "I've never vomited that hard in my life. It hurt my stomach so bad that I didn't even feel Rick's gun in my mouth." She struggled to sit up. "What happened to Rick? I thought he was going to kill me. How did you guys get in here so fast?"

"Thanks to Von and his amazing technology, he took Rick and his men out in a matter of seconds." Trevor didn't have the heart to tell her that the same technology had also made her throw her guts up, but he figured he had plenty of time to tell her about it later.

After finishing untying Melanie's wrists and ankles, Trevor helped her to get to her feet. Nothing seemed to be broken. Turning, he noticed that Von's men had gathered Rick, Shannon, Austin and all of the guards into the kitchen behind him. They were all seated in a circle with their backs to each other. A rope was looped around their waists to hold them in place in the circle. Each of their wrists were tied to their ankles. Trevor helped Melanie to hobble over to where Von stood, directly in front of Shannon, Austin, and Rick. They looked terrible with vomit still sticking to their faces and mixed into their hair. The guards looked just as bad.

"They don't look so scary anymore, do they," Von said.

"Just you wait," Rick said with his lips tight. "I'm going to make you sorry that you were ever born.".

"I don't think you're in a position to inflict any more pain and suffering on anyone," Trevor said.

"And once the law gets done with you, you'll be so old that you won't have the strength even to push your walker," Von said.

Ignoring the men and their endless need to sound tougher than each other, Melanie concentrated on Shannon. Shannon was still looking down at the floor dejectedly with her shoulders slumped. "Why did you do this, Shannon?"

Shannon gave no sign that she had heard Melanie.

"What made an intelligent girl with looks and talent galore get mixed up with a guy like Rick?" Melanie paused, waiting for Shannon to answer her question. "Was it for money? Or was it for love?"

Shannon ignored her and looked away.

Melanie continued, "Most people realize that the pursuit of wealth, possessions, and power just brings emptiness inside. It seems exciting while you are trying to get those things, but once you have them, they don't make you happy. The only true happiness comes from caring about and nurturing the people and the causes that you love."

Shannon said, "You have no clue about why I do what I do."

Trevor interjected, "She doesn't know what you're talking about. Maybe a few years in the slammer with people just like herself will teach her a thing or two."

Melanie and Shannon continued staring at each other.

"Melanie," Trevor said. "We have to get going. Von has called the police, and we need to be gone before they get here."

Trevor turned to go, but Melanie and Shannon stared at each other for a moment longer. Then Melanie shook her head, looked away, and turned her back on Shannon. She put her arm in Trevor's, and together they left the house.

CHAPTER 75

THE LAUGHTER OF the small children playing on the playground at the park was like a breath of fresh air in the otherwise stifling heat of another midsummer Phoenix scorcher. It was supposed to hit one hundred and fifteen degrees again for the twentieth day in a row. In spite of the heat, there was no way that Trevor and Melanie were going to miss their annual Labor Day picnic with Becky and George. Especially after what they had experienced together six years ago. At times, the horror of it all was still so raw in their memories that it seemed like just yesterday. However, most of the time, including today, it seemed like a long time ago.

"Your kids are so cute," Becky exclaimed as she watched Trevor and Melanie's four-year-old Spencer and two-year old Jessica running from one slide to another.

"And so are yours," Melanie said as she watched Becky and George's three-year-old Jonathon run to keep up with now eight-year-old Spencer.

"Thank you, but Trevor and your genes together make for some really beautiful children."

"You are always so sweet."

"Speaking of compliments, I wanted to tell you that I am really impressed that you have lost so much weight since the last time I saw you."

"Thanks, but I really didn't lose that much."

"Oh, yes she did," Trevor said. He was sitting on the wooden bench next to Melanie. "She is down thirty pounds since her pregnancy, and she is only twenty pounds over her ideal weight. She has been working very hard."

"I've been taking Reductol, or else I would have never been able to lose it. Without it, I am so hungry that I can't help but eat everything in sight."

"Me too," Becky said. "I'm also on Reductol, thanks to Trevor. I think that I'd weigh three hundred pounds without it. As long as I take it at least every other day, I stay right at twenty-five pounds over my ideal weight."

"Don't forget the hour a day that you spend at the gym," George reminded Becky. "I think that it's amazing how well the two of you have done, in spite of what Rick and his men did to you. I've heard of people from Las Vegas and Los Angeles, including some movie stars, have gained two hundred and three hundred pounds since Rick killed their appetite centers with his drug."

"He deserves to suffer in prison forever for what he did," Becky said. "By the way, do any of you know what's happening with Shannon?"

"Do we really want to know?" Melanie said.

"Brittany Adams, a.k.a. Shannon Lowry, got out of prison a year ago," Trevor said quietly.

"You've got to be kidding." Becky said. "After what she did?"

CHAPTER 76

A SHINY, CHERRY-RED ROLLS-ROYCE came to a stop in front of a mansion. Both the mansion's doors abruptly swung open, and two men in their thirties, wearing white shirts, black pants, black vests, and black running shoes sprinted to the driver's door. The first one to arrive grabbed the door handle without delay, yanked the door open, and then held it while he stood straight as an arrow. The second man arrived barely a second later and quickly came to attention next to the rear driver's side passenger door, ready at a moment's notice to assist the driver.

A sleek, polished, jet-black shoe, closely followed by a nylon-clad ankle, slowly and seductively crossed the threshold of the driver's door until the shoe lit softly on the immaculate marble driveway. The ankle above the foot was thick and hung over the edge of the shoe on both sides like dough that had been allowed to rise too long in a bowl that had been too small to start with. The double roll of fat around the left knee that followed the ankle shouted that things were not as they seemed. The leg protruded farther from the car and then was abruptly joined by another leg. To any observer, it was painfully obvious that the woman to whom the appendages belonged was either suffering from a severe case of elephantiasis or was enormously obese. Tightly stretched nylons did little to cover the myriad of dimples in the woman's skin where the body was straining to hold the epidermis attached to the underlying tissues.

A pair of massive thighs followed the knees. The material of the nylons was stretched so much that the individual threads stood out against the woman's pale skin. The thighs kept coming and with no skirt in sight, the two men quickly looked even farther away.

The woman in the driver's seat reached out a pudgy hand that was sporting a white driving glove. She only had to wait for a half a second for the man standing next to the passenger door to come to her aid. With his help, she heaved her torso out of the seat of the car and on to her legs. Aided by gravity, the woman's pup-tent-sized, red dress slid down her bare legs, hiding her partially-visible underwear. Only then did the two men dare to turn their eyes back to the woman. They carefully concentrated on her face, afraid to be caught starring at her massive torso that seemed to be threatening to burst through at every seam of her large, but not large enough, red dress.

"You're looking radiant this morning, Brittany," the man holding the door remarked cheerfully.

"She always looks radiant," the second man said sharply. Then, to Brittany he said, "Brittany, is there anything that I can carry for you this morning?"

Expressionless and unblinking, Brittany Adams fastened her stunning blue eyes on the second man. He smiled awkwardly and tried his best to look eager to please.

Shaking her head in disgust, Brittany turned her attention to the front door of her mansion. "You guys are too desperate. Chill out a little. I just got here, and you're already suffocating me."

The first man couldn't restrain himself. "But it's been almost twenty-four hours since my last dose, and I've been really good. I can't take this anymore."

"I've been really good, too," the second man said. "I finished painting the hall, and then I helped with weeding the—"

"I know. I know." Brittany said as she cut him off. "If you'd just behave yourselves, then you wouldn't get in this predicament, would you?" Brittany noted the beads of sweat on each of the men's brows. In addition, the first man that had helped her out of the car was trying, but failing, to hide his trembling hands. Feeling unusually magnanimous this morning, she decided that they had both suffered long enough.

"I'll reset the machine for both you in a few minutes. Now who's going to carry my briefcase?" The men almost fell over each other in their haste to reach for her briefcase. The second man got his hand on the handle of the briefcase before the other and then quickly yanked it away, winning himself a downright menacing glare from his partner.

Brittany impatiently ignored their childishness.

Hefting Brittany's briefcase, the second man sprinted for the front door of the mansion and swung it wide open. He then turned, stood at attention, and smiled as best he could.

His abject discomfort wasn't lost on Brittany. These two men, as well as the thirteen other men that worked for her at her mansion, were so completely dependent on these pills. It still amazed her that just having control of the pills gave her complete and unquestioned control over the men. They would do anything for her just to be sure that the pills came out of the machine every eight hours. She was sure that if she demanded it that every one of them would crawl on broken glass, rob a bank, or even take a life. It was a total thrill to have such absolute power over these dumb men. What was even more of a thrill to contemplate were her plans to increase her control over an ever-widening circle of men that might ultimately include a certain doctor in Phoenix, Arizona.

CHAPTER 77

"BRITTANY; AUSTIN; AND Rick's old girlfriend, Candy, plea bargained for lighter sentences in trade for testifying against Rick," Trevor said. "There never was enough evidence to convict Austin of any of the murders he had committed. Brittany, Austin and Candy were each sentenced to five to ten years for the only charges that were ultimately brought up against them: racketeering."

For Trevor, the years following the arrest of Rick and his accomplices had been long and frustrating. He had given depositions and been a witness in court multiple times. However, without witnesses that were willing to testify, most of the charges that had been brought up against Rick and his accomplices had been dropped. In spite of the long list of charges with which the Feds had considered charging Carl, there hadn't been enough evidence to link him directly to any crime. At the insistence of his attorneys, he had been released on bail, pending further investigation. Even though he had been ordered to remain in the LA area, he had instantly disappeared and had never been seen again. The other escort girls that Austin and Rick had hired to sell Waitnomor scattered like leaves in the wind as soon as they heard of Austin and Rick's arrest. The few that the

FBI had tracked down were given immunity against prosecution in exchange for testifying against Rick.

In an effort to try to save face, Pharmplus had fired Rick immediately upon hearing of his arrest. Rick's trial had been delayed for a year while evidence based on Shannon, Austin, and Candy's testimonies was gathered. He had remained in jail without the possibility of bail until the trial. After a lengthy trial and in spite of the web of lies told by some the best defense lawyers that Austin's father's money could buy, Rick was convicted of racketeering, domestic terrorism, and being an accomplice to Dr. Fife and Jennifer's murders. He was sentenced to life in prison without possibility of parole.

Not long after Rick's trial, the thousands of lawsuits against Pharmplus for damage to patients that had taken Waitnomor had been gathered into a class-action lawsuit. The jury had returned a unanimous decision that the company was guilty. Already suffering from the loss of profits from Waitnomor being taken off the market within days after Rick's arrest, the company was unable to pay the resulting multibillion-dollar award for damages. The company declared bankruptcy and was liquidated. The proceeds from the sales of its assets went to the thousands of injured patients.

Trevor said, "Candy and Austin were also released last year. All four had been model prisoners, from what Officer Walter Swallow tells me."

"That just makes me sick," Becky said. "I had no idea that they are out of prison. Are we safe? Are Shannon and Austin going to come after us?"

"Trevor didn't tell me until just a few months ago," Melanie said. "He said that he didn't want to worry me. However, since he told me, I've had lots of horrible dreams about those two."

"Any threat that we were to them has long passed," Trevor said. "I'm sure they are getting on with their lives and that we'll never hear from them again."

ABOUT THE AUTHOR

Derek Muse is married and has seven children and two grandchildren. He spends most of his free time with his family, but during the remaining moments left each week, he enjoys baking, ballroom dancing, walking with his wife, and throwing pottery.

www.ingramcontent.com/pod-product-compliance
Lightning Source LLC
Chambersburg PA
CBHW022240020726
47496CB00004B/999